*For Rhonda,
Remember —
Question Everything!*

CHYMIST

The Coelacanth Project
Book II

Sarah Newland

This book is a work of fiction. Names, characters, places, and incidents are products of the author's imagination or used fictitiously.

Copyright © 2021 by Sarah Newland.
Cover art copyright © 2021 by Sarah Newland.
All rights reserved, including the right to reproduce this book or portions thereof in any form whatsoever.

Books may be purchased in quantity and/or special sales by contacting the author at
SarahNewland@SarahNewlandBooks.com.

Connect with Sarah on Goodreads, Instagram, and Patreon.

ISBN: 978-1-7333458-3-5

LCCN: 2021905935

First Edition

Hiking Hedgehog Press, LLC is dedicated to promoting thoughtful living and celebrates the right to read.

For Autumn, Chloe, and Dean.

Test your thoughts,
Trust your feet.

And when in doubt,
Read a book.

heavy is the heart
of those who bear the weight of
mind - whose hopes grow dim

Craig Randall
@craigrandallwriting

The Coelacanth Project
October 6, 2005

It is with great enthusiasm and reverence that I formally welcome you to the Coelacanth Project. Although the world will never know of your sacrifice, I hope you find peace in the essence of our mission. The Coelacanth Project is a private program dedicated to the prevention of nuclear war and other catastrophic events through the service of five biochemically unique individuals.

These individuals, who will ultimately become global sentinels for peace, are equipped with additional cellular receptors. These exclusive receptors enable their bodies to interact with the special metal aurichalcum in a solid, concentrated form and in a dissolved ionic state in seawater. This interaction permits a conduction of charge that elevates the atoms that comprise their bodies to a higher state of excitement. The subsequent release of this energy allows them to transport the electricity and themselves from one place to another via a connection of seawater and driven intent.

As you well know, this power has vast potential for peacekeeping efforts in an era of growing global tension. However, we must also consider its capability for exploitation. I implore you to unite with your fellow Coelacanth associates and conserve the obscurity of our mission.

Your charges will be as follows:

Brant - Mr. Frederick Hutchinson and Ms. Nora Delacruz, henceforth known as Mr. Robert Smith and Mrs. Jennifer Smith.

Leonidas - Dr. Philip Kurr and Ms. Suzanne Sharpe, henceforth known as Mr. Michael Merrick and Mrs. Elizabeth Merrick.

Natalie A. - Mr. Benjamin Shepard and Dr. Madison Finch, henceforth known as Mr. John Morrigan and Mrs. Mary Morrigan.

Owen - Dr. Caleb Randolph and Ms. Avery Kinney, henceforth known as Mr. Thomas Johnson and Mrs. Margaret Johnson.

Tawney - Mr. Wyatt Barnett and Ms. Natasha Morin, henceforth known as Mr. Samuel Davis and Mrs. Patricia Davis.

Let us embark on this grand adventure together and secure a peaceful future for humanity.

I am forever indebted to your service and your sacrifice.

Christopher E. Reyes

Executive Director
Coelacanth Project

CHYMIST

CHAPTER 1
NATALIE

*B**reathe.*

Black waves rose and spilled overhead. The frigid water engulfed her, stinging her skin and piercing her lungs. Weightless and blind, she stretched for the sky. She kicked, and kicked, and kicked, numb save for the agony in her chest.

Hope isn't a bird. Fireflies streaked her vision as she clung to consciousness. *Hope is an anchor.*

Her pulse drummed in her ears as chains crept up from the depths. They snaked up her legs to clutch at her throat. Cradling her underwater with the patience of death, they allowed her to skim the surface, letting her feel for freedom yet never taste it.

"Breathe."

Natalie gasped. Blinking back to life, her lungs flooded with sweet, salty air. She stumbled away from the water's edge and collapsed in the safety of the sand. The fear that fogged her mind dissipated as pieces of the world dropped back into focus. Vines crept up the aluminum walls of Morning Sun Marina. Crickets sang in the reeds. Water slapped the vacant docks. Behind her the cinder block cottage lurked dark and empty, and even from the beach she could hear the clock inside.

Tick-tock.

"You're resisting." A portly figure marched down the dock, moonlight reflecting off his salt and pepper stubble.

"I can't do it."

"You already have."

"Once!" Natalie argued. "Weeks ago. It's harder than it looks."

"So's ballet. Ask Tawney," Uncle Chris loomed over her, declining any effort to help her up. "The art is making it look easy."

Tick-tock.

Natalie pushed her clammy fingertips against her forehead. Three months ago, she wouldn't have even noticed the damned clock, but that was before.

Before I cost my family their freedom. Before I tacked across oceans. Before I traveled back in time and lost—

"Again." She forced herself to stand, adjusting the stone spark on her wrist out of habit.

"You need a break."

"No."

"Time travel's no cakewalk. You need sleep, kid."

"Don't call me that."

"Listen—"

"Listen?" Natalie hissed. "Listen to what, Chris? The bombings on the news? Amir's taunts in my nightmares? The utter absence of guidance in this *mess* you've given me?" She dropped her head back, desperate to see something stable, something stagnant, something as reliable as the permanence of stars.

A lie, she scolded herself. *They burn until they explode and die. Too powerful for their own good. Maybe that's how I'll go, too: the spark that implodes the world.*

"Your silence is suffocating." Intended to be accusatory, her words crumbled to a plea.

"Listen to what I've already told you." Christopher advanced until she could see the wrinkles around his black eyes. "I've given you everything I have."

"You mean this?" Natalie fished a roughly hammered key from her pocket. Ancient in every way save for the iridescent metal inlaid in the bit.

Christopher rubbed his leathered neck. "Doin' this again, are we?"

"What does it open?"

"I told you before: I'm not tellin' ya."

"Because you can't or because you already have?"

"Precisely."

A hundred questions battled for her tongue. Why did he arrange their adoption? Why had she and her friends been chosen for the Coelacanth Project at all? Who were their real parents? Were they even still alive? What was she missing? Natalie choked down every query. Christopher had given all the help he would. She couldn't rely on him to fix her problems, not even the ones he created.

It doesn't work that way anymore.

"I won't have to keep bothering you if you tell me the truth."

"Ah," Christopher admired the open ocean. "Then only the birds would visit. How long do you have anyway?"

"Until dawn."

"Be quick about it then." Chris leaned against a pylon. "Tell me everythin'. How's Angie?"

Natalie forced herself to participate in the pleasantries. "She loves Tawney. And Enzi makes her feel braver, I think, like she's more than eight inches tall."

"Hmm. And the boys?"

"They're fine." Natalie didn't trust herself to elaborate. Brant's tactical course and Owen's satellite search were not on the morning's talking points.

"Leo?"

His name stung like a papercut that spanned Natalie's entire being. She clenched her jaw against the pain and shook her head. The truth was Natalie hadn't seen or heard from Leo since she lost him in that frigid sea forty-seven days prior.

And tomorrow will make forty-eight, and the next day forty-nine...

"And what about you?"

Me? I don't even know me. Natalie shuffled her feet in the sand. She missed the Eastern Shore more than she admitted. She longed to see it in the sun again, the marshes and seagrass, and the blue crabs roaming the beach. However, daylight threw into sharp relief truths she would rather leave buried.

"I'm...hoping."

Uncle Chris's arms folded atop his round stomach. "For what, exactly?"

Leo. My parents. The truth of what I am. To remember what it means to be home. To spare the world the chaos we've caused. It all bubbled to a halt in her throat. She couldn't say any of it, not out loud, not to him.

"To breathe," Natalie answered finally.

On the horizon the clouds churned from charcoal blue to burgundy. Gulls scoured the beach and in the distance porpoise fins rippled the glass-calm water.

"Hmm," Christopher squinted at the rising sun with distaste. "Red sky in morning..."

"So superstitious." Natalie nearly smiled. "I think there's a joke in there somewhere."

"Where's Brant when you need him?" Christopher chuckled, the sound echoing his isolation.

She drove her toes into the sand, digging for the strength to do what had to come next. "I have to go."

Natalie leaned in to kiss the scruff of his beard, something she'd done a thousand times, only to stop just before they would have touched. After their escape from Nautilus's Antarctic prison ended in a shootout, after she dragged him bleeding onto that beach, she still couldn't bring herself to ever say goodbye.

"See you," she promised instead, turning sharply for the water before she lost her nerve.

"Hey."

She faced him, trotting backwards towards the covered fueling station.

"Chin up, eyes open, kid," Christopher thumbed towards the cabin. "I'll be waitin'."

With the awning obscuring the sky, Natalie rolled the spark against her wrist. She had only known her power a short time yet tacking already felt as natural as walking. She pictured the lighthouse: Ancora's turning beacon, its two-toned spiral stripes, and the murky waters of the cape.

Stepping to meet the oncoming wave, she tacked faster than she could blink. Where there should have been water, a blinding light embraced her, and a tingling raced up her skin. For an instant she was weightless.

Then she was gone.

CHAPTER 2
NATALIE

Unlike the marina, Ancora's dock didn't bow or splinter as Natalie scaled the sheltered ladder. The lighthouse beacon had already begun to fade against the baby blue sky and, cursing her tardiness, Natalie ran for it. The sight of the so-called sanctuary made the hairs on her neck stand on end. Every day she expected navy jumpsuits to overtake them; yet, every day they stayed.

Far longer than we should have.

Leaping over the *'Closed for Renovations'* sign, Natalie tip-toed inside. The round room was vacant and, with so few possessions to have out of place, remarkably neat. A sterile kitchen opened to a sitting room where she passed a soot-soiled fireplace, ignoring the photographs on the mantle. Unfinished floors and exposed wooden rafters made Ancora III resemble a warehouse more than a home, but Natalie preferred it that way.

The less comfortable we get the better.

Paws descended a spiral staircase, followed by a white body and fluffy tail until a tall German Shepherd balanced nimbly on the narrow bottom step. He cocked his head.

"You're supposed to wait for me in bed," Natalie reminded him.

Enzi bounded up ahead of her as Natalie climbed more carefully, hugging the center pole to prevent the metal from creaking.

The first landing she reached was a maze of dirty clothes and thick foam mats. Somewhere in the tangle of bedsheets Tawney slept soundly and Angie, a matted ball of black fur, barely lifted her head as Natalie continued sneaking upwards.

Despite having more in it, Owen's floor was meticulously organized. Computer wires laid snaked in thick coils across the floor, while Owen snored on his desk, his glasses askew and a puddle of drool under his chin. Projections brightened his southern wall, flashing between satellite images of the earth and media feeds. Shattered storefronts in Spain and overturned cars in Germany echoed an unrest that clutched the globe. Every nation blamed the violence on another, turning borders into fissures and neighbors into enemies.

Natalie paused beneath the next room. Willing her feet to be swift and silent, she scaled the stairs two at a time and Brant's barren floor passed in a blur. Besides a creased photograph of his parents propped against the window, the only evidence of life was a transient shifting in the mound of bedsheets.

Passing without incident, Natalie's shoulders relaxed down her back. Book stacks carved a path to her bed and, though they were primarily academic titles (marine biology textbooks, self-defense basics, astrophysics, and psychology studies), a few novels had found their way into the mix. They made Ancora as close to a home as it could be.

Two large maps plastered a flattened globe to her walls. She had replicated Uncle Chris's notes from Ancora I to the best of her memory and added her own irritatingly limited knowledge to the pages. Nautilus shells and Coelacanth symbols branded various shorelines across the maps and sketched alone in the blue ink, as far north as the Atlantic Ocean allowed, was a faint triquetra. Natalie mindlessly tapped the looped symbol as she passed, not sparing the useless map a second thought.

Enzi sprawled across her mattress as she eased open the bottom drawer of her wardrobe. She rested Christopher's key atop her worn copy of *Jurassic Park* and, digging deeper, she brushed against the bloodstained cover of *Oh, the Places You'll Go!*.

"Caught in the act, Morrigan." Brant stood on the spiral staircase, his torso level with the floor, smirking with his chin on his palm.

Enzi's tail thumped excitedly, sending the covers rippling across the bed. Natalie kicked the drawer shut as Brant plopped down beside her. Wearing the same jeans and ripped shirt he had the night before, a red knit cap forced his brown curls flat against his forehead.

"Visiting him again?"

"I don't know what you mean."

"Liar." Brant sniffed her. "You smell like charcoal and sugar."

"No, I don't."

Brant leaned closer until she could feel the heat of his breath on her neck.

Don't tell yourself it's something when it's nothing, she chided herself. *He's just being...Brant.*

"Definitely Christopher," he decided.

"Don't do this."

"Fine," he conceded. "Whenever you're ready to talk, I'm ready to listen."

Natalie began to respond but the brush of his hand on her cheek stopped her. *Okay, that is something.*

"My dad became a counselor to help people." Brant said openly. "After Mom died...I guess it's hard to lift others up when you're drowning."

You don't know what I know. Natalie peered at the wardrobe where the papers outlining their adoption laid hidden. *You don't even know your last name.*

Brant leaned away and she breathed out in relief. "Make breakfast with me."

She wanted to refuse, however her stomach spoke first. "Alright."

"So, we're ignoring the buddy system now?"

Natalie cringed as she followed him downstairs. The first thing they'd done in Ancora III was establish ground rules.

Rule number one: No Christopher.

Rule number two: Tack with a buddy.

Though Natalie wasn't great at sports metaphors, she was fairly certain she was 0 and 2.

"I had a buddy."

Brant's eyebrows disappeared beneath his cap. "Christopher doesn't count, Nat. He can't protect you."

"A penguin can't fly. It's still a bird."

"That's irrelevant."

"It's entirely relevant; right, Owen?"

"Affirmative." At the kitchen table, Owen gingerly massaged his neck.

"You don't even know what we're talking about!"

"Like that matters." He yawned and Natalie took the seat next to him. Brant mixed up a bowl of batter as Tawney sauntered in.

"Well, well, well." She bounced in the center of the circular room. "Everyone's up for sprints!"

Brant and Owen synchronized a groan.

"Not everyone shares your love of self-torture." Brant flicked batter at her.

Tawney faked a jab to his ribcage. "Which is why none of you can out-sprint me."

"I'll run," Owen gave in.

"I bet you will," Brant snickered. "Spritely leprechaun chasing that pot o' gold."

Natalie frowned. It was unsettling how little had changed in light of how much had changed. Not eager to mull over those thoughts, she joined them.

"I'll have waffles ready when you get back," Brant said.

Tawney pointed a stubby finger at him. "No blueberries."

"Yeah, I know," he grumbled under his breath. "I'm still bruised from last time."

Natalie followed Tawney and Owen to the door until Enzi halted, struck by Brant's proximity to the stove. His muzzle jerked from Natalie to Brant and back again.

"Up to you." Natalie waited. Enzi looked to Brant once more before padding outside with his tail down. "Good choice," she patted him.

Angie's fluffy black figure dropped down the stairs like a slinky and Tawney snapped the door shut, locking her inside.

"She can't manage the heat."

"Neither can we." Owen's tone carried more than a hint of dread. "How far today?"

"There and back." Tawney nodded towards the tip of the cape. She took off, sending sand flying up around her ankles.

Already resenting the humidity clouding her lungs and sweat caking her neck, Natalie settled for a jog. Enzi blurred past her and Owen shouldered his glasses onto the bridge of his nose, barely keeping pace.

The only thing Natalie enjoyed about running was the inability to worry about anything other than breathing. The struggle for oxygen overrode any question of where her parents were or whether Leo was alive. The cramp in her side forced out the fact classes at Oxford had started and, in a kinder universe, she would have been a college freshman. Running forced her to trade reflection for survival.

But she could hardly keep it up forever.

Conquering the cape without pause, Natalie collapsed back against the cool paint of the lighthouse. Her chest heaved as she beckoned to Owen who lagged far behind. She'd settled in to wait for him when a disturbance inside Ancora sent her stomach to the sand. Not even Angie's piercing bark could mask the thud of fists on flesh.

Rushing inside, she caught Tawney with a frying pan aimed for the figure pinned beneath her. Natalie whisked the weapon away on her downswing.

"Hey!" Tawney jumped for it. "It's his bloody fault!"

At the table, a hot waffle steamed on Tawney's plate and a single blueberry oozed in its center.

"There goes…your record." Owen gulped down air in the doorway.

Brant scrambled to his feet and snatched a chalkboard from the counter. "This Ancora has gone," he erased a messily scribbled number seven, "zero days without incident."

"You know what, Brant?" Tawney scowled. "You really are an ass."

The rest of the morning was a blur. Breakfast's conversation dissolved into white noise and, though Natalie did her best to participate, she awaited any opportunity to leave the table. She hated breakfast. She hated dinner. She hated anything that forced her to sit beside Leo's empty chair.

She still felt him there. She knew which of Brant's jokes would make him laugh and that he'd slip Enzi bits of waffle under the table. If they did leave, if they made the safe choice to keep moving and find another Ancora, she feared the chair would remain empty. It would no longer belong to Leo, but to his ghost.

"It's settled then!" Tawney leapt up.

"Hmm?" Natalie's troubled thoughts stumbled their way back into the kitchen.

"It doesn't count," Owen said. "She didn't know what she was agreeing to."

"Don't care! She agreed; therefore, we are going." Tawney skipped up the stairs. "Get dressed!"

"What's happening?" Natalie sat up straight. "Where are we going?"

"Should we keep it a surprise?" Brant asked shrewdly.

"No!"

"Tawney's found a festival." Owen tried to calm her as he cleared her plate. "It's a few states south."

"A festival." She wetted her lips. "That's risky."

"Honestly, Nat, I don't see how it's any riskier than squatting here like sitting ducks for weeks on end," Owen spoke rationally. "The distraction might do us some good."

"Or get us killed."

"Loosen up!" Brant insisted. "We don't have to stay long."

Natalie sulked as they prepped to leave. She begrudgingly shoved her bolt, *Chef's* bolt, into her backpack before Tawney herded her out the door and down the dock.

"It'll be great," she said dreamily. "Kettle corn, fair rides with questionable stability, live music!"

"Nautilus bolt-frying our brains out," Natalie muttered.

"The radio ad said it'll be the biggest party on the east coast!" Tawney ignored her. "And we haven't been to Florida in ages."

"Florida?" Natalie gaped. "We're going all the way to *Florida* for this?"

Brant shrugged. "Florida, France; it's all the same if we're tacking."

"Twenty bucks if you can find France on a map," Owen challenged.

Natalie lifted her chin, "It's still risky."

"If you're not careful, they're going to change the phrase from 'Negative Nancy' to 'Negative Natalie,'" Tawney pouted.

"My legacy." Natalie bit down her irritation. "You all want to do this then?"

Reaching the covered end of the dock, Brant and Owen both nodded.

"It's time to blow off some steam," Brant explained.

Or at least tried to explain. She still didn't get it. How could they go chasing festivals when their parents were still captured and Leo missing in action? Yet as excitement radiated off her friends, Natalie knew Leo would be on their side. He would have told her to make it memorable, to find a spot of happiness in the chaos.

"Okay," she caved.

"Lead on, Macduff!" Brant high-fived Tawney.

"It's '*lay on*, Macduff,'" Natalie corrected dryly.

Brant scowled, confused. "Why would I lay on him?"

"No, you don't...nevermind," Natalie sighed.

"Stay, pups," Tawney petted each dog in turn before taking Natalie's wrist and dragging her into the sea.

CHAPTER 3
NATALIE

The spell of tingling weightlessness was not nearly long enough to ease Natalie's nerves. Stifling humidity engulfed her before gravity did. When solid ground rose underfoot, she found herself in a boat repair center. It reeked of oil and cleaning chemicals, and propellers hung from metal poles overhead. A single, storm-beaten ship occupied the concrete-bottom slip she climbed out of.

Tawney's squeal echoed off the aluminum walls, briefly drowning out the tinkling of carnival games. She burst out of the boat shop so fast Natalie had to run to catch up.

"Tawney!"

Her wild head of curls disappeared in the flood of festivities on the boardwalk. Bright tents lined the beach, exhibiting oversized stuffed animals and bags of cotton candy that would dwarf a small child. The sweet scent of funnel cakes and fresh popcorn accented the delighted screams of ride enthusiasts. Natalie jumped up and down, trying to spot her friend in the carnival jungle.

"Kettle corn?" Tawney offered at her side.

"Don't do that!" Natalie barked. "We can't lose each other here."

Tawney threw popcorn at her. "Good luck misplacing that walking torch," she nodded at Owen's hair. "I can spot him from the other side of the party."

"Nat's right." Owen stole a handful of Tawney's snack. "At least use the buddy system."

"Fine." Tawney pulled him after her. "Keep up, *buddy*."

"Wait!" Already out of sight, Natalie chewed her cheek.

"Shall we?" Brant formally offered his arm.

"Don't suppose I have much of a choice."

"That's not true." He led them through the festivities. "It's not Tawney's fault you were too lost in your own world to notice what's happening here on Earth."

Unable to argue his point, Natalie changed the subject. "How'd she even find out about this?"

"Radio ad." Brant booped every nose in a line of stuffed sea turtles. "They've been selling tickets for weeks."

"Tickets? Did we buy tickets?"

Brant smiled.

"This is a bad idea." Natalie tightened her grip on him.

"We completely by-passed the ticket booth," he gestured around them. "We're another couple in the crowd."

Despite his assurances, it took nearly an hour for her uneasiness to fade and another two before she could actually enjoy herself. She even devoured an entire bag of cotton candy despite the fact that the intense August heat melted most of it to sticky goo. Catching sight of Tawney and Owen, Brant cut through a line to hijack their ride on the Ferris wheel.

"Well, well," Tawney draped her legs over Owen's lap as their cart rose in the air. A cheap golden crown adorned her head and edible jewels glittered on her fingers. "She does remember how to smile!"

"Yeah, yeah, I hear you." Natalie suspected her friends had been right: they needed a break. Up high, the air was cooler, and the world was smaller. Natalie leaned into the breeze. She couldn't remember the last time she had simply enjoyed being on the ocean, watching the birds and squinting against the sunlight on the water. It felt *good*.

"We should do this every week," Tawney suggested.

"I'm not sure enough carnivals exist to satisfy you." Brant reached for her crown, making their cart sway.

"Are you kidding? We have an entire *world* of carnivals to conquer." Tawney kept him at bay with her foot. "And they're all only an ocean away."

"I wouldn't mind seeing the Netherlands," Natalie admitted. "Oh, or Italy."

Tawney plucked off her crown and put it on Natalie's head. "Not or," she corrected. "*And*. We can have it all."

"Well, what's next?" Owen scanned the festival as they neared the peak of the wheel. "Ring toss? Or we could walk out to..."

"There!" Brant rocked the entire carriage pointing to the other end of the carnival. "By the stage! They're giving out prizes or something."

"Nice!" Tawney reached for the sky. "Give me the freebies."

"It's all free to you lately," Natalie nudged her.

When their cart returned to solid ground, Brant beelined down the boardwalk. Natalie trailed behind, watching kids play larger-than-life chess with their parents. She became so captivated by a family of four sharing what might be the biggest sundae she'd ever seen that she failed to notice Owen stop short. She collided into him, catching herself on a stranger next to her. She turned to apologize when the performance on stage finally registered.

"Peace will be made in our time because of you!"

The ground swayed. A cheer rose nearly as loud as the blood pounding in Natalie's ears.

"Probably a coincidence," Brant muttered.

Question everything. Christopher's warning rang with the enthusiasm of the crowd.

"For years we've cultivated peace in the shelter of our union. Now, with you joining our society, with your continued donations and unyielding commitment to our vision, Nautilus will give peace to the world!"

"What is this?" Tawney's hand found Natalie's and she clung to it.

"You've brought us to a Nautilus recruitment fair," Owen blanched.

"Why? Why would anyone want to be one of them?" Tawney started to yell. "Don't they know what Nautilus does?"

"No," Owen surveyed the audience. "I suspect they don't."

We have to get out. Natalie was certain she had said the words aloud, yet she didn't hear them.

"Peace is not given!" the speaker roared. "It is taken! See the violence we endure! Witness the innocent drawn into war!"

A screen materialized behind the speaker; a shimmering projection Natalie recognized as a hologram. Eight figures knelt in a glass cell, their wrists bound, and clothes torn. People moved about freely behind them, blurred except for the sharp outline of their weapons. The hostages avoided the camera, averting their faces over their shoulders or towards the ground. For Natalie it made no difference. She had known them her entire life. Bound, bloodied, bruised, it didn't matter.

She would know her parents anywhere.

Natalie snagged Tawney's shirt and dug her heels into the sand to hold her friend back from the stage. Tawney bit and scratched like a wild animal until Natalie eventually gave in, letting Brant and Owen handle her.

Tawney's mother filled the screen, her cut lip curled in a snarl not unlike her daughter's. The camera focused on each hostage in turn as the narrator's statement fell on deaf ears. The names they gave were invented. The story they told was fiction. Nautilus was using their parents to make headlines, to show Americans held captive by the reckless evil of the world. She didn't catch who they blamed out loud. She knew it didn't matter; Nautilus would keep the truth far off-screen.

Natalie's own mother and father came into view and she smiled in spite of herself. They were alive. *Alive.* Her mom struggled to turn away and Natalie's relief evaporated when someone slapped her.

"See the violence that plagues our world? We must stand! We must bring peace!" Elated shouts reverberated against Natalie's skin and bodies rocked her as the crowd cheered.

"Nautilus KILLS PEOPLE!" Tawney screamed until Brant covered her mouth.

"Nautilus is using them." Owen squatted with his elbows on his knees. "It's manipulation. It's propaganda."

Natalie stared at the ground, uncertain how the pavement could appear so solid and feel so unstable. The Florida sun beat down on her, its heat making the beach blur. There wasn't enough air. She couldn't stand it. Dark clouds dotted her vision and she stumbled backwards, desperate to escape. She pushed through the crowd, not caring who she shoved aside in her haste. She nearly had the space to run when someone blocked her path.

"Woah, woah!" A broad grin snapped into focus. "Don't forget your invitation!"

"Invitation?" Natalie parroted.

Flipping back stray strands of blue hair, their host passed her a pamphlet. She read the text four or five times before processing what it meant.

"Now then," he continued cheerily. "Have you already made your donations?"

"No." Natalie's head spun too fast to formulate a lie. "I'm sorry, is this...is this invitation…"

"You—"

Owen cut Tawney off with a quick move of his foot. She fell flat on the cement and glared up with such fire that he squeaked out a swift apology before helping her up.

"It's for the Adoption." The man's jovial mood slipped, and his navy-lined eyes narrowed. "Aren't you here to join?"

"To join Nautilus?" Owen's voice cracked.

"I'm sorry." He flipped his hair back again. "How'd you get in here? Our guest list was strictly enforced." He motioned to take back the pamphlet until Natalie slapped on a smile.

"Sorry," she said emphatically. "That footage was so," she looked back to the stage, "enlightening. To be honest, we'd heard rumors about…about Nautilus. After that display, well, we can't wait for peace to come to us." She clutched at the paper. "We have to go get it."

"I'm afraid the Adoption is reserved for inductees who have already confirmed their recruitment with a donation."

"Will this do?" Brant produced an envelope bursting with cash, one of many found stashed in the lightroom of Ancora III. No doubt Christopher's work.

Fanning the heap of hundreds, the Nautilus member lifted one shoulder. "Our entry fees are quite substantial. Ordinarily, this might have covered one or two of you. However," he passed Tawney, Brant, and Owen their own invitations, "it seems fate knew you needed to find your peace with us today."

He might as well have driven a knife between Natalie's ribs. She sucked in sharply through her teeth.

"Retrieve your welcome package there," he turned their attention to a silver tent. "Arrive in uniform tomorrow and don't be late!" He strode away, distributing invitations as he went.

Natalie trembled, unsure if it was the relief of seeing her parents alive, the rage of their treatment by the Ward's hand, or the terror of finally finding Nautilus again. Perhaps it was some sickening combination of the three.

"What are you playing at?" Tawney shoved her. "Nautilus is torturing our parents and you're snuggling up with their peons!"

"Look around!" Natalie urged. "The Ward's using their own hostages as a ruse! These people are brainwashed by propaganda and perception."

"I don't like this," Owen flicked the invitation. "Our parents on international news? We're being baited. The Ward wants us to come to them. They'll know we're coming."

"Our narcissistic hunter," Tawney mumbled.

Brant tousled her hair. "Big word."

"The first on your list of social ineptitudes," she retorted.

Natalie ignored them, studying the silver foil shell inlaid in the invitation. "But Nautilus isn't expecting us to come as *one of them*. The plan was never to meet them in an outright fight anyway. We wouldn't stand a chance. We needed to find a way inside. Now we have one."

"This wasn't exactly what I'd had in mind," Owen read the pamphlet again. "Though I'll admit, it could work."

Tawney clenched her fists. "It's more fun to punch your way through."

Chin up, eyes open.

"It's perfect," Natalie blurted.

"Nat—"

"If we can get inside their," Natalie fumbled for Nautilus's phrasing, "Adoption, we can find information on our parents. We can stop *that*." She pointed to the hologram.

"Nat—"

"This is it." She shook the invitation as certainty set in. "We get in, we get answers, we get out."

"We get it, Nat!" Tawney spun her towards the tent. "I better get credit for this disaster."

Tawney buckled the back of Natalie's knee and she moved with the momentum, terrified she'd lose her courage if she stopped. Beneath the silver tarp a clutch of older women cooed at their approach.

"Such young blood! Come, come, let's see your invitation."

A bundle of fabric wrapped in silver ribbon dropped into Natalie's arms. The last time she'd worn Nautilus blue she'd shattered her family. Now the uniform felt heavier than she remembered, as though every fold of cloth was woven thick with hope. She tucked the invitation on top, sealing her decision.

3 DOVE DRIVE, ST. AUGUSTINE, FLORIDA
10 AM TOMORROW
MAY YOU FIND PEACE

Tawney kicked up a cloud of sand. "Welcome back to Seashell Sisterhood."

CHAPTER 4
LEONIDAS

*P**ainless.*
It was a strange concept and, admittedly, not as smooth a transition as he had hoped. Every step harbored the trepidation of dragon fire in his gut, while every drawn breath remained wary and shallow. Yet Leo forced himself to walk far and breathe deep the Scottish air because no one, not even pain, would hold him there forever.

He survived a bullet to the belly. Escaping Scotland should be child's play.

Pale sunlight soaked the hillside, painting the white cottage gold as its muted warmth stretched across the hills. Green fields dotted with clouds of grazing sheep softened the rocky isle and footworn paths wound through high grasses to a spit of sand where the North Sea drenched the cliffs.

Leo never missed a sunrise, mainly because he hadn't had a full night's sleep in weeks. Scotland lived up to its iconic legend: every day the hills sang their siren song, inviting him to rest forever in the cradle of their sanctuary. So, every dawn greeted him among the sheep, providing an illusory escape from the truth.

War was coming. And he remained trapped with his hosts in their beautiful prison.

Trust meticulously manufactured over decades of diplomacy had dissolved in a matter of weeks. Bombings in France and Russia pushed Europe to a precipice. World leaders waited to see who would move first, while many stubbornly sealed their borders: no one in, no one out. And no matter how impossible it seemed, Leo couldn't help feeling he and his friends were to blame.

Tacking could change war as we know it.

Still, Scotland's secluded cliffs and stormy seas promised to keep all that misery at bay. It was a hard offer to refuse, which gave Leo all the more incentive to leave.

Reaching the squat cottage, Leo muscled his way up the trellis of vines to the balcony. The effort left him slick with sweat, trembling against the rail. He reminded himself to be grateful. Afterall, weak was better than dead.

A prompt tap on the door inspired him to straighten.

"Yeah, come in." Leo entered the peasant-style bedroom, stretching tall to slap the rafters that spanned the ceiling.

Painless.

A wisp of a woman floated in, her bare feet silent on the worn wood floor and her cloak blood red against porcelain skin.

"Good morning, Leonidas." Ice blue eyes pierced him. "Did you sleep well?"

Cordial. Careful. After six demandingly intimate weeks, this was still their dance.

"Never better."

"I brought salve for your scar." She tossed her curtain of silver hair over one shoulder. Her presence was otherworldly, like reaching out and touching the moon.

"Thanks, Lache."

"Thank Atro and Clo," she insisted. "I would have left you to bleed on our beach." Her words were short and sharp as butcher's knives.

They were also lies.

"No hard feelings." Leo lifted his shirt, exposing the line of pink flesh branded across his abdomen. "If you washed up on my beach with nothing except a Nautilus uniform and your name, I would have drowned you myself."

Though I doubt you would have been incompetent enough to lose your only ticket out. Leo rubbed his bare wrist. How he'd managed to lose his spark he still had no idea. In fact, with his memories slurred through a cocktail of blood loss and oxygen deprivation, what he knew of his arrival was only what Lache and her so-called sisters had been willing to share with him.

Leo shivered as Lache worked the minty salve against his tender skin. A devoted soccer player, Leo was no outlander to injury. But this was no broken wrist or sprained ankle. He had been torn apart and sewn back together and for what seemed like a lifetime, pain had been his closest companion. His shepherd through surgery and director of his nightmares, pain remained steadfast by his side through four weeks of grueling physical therapy.

Who knew you used your abdominal muscles to open a pickle jar? Or pick a sock up off the floor? Or pet the excitable therapy dog that frequented the hospital?

Pain did. Pain always knew. Pain was always there, eager to remind him he no longer belonged to himself. Even the memories of his friends left a bitter taste in his mouth. Most were fuzzy and blurred, tarnished by time, though one remained almost tangible.

Natalie.

He could picture her brows pinched in thought and hear her hesitant laugh. He could still smell the coconut in her hair and taste her lips. She was so real, but when he reached out to feel her there was only pain, and it tricked him every time. He was the mouse that would take the shock to get the cheese. He would succumb just for a glimpse of her.

In short, his recovery had been hell and Lache never let him suffer through it alone. Now her diligence had finally paid off. Deep breath in. Deep breath out.

Painless.

"You are still intent on leaving us?" Her tone was cold. The contrast in dialogue and body language made her a paradoxical being most hours of the day. At the very least, she ensured he was rarely bored.

"You know I am."

"To find your Nautilus friends."

"No." Leo took a breath. They had been through this a million times. "I'm not Nautilus."

Lache squinted up at him. "And your parents?"

"Yes, my parents. I imagine you'd want to save yours if they'd been captured trying to rescue you."

"Unlikely." Lache's smooth features remained expressionless. "I am an orphan."

Leo froze. More information hung in those four words than he had squeezed out of her all summer.

Her shadows, Atro and Clo, hovered in the doorway. Clo's silver pixie hair stuck out wildly as she bit her nails to hide her smile. Atro pulled Clo against her. Swirling, fractal scars glowed against the other sister's charcoal skin. From what Leo could see, they wrapped around her bald scalp and extended to the back of her hands. As their complexion made the markings less obvious, it had taken days for him to notice Lache and Clo wore identical scars.

Identical scars to the one on Natalie's wrist. Which enlightened Leo to exactly what had made them.

"He has changed his mind?" Clo asked hopefully.

Lache shook her head. Together, the three girls forged an eerie sight. Each tall and thin, with irises so brilliantly blue they were nearly white.

Atro retrieved a filing box from beneath the bed. Leo did his best to appear indifferent as she arranged the magazine clippings and computer printouts across his mattress. He figured they must think him insane. Perhaps he was.

"I like lighthouses." Leo crossed his arms, annoyed with the weakness nearly two months of bed rest had inflicted on his body. His muscles were heavy and sluggish, and every menial task proved a test of his stamina.

"It is incredible," Atro cocked her bald head, "the effect physical trauma has on the mind." She studied him as though he were a particularly tricky calculus problem, inching closer and closer to her subject matter. Lack of personal space was another quality the girls had in common. Atro leaned in until they were sharing the same sunbeam, the light turning her silver scars gold.

"Why leave us when you have no idea where to go?" Lache questioned.

Leo swallowed his frustration. They knew he could not remember Christopher's lighthouse. The details were muddled by pain and cold and unconsciousness, until the image of Ancora III had faded. Hope his memory would return was what pulled him through his recovery. He wasn't about to give up now.

"I will find them," he swore. "Even if I have to scour every shoreline on the planet. I can't stay here."

"Perhaps you would consider a third option."

Leo hesitated, considering the cost of hearing them out. "I'm listening."

"You say Nautilus has taken your parents. As you have undoubtedly guessed, we too have suffered from the Ward's hunger for power." Lache pursed her thin lips. "We offer an opportunity to strike back."

Intrigued, Leo asked, "What exactly did you have in mind?"

"We cannot return to Nautilus without being recognized." She chose her words with care. "However, with our help, you could blend in. You could return not as a prisoner," Lache opened her palms, "but as a spy. We can give you an opportunity to find your parents in exchange for your help."

"What is it you want, Lache?" Leo wished she would speak plainly instead of spinning webs out of words.

Unable to contain herself, Clo bounded forward and took both of Leo's hands in her own. "We want to kill Nautilus," she giggled. "Every member we can find."

CHAPTER 5
LEONIDAS

Leo nearly choked. "You're insane."

"I thought you wanted to find your parents. And your friends?" Lache challenged. "Are you not willing to kill for them?"

"Of course, I am." The truth of his words sent a chill down his spine. He would do whatever it took to save his family. The likelihood of killing a Nautilus thug or two along the way had crossed his mind, but all of them? That was more than undermining a wicked organization or coordinating a rescue mission. "That's genocide."

"It is necessary," Lache responded plainly.

"It isn't."

"Nautilus is a plague, Leonidas. They conceal an army behind their promise of prosperity." Lache pulled up the sleeve of her cloak, exposing the matrix of white scars crisscrossing her skin like light refracted on the bottom of a pool. "They mask violence with an illusion of peace. You are foolish if you believe Nautilus deserves anything less than death."

Leo tried not to move or make a sound or even breathe. It had been nothing short of unsettling living with his rescuers for nearly two months and learning no more than their names. He was desperate to keep Lache talking. The three bolt-scarred teens had screamed 'on-the-run' from the beginning. Now he was certain.

Lache leaned closer until he could smell the lingering notes of orange tea on her breath. "Perhaps most importantly, they know where your friends are."

Fear tugged at Leo's stomach. "You can't know that."

"I guarantee it," Lache seethed. "Nautilus destroyed us, and they will destroy your friends, in time."

"So, you were prisoners, too?" Leo struggled to focus on the rough clues she threw at him rather than the possibility Nautilus had already won.

"We were the Moirai," Clo blurted before anyone could stop her.

The Moirai? For the thousandth time that summer, Leo wished Natalie was with him. She would have known what that meant.

"And, what? They just…let you go?" he asked in disbelief.

Silence answered him.

"How has Nautilus not found you here?"

The girls exchanged a loaded glance before Atro deflected his question. "Are you in?"

No matter what Nautilus had done, annihilation seemed extreme. Those people were still people.

At what point do we become like them, pointing to purpose as justification for violence?

"Going back, they would recognize us instantly, but you," Lache tapped Leo's chest. "You could tear them down from the inside out and when the Helix falls, its secrets fall with it."

"Secrets?"

"The Helix is Nautilus's center. Everything is stored there," Clo rocked onto her toes. "Including prisoner records."

So that was their offer: a massacre in exchange for his family. Assuming he could even pull off such a thing.

"What you're describing," he shook his head, "it's nothing short of suicide."

"I am not afraid of death," Lache assured him.

Well, snaps to you, Leo huffed. Still, he was more than tempted. He couldn't walk away from a chance to find out if Nautilus still had his parents or knew where his friends were hiding. Rubbing his palm against the scar on his side, he mulled over his options.

"What if we can stop them without devolving to mass murder? What about taking out the Ward?"

Expressionless, Lache blinked at him.

"Hear me out," he begged. "All of Nautilus acts on the Ward's orders, yeah? Take them out and the organization will die on its own." He chose his words strategically, taking care not to commit to murder.

If I get the Ward out of the picture, the so-called 'Moirai' would never have to know one way or the other.

"You said you wanted my help," he pressed. "This is how you get it. We'll take Nautilus down as cleanly as possible." *While getting what I need to find my mom and dad, and maybe Natalie, too.*

Lache looked to Clo and Atro before replying. "You will never reach the Ward," she insisted. "Though another could take their place. There was a man in charge of us, a Legate. Everything done to the Moirai was on his command."

From the scars that laced their bodies, he couldn't bring himself to argue. "Okay," he said. "Who is it?"

"Legate Amir Amani."

Leo froze.

"You know this man," Atro realized.

"Yeah." He wasn't sure if his scar had truly begun to throb or if he imagined it. "We've met."

"You still will not agree?" Lache adjusted her robe, trapping her silver hair against her body.

"Give me a minute," he worked through the play, searching for weaknesses. The Moirai were clearly calling the shots, forcing him on defense. He agreed that, of anyone, Amani should pay for his cruelty. Leo just didn't want to be the one to kill him. So where could he turn the advantage? How could he decline their demands and still garner passage into Nautilus's halls?

"Show him," Atro suggested.

Lache dug in her robes and Leo's adrenaline kicked up a notch. What did she have sealed away in there? A gun? Poison? A shrunken head? But when her hand emerged there was nothing threatening clutched in it. Instead, a polished five-sided stone hung by leather straps. Leo's anticipation flamed into anger.

"My spark." His entire body trembled with rage. He had been trapped on that green island for weeks thinking he'd lost it, that he'd be scouring the planet for his friends on foot, but his rescuers had stranded him there in the first place. "That doesn't belong to you."

"Relax, Leonidas. It disgusts me to merely hold this cursed stone," Lache held the spark as far away as she could from her body without allowing Leo to grab for it. "Agree to our terms and it is yours once again."

No, Leo's pride rallied. He had been bed-ridden for months, doomed to exist at the grace of others. He'd endured the humiliation of being spoon-fed, bandaged, and medicated by strangers' hands, utterly unable to help himself, and now Lache demanded he compromise for his freedom? He would not.

"Why now?" Leo growled to keep from screaming. "You've had it for months. What's changed?"

"You convinced me." Atro slid the stack of lighthouse clippings across the bed. "You do not know your way home. Your spark will not change that."

Leo clenched and unclenched his fists. Every word she said was the truth. Their pretending he had a choice at all was mere pity.

"Do you even know what it is?" he asked through gritted teeth.

Clo bounced forward only to have Atro yank her back.

"We both know that does not matter." Atro tucked Clo behind

her so only her spiked pixie points poked out over Atro's shoulder. "It does not matter how we came to have your spark or how you washed up on our beach. What matters is what you do next."

"You can leave this place right now," Lache offered. "You can search for your friends by boat, hoping to one day land on the same beach at the same time. Or," she held the spark up to him, "you can help us. And we will all get what we want."

Leo glared at them. He did not like being backed into a corner, tricked into playing a game before he knew the rules. But Lache was right.

"Okay."

Not following, Clo produced a rare frown.

"Okay?" Lache probed.

"I'll do it. Get me inside the Helix, help me find out where my parents are, or my friends, and I'll kill Amir Amani." Hardly believing his own words, he reached for the spark. "Hand it over."

Lache tucked it close to her chest. "Soon."

"Soon?" Leo breathed in sharply through his nose. "You said if I helped you it's mine."

"And it will be." Lache pinched the stone by its leather straps as though holding a mouse by its tail. "When it is time."

For the first time since he met her, Atro smiled. "Let us get started."

Leo begrudgingly followed his caretakers downstairs where the cottage was sparsely furnished and breezy with every window open.

They didn't nurse me back to health to save me. They intended to use me all along. Moirai. The word stuck in his mind. As curious as he was, he hardly spared a thought about their past. Still fuming about his spark and the weakness of his memory, Leo forced himself to focus on the task ahead. The Moirai would arrange his passage into Nautilus's information center, and he would take care of Amir in return. It was simple.

His father would have said it was business.

The plan Lache, Clo, and Atro laid out came in the form of blueprints concealed in linen closets and diagrams tucked under coffee tables. He studied roughly drawn layouts of the Nautilus compound like field plays until he could replicate them. The bullet hole in his uniform was sewn, and the sand and blood caked into it scrubbed away. They made him recite his tightly woven background story until he could do it in his sleep.

At night, when the cottage fell silent save for the distant sighs of the sea, Leo snooped through cubbies and cabinets for his spark. His fruitless search took him into the girls' room. He eased open the nightstand drawer and nearly jumped out of his skin when Clo's cold fingers clasped around his wrist. She didn't make a sound, content to fix him with her glacial stare until Leo retreated silently the way he had come.

The morning met Lache admiring their table of notes on everything from Nautilus etiquette to the location of compounds across the globe. Photographs of senior members, or 'Legates,' formed a pyramid with the imageless Ward at its point. One of the images drew Leo forward and Atro snatched the glossy paper from his grasp.

"Amir Amani," Clo pouted. "They say he was a Captain before the Ward made him Legate and supervisor of the Moirai—"

Atro hissed. Clo waved her away.

"How do you know all of this?" Leo gestured to the table so full of schematics it appeared as though they were about to rob a bank. Which, Leo figured, would probably be easier.

"We lived there." Clo earned another one of Lache's frigid looks.

"This is not any Nautilus institution." Lache referenced the drawing of a cylindrical building with eleven floors, the majority of which stretched underground. "This is the heart of it: the Helix."

Leo pictured Uncle Chris's reaction to what he was agreeing to. *He's going to blow a gasket when he finds out.*

Every waking moment they practiced Nautilus's routine. How to greet a superior, how to stand with respect, and understanding why Curtanas and Doves never shared a meal. Ever.

To Leo's amazement, he found the process rejuvenating. Chained down by his injuries for weeks on end, it felt good to have purpose again. However, the more he learned, the harder it became to swallow his questions.

What part of the facility housed the Moirai? Did they ever leave the compound? How long were they prisoners? Why did Nautilus call it 'The Helix'? Why were so many floors below ground? And there was one question in particular that ate at him constantly. Finally, as Clo nimbly braided the top half of his hair the morning he was to leave, Leo secured a moment alone with her to ask.

"How'd you escape?"

Clo hesitated for a shadow of a second before resuming her work. In the mirror, her reflection was agitated. Her sisters would return any moment, and if anyone was going to answer his questions it was Clo.

"I only ask," Leo coaxed, "because I was Nautilus's prisoner, too. They locked me in a cell hundreds of miles away from anything. I couldn't get out. I couldn't help them." Leo squeezed the seat of the chair until his knuckles shone white.

"What does this have to do with your question?" Clo whispered hastily.

"I was held in a pathetic compound in the middle of nowhere and would probably still be there if I hadn't had help. So," Leo leaned forward as Clo tied the remainder of his hair up at the base of his neck. "How'd you escape the center of their operation? And why haven't they come for you?"

Clo met his gaze in the mirror, and everything came out in a stumbling rush. "We had help. Nautilus has not found us because they do not know to look!" She breathed out a laugh. The sound floated across the room like the turbulence of a butterfly.

Though what she was saying didn't make much, if any, sense, he wanted to keep her talking. "Someone helped you?"

Clo nodded, her spiked hair a blur atop her head. "My sisters, well you know they are not *really* my sisters, they do not trust you. They still worry you are one of them." She tapped the neatly folded navy uniform. "They say it is still possible you will turn us in, that we will be caught and executed. But," she put her face so close to Leo's the tip of her nose brushed his. "I think you are telling the truth. I can feel it. Here," she pressed against his scar.

"Whoever rescued you, were you planning to kill them along with everyone else?"

"Yes." Lache strode in with Atro tucked close behind.

"Then your rescuer's actions count for nothing?"

Lache tossed him his uniform. "What is a drop of water among flames?"

Chef was Nautilus. He remembered her eccentric purple lipstick, the Antarctic snow blushing red with her blood. He doubted he would have escaped without her. *Nautilus would have tacking at their disposal and where would the world be then? Chef didn't only set us free; she gave us the chance to fight back.*

"Hope," Leo argued. "It's hope."

"We do not rely on hope. We rely on ourselves," she pressed his spark into his hand. "And now you."

The roughly cut stone was heavier than he remembered, though not in the way of a burden. The weight felt good. A lost part of himself had been returned, making him whole again. He slipped the straps over his wrist and breathed out in relief.

Lache's mouth still moved. He ignored her. He didn't care anymore. He had his spark.

So why was he still talking to them?

I'm going home.

Leo fled the room. By the time he reached the arched cottage door he was running. Half stumbling, half sliding, he descended the cliff's trail and cleared the thin stretch of pebbled beach. An overhang of cliff-face blocked out the sky, providing what he decided would be sufficient cover. Not that the threat of exposure would have stopped him.

He was going home.

He willed forth the memory of Christopher's photograph: a painted lighthouse beckoned over murky water, and hadn't there been dunes collected around its base?

Meeting the surf head on, the water never touched him. Instead, a flash cracked the morning sky like lightning. A tingling energized every inch of him, and gravity leached away. In less than a second, the sensation faded, and his toes curled to grip the smooth stones underfoot.

Cautiously, Leo opened one eye. Familiar craggy cliffs rose to dizzying heights above him, capped by lush green fields.

No. He spun on his heels to confront the ocean again. Once more the light came and went and left him stranded on Scotland's shore.

"No!" Leo ran in again.

And again.

He slammed his fists against the cliffside. He was so *close*. Yet the memory of the lighthouse flickered and shifted like smoke.

Clo gingerly applied adhesive bandages to shallow cuts made by his assault on the cliff. He had no idea when the girls had followed him to the beach, nor did he care. He glowered at Lache as his chest heaved. A tidal wave of hatred surged through him.

"You had to recover," she said bluntly.

"If you'd given me the spark sooner—" his excuse fell flat.

"We did not know if we could trust you."

"And you trust me now?"

"No." Lache's lips pressed into a thin line. "Though I trust our fates are aligned."

He was not angry with her, or Clo, or Atro. Not really. It hardly mattered if they surrendered the spark six weeks or six seconds ago. In the end, it was his own failure anchoring him to the beach. It was his weakness that separated him from his family. *Weak of body, weak of mind.* Leo cracked his knuckles, seeping blood around Clo's bandages.

"I won't stop searching for them," he swore more to himself than the Moirai.

"I believe you." Lache's silver hair whipped in the wind like a ribbon. "In the meantime, shall we proceed?"

Leo shrugged in resigned agreement.

"You need to better look the part."

"What do you mean?"

"Nautilus's Captains lead their Chamber into battle. They start riots, they assassinate, they fight."

"I have a gunshot wound," Leo spat. "What more do you want?"

"Something visible." Lache nodded to Atro.

Leo turned in time to see Clo cover her face before Atro's elbow collided with his forehead. There was a flash of pain, then he succumbed to darkness.

CHAPTER 6
NATALIE

Starlight dripped down the wings of a shadow perched on the farthest pylon of the dock.

Crow or raven? The bird preened as Natalie flicked the weak candle flame. Its glow darted across the rough wooden table, seeking sanctuary in cracks scaling the marina's walls. The bird turned and cawed.

"Crow," she grumbled.

"Were you expectin' anythin' else?"

Natalie leapt from her seat, clutching her bolt defensively across her chest.

Christopher chuckled. "Gonna kill me, are you?"

"You aren't supposed to be here." Natalie returned the bolt to her back. She couldn't believe she'd let him sneak up on her. Again.

"It's my house!" Christopher peered into the bowl of brightly colored taffy between them.

The crow cawed again, and Natalie smacked the window.

"Why are you back so soon?"

"I'm going to find our parents—"

"'Cause that worked out well last time."

"—and then I'm going to find some answers. Real ones."

Christopher said nothing.

"I know you think if Nautilus catches me, they'll have tacking and," she still stumbled over the term, "time-travel at their disposal, but them holding onto our families isn't any better. Our parents created us. They made tacking and time-travel possible." Natalie reached for him, then promptly stopped herself. "If Nautilus is torturing them," she paused, "time-travel will be theirs just as fast."

"Your parents knew what they signed up for, kid." Uncle Chris offered a sad smile that never quite reached his eyes. "Give it time."

Time. She hated time.

Time was exactly what had landed her in this mess in the first place.

The crow cried and abandoned its post and Natalie wondered how light she would be without the weight of her hopes grounding her. She hoped to free her parents before Nautilus broke them, or worse. She hoped she could keep her friends safer than she kept her family. She hoped to find Leo alive. She hoped to find Leo at all.

A sharp tap on the door sounded and, though she'd been expecting it, Natalie jumped.

"Who's that?"

"An old friend." Natalie ushered in a petite girl with pin-straight auburn hair.

"Nat!" She dropped a tattered duffle bag and threw her arms around Natalie's neck.

"Nora!" Chris greeted her warmly.

Natalie gingerly pried herself away. "Get everything?"

"Of course. Have you done this before?"

Natalie shook her head as Nora unzipped the bag, revealing a bounty of beauty products. Natalie bypassed a bulging bag of makeup in favor of a case of black hair dye.

"I hoped you'd pick this one." Nora clapped. "And be sure to use this liner: heavy on top, light on the bottom. Okay? And any ideas on the new cut?"

Thinking, Natalie poked the pointy end of Nora's barber scissors.

"Don't go doin' that!" Christopher fussed from the corner. "You won't change a thing by changin' your face or your hair."

Natalie stared at him. If he was right, she didn't stand a chance.

Nora spared a glance towards Uncle Chris before looking expectantly at Natalie. "Well?"

"No cut," Natalie decided. "Just show me how to use this stuff."

Nora held up the bottle. "Work in a palmful of dye after you wash your hair. Oh gosh, be sure you use the gloves." She went on. "You can get it wet, no problem, so when you're ready to be caramel again, be sure to wash with the dye-stripper. Rinse and repeat and ta-da! You're you again."

Me again, Natalie thought skeptically. *Must be some pretty magical stuff.*

"And don't be stingy. I can get y'all more whenever you need it. No problem."

Natalie shifted impatiently. She could clearly see the sprinkling of freckles across Nora's nose and the shine of old water rings on Christopher's table. Dawn was breaking.

"How are you holding up?" Nora asked as Natalie stuffed everything back into the bag.

"Fine." Natalie's bottom lip quivered with the lie.

"Keep your head up, kid." Uncle Chris blinked slowly at her. She couldn't take it anymore. She had to leave.

"I have to go." Natalie slung the bag over her shoulder and fled the cottage. Crisp, salty air blew off the Atlantic, ignorant of the sticky Virginia heat accompanying the rising sun.

"Do you still think Leo's coming back?" Nora hurried to keep up.

The anchor in Natalie's stomach gave a sharp tug and she felt herself sink a little deeper. Leo could have drowned in that fjord. He could have been dredged from the sea by Amir Amani and his crew. He could have—

"How's your mom?"

"As well as anyone these days," Nora hugged herself. "Have you seen the news?"

"Only headlines." Natalie watched a flock of sandpipers dance back from a breaking wave.

"People are scared. My brother's elementary school is practicing bomb drills," she scoffed. "Like a wooden desk will save them. It's the only hope they have I guess."

Sometimes that's worse. Natalie shifted her weight. She had stayed too long.

"I don't want a war," Nora added quietly.

Christopher's warnings of another world war had once seemed alien: foreign and out of context. Now the world waited, anxious to see if diplomacy or discord would reign.

"Some people call them a 'time-step,'" Nora noted as the sandpipers outpaced another wave.

"Guess my parents should have called me Piper."

"Oh, you are listening." Nora elbowed her. "Why Piper?"

"Long story," Natalie adjusted the bag on her back again. "Listen, I've really got to go."

"These people you're trying to fool," Nora went on, "how dangerous are they?"

That depends, Natalie chewed her cheek, *on whether you stand in front of them or behind them.*

"Keep your head down," Natalie warned aloud. "Just in case."

Nora nodded and Natalie forced her anxiety for her friend and her mother aside. They helped with Christopher when no one else could. They'd accompanied him to the hospital after he was shot and stuck around ever since. It was a debt she'd never be able to repay.

"Will you..." Natalie didn't know how to ask Nora and Mrs. King for more than they'd already given. She glanced back at

Morning Sun Marina.

"We're taking care of things here," Nora promised. "I still think this whole tacking thing is magic."

"Don't let Owen hear that."

"It's hard to insult someone I've never met."

"Soon," Natalie hugged her.

As they parted, Nora eyed the black pistol strapped to Natalie's waist. "Be careful."

Hurrying to the covered fueling station, Natalie dropped towards the water as the first rays of sunshine flowed over the horizon.

CHAPTER 7
NATALIE

Natalie stifled a yawn.

"The Adoption," Owen admired the rising sun. "How insulting."

And ironic.

"It's kind of clever." Brant laid on the floor with Nora's black duffle on his chest. "Unlike this bag of tricks."

"Make-up." Tawney wrinkled her nose.

"If there's any sign we've been discovered, we'll bail, but this is our best shot to find our," Natalie steadied herself, "our parents."

Brant rolled over, dumping the contents of the bag across the floor. "Contacts! For you, my good sir!" He tossed a box to Owen, who blanched.

"I *cannot* touch my eyeball," he covered his mouth with his fist. "I'm going to hurl just thinking about it."

Upside down on her hands, Tawney lapped around the circular room. "You'll tack around the globe and time-travel to see man-eating dinosaurs, but you won't—"

Natalie's head snapped up. "You *what?*"

Tawney collapsed in a heap. "What I meant to say was: he was *thinking* about—"

"We discussed this," Natalie's rage boiled up like lava. "You, Owen? *You* of all people!"

"I know what you're thinking—" Brant's attempt to calm her was cut off.

"We don't know what happens when you mess with the timeline! Christopher said so himself. We have no idea how to time-travel, let alone *control it*. What you did was…was," she stuttered over her fury. "Irresponsible!"

"Oh please," Tawney slumped into a chair. "Why shouldn't we at least try?"

"Because we don't know what we're doing!"

"You did it."

Natalie balked at her. "On accident! You could have exposed Ancora III to Nautilus instantly." She turned back to Owen. "You were the one who said a time-traveler's energy signal could be a thousand times more powerful than tacking. Not to mention the possibility of igniting a catastrophic chain of events." She could feel her pulse in her temples. "How many times did you try?"

"Doesn't matter," Tawney leaned forward with her elbows on her knees. "It didn't work. Maybe if you shared with the class how you managed—"

Owen kicked her and the sheer fact Tawney didn't lay him out was enough to crack Natalie's anger.

"We couldn't figure it out," Owen held his palms out in surrender. "We went nowhere every time, never even left the beach." His guilty defense turned wistful. "I just wanted to see it, you know? A real dinosaur. That it's even a possibility…" He shook his head.

Natalie inhaled her frustration into her chest and out through pursed lips. Owen had been presented with the scientific advancement of the age, the key to unlocking the secrets of history, and then asked not to use it. It was like giving a kid a chocolate bar and telling them not to eat it. Natalie's power weighed on her every day: a responsibility she didn't want demanding control she didn't have. It wasn't fair for any of them.

"If I knew how I did it you'd already know," Natalie assured them. "And if you were trying to go anywhere, you should've been searching for Leo."

She regretted the comment the moment she said it. Tawney scowled at her shoes while Owen studied the wood grain of the table. She wasn't surprised it was Brant who snapped back.

"We've nearly drowned splashing around in that ice bucket." Brant wrung his cap. "Hell, time-travel, we were trying to have a little fun. Don't you remember fun? That thing that makes you forget your life is completely botched. A freaking second of peace."

Natalie deflated. What would she give for a second of peace? The fate of the world?

Maybe I would. Her family had sacrificed everything to keep her safe, but she wasn't sure she was like them. She was selfish. She wanted to feel stable again, to take it all back, to have something as simple and concrete as a home.

But if Nautilus figures out how to manipulate us, to manipulate time-travel, fate will be in their hands.

And her home in their dungeons.

"Why didn't you tell me?"

"Exhibit A," Tawney gestured at all of her. "Like we said, didn't work anyway."

Her notes of jealousy made Natalie's heart ache. If she knew what Natalie was really hiding…

She deserves to hear about the adoption from her parents. Not me, not a stupid piece of paper. They owe her that much.

"We can't afford taking chances on time-travel." Natalie decided to move on. "Agreed?"

"Agreed," they echoed.

Refocused, her gaze fell on the table's empty chair. "I want to make sure everyone's comfortable with what we're about to do."

"We get in, we find what we need, and we get out," Owen nodded.

"Brant?"

"I'm going to save my family," he promised. "And yours, too."

Tawney pulled a hair straightener from Nora's bag, pinching it cautiously as though it might bite her. "This is going to take a while." She frowned at her curls.

"Then we'd better get started."

Hours later, Natalie braved the mirror. She blew back a stray strand of black hair. Her eyes watered incessantly, protesting the blue contact lenses. She was no longer herself. She was no longer anyone. She saw a stranger wearing her mannerisms.

"Want it up?"

"You're joking, right?" Tawney's once wild curls shone fire-engine red and fell straight to her hips. "What else am I supposed to do with it?"

Natalie worked Tawney's hair, struggling to find something to talk about. They'd been friends so long silence was as comfortable as laughter. At least it used to be. Before secrets carved a chasm between them.

"If you keep furrowing that hard your eyebrows are going to fuse together."

Natalie tried relaxing her forehead.

"Are you sleeping yet?"

"Sometimes."

"You can actually talk to me, you know," Tawney's new reflection reminded her. "We're all going through the same thing."

Not quite. Though Natalie wanted to confide in Tawney more than anything, how could she tell her best friend she was adopted? How would Tawney react? Would she still be ready to go hunting for answers or would she prefer to leave their lying parents to their fate? It was a risk Natalie couldn't take.

Securing Tawney's red mane into a high ponytail, she stepped back to admire her work. "What do you think?"

"That girls take forever." Brant poked his head into the washroom. His chestnut mop of curls was painted golden fair with the top half twisted back.

"You spent forty minutes deciding on a color for your man-bun," Owen countered from the couch. He pretended to survey the room, blind as a bat with his glasses tucked on his collar.

"I think it was better before." Tawney inspected Owen's newly browned locks so openly he flushed pink.

"We're going to be late," he deflected.

"What are you talking about?" She spun her ponytail like a bloody helicopter blade. "We'll tack to the Adoption lickety-split!"

"We can't," Owen squinted in her general direction.

"There has to be somewhere by the Adoption that's covered," Brant insisted.

Tawney pointed at him as though this was obvious however, as happy as Natalie was to see the two getting along, it simply wasn't possible.

"We'll tack to Florida," she agreed. "Only the address on the invitation is ten miles inland."

Tawney burst out of the bathroom. "What are you saying? That we're *walking*? Ten miles? In that devil's sauna they call a state?"

"Ten-point-seven miles actually." Owen pushed his frames back up the bridge of his nose.

"Fat chance," Tawney argued.

Surrounded by navy jumpsuits, Natalie took the spiral stairs two at a time, leaving her friends bickering. Enzi bounded ungracefully ahead of her to the wardrobe, his ears two perfect triangles atop his head.

"Fine," Natalie conceded. "You're going to have to work for it." She retrieved a biscuit from the drawer and, before she could give a single command, Enzi offered each of his paws, laid down, rolled over, and army crawled. Sitting up again, he ogled the treat intently.

She tossed him the cookie. "We need to challenge you more."

Natalie pushed past the weathered uniform forced on her in Antarctica and pulled on the new one from the Nautilus festival. It would be brutal in the summer heat, but she wasn't about to challenge protocol. If blending in meant sweating a bit, she would gladly glisten.

Finally, she adjusted the pistol tucked against the small of her back. Though not part of the uniform, her promise to Christopher required she take it.

A deal's a deal.

Tucking Chef's bolt safely inside the wardrobe she gave Enzi her parting instructions. "Water bowl is full. Take care of Angie. The door will be cracked for you to go out. I'll be back before dark." She kissed the top of his muzzle. "Don't talk to strangers."

Downstairs, she found Ancora abandoned. Savoring a few moments of quiet, she drifted to the mantle and the largest photograph propped upon it. Immortalizing a Formal Friday long past, the last one to see them all together, the scene was bittersweet. It reminded her they'd been happy once, before the bombing in Norfolk wrenched them from their parents, before Mrs. Smith lost her battle with cancer, before Christopher ghosted them in junior high. More importantly, the image hinted to answers lurking beyond her reach. As far as Natalie knew, everyone involved in the Coelacanth Project was present in the photograph.

So, who took it? Chef?

Yet another question she would ask her parents as soon as she was able.

Outside, three strangers waited around a line of brand-new bicycles. Angie dashed in and out between their ankles until Enzi skidded out of the lighthouse and trapped her between his paws. Natalie let out an impressed whistle.

This might actually work.

"How do I look?" Tawney asked.

"Like a wanted thief."

Tawney ripped the price tag off one of the gold bikes. She had stolen small things at first: Japanese candy, bullets for target practice, wiring for Owen's computers. And it was not for lack of funds. Though Natalie didn't agree with Tawney's methods, she let it go. She figured everyone needed an outlet. Tawney's was stealing.

Hers was Christopher.

"I haven't ridden in forever." Brant rocked his bike in the sand.

After six weeks of stagnant misery, they had a plan. It hung on the strength of navy thread, and still hope battered against her dammed heart with the force of a tsunami.

Or our parents are already dead and this is for nothing, she fought against the swell. *They aren't our parents anyway. Not really.* She recited the facts only to weaken the hope that threatened to overtake her. Sand shifted beneath her shoes as she walked the bike towards the water. *From one adoption to another.*

Beneath the shelter of the dock, she stepped into the blinding light and out under a busy fishing pier. Sweat beaded the back of her neck as three more flashes followed close behind.

"Ladies first." Tawney ran out and jumped on her bike the moment her tires hit the parking lot.

Natalie mimicked her and welcomed the rush of the wind. It wicked away the heat, sending goosebumps down her body. She pedaled faster.

"Don't let go!" she giggled with delight. Scabbed, stubby legs pedaled hard beneath her and the handlebars' sparkling tassels whipped her wrists. Finches fled the safety of the bushes and she flew with them.

The bike disappeared beneath her and she was sky bound. She was weightless, free, a bird all along.

She slammed into the ground, rolling to a stop on the sidewalk. Blood bubbled up from her palms and dripped down her knees to her socks.

Uncle Chris sprinted for her. Her knee burned, and the blood running down her leg itched, and she wailed until soft hands lifted her from the earth. She melted

against her mother's chest.
"I flew!" Natalie sobbed.
"I know," Chris called to her. "I know, kid."
He let her go.
Mother would never do that.

"Watch it!" Brant's shout pulled Natalie out of her memories. She jerked her handlebars, barely avoiding a pothole.

"Are you blind?" he teased.

"Only for most of my life," Natalie muttered under her breath.

Tawney raced ahead and stood high on her pedals. When her bike slowed, Owen bumped her back tire. Tawney grinned.

"Don't start something you can't finish," she taunted.

Natalie nearly fell over. Tawney was flirting.

They'd been cycling for almost an hour when Tawney skidded to a stop. A field of solar panels stretched before them with a cylindrical building at its center. Natalie didn't care for the layout; it would be impossible to come or go unseen.

"Remember," she warned aloud, "blend in. The less you speak, the less you lie, and the less likely you are to slip up. We'll meet back at Ancora III tonight. If anyone doesn't show…"

"Leaving Ancora III is a last resort," Brant rubbed her back and she subtly arched away.

"Here we go," Tawney set off down the hill, a red blur between two queues of solar panels, and Owen followed several rows over.

Meanwhile, Brant hesitated. Thrumming on his handlebars, he leaned towards her. "We should…well, maybe later we can—"

Natalie refused to let him finish. "You're next."

If her deflection offended him, he didn't show it. With a mock salute he pedaled in the opposite direction of Owen.

One crisis averted. A flood of Nautilus members and recruits funneled down the field of panels. She dried her palms on her pants, steeling her nerves. Dizzy with adrenaline, Natalie floated down the hill and as Nautilus's compound loomed over her, she clung to one

reassuring fact.
This is the beginning of the end.

CHAPTER 8
NATALIE

Uncut grass tickled Natalie's ankles as she propped her bike against the building. She immersed herself in the crowd, falling in line behind a group of college-age boys just boisterous enough to keep attention away from her.

"Better than the animal shelter," one argued.

"Or the food pantry."

Another of the boys puffed out his chest, prematurely proud of all the things he'd yet to accomplish. "Did you even listen to the guest speaker?" His torso inflated so wide his gate mimicked a penguin's waddle. "Nautilus will be calling the shots soon and I'm going to be the one making them. I'm going to be a Legate."

"Yeah, and I'm going to be the Queen of England," a broad girl sneered at them.

"Shove off, dragonette."

Natalie couldn't disagree with his assessment. The gelled green hair, plethora of piercings, and bulky body did invoke a dragonesque vision. And that was before the smoke coiled from her nostrils.

"You slugs may be too dense to notice," she inhaled deeply from a metal box, spilling vapor out of her grin, "but women run the world."

"Hate to burst your bubble," the first boy scoffed. "There's no way the Ward's a woman."

The girl ignored him. "When Nautilus manages to light a real fire in you, you'll be serving peace by serving our meals."

To Natalie's horror, the dragonette wrapped an arm around her shoulders. Natalie had no intention of joining their conversation, particularly not so physically, and a squeak of alarm escaped her. She suddenly understood how Enzi's toys must feel trapped between his jaws.

Bored or intimidated, the guys retreated to their own conversation.

"What's your name?" the dragonette asked her.

Natalie's stomach sank and, much to her alarm, she let out another squeak.

"Mouse?" the girl teased.

My name? She was keenly aware of the sweat stinging her eyes. Away from the sea the air was stagnant and stifling, even worse with the solar panels firing up the hillside like a kiln. She uttered something inaudible, trying to buy a few seconds in the eternity that stretched between them.

"What's that, Mouse?"

Normally, Natalie would have slipped away, simply disappeared into the crowd with her awkwardness in tow. However, if she couldn't con her unsuspecting peers, she would never fool the Nautilus members inside. Flustered by her ineptitude and the debilitating heat, Natalie went for the first tangible thing that blew by: a shiny black lock of hair.

"Raven!" she exclaimed. "It's Raven."

"Raven. Pretty," the girl let go of her. "Mine's Max."

"Pleasure." Natalie tried to separate herself into the crowd. Max stuck fast by her side.

"So, what brings you here?"

"Oh, you know. Peace."

"Right." Max stuck the stud in her tongue out between her teeth. "Why are you really here?"

"I told you." *Wrong,* Natalie bit her cheek. *That's no way to make friends.* "Look, I really am here for peace." She gave Max her full, sweaty attention. She needed the girl to believe her. She also needed a distraction from the fact she was entering the lion's den reeking of fear and undoubtedly a fair amount of body odor. "My life has been...messy. I want to sort it out. I want to prevent the same from happening to anyone else."

Though I doubt mine's an experience to be duplicated.

"Wow," Max sucked on a metal ring around her lip. "How sickeningly noble of you."

"I guess so."

"Well, I want to lead," Max said bluntly. "I want people and tanks lined up behind me. *Me,*" she emphasized, pointing to her hair and jewelry. "Not some image of what society wants me to be. Nautilus says they don't care," she snorted, making the dragon evolution complete. "We'll see soon enough."

They passed through the open doors together into a wall of cooled air. Natalie leaned into it. The chemical scent of bleach and lemon burned her nose and she hardly cared. It had never felt so good to be so cold.

Eyes open. Her heart hummed in her throat. She had one day inside. One day to find anything she could on her folks. She couldn't afford to miss a single detail that might lead to where Nautilus was holding her parents. *Pay attention.*

Natalie spun, intent on absorbing everything as she was jostled in deeper by the swarm of recruits. For all the fanfare at the festival, the compound was unsettlingly bare. The main room formed a semi-circle with halls vanishing far off on either side. Everything was white: white tile, white chairs against the walls, white tables, white paint. Only the railings, doors, and security pads shone silver under the fluorescent lights. The navy uniforms stood out plainly in contrast, leaving nowhere to hide outside the crowd. She felt like a guppy in a school of fish; one step out of line and she'd be picked off by the sharks. Two Nautilus members closed the doors behind them, and an unexpected swell of claustrophobia rocked her.

It's not the same. She forced herself to breathe. *It seems the same, it feels the same, it's not. This is not the White Room. This is not Antarctica. Control your fear.* Amir Amani's sharp features swam before her. The screams of her friends echoed in her ears. Panic paralyzed her. There was no sun; she was trapped beneath the earth, destined to die in their pit.

"You okay?"

Natalie blinked. "Fine." *Same organization, different place. Different me.* "Just...a lot of people." A lot of Nautilus.

"Ah." Max let it drop, captivated by the assembly awaiting them. Nautilus members mobbed a balcony that spanned the second floor, beckoning them forward.

"Welcome to Nautilus! Welcome to Peace!"

Someone stopped in front of her. Their uniform glinted with a line of silver bars, each about an inch in length. He passed an identical pin to her before moving on to Max. By the time she gathered enough of her wits to question what the pin was for, the distributor was long gone.

A hush crept through the mass of bodies. A woman on the balcony opened her arms, as though aspiring to embrace the whole of them at once. Instead of Nautilus blue, she towered in a tailored charcoal suit and polished heels. Her dark hair was pulled back, assuring an unobstructed view of those beneath her.

"It gives me great pleasure to welcome you on behalf of our Ward. Welcome to the Helix, welcome to Nautilus, welcome to peace, and welcome home!" Her diplomatic demeanor jarred Natalie's memory. However, it wasn't until the woman spoke that she placed the resemblance.

Amir Amani. Same poise, same velvet smooth tone. The only discernible difference was that this woman sported three Nautilus shells pinned to her collar. They were no doubt some sort of honor and, if Natalie's memory was correct, Amir only had one.

At least he worked for it. He had to catch me. I marched right into this woman's blue and silver web.

"You come to Nautilus on different paths. No matter what brought you here today, we'll guide you on your journey to peace.

"My name is Legate Shaye. I oversee Inductee Assessment and Adoption to ensure your smooth transition into Nautilus. We will remake you in Nautilus's image and fight together for a greater good.

"Only the Ward knows the path we must take to find peace. It will take your dedication, determination, and donations to see us through. Nautilus will rise so we may bind together in a new world of prosperity!"

Natalie balked at the sentiment. Yet, as she looked around the room, every recruit admired Shaye as though she wove gold from her breath.

"Now that you are home," Shaye continued. "You will be Assessed for how you will best serve our cause and be Adopted into our family. In two weeks' time, after you have learned the ways of our society and trained for your role, you will graduate as honored members of Nautilus!"

A roar of applause erupted.

They're actually buying this? Studying her fellow inductees, they were all incredibly and inexplicably normal. Neighbors, doctors, and students stood shoulder to shoulder. Pierced, wrinkled, and sunburned skin formed a mosaic lined in navy blue and it was undeniably beautiful. In them, she saw herself. She recognized the strained squint of their eyes and hesitance of their smiles. They were all burdened with the same weight that threatened to pull her under every day.

Hope.

She wasn't surrounded by the enemy. She was surrounded by people.

This is Nautilus's game. They transform recruits into the hunters that burned my home and abducted my family.

"Nautilus will do whatever is necessary to keep you safe. Strict surveillance is in place and we will extricate all obstacles on our journey to peace, whether external or internal in nature."

There's a chocolate-covered gut punch. Natalie swayed, swept up in the growing excitement of Shaye's audience.

"By joining us today you have earned your first Prestige: a recognition of your service to the Ward. Don it now as a symbol of your vow to pursue the path to peace no matter the cost."

Natalie affixed the silver pin to her chest and its weight seemed to multiply tenfold.

"Let us proceed with your Assessment!"

For the first time since their arrival, doubt rippled through the recruits. No one had mentioned anything about a test. *Blindly follow an obscure leader shrouded in peaceful promises? Sure. Submit yourself to their judgement of whether or not you're worthy? Not likely.*

"The Assessment," Legate Shaye spoke over the restless shuffle, "is only to determine where Nautilus will be best served by your contributions. You found your home the moment you walked through those doors. We will help you find peace."

Comforted by her words, the crowd trickled deeper into the Helix. Passing through a tunnel beneath the balcony, Natalie shuffled along, her anxiety building with every step. Through another large, semi-circular room and several passages, she descended a grand spiral staircase. The white marble stairs sparkled with all the finery of an art museum. But Natalie knew better.

"Before we get started," Shaye's projected voice drifted among them. "Allow me to introduce your Legates. These members will oversee your Adoption and prepare you to fully integrate into your

Chamber."

Chamber?

A blue hologram flickered near the ceiling, flashing through Legates as Shaye introduced them. Although normally gripped by detail, Natalie struggled to pay attention. Her legs dragged as though they'd congealed to lead. She wanted nothing more than to push against the flow of bodies channeling her down. She wanted to see the sky. She wanted out.

Someone pried her death grip from the rail. Searching far ahead of her, she spotted a familiar figure. Brant winked.

Be stronger than your fear, Christopher's words resonated in her mind.

Natalie inhaled, hoping clarity would accompany oxygen. She made herself taller, if only by an inch, to descend with more control. She catalogued the few facts she managed to catch from Shaye's speech.

Legates, like Shaye, formed the Ward's inner circle and served as leaders for each division, or Chamber, of Nautilus. Natalie was certain she explained what each Chamber was for, but the details were too foreign and slippery to find purchase. Even the names of the Legates bounced in Natalie's skull without sticking. The Helix, the Assessment, the hundreds of people: it was too much to take in.

Natalie constantly reminded herself to keep moving with the other recruits. One step, then another, and another. Eventually, the staircase would end. Eventually, she'd come across a passage and slip away to dig up whatever information she could.

The only way out is through.

Shaye continued speaking as the end of the spiral staircase approached. Another hologram appeared but Natalie focused on the metal doors ahead of her.

"Finally, I present the head of the Legate Chamber: the fearless Eleanor Deluna."

Natalie missed a step. The crowd blurred and Shaye's words

muffled up like thick cotton in her ears. Above her, pixels arranged into a wrinkled face framed with wild grey hair. She waved down at the recruits. Two fingers were missing from her left hand.

Eleanor had stalked them in Ancora I. She invaded Natalie's home, burnt it to the ground. Fooling a room of strangers was one thing, but Eleanor? Natalie clung to the rail with clammy palms to save herself from tumbling the rest of the way down.

I've marched us to our tomb.

CHAPTER 9
NATALIE

The metal doors opened and Natalie stumbled into an expansive white abyss. The ceiling floated somewhere high above her, out of reach of the silver and blue lanterns casting light up their columns. She barely noticed anything else; the lingering chill of Eleanor's presence blurred the details.

She'll recognize me and then what? Torture me for information? Kill me on the spot?

Someone guided Natalie to stand with a few people she recognized, most notably dragonette Max who tapped her tongue piercing against those on her lip.

"Different aspects of the Assessment will be conducted simultaneously," Shaye's disembodied words explained. "Follow your senior members and remember: no matter where your Assessment assigns you, you are already home."

Maybe I won't even see her. Natalie bit the inside of her cheek so hard she tasted the metallic tang of blood. *The second I can slip away I'll find what I need for my parents, get out, and never come back.*

She was led out of the cavernous room and down a winding hallway. Other than Max, she journeyed alongside a young girl with flawless bronze skin, two guys Natalie guessed were twins, and a shuffling elderly couple. The girl watched Natalie curiously.

"What brings you here?" Natalie asked, partly to distract herself and partly out of genuine curiosity.

"Peace."

"Wouldn't you rather be at school?"

She swished her dark braid, exposing purple and yellow bruises patchworked down her neck. Natalie shied away from the sight; the girl could hardly be older than thirteen.

Violence knows no age limit.

"My name is N—," Natalie caught herself, "Raven."

The girl side-eyed her cautiously. Before she could answer, they were ushered down yet another corridor branching off the gallery. The more Natalie saw of the Helix the more it reminded her of a hive.

Another labyrinth to get lost in. She wasn't sure she could retrace her steps, let alone remember all the different paths they had crossed. Every turn took her deeper into a uniquely familiar prison. How was she supposed to find anything on her parents if she couldn't even find her way out?

They emptied into a round room packed with twenty square desks. Natalie claimed the first she reached, grateful for something solid to sink into. Fluorescent lights hummed from the ceiling, illuminating the source of a rhythmic ticking. Natalie white-knuckled her seat.

Damned clock.

"You have an hour to answer as many questions correctly as you can," their proctor explained, conveniently blockading the only exit.

I'll never find anything with them hovering like this.

"You may begin."

At his command, the surface of her desk glowed to life. She tapped a white button labeled *'Start'* and an outline of a hand appeared on the screen. Mimicking the recruits around her, she aligned her palm with the image. The computer scanned the length of her hand, ending with a sharp pinch at the base. She yanked it back, expecting to see blood, and found no mark at all. Before she could inspect it further, the first question appeared.

Name?

Natalie drew *'Raven'* across the screen.

What is the square root of twenty-five?

Tick-tock.

What fatal virus is spread through the saliva of mammals?

What were the three trials of Odysseus?

Tick-tock.

Natalie alternated between answering the questions and imagining all the ways to destroy the clock.

Who is considered the founder of modern chemistry?

Tick-tock.

How do you define success?

Tick-tock.

Nautilus had taken everything from her. Her family. Her home. The simple pleasure of her safety.

Tick-tock.

But she would obliterate their bloody clock.

"Hands below your desks," their proctor announced. "Remember, your score is for the Legates alone and solely for the purpose of finding your perfect fit in our family. You are already home; the Assessment has no power over that."

I doubt Eleanor will care about test scores if she sees my face.

His words, surely intended to be reassuring, only reminded Natalie she had lost another hour she could have been searching for information.

"The next phase of your Assessment is physical."

Oh good, one last humiliation before my death.

Passing through the white cathedral hall, they plunged into another narrow tunnel. Most of those around her chatted excitedly about life after the Assessment, apparently at ease in Nautilus's chambers. Natalie hung towards the edge of the group and when the first empty passage finally appeared, she didn't hesitate.

Side-stepping into the shadows, Natalie pressed her back so hard against the wall she thought it might open and swallow her whole. Five seconds passed. Ten. After fifteen, she finally exhaled.

I did it.

Staring down the dim hall, she drew herself up and blew out a puff of air. Six weeks had passed since her escape from the Ward's Antarctic hell; yet that night clung to her like a ghost. Finally, after causing their parents' capture, Leo's disappearance, and more, she was exactly where she needed to be to set things right.

Find something, anything, and get out.

She took her first step when the guide grabbed her.

"Recruit?"

Natalie spun, ready to fight. Wrenching out of his grip, she raised one arm to defend herself while the other reached for the pistol tucked into her waistband.

"Hey."

She stopped. What she saw in his face was...concern. Genuine *concern.*

"I know this can be overwhelming." He squeezed her shoulder. And not to push her down or subdue her, but to comfort her. The action was immobilizing.

"I'm fine."

He grinned until dimples appeared in his cheeks. "If you need to talk to someone—"

"No." Natalie released her grip on the pistol, leaving it hidden beneath her uniform. The last thing she wanted to do was talk. "I just needed to breathe was all."

Satisfied, he led her back to the group, and she trudged alongside her fellow recruits. She had blown her chance and managed to catch the attention of their proctor in the process. Wound up in her frustration, she failed to notice they had stopped in a gymnasium until their guide addressed them again.

"You will travel individually from station to station where your physical capabilities will be evaluated." He gestured to dozens of Nautilus members spread out around the gym. "These measurements are a formality. Your place in Nautilus was secured the moment you entered our doors."

Scanning the room there were too many Nautilus members to count and no exit was left unattended. She wouldn't be slipping out of the gym unnoticed. Resigned, she stepped to the closest attendant: a plump woman with a tablet and a wooden box.

"Scan," she demanded, already pulling Natalie to her.

Her palm flattened against the tablet and, like the desk, a bar of light scanned it and ended with a sharp prick. Satisfied, the woman directed Natalie to sit with her legs out and her feet flat against the box.

"Now lean forward as far as you can across the top."

"I'm sorry," Natalie pointed at the box. "Are we doing the sit-and-reach test from Phys. Ed.?"

"Reach forward, Raven," the woman deflected. "We have many recruits to get through."

Natalie did as instructed, her reach extending a few inches beyond the tips of her toes. It wasn't until she arrived at the next station that she realized she'd never given the woman her name.

My information's in their system. She massaged the base of her palm. *My name, my scores, my measurements...*

The attendant at the next station was so old and frail, she quivered holding the biometric scanner.

"Remember, love," the lady worked a pair of calipers over Natalie's body, pinching the skin around her triceps. "None of these numbers mean anything." Her pinching traveled to Natalie's thighs and stomach. "Nautilus simply needs to know all the wonderful things you bring to the family."

I see how they could believe you. Natalie skimmed the various tests conducted across the gymnasium. *If I hadn't seen the blood spilt by your leaders, I might believe you, too.*

"You're quiet."

"I'm sorry, ma'am. That exam exhausted me more than I thought."

The old woman chuckled. "We may be in the south, love, only here I'm a Dove, not ma'am."

"Dove?"

"It's my Chamber. Doves spread Nautilus's word and the promise of peace."

Working through the stations, Natalie searched for an opening, any lapse in security that would allow her to sneak off.

And wander around aimlessly? Even if she did manage to get away, which did not look promising, she had no idea which way to run.

Meanwhile she was weighed, held her chin above a metal bar until her muscles gave out, and did as many sit-ups as she could in a minute. She walked ten yards balanced on a four-inch beam and ran a timed mile.

Eight minutes, Natalie caught her breath. *Tawney will say I should've made seven.*

She lined up behind recruits who finished before her, most of whom silently watched their companions. No matter how much Nautilus said their scores didn't matter, it was obvious they were being ranked.

They know they're competing, Natalie watched the quiet girl with the dark braid sprint around the track, *but not what for or what it takes to win.* Eventually, their faithful guide led them into yet another passage. Its floor inclined slowly, and the walls curved perpetually to the left.

We're going around the spiral staircase, she guessed. She trailed the smooth wall next to her. There were no turns, no side tunnels to hide in, no escape from the inevitable fate waiting at the peak.

Abruptly, their march stopped. Natalie clutched a cramp in her side and for several minutes nothing happened. Every now and then the line advanced a pace or two. After an hour, her adrenaline dissipated, and frustration set in. After two, she slumped against the wall, her muscles aching in ways Tawney's workouts only dreamed.

She had no idea how much time had passed when she finally stood before a door. Recruits closest to her babbled excitedly as their turn to exit the passage approached. The guard's eyes were unfocused and glassy, his mind busy elsewhere, and not giving any hints to what awaited them.

Natalie bounced on the balls of her feet. No one who had gone beyond the door returned, and a rumor rippled up the line that this was the last trial of their Assessment.

I must make it through this. Focusing on her parents, she readied herself. *I can still get what I need and get out.*

Without any cue she could see, the guide pressed Natalie's hand flat against the scanner mounted to the door. Light flowed down her palm, pricked her skin, and he shoved her through. She hovered in a shadowed foyer, unable to hear anything over her heart pounding in her chest. Without a single other recruit in sight, she figured she would endure this test alone.

Her jaw set, Natalie forced herself to move forward. Beyond the shadows, a large platform illuminated the center of a familiar semi-circular room.

I'm back at the entrance to the Helix. A tiny part of her managed to relax. At least she had sort of found the exit.

"Come forward, Adoptee."

Digging her nails into her fists, Natalie stepped onto the platform. It rose into the air, levitating her to meet the assembly of Legates occupying the second-floor balcony. The elite members draped themselves over velvet chairs, each with their own personal holographic screen projected before them. Though she couldn't read the tiny lines of code, Natalie was willing to bet her Assessment scores were on display.

"Welcome, Raven, to the capstone of your Assessment," Legate

Shaye peered down at her like a hawk admiring its prey. *Eleanor is up there.* Natalie resisted the urge to search for her. *The faster I get off this stage the better.*

"We evaluated your knowledge on mathematics, world history, science, and the arts. We assessed your physical capabilities and opportunities for growth. Now we will see your personality and ambition."

Six tiles on the levitating platform receded and pillars rose in their place. Stopping level with Natalie's chest, each presented a single object.

"Choose one item. It works best if you go with your first instinct."

That's it? Natalie spun in a slow circle, evaluating each item. *All I have to do is choose?*

The pedestal directly in front of her held a handblown glass poppy that flawlessly reflected every speck of light in the room. Beside it rested a silver shafted arrow and then a circuit board with a blinking show of lights. Each was so beautifully crafted she nearly overlooked the final pedestal.

A book bound in black leather glinted with silver-painted pages. No title marked its surface, and no author branded its binding. She turned the book over, eager to look inside, when Legate Shaye interrupted her.

"You have decided?"

"Yes," Natalie answered without lifting her attention from the book.

A murmuring picked up and was quickly subdued by Shaye's applause.

"Congratulations on completing your Assessment, Recruit Raven. Please help yourself to refreshments in the adjoining hall whilst awaiting your fellow recruits."

It's over? The floating platform returned to its rightful place on the ground and Natalie made for the indicated exit, light and giddy as

67

though walking on a cloud. *There's some daylight left, I can still slip away and search for—*

"Recruit Raven."

Natalie froze.

"The book, please."

"Oh." She returned the book to its pedestal and hurried through the passageway beneath the second-floor balcony into the adjoining chamber.

Its half-rounded shape mirrored the room before, with dozens of cloth-draped tables offering fruit, desserts, biscuits, and even towers of champagne. Recruits mingled; no doubt grateful the Assessment was over. A fiery redhead crossed nearby and, though she wanted nothing more than the comfort of Tawney's company, Natalie set off in the opposite direction. She drifted through pools of strangers in a haze, overwhelmed by the scent of sweets and alcohol. Carbonated with anticipation, the atmosphere buzzed as everyone waited to begin the next chapter of their lives, to start over, to be adopted by Nautilus.

Natalie nibbled on a biscuit, more to avoid conversation than to sate any hunger. The Adoption posed as a cocktail party complete with guards stationed at every exit. Taking a tour of the room, Natalie watched them warily. The guards blocked each passageway and, smiling pleasantly, they almost appeared casual. Yet she caught the strategic positioning of their feet, the soft bend in their knees, and the bolts on their backs. Was this standard Nautilus protocol or did they suspect something? Maybe Eleanor had already recognized her. Maybe they'd somehow matched her DNA.

Her steps quickened as she searched fruitlessly for any unguarded escape. After two laps she stopped, clinging to a table for support. A mountain of champagne sparkled over her and she wanted to shatter every glass.

I'm not getting out of this room. She clenched her fists. *I'm so close; I'm right here, and I won't be finding anything on our parents. Not like this.*

Applause broke out as the final recruit entered with the elite Nautilus members following behind. Ascending the stage propped against the only straight wall of the room, Natalie spotted Eleanor's hunched stature among them. Despite the fact her hands were shaking, Natalie forced herself to clap along.

I won't be leaving this room alive at all.

CHAPTER 10
LEONIDAS

Leo paused outside the massive glass doors guarding the Helix. Tacking from Scotland to the Florida coast took less than a second and before he knew it, the bus from the oceanfront spat him out on Nautilus property. Despite the Moirai's training, and his relief to see anything other than Scottish cliffs, he didn't feel ready.

They have my parents, Leo reminded himself. *Only a few hundred Nautilus guards stand between us.*

His forehead throbbed from the cut Atro had so graciously bestowed upon him. How had he, of his own free will, run right back into Nautilus's bloodstained hands? Rocking from foot to foot, adrenaline twitched his fingers.

The Helix wasn't what Leo expected. Under the overcast sky, its white dome dominated a field of solar panels. Though there was no flashing neon sign, Nautilus wasn't exactly hiding. The Helix was more akin to a five-star hotel than the headquarters of an undercurrent cult.

Leo snapped to attention as the doors swung open and a man marched out, his expression sour.

"The sentries informed me a man in blue lurked on our stoop."

CHYMIST

He tapped the bolt fastened to his hip as he approached. "You're tardy, recruit. The Adoption started hours ago."

"I'm not a recruit," Leo said evenly. "I'm transferring."

The man stopped inches from him. "Oh?"

"I have my paperwork here." Leo presented the wax sealed envelope Clo had crafted. "On my last mission I was honored by my Legate and promoted to Captain. I'm ready to command my team at the Ward's pleasure and pave the path to peace across the globe."

Painless.

Analyzing the contents of the envelope, his meager welcome committee ignored him. Leo figured the stranger wasn't much more of a man than he was, maybe five or seven years older at most. Three silver hoops capped his right ear. He put a cigarette between his lips and flamed the end with a silver lighter.

"We weren't expecting a transfer today," he puffed.

"Apologies Legate," Leo bowed his head as Lache taught him. "I simply follow where my orders lead me."

"Hmm."

A silence stretched between them and Leo resisted the urge to hold his breath.

Never appear uneasy. Atro's advice resurfaced. *You are there to serve for peace. There is no guilt in peace.*

"Is the Helix entirely solar powered?" Leo feigned curiosity.

"Partly. It's a work in progress."

Leo whistled. "Talk about peace in our time. Shattering the coal ceiling would really be something."

The man looked up, surprised. "It would be, wouldn't it?" He folded Leo's falsified paperwork away with a shrug. "As for your transfer, we've already informed the EuroUnits documentation is to be sent prior to transfer completion, not after. However," he smirked, "there is little to be done for incompetence. Welcome, Captain Lev. Let's find our way inside before the sky falls, shall we?"

Thunder cracked overhead. With one last draw on his cigarette, he put out the butt and threw it away.

Getting in is the hard part, Lache had warned him. *If we can get you past the gates, the rest will be easy.*

Leo rolled his eyes at the memory. *It's only murder. No big deal.*

The Helix doors opened as they approached. From the moment Amir Amani announced their parents' capture and shot Chef on the spot, Leo knew the time to fight Nautilus would come sooner rather than later.

But this, his pulse quickened. *This is manic.*

The cold interior of the Helix was surprisingly empty. Where Clo had promised groups exchanging idle chatter, there were only ceiling-high columns. A muffled noise floated to him, broken regularly by applause.

"The Adoption." The man nodded towards a loft with an impressive overlook spanning its length. "They'll be done in a few hours."

"Right." *Adoption. New recruits.* Leo ran through the details like positions in a playbook.

The few people they did encounter ignored them and a seed of doubt rooted in Leo's stomach. Legates were the most elite members of Nautilus society, expected to be treated with reverence and greeted with a modest dip of the head. So why did everyone pass them by? Was the Moirai's information outdated? Where else had they been wrong?

Stopping at the corridor, the guide blatantly looked him up and down, fiddling with his earrings.

"Legate?"

"What brings you here, Lev?"

"My papers."

"Uh huh, but what brings you *here*? Now, in this moment?"

"I don't understand."

"Most people never do." The man squinted at him. "Your name, derived from the author?"

"No, actually—" Leo frowned. It was possible the Moirai's information wasn't wrong at all, and if that was the case... "You're not a Legate, are you?"

The man laughed. "You are awake in there! Good show, man. No, I'm afraid I'm no Legate; they're all preoccupied with the Adoption. I hope you'll forgive me. It gets a smidge boring in the seashell parade, eh?"

Leo relaxed a little. In the grand scheme of things this guy was next to nothing. It was the Legates he had to worry about.

The man's laughter died in his throat like the cut-off croak of a toad. "Legate Shaye," he bowed his head.

"At peace, Captain." The real Legate stood tall on polished heels, every line of fabric and angle of her composure pressed straight. "Who is this?"

"Transfer, Legate." He mechanically handed over Leo's papers. "A Captain."

Leo watched her sharp features for any hint of suspicion as she scanned the document.

She glazed over him the way an eagle might regard a sparrow. "Captain Edwin, assist Lev in learning his way around the Helix and conforming to our practices here. I want him acclimated in time to coordinate with you on your next assignment."

The Captain nodded curtly, and Leo bowed his head in dismay. The last thing he needed was a babysitter.

"Captain Lev, Edwin will be your primary contact going forward. Peace be with you."

"And with you," Leo answered.

Legate Shaye disappeared beneath the balcony with a swish of her dark hair and Leo cleared his throat.

"I'm not here to step on your toes."

"You're incredibly apologetic for a Captain."

Leo attempted to appear annoyed. "We're a little less abrasive across the pond. You Americans tend to take everything so...personal."

Edwin loosed a sloppy sideways grin. "The ceremony here is a bit much for me. Fancy a tour?"

"Not sure I have much of a choice."

Edwin clapped Leo hard on the back. "Not in this Helix."

He led Leo away from the wide central room and into a corridor where the walls pressed close around them. The ceiling hung low enough to inspire Leo's pulse to quicken.

It's not like before. I'm exactly where I'm supposed to be.

"There's no way you hail from the EuroUnits," Edwin decided.

Leo nearly tripped over his own feet. "What makes you say that?" he asked, ascending a flight of stairs.

Edwin stopped mid-stair. "Oh, I dunno." He thumped Leo hard in the chest. "Lack of mannerisms, lack of training, lack of accent. Shall I go on?"

Leo wasn't sure why Edwin was challenging him, but he wasn't about to lose. "I'm American," Leo confessed. "Recruited in Scotland, thank peace, since American training centers seem more concerned with their status than results."

Edwin frowned at him; his black eyes were cold as coal until he finally grinned. "Couldn't have said it better, brother. You're alright." Continuing up the stairs, his gait relaxed, and he walked a few paces ahead of Leo instead of behind.

Thank you, Moirai, Leo silently praised them.

"Alright," Edwin rubbed his hands together on the second-floor landing. "Let's start with the 'Boring but Necessary,' shall we?"

Leo shadowed him for at least an hour and decided, in a word, the Helix was confusing. He'd understood the Moirai's maps but in reality, the corridors crossed and doubled back, and somehow all halls eventually led to the semi-circular entry room.

Assessing the second-floor balcony, he knew it was the most advantageous spot in the Helix. What he missed from the ground floor was that the balcony divided two massive chambers and overlooked them both. The first was the entry hall, framed with the glass doors that led to freedom and the sticky Florida heat.

"That's the Core," Edwin explained. "If you want to find someone, the Core's the best place to do it."

"Why's that?"

He huffed. "Pure laziness mostly. Nine times out of ten, your route in the Helix is going to pass through that room."

Leo tapped his thumb on the banister. *That's no coincidence,* he knew. *If every member passes through this room every day, monitoring them becomes a hell of a lot easier.*

"And over here is the Focus."

Leo weaved his way between passing Nautilus members to peer over the other side of the catwalk. The Focus was *packed*. Columns lined the curved wall and between them rocked an ocean of navy blue. Hundreds of members huddled on a stage beneath different holograms: a spear, a flower, a miniature tree, and a circuit board.

Curtanas, Doves, Legates, and Artisans. The Moirai's efforts hadn't been for nothing.

"This year's recruits," Edwin noted. "Don't miss training, eh? Peace be with them."

Leo passively studied a clutch of Legate recruits gathered around an elderly woman. He might have glazed right over her if not for the fact she was missing two fingers on her—

Eleanor!

Leo turned his back on the scene. He tugged at the collar of his uniform, playing bored as his heart attempted to escape his chest.

Edwin leaned against the banister expectantly. "Problem?"

"Heights freak me out."

Edwin steered him away. "Then let's crack on."

Leo tried to shove the old woman out of his mind. If he was being honest, it wasn't truly Eleanor that set him on edge, but how quickly he'd encountered a familiar face. And in his experience, wherever Eleanor went, Amir was never far behind.

If he's here, I'll have to find somewhere in this maze to take him down quietly. And I'd better figure out if Nautilus knows anything about my friends before—

"And what's different about this column?" His tour guide scuffed the marble cylinder.

"Uh…"

"Tisk, tisk! I warned you it's the boring part of the bit." Edwin pointed up at the top of the column where its plain square embellishment met the ceiling. "This one's Doric instead of Ionic. Now open your eyes and *pay attention.*"

Captain Edwin pointed out several other things Leo never would have noticed. A crack in the tilework, no doubt the result of a rush job. Sorting members of Nautilus society by their quirks before being close enough to analyze their pins. The passageway that was actually a short-cut to a different passage three floors down where shipments were received.

He sees everything, Leo realized with dread. *He can see the hole before I've identified the play.*

"Don't panic too much if parts of the Helix go dark. We get rolling blackouts."

"Why?"

Edwin frowned. "Not sure yet. Point is, if you come across a dark hall there's most certainly another way to get where you're going. It'll take you a few months to learn which passages lead where anyway."

Leo balled his fists. He didn't have months.

"I figured all those solar panels would save them some money on the power bill."

"With all that money they get from members every month? The bill isn't the problem," Edwin huffed.

Before Leo could ask more, his companion tapped the breast of his jacket.

"No Prestige."

"Not something appreciated in the EuroUnits." Lache's training made the lies practically flow off his tongue.

"No worries. An easy fix." Edwin stopped before a weighted door and pressed his palm against a square matte screen. It lit up and the door popped open. "Suppose you didn't have these beauties in the EuroUnits either?"

Dismayed, Leo shook his head. How did Lache expect him to get past biometric scanners?

"These types of things were debunked years ago," he flicked the scanner. "Too easily fooled."

Leo's hopes rebounded. "Then why do we use them?"

Edwin directed Leo to a chest of drawers inside the doorway. "Well, Nautilus took it a step further of course. Those beauties sample your DNA." Edwin showed him the base of his palm where Leo saw...nothing. "Cool, eh?"

"Great," Leo mumbled.

Edwin rummaged through the cabinet, cursing under his breath. "Where the devil—ah! Here you go."

He pinned three straight bars and the outline of a spear onto Leo's uniform, directly over his heart.

"Captain Lev," Edwin mockingly saluted him. "Wanna go have some fun?"

CHAPTER 11
LEONIDAS

As much as Leo knew he shouldn't enjoy hanging out with Edwin, he was having a blast. Locked away with the stoic Moirai sisters had left him desperate to do anything.

Even play ball with the enemy.

Though he'd seen hundreds of members on his tour, the massive gymnasium Edwin took them to bordered on empty.

"People rarely take time to burn off steam around here," Edwin explained. "We're mission-based. The path to peace isn't paved with pick-up games."

"But you come here?"

"I'd go crazy if I didn't." Edwin passed him a basketball. "You play?"

"I'm more of a soccer player." Leo dribbled the ball as the thrill of the game overtook him.

"Ugh," Edwin twisted his face in mock disgust. "Soccer. You do hail from the EuroUnits after all."

They divided the court in half and played one-on-one. A quarter game later, Leo dripped with sweat, and his breath came in quick bursts. With a hard chest pass to Edwin, he signaled for a break.

"Jeez," Edwin mocked as Leo unzipped the outer jacket of his uniform. "Did they not train you overseas? What kind of Captain can't outrun his Curtanas?"

Leo took a deep breath in and a slow breath out. Two months ago, he would have been embarrassed. A lot had changed since then.

Painless.

"Still recovering." He slipped his shirt off over his head and Edwin grimaced at the ugly pink scar branding Leo's stomach. Taking advantage of his distraction, Leo slid his spark off his wrist and into his pocket.

"Ouch. That's still fresh, man. Gunshot?"

Leo nodded and downed half a bottle of water. His chest was on fire. It felt amazing. Part of him was back in team conditioning, playing the fourth quarter a goal up. He'd done some light jogs around the Moirai's house in recent days, but nothing compared to this. And Edwin wasn't even breathing hard.

"You should have told me." He tucked the ball against his side. "I wanted to have a little fun, not kill you on your first day."

"It's good," Leo insisted. "I've been benched for two months. This is the most fun I've had in weeks."

"Take a breather at least. How'd it happen?"

"I was trying to protect my family. It got messy. Complicated."

"Did you succeed?" Edwin bounced the basketball and Leo watched it go up and down, floor to hand, hand to floor. Rhythmic and steady.

That was the million-dollar question.

"I don't know."

"That's a heavy weight to carry, my friend."

Edwin was Nautilus. He was, by definition, the enemy. Yet Edwin was right. In their own strange way, maybe they were friends.

"That's how you got the cut as well?" Edwin gestured to Leo's forehead.

Leo stole the basketball back. "Pft, no."

Edwin barked out a laugh. "Lev! Was she beautiful, at least?"

Leo dribbled the ball between his legs. It was a fair question, though his teammates back home would have chosen more vulgar descriptions before landing on 'beautiful'. His thoughts drifted to the Moirai, to their expectations of him, to their icy stares and swirling scars.

Then he thought of Natalie. The softness of her smile. The stubborn pinch of her brow. He wanted more than anything to know where she was, how to get to her, if she was even still alive.

Leo guillotined the thought.

He didn't go there. Ever.

Edwin chuckled at his silence. "I think you're in love, Lev."

"Nah." Leo passed the ball, eager to deflect the conversation. "What brought you here?"

Edwin swished it through the net. "Same as you, actually." He jogged to retrieve the rebound and repeated the shot. "My family's at risk. Nautilus is the solution. You'll find it's the same story for most everyone. Except maybe the Legates."

"And the Ward?" Leo attempted to sound casual.

"Yet to be determined."

"What about Amir Amani?"

Edwin's shot missed the basket, skirting off the backboard. He watched the ball roll away without going after it. "You ask a lot of questions."

"He's kind of a legend overseas." Leo backtracked, sensing he'd crossed a line.

Edwin watched him for a long second before finally letting out a snort. "A legendary failure? You must have low standards out your way."

"Why's that?"

Edwin squinted at him.

"Like you said," Leo tapped his temple. "I'm awake in here.

Curiosity's a habit."

"One I'd advise you break." Edwin said seriously. "There's a reason you won't see any cats around here."

"Cats?"

"Oh, come on! Because curiosity killed the cat?" Edwin's laugh sent a pang of loneliness through Leo. It was the kind of joke Brant would've made.

"Ah, forget it." Edwin moved on. "Nice and relaxed, like you've returned from battle. Perfect time to meet your team."

Leo began to redress when Edwin stopped him.

"Wait on that."

Leo raised a brow.

"Trust me, you'll earn more respect in the first five seconds than you could in a year when your team sees you're willing to take a bullet for them."

Reluctantly, Leo followed Edwin out of the gym. He wanted to forget his promise to the Moirai, to abandon his hope of finding Natalie. He didn't want to think about his parents or Uncle Chris. For one afternoon, he didn't want to have any responsibilities to anyone. For a little while, he only wanted to play a game.

You are playing a game, Leo fumed. *One wrong move and you're dead, Natalie is dead, your parents are dead, and Chris is dead. Find the play.*

The hallways wound together like a ball of yarn: intertwined and tangled. Without a single sign posted anywhere, he gave up memorizing the turns and focused on his guide.

"What mission does Legate Shaye want me to assist you on?"

"I'll brief you when I get the call." Edwin led him up a wide spiral staircase that ascended farther than Leo could see.

Unable to respond past the stitch in his side, Leo nodded. His spark pressed against his thigh with every step and, despite being miles away from the nearest ocean, he longed to have it back on his wrist where it belonged.

"Here we are." Edwin opened a door and Leo found himself in

the Focus.

Nautilus recruits were everywhere. They swarmed in groups, all generally fixated on the central stage that was commanded by the Legate he'd met earlier. She spoke confidently, gesturing occasionally to the few members gathered behind her. He spotted Eleanor and ducked his head.

"Ah, damn recruits." Edwin forced his way through the mass of people. "This way."

Gladly.

They slipped behind a hanging curtain to meet fifteen Curtanas arranged in five neat rows. Quiet and still, they harbored none of the nervous energy emanating from the room beyond. These were not new recruits. They were every bit the hardened and refined soldiers the Moirai promised them to be.

"Curtanas." Edwin's tone was sharp as metal, all friendliness gone. "Captain Lev will serve you as dutifully as you serve him. Demonstrate yourselves in preparation for your first mission together. Begin."

At his word, the team dispersed over a foam sparring mat. Some stood one-on-one, others two-on-one, and a few prepared to challenge three or four opponents at once. For a moment they were still.

Then there was blood.

The smack of flesh against flesh overpowered the noise of the Adoption next door. Flashes of bloody grins and whoops carried a thrill as the Curtanas punched and pinned and rose to do it again.

Blood had never bothered Leo. He'd had his fair share of busted lips and scraped elbows but watching the Curtanas bleed for his pleasure sickened him. He was grateful when Edwin called the fight.

"Enough," the Captain's mouth pinched tight. He appeared menacingly commanding. Leo tried adopting the expression; however, he doubted it carried the same effect.

As the team aligned themselves again into five rows of three, a pattern emerged. Those who had performed well claimed the front, while those who had not took their place at the back. They ranked themselves honestly, abandoning selfish pride for the success of the team, all without ever speaking a word.

"Serve your Captain, serve your Ward. In success or in death, peace be with you." Edwin stepped back, leaving Leo to contend with fifteen strangers prepared to die for him.

As they simultaneously bowed their heads in respect, Leo knew the Moirai would be proud. But would Christopher? Would Natalie? Would they understand he was doing this for them? Would his parents?

Leo acknowledged his team, releasing them to clean the blood off their uniforms. Only then did they converse with one another, praising performance and giving advice.

"Permission to dress?"

"Please," Edwin shielded his eyes. "Your skin is blinding. Don't you ever go to the beach?"

"Shot." Leo donned his shirt and jacket.

Painless.

"Exactly. Sounds like weeks of tanning and mixed drinks if you ask me." He stalled as the Curtanas exited the Focus. "Now, let's register your uniform and find some grub! The cafe serves breakfast all day. It's the brightest thing about this hole in the ground."

Away from the crowd, Leo slipped the spark up under his sleeve. Its weight brought a shot of relief chased by a gut-wrenching dose of reality.

Edwin seemed nice enough, fun for a pick-up game or two. But they could never be friends. It wasn't possible, not while each fought for a different side. For the first time since the Moirai discovered him bleeding on their beach, Leo had no one to turn to.

In a Helix full of Nautilus, he was truly alone.

CHAPTER 12
NATALIE

Legate Shaye spoke flawlessly.

"Every member, every Chamber, is essential to fulfilling Nautilus's mission. The Doves spread our message of peace, while Artisans advance our technology. The Curtanas selflessly fight for our cause when words fail, and our Legates report directly to the Ward."

Applause rose at the name of their leader and the collection of Legates behind Shaye nodded their approval.

Keep your head down, Natalie calmed herself. *Maybe Eleanor doesn't care that Christopher shot off two of her fingers.*

"So, let us learn how you will serve!" Shaye summoned the first inductee to the stage. "Recruit Francie."

A middle-aged woman picked her way timidly across the banquet hall to stand before Legate Shaye.

"You leave your old life behind and begin anew. Nautilus welcomes you into our family. You will bring peace as a Dove and work to spread our message far and wide, expanding our family and our reach." If Legate Shaye said anything else, her words were drowned out by the crowd. She pinned a Prestige badge to the recruit's jacket and gestured her towards her new Legate. The woman had hardly taken her place when Shaye summoned another.

"Recruit Maxine."

Max's green hair practically glowed beneath the stage lights. Her chest puffed out with pride as she met the semicircle of Chamber leaders.

"Your Assessment results have been evaluated. You will bring peace as a Legate and will be taught to lead our Chambers down the path the Ward has set for us." Cheers echoed as Shaye fastened Max's new Prestige to her uniform.

With hundreds of recruits to process, Shaye wasted no time. Newly inducted Nautilus members were called onto the stage and Adopted into their new families in a matter of seconds and in no apparent order.

Natalie tensed. It was never supposed to go this far. She should have been rummaging through Nautilus's files, getting any and all information she could on her parents' whereabouts, yet she was trapped.

She recognized two of the boys she'd met outside as they were Adopted, as well as the elderly couple from the Assessment. The lines of recruits behind the Legates grew as the crowd around Natalie dwindled. Around her, the walls seemed to grow taller, towering over her until she began to lose herself in the fact there was no way out.

"Recruit Patricia."

A tiny figure with swishing red hair marched across the stage. Her every step resonated in Natalie's chest like a drum.

Tawney.

"You will bring peace as a Curtana, leading your Brothers and Sisters to fight when diplomacy hinders peace."

She's in. Natalie picked at her nails. With no viable escape route, she'd have to stand on that stage. She'd have to meet Eleanor head on.

"Recruit Thomas."

Borderline blind without his glasses, Owen stumbled his way to the Artisans. Seconds later, Shaye called another.

"Recruit Raven."

Natalie's body moved mechanically towards the stage, her thoughts fleeting and disjointed. Her head rotated on a swivel. Though desperate for an exit, or a passageway, or some hole in the ground she could bury herself in, there was nowhere to hide from Shaye's summons. She didn't remember climbing the steps, yet the Legate stood before her. Her painted red lips somehow moved faster than her words and the sound came and went like waves crashing on the shore.

"Welcome...Nautilus..."

Natalie spread her toes in her sneakers, desperate to feel the stability of the stage under her feet. Steady. Firm. Unyielding. She focused on Shaye's sharp cheekbones, on the smell of sugar that filled the banquet hall.

"...Legate family."

Terror clawed at Natalie's chest. She couldn't move. She couldn't think. Shaye pinned a Prestige bar to her chest, and she was numb to it. Every shuffling step Eleanor took towards Natalie hammered through the floor. Somewhere beyond the roar of her pulse, people were clapping. Eleanor wrapped her in a frail embrace. How could this woman, who smelled of roses and mothballs, who weighed no more than a child, have so much blood on her hands?

"Raven," she cooed.

Natalie might have collapsed on the spot if not for Eleanor's feather-light grip. It took everything Natalie had to meet her grey stare. If this was her death, if this was how her struggle to reunite her family ended, she would meet her fate on her feet. Determined to conquer her fear, Natalie lifted her chin, but it seeped into every crack of her being.

And Eleanor saw it.

"There's nothing to be afraid of, dearie." She brushed a lock of hair behind Natalie's ear.

What else do you see? She studied Eleanor's expression. Powder filled her wrinkles and, now that she was closer, Natalie could see her figure shake lightly like a leaf in the wind. Any second, the recognition would surface. Any second, Natalie would be captured or killed where she stood.

"We'll help you find peace." Eleanor retreated to her station, leaving Natalie rooted to the spot with the words branded into her memory. She'd heard them weeks before, sinking into a medicated sleep in the prison of Eleanor's embrace.

I'm not a prisoner. Natalie watched Eleanor's retreat in disbelief. *I am not a prisoner.*

Several more recruits were Adopted before Natalie regained composure. The final adoptee assumed his place on the stage before Legate Shaye even called him forward. After working tirelessly for over an hour, she fumbled.

"Recruit," Shaye checked her tablet. "Recruit Bobby."

Natalie stood straighter, allowing the Legate's second of uncertainty to pull her up. Nautilus wasn't a machine: they were people. They were flawed.

Before the Legate, Brant nodded curtly, his blond bun bobbing her acknowledgement.

"Welcome to Nautilus," Shaye presented his pin. "May you bring peace as a Curtana."

Brant paled and Legate Shaye dismissed them, freeing the recruits to enjoy their spoils and return fresh for training the next morning. It wasn't until she vacated the stage Natalie released the tension in her neck. She introduced herself to her fellow Legates as she waited for the room to stop spinning.

Max, of course. And the young girl from earlier; still don't know her name. And about twenty more...

Recruits toasted champagne with their new families and Natalie shared no interest in it. For the first time since her arrival, the front doors were unguarded and if she couldn't dig for information, she'd settle for breathing. Natalie left the banquet hall and slipped out of the Helix. Rain fell in sheets on the concrete slab and steam rose in thick coils from the ground. The smell of earth and rain washed away the sterile scent of Nautilus marble and steel.

"Raven."

Eleanor's voice doused her like cold water. Her stomach sucked her ribs in close like armor and her spark suddenly felt heavy on her wrist. Staring out at the field of panels, Natalie sensed how far Nautilus had taken her from the sea.

"It is Raven, isn't it, my dear?"

"Yes." Her own strength surprised her.

"You rushed out in a hurry, child."

"I like the rain."

"Me too." Eleanor patted Natalie's back with the strength of a battering ram. "Legate Shaye couldn't share the truth of your Adoption with the reception hall, so I would like to."

Natalie rolled her wrists. *I can drop her right here and run for Ancora. We'll have to leave. We'll have to—*

"To be a Legate Recruit is an honor," she continued. "Yes, you will learn to lead our members, but you may do so much more." Eleanor exuded a mixture of joy and excitement. It made Natalie sick.

Why doesn't she just say it? What is she playing at?

Eleanor straightened the pins on her jumpsuit. Natalie flinched.

"If chosen," Eleanor explained, "you will enter the Ward's inner circle."

"Wh-*what?*"

"All Legate recruits will be evaluated for only five available positions. Don't you worry, dear. You've found your home no matter what Chamber you keep in the end, Legate or not." The old woman's embrace packed surprising vigor. "They'll announce the chosen Legates at Graduation."

"Graduation?"

"Yes, it's a huge celebration. Puts this little soiree to shame. In two weeks, you'll become full members. All rights and responsibilities will be yours, including full access to the Helix."

Full access to the Helix. Natalie's train of thought left the station at freight speed. *Two weeks. Can we keep this up for two whole weeks?*

"You'll be happy you were here today," Eleanor assured her. "Trust me, dearie." She reached into the rain, letting water pour through the space her missing digits had once been.

"Does it hurt?" Natalie couldn't believe her own words. Had all of the adrenaline gone to her head?

"Sometimes," Eleanor said thoughtfully. "Strange how things gone still have the power to cause pain."

Though she agreed, Natalie didn't say a word.

"We mustn't let that keep us from moving forward, hmm?" She pinched Natalie's chin without seeming to notice her shudder. "We keep going with the best we have, and the Ward is truly the best we have. See you tomorrow, child."

As she pulled away, Natalie couldn't help herself. "What's inside the book?" she blurted. "The one from the Assessment, with silver pages."

"Ah," she winked one watery eye. "Why don't you take a peek?" Eleanor produced the book from her jacket.

Natalie took it cautiously, fearing the woman's hands would snap shut like a trap. She turned it over, admiring the beauty in its simplicity. She wondered what Nautilus would think so important to present at the Adoption. She hoped, if she was lucky, she'd find something useful inside. So, when the soft leather cover fell open to hundreds of blank pages, Natalie slouched.

"Huh."

"Knowledge is a privilege, dearie," Eleanor returned the book to her jacket. "The Ward will tell you anything you need to know. Peace be with you." She shuffled back inside the Helix, leaving Natalie dazed.

She skimmed over the field of drenched solar panels without truly seeing it. Though she hadn't found any clues to her parents, her ruse had more than done its job. It was just going to take time. And if she was chosen to graduate as a Legate, if she could infiltrate the Ward's inner circle, she wouldn't need to sneak around to find their secrets.

Nautilus will take me right to them.

Natalie tore into the storm. Soaking wet, she mounted her bike and raced up the rows of panels, flinging mud and grass behind her tires. Yet the further she pedaled from Nautilus and its Ward, the more she sensed herself falling back in, sinking further into an abyss she'd never escape from.

I have to get out.

CHAPTER 13
NATALIE

Natalie stood on the dock of Ancora III. She'd expected the rain to stop after tacking back to North Carolina's shores, but heavy raindrops drenched her skin and thunder shook the earth as Ancora's yellow beacon glittered through the storm.

"*Look there, princess.*"

She bounced in the driver's seat as the boat flew across the water. Her father tracked the horizon. He trusted her to listen without taking the wheel. She trusted him not to let her capsize them.

"*See the storm?*" *her father asked.*

There was blue sky and the sun, and ospreys flying overhead.

"*There,*" *he pointed to where the sky met the sea.* "*Where the cloud is darker. Beneath it, that's—*"

"*A shadow.*"

"*Rain.*"

It seemed like a shadow, but he must be right. Her father knew everything and, if she paid attention, one day she would too.

Sopping wet fur brushed her clenched fist. The dog's tail drooped, and his ears flattened against his head.

"Go inside, Enzi."

"You should do the same. Or do you fancy yourself a fish?" Natalie thought the rain was warm until Brant pulled her against him. "You already went twice this week," he said in her ear.

"I don't know what you're talking about," she lied. She was desperate to unload everything off her shoulders and onto Christopher's. He could carry it better.

"Come inside, Nat." There was something heavy in the way he said her name. It filled her with dread. "I want to tell you—"

She already knew what Brant wanted to tell her. His stare lingered a few seconds too long. His touch was frequent and his smiles coy. She couldn't deal with his affection on top of everything else, not now. Natalie pulled away from him.

"Come on. Get dry. Tell us what you want to tell him." Brant guided her towards the lighthouse. "And then, if I deem you worthy, I may even share my newest laughable."

She thought the pouring rain would obscure her lack of excitement. It didn't.

"Hey!" Brant shoved her. "This one takes the cake! Speaking of which, we're awfully low on sweets."

"Well, you can tell Tawney." Natalie relaxed, content to talk about something as mundane as groceries.

"No thanks. I prefer my face to remain in its current conformation," Brant held open the door and Enzi rushed in.

Natalie hovered on the stoop, dripping onto a pile of towels. Brant's mop of golden-dyed hair spilled down his neck. He ran his thumb across Natalie's forehead and presented her the evidence: not a drop of color.

"Your girl Nora knows her stuff."

Natalie draped a towel over Enzi while keeping Angie at bay with her foot. One wet dog at a time was plenty. Meanwhile, Brant stripped and puddled his uniform at their feet, leaving him flexing like a fool in his boxers. He was growing bolder by the minute and Natalie refused to give him the satisfaction of her peeking. It wasn't that she didn't find Brant attractive, she simply wasn't interested. *I'm only keeping a life-altering secret from him and lying fluently through my teeth about it. Then there's Leo...*

Brant halted Natalie's hands. "Can you be still for one second?"

"No."

"Ugh!" Tawney burst inside, her arms out wide and her red hair pouring down to her waist.

"Woah," Brant backed away. "Who invited rabid Raggedy Anne?"

Before Tawney could snap back a response, Owen slipped inside and crashed to the floor.

"Lovely evening," he commented from the comfort of the cement.

Brant threw a towel over him. "You're worse than the dogs."

"What's this?" Tawney looked from Natalie to barely dressed Brant.

"Brant was telling me what he'd like to add to your grocery list."

He gasped at her betrayal.

"You can damn well go to the store yourself. No one's stopping you," Tawney peeled her feet out of her squishing shoes. "Bloody hate grocery shopping."

"I know we didn't get what we went in for," Natalie refocused their squabbling, "but we did well today."

"Well?" Still on the ground, Owen dried his glasses. "I'd say we did a fair bit better than that. We're in the long game. And being in different Chambers will deliver a wide range of data."

"Especially since one of us is training to be a Legate." Brant's pride made her cringe.

"No more 'til I'm dry." Tawney dripped her way to the stairs and, already shivering, Natalie followed.

She tip-toed across her bedroom, avoiding the scattered books. Propping open the wardrobe door for a smidge of privacy, she stripped free of her wet clothing and melted into a thrift store sweatshirt and jeans. The fractal scar on her wrist peeked out and she adjusted her sleeve to cover it.

Downstairs, Enzi sprawled on his back to bask in the heat of the freshly lit fireplace, curling his white paws over his belly.

"What a goof," Tawney sat, and Angie promptly occupied her lap.

Natalie relaxed into the couch and rested her head on Tawney's shoulder. Her friend brushed the overgrown fur out of Angie's eyes.

"She's due to be groomed," Tawney noted.

Natalie knotted the long fur on Angie's face up on top of her head. "There. Groomed."

Brant commented from the stairs, "Aren't we a little old to play dress up?"

"Aren't you a little old to have a crush?"

In a rare turn of events, Brant blushed. Natalie fiddled with the sleeve of her hoodie, drowning in embarrassment.

Owen sat cross-legged at Tawney's feet. "We have more important things to do than bicker."

Enzi didn't even flinch as Natalie placed a foot on either side of him to address the group.

"Graduation is two weeks away," she started. "After that, digging for information on our parents should be much easier."

"Well, their hierarchy is pretty clear," Brant sprawled on the floor next to Enzi. "Artisans, Doves, Curtanas, Legates, and then the Ward."

"Rock bottom," Owen grimaced.

Natalie shook her head. "You're probably the best positioned out of everyone."

"She's right," Tawney poked Owen's leg. "You're a fiery virus set to destroy their internal systems."

"A virus..." Owen repeated.

"Tawney and Brant will learn how they fight." Natalie thought aloud.

"We'll all learn how they fight." Brant fanned out Enzi's tail. "I'm going to learn how they kill."

"It won't come to that," Tawney promised.

"Sure." He didn't sound convinced.

"Did anyone see anything worth noting?" Natalie changed the subject.

"You mean other than that old woman whose favorite pastime is tormenting us?" Tawney scowled.

Natalie leaned against the mantle. "Eleanor was…unexpected."

"Understatement of the year," Brant pointed finger guns at her.

Natalie shivered, reliving their conversation. "She caught me outside. Alone."

Tawney sat bolt upright. "She didn't recognize you?"

"No." Natalie suddenly felt tired and sluggish as the full weight of the day settled in her mind. "She said the Ward will tell us anything we need to know."

"Speaking of," Brant propped himself up on his elbows. "Anyone see the Ward? A photo of him, or hologram? Anything?"

Everyone shook their heads.

"Me neither. So, I was thinking," Brant paused, "what if it's all fake?"

Owen wiggled his nose to adjust his glasses. "You mean maybe the Ward isn't real?"

"Exactly. What if it's a placeholder? What if Legate Shaye is actually calling all the shots?"

"It's possible," Owen sounded unconvinced. "Regardless, we'll need to tread carefully. Getting in and out in a day is one thing; maintaining this ruse for weeks will be difficult."

Natalie's expression hardened. "I won't quit on our parents because there's a chance we could fail."

Because they've never quit on us, she added silently. *Even if we were just an assignment, a project.*

"No one said anything about quitting," Owen backtracked.

"The Helix will be a challenge," Tawney bounced one of her countless curls. "It's more twisted than that shithole in Antarctica."

"Filthy mouth, Tawney," Brant chastised.

"You think?" She leaned over and licked Brant's cheek. He swung for her. Tawney was faster. She whipped off his red cap, licked her pinky and stuck it in his ear.

Howling with laughter, Brant flipped her onto the floor. There was a blur and Brant landed face down with Tawney's knee on his back.

"Unfair," Brant complained.

Tawney covered his bun with his cap. "Pick your battles better."

"Duly noted." As she let him up, he said, "It's weird, right? When did it become wrong for us to want peace?"

Tawney looked like she might pin him again. "Why don't you ask your dad?" She snapped her fingers. "Oh, that's right. Nautilus *abducted him*."

"I only meant—"

"Of course, we want peace," Natalie cut in. "I've never wanted peace more than I do right now. But it's not peace they're after, it's chaos and power. It's *us*. We've seen it. The Ward's methods will end with Nautilus calling the shots and thousands dead, including our parents I'm sure. Don't get caught up in the lies they're selling."

"I need to work on something." Owen said abruptly, retreating to his cave of computers.

"Good." Tawney took two leashes from the wall. Enzi and Angie dutifully followed. "If we're done, I'm going for a run."

"We ran this morning!" Brant marveled. "What are you made of?"

"Anger, mostly."

"Not 'sugar, spice, and everything nice'?"

"Maybe in the next life." Tawney opened the door and jogged into the haze of steam baking off the earth.

A familiar, uneasy sensation crept up Natalie's spine, completely separate from the fact she was once again alone with Brant.

"You look like you're a thousand miles from here and it doesn't seem any more pleasant."

"It isn't," Natalie bit her lip. "I feel like we're missing something. More than our parents, and Christopher, and…" *Leo,* she choked on his name. "What about the key Christopher left us? There has to be more going on than tacking and time-travel, otherwise Nautilus would be hunting us relentlessly."

"Maybe they are."

"I don't think so," Natalie countered. "They found us at Ancora I in a matter of days. We've been here nearly two months. We're missing something." She flipped through a textbook on the kitchen table, *The Chemistry of Biology*. "Can I ask you something personal?"

"I'd like nothing better."

Though they'd been friends their whole lives, she'd never broached such a sensitive subject with him before. She wetted her lips, not entirely sure how to begin.

"When your mom…when she…"

"Died."

"Yeah," Natalie slumped in her seat. "I know Christopher and Leo's," she fished for the right word, "*situations* aren't even close to the same as losing your mom." She cradled the pit in her stomach, unable to voice the question. "I guess…I thought it wouldn't hurt by now."

Brant moved to sit in the chair beside her. "What are you getting at?"

"When does it stop?"

"It doesn't," he said bluntly. "It's going to hurt every day for the rest of your life, as bad as it does right now, as bad as the moment you lost them. So, our parents lied about a lot. We all lie to each other every day. People, therapists, even my dad promised the pain would fade in time." He picked a frayed thread from his cap. "It doesn't."

She glazed over the paragraphs of facts in the textbook before her. "Then how do we carry it?"

"One day you wake up and a month's gone by. Then two. Then a year. One day you accept the pain isn't enough to kill you. You stop waiting to heal or feel whole again because it's not going to happen. You must *decide* to move forward."

"It's like," he surveyed the room, "it's like carrying a giant backpack of books, yeah? It never gets lighter but eventually you get stronger, eventually you find someone to help hold the weight, so it gets a little easier to carry." Brant shrugged. "You start smiling again because you're not alone."

Natalie pulled her knees to her chest as a dark, pulsating knot of anguish twisted her stomach. She realized Brant was the strongest person she'd ever met.

"See," he peered sideways at her. "You don't need to run to Chris for everything. You can't. I've got you."

Natalie shifted uncomfortably as Brant fanned the pages of the biology book.

"Did you already finish the books he sent here ahead of us?"

She imagined the bottom drawer of her wardrobe where the books, logic puzzle, key, and her immense guilt stayed tucked away.

"No," she confessed. *I can't seem to get past the bloodstains on the covers.*

"Maybe you should start there," Brant suggested. "Or you could get some new ones. Maybe visit that bookstore?"

Natalie stiffened. She had only told Leo about the bookstore in a moment she'd believed to be private. "How do you know about that?"

"We could go together."

"That would be irresponsible."

"If you aren't going to time-travel, or tack to go see your most desired place in the world, then what's the point?" Brant retreated towards the stairs.

"Staying alive long enough to save the people I put in danger."

"It's no more dangerous than a group of genetically modified teens infiltrating the very organization that seeks to manipulate them, miles away from the nearest spit of sea spray." He ascended a stair, his tone uncommonly cold. "Every day for the rest of our lives is a gamble: high risk, high reward. Don't waste your bets on someone who's never coming back."

Furious, Natalie marched over to him, facing off between the railing's wrought iron bars.

"I would *never* risk our family for a fantasy."

"Oh, I know," Brant whispered. "However, while you think it over, and we both know you'll think it over, consider this." Leaning through the bars, Brant kissed her square on the mouth. Before she could blink, it was over, and he was climbing up away from her. "I almost forgot," he called down. "Where does King Midas keep his horses?"

Natalie hardly heard him. Her head spun and her lips tingled, and she didn't care one bit about King Midas or his bloody horses.

"Golden Corral!"

The round walls surrounding her seemed to shrink. Or perhaps her thoughts were getting too big. Taking the stairs two at a time, she climbed past her floor and those that would have belonged to Christopher and Leo without sparing them a glance. They were empty. And Brant was right: they would remain empty.

The hatch at the top of the stairs opened to a narrow platform that surrounded Ancora's light. In the distance, the shadow of the storm hung above the sea. For weeks she'd held onto the hope Ancora's beacon might guide Leo home, and now that hope was weighing her down, pulling her under.

Her family was counting on her to find them. Her friends trusted her to keep them safe. She couldn't fail them, not again.

Leo was a distraction she couldn't afford.

CHAPTER 14
LEONIDAS

The metallic shell on Leo's uniform blinked and vibrated. It sent a thrill through his veins. He was going on his first mission.

"You are distracted," Lache observed.

Leo spun, searching for his other shoe. "I am not."

"You are there all the time," Clo whined.

"And have yet to do what you promised," Atro relaxed against Clo, her white fractal scars practically glowing on her bare brown skull.

"It's only been a few days." He spotted a shoelace peeking out from beneath his bed. "Ha!" Slipping on the sneaker, he straightened the pins on his jacket as the shell buzzed insistently. "I know you want Amir dead last year. I have to be careful." Leo grabbed Lache firmly. It was like shaking a sculpture, she was as stiff and cold as marble. "If I give myself away, I'll be killed or worse. I can't risk blowing my cover with murder. Besides, I haven't found him yet."

He avoided thinking about their arrangement as much as possible, so confessing his assassination contract aloud filled him with dread. When the time came, he still wasn't sure he'd be able to pull the trigger.

As though sensing his doubts, Lache sulked. "We agreed you would take down Amir Amani first."

"Yes, I know. I have to think about my family—"

"We have no family!" She erupted, quieting the birds in the garden. "We have no teachings outside of the Helix. We have no names other than the irony Amir bestowed upon us. We could not even acquire the abilities—" her mouth snapped shut.

The Nautilus shell buzzed again. Leo fidgeted.

"I made you a promise. I can't keep it if I'm dead. If I prove myself today, I may earn some independence to explore the Helix. Once I find out where my parents are being held," he frowned, "I will honor our agreement."

Lache moved out of his path.

Leo wasn't sure if she believed him or had simply grown tired of fighting. Ultimately, he decided it didn't matter.

"You just got here!" Clo pouted.

Already out the door, Leo threw her a wave. The pebbled pathway crunched underfoot as he ran down the hillside. With the sun and its warmth tucked behind thick clouds, he pulled his jacket tighter around him. Beneath the rocky outcropping, Leo barged into the sea.

The white light rushed up and flashed against the afternoon sky. Every atom that made him fluttered with energy. He pictured the pier tucked against Florida's eastern coast and he was weightless. Then he emerged onto a covered dock in the stifling southern heat.

Cold chills ran the length of his body as he adjusted to the abrupt change in climate. A twenty-minute bus ride and several jolting bumps later, he jogged through the field of solar panels and into the ominous Helix.

"Edwin!" Leo flagged down the dark-haired Captain hurrying across the Core.

"You're late," he shouted back. "This way."

Leo shoved past idle groups of Nautilus members to catch up.

"Amigo," Edwin's features pinched together when Leo finally reached him. "You didn't bring your bolt?"

Leo was fairly certain 'I don't have one' wouldn't qualify as an appropriate response.

"Oh, uh..."

"No worries, man, we have spares."

Leo caught the metal rod Edwin tossed him. Without a bolt of their own to practice with, the Moirai had lectured him on how the weapon worked. He knew it had to be spun for the magnets inside to generate the electric charge on either silver-capped end. He knew how easy it was to kill someone. Unfortunately, the closest he had come to using one was when the Moirai had beaten him with some driftwood on the beach. Knowing how something worked and appearing to be an expert were two vastly different things. Leo held the bolt awkwardly, testing its weight.

"What?" Edwin folded his arms. "Don't tell me you prefer a gun?"

After having nearly died from a gunshot wound, it didn't make sense to Leo either.

Edwin took back the bolt and kicked open a storage chest. "Pick your poison."

Leo assessed the intimidating selection of handguns before settling on a light model that clipped easily to his belt. He expected his body to recoil from the cold metal, for his muscles to clench at the memory, however his hands were steady and sure. More sure than they'd ever been before he was shot.

"You're right to follow your gut. It's the weapon you know that'll save you," Edwin stopped short. "Rings true for anything, really."

Regardless, Leo resented how natural the gun felt. He wondered if Natalie would hate him for it, too.

I know the pistol better than I know myself. I know what it's like to be on the other side.

Edwin rushed away again and by the time Leo matched his pace they were several turns and a flight of stairs away from the Core.

"What's the rush?" Leo managed, already winded.

"Big day today," Edwin's carefree features were drawn and strained.

"Yeah," Leo nodded. "First mission."

"Excuse me?"

"Here at the Helix, I mean," Leo amended quickly. "What's the play?"

The Captain stopped abruptly outside a set of heavy iron doors. Their medieval carvings stuck out starkly from the shining silver of everything else Nautilus owned.

"Beyond these doors the highest-ranking Nautilus members outside of the Helix will be meeting for the last time before Graduation." Edwin worked his jaw. "The Ward is prepping them for their part in the show."

Leo straightened so fast he nearly popped out of his shoes. "The Ward will be in there with us?"

"Of course not," Edwin scoffed. "The highest positioned political members and the Ward all in the same room? That's an assassin's dream."

Leo prickled with unease. *Assassin.* The title didn't fit right against his skin.

"Right," he redirected the conversation. "So, what's the big deal about a bunch of recruits graduating to member status? Don't we do that all the time?"

"Annually," Edwin flicked the three hoops that capped his right ear. "So that's exactly what I'd like to know myself. This time is different. They're planning something big. Huge." He turned his back to Leo and placed his palm on the biometric scanner beside the doors. It pinged pleasantly and as the metal doors clicked open, Leo still had no idea what was expected of him.

"What's my position?"

"I'm the protection detail to a senior member attending the meeting. Though we're in the Helix, Nautilus isn't taking any chances. This is too big to screw up now." Edwin stepped inside and peered at him between the two heavy doors. "You, my good man, are standing watch."

"Oh," Leo deflated, which must have been evident because Edwin punched his arm.

"Buck up," he teased. "You can't expect to be in the room where it happens your first week. Trust me, even standing outside the door is an honor."

Not long after Edwin disappeared inside, a string of black suited politicians silently filed in after him. Leo studied each one, determined not to let his sour mood sully an opportunity to glean anything of interest. One by one they hurried past. He vaguely recognized a few from news reports: that old dame was the Prime Minister of somewhere, and the beauty whose black dress hugged her every curve was certainly some country's princess.

There was only one figure Leo knew instantly. The man stomped towards him and, before he could stop himself, Leo blocked the politician's path, forcing a clear view of his face. Round and squinty, the man held a finger to his lips and brushed Leo aside.

It shouldn't be possible, yet there he was, strung along by the world's most covert cult to date.

The Ward has the President of the United States.

Standing guard outside the armored doors, the President was all Leo could think about. He tapped his foot anxiously. Denial soon set in and he welcomed it. Surely, it was a mistake.

The President can't be with Nautilus. Leo thrummed against his thigh. After the inaccurate reporting of their parents' disappearance, Christopher had accused Nautilus of manipulating the media, and maybe even the local police force, but the White House? No. It simply wasn't possible.

If Nautilus has him, our problems just got a whole world bigger.

Another of Christopher's warnings lingered in the back of Leo's mind. It weaved in and out of his thoughts, haunting him with its weight.

War. Weeks ago, when Uncle Chris had first proposed it, a third world war had seemed an impossibility. Now...

Now Nautilus has the President of the United Freaking States.

Engrossed in his thoughts, Leo was surprised when the doors burst open. International figureheads scurried past him, their legs trained to outpace the probing questions of reporters, though none were fast enough to hide their satisfied smirks. Leo's heart sank.

Nautilus's satisfaction rarely boded well for anyone else.

Several Captains and Legates followed behind with their heads bowed in silent respect for those they escorted. Leo was drifting after the President when Edwin caught up to him.

"Follow the gulls." His eyes shone wild with excitement and his brow shimmered with sweat. Frantically, he bent close to Leo. "That mean anything to you?"

The President slipped around a corner and out of sight.

"I don't know." Leo thoughts scattered like marbles. "Like the birds? There's a Gull hockey team—"

"Ah! Catch you later, man." Edwin sprinted into the labyrinth of passages and Leo didn't hesitate. He took off after the President.

What would he say when he caught him? *Why are you doing this? Why would you abandon your people for Nautilus? What's going to happen at Graduation?*

Leo turned the corner and all his questions evaporated. The President was gone, long absorbed into the maze of the Helix.

Only Leo wasn't alone.

A towering figure hurried towards him. His head of gelled hair was bowed, and his polished shoes clicked against the tile with every step. Leo's blood turned to ice; he froze. The man was only steps from him and still Leo couldn't move. He hadn't expected his fate to find him so quickly, yet Amir Amani rapidly closed the distance between them. The Moirai demanded murder. His vow put this man's blood on his hands.

Amir's every footfall echoed with his sins. He'd kidnapped Leo and his friends. He'd tortured them. He'd taken their parents. He shot Christopher. He killed Chef. And then there was the Moirai. Their scars blurred Leo's vision.

Leo clenched his fists. Amir was so close Leo could smell his cologne. Five more paces and Amir would be on him.

Four. Three. Two.

Leo could hear him speaking feverishly under his breath.

One.

Leo stepped aside. Amir passed by without a word and, turning the corner, the Helix consumed him. Leo leaned against the wall and a cold sweat set him trembling. Or maybe it was his nerves. Or general self-loathing.

What is a man without his word? Leo looked at the ceiling. It was as perfectly polished as the floor. *Nothing.*

He had never hated himself more than he did right then. Whether or not he wanted to be an assassin didn't matter. It was no longer a choice. The Moirai saved his life and gave him a chance to find his family. They trusted him to honor their agreement. How had he repaid them?

Irritable, Leo returned to the iron doors. He searched for Edwin, but his friend was long gone.

Follow the gulls. Leo suffered a pang of longing that nearly brought him to his knees. He wanted to go home. Not with the Moirai, not stuck in the Helix. *Home.* Natalie would know what the gulls meant, or Owen. Brant would joke about it. Tawney would brush it off.

Assassin.

He wondered who he had become without them.

CHAPTER 15
NATALIE

Max slammed Natalie down on the sparring mat. Again. Fuming, Natalie rose. She wasn't angry that she was pinned. She wasn't angry Max had developed some personal vendetta against her, morphing from friendly to bloodthirsty overnight. Natalie was angry that, thanks to seven weeks in Tawney Davis Boot Camp, she knew how to flatten Max like a pancake, and she had to hold herself back. If she did too well in combat, Nautilus might deem her more fit to be a Curtana than a Legate, and she couldn't risk being skipped over for the Ward's inner circle.

Play the game. Let her win.

What irked Natalie more than playing the victim was that she'd yet to see anything beyond the Core and the Focus since the Adoption. In fact, sparring was the first thing she'd done other than be showered in gifts and relinquish wads of Christopher's cash. The ceremonial love bombing of the new recruits had lasted days. From their arrival in the morning to their departure in the evening, Nautilus spent every moment doting upon their newest members and inventing miscellaneous dues.

Max slammed her into the mat again. Lost in thought, Natalie bit into her tongue. She tasted blood. Her eyes watered.

Stupid.

"You're nothing," Max said in her ear.

Max is innocent, Natalie reminded herself. Still, Natalie dreamed of shoving her green-haired head flat into the floor.

"Recruit Raven," Eleanor called.

Unable to reply, Natalie swallowed a mouthful of blood.

"I hardly believe you are trying."

"Apologies, Legate," Natalie winced. "Fighting isn't in my nature."

"Understandable," Eleanor circled her, a vulture coming to claim Max's leftovers. "And untrue." Eleanor squeezed one of Natalie's biceps, flicked her abdomen, and, finally, cradled her right hand in her own with the palm facing upwards.

Natalie forgot to breathe.

Eleanor had witnessed the moment that scar had blossomed across her wrist, spiraling down to her fingers and up her forearm. It had come from a deflected blow of Tanaka's bolt; a grazing wound instead of the killing shock that was intended.

"You are strong. You are fast. You burn with the desire to protect yourself and your people."

Natalie identified the exits, all too far away. She wouldn't beat hundreds of recruits and a swarm of Legates to the door. She doubted she'd make it two steps.

However, when Eleanor looked up from the bolt's scar, there was no recognition in her eyes, only an immense sadness.

"My dear, you've had such pain in your life," the old woman nodded. "Such suffering. It has not beaten you, as you would lead us to believe here on the mat. Show your brothers and sisters how life has prepared you to fight for them and for peace."

Several other recruits had paused in their assignments to watch whatever was developing over in the Legate Chamber. Owen squinted at her from several mats over. He gave the subtlest shake of his head.

On the opposite side of the Focus, Tawney was calmer than Natalie expected. Her fire-red hair was straight and still. She didn't bounce on the balls of her feet or pace in irritation at the beating Natalie endured. Instead, she winked.

Behind Natalie, Max moved fast. She felt the girl's grip on her and leapt into the air spinning. As Natalie expected, the change in direction caught Max off-guard. She lost her hold. Without breaking stride, Natalie pushed her momentum into the girl while kicking her feet out from under her. Natalie dropped her knee onto Max's back and, with a fistful of green hair, saved Max from smacking her face on the floor.

A few people in the crowd clapped while Max shook with rage. A drop of blood fell from Natalie's mouth onto Max's forehead. As she reached up to staunch the bleeding, Max flipped beneath her and closed her hands around Natalie's throat.

"Enough!" Eleanor called from the sidelines.

Max's grip tightened. Natalie couldn't breathe. She clawed at Max's fingers as black and silver dots sparkled in her vision.

Eleanor screamed for Natalie's release. She sensed recruits and senior members approaching from around the Focus. They wouldn't make it in time.

Don't fight, Tawney's lessons resurfaced. *You'll only pass out faster. She'll mess up. Give her time.*

Natalie let her head fall back. She slumped and listed to the side, abandoning all form.

"I said *enough!*" Eleanor stomped across the mat.

"She is weak," Max spat. Her grip fell away from Natalie's neck.

Natalie caught the unmistakable slap of high-fives as Eleanor hovered over her.

"I'm okay," Natalie croaked. Standing, a painful cough tore at her throat. She bowed her head respectfully at her Legate.

"Ah!" Eleanor said with relief. "She is clever!"

Max's victorious smirk dissolved.

"Let us mend." Eleanor motioned for the entire Legate Chamber to sit around the blood-stained center of the sparring mat.

Please not a sharing circle, Natalie begged.

"After breaking bonds of brotherhood it's important to mend our family by remembering our purpose. This is best accomplished by sharing your struggles with your brothers and sisters."

I'd rather she hit me again. Natalie leaned back onto her elbows. She pushed her bleeding tongue against the roof of her mouth, encouraging a clot to form, while still having to clear her burning throat every few seconds.

Eleanor knelt among them and nodded to the unlucky recruit chosen to go first: the young girl Natalie had spoken to at the Assessment.

"Recruit Ignis."

The girl peered down at her shoes. A purple bruise stained her otherwise flawless brown skin, blossoming up from her chin.

"I came to Nautilus to find peace," Ignis said.

"More."

Natalie noted the dozens of security cameras mounted around the Focus and, for the first time, Natalie suspected they recorded audio as well.

They're finding us out. That's why we haven't left the Focus. That's why we're still labeled 'Recruits'. The rise in her blood pressure set her tongue bleeding again. *We're being interrogated under the guise of bonding.*

Meanwhile, Ignis was cracking under Eleanor's grey scrutiny. She curled up as tight as possible, as though attempting to shrink right out of existence.

"I'm here for my family." Natalie's sympathy won out and the attention of the Sharing Circle fell to her.

Oops.

Ignis relaxed a smidge, so Natalie looked at her when she spoke.

"I'm here for my family," Natalie started again, "because they were taken from me."

You don't have to lie, just don't tell the truth.

"My home was destroyed," Natalie uttered each word with care. "I lost everything. It's shallow, I know, to mourn the loss of a building, of paper and plastic things, but I do. I mourn the life I had. School, homework, family dinners. I watched it burn. And I lost them, too. My parents...my family...I lost them. Despite who I still have...they don't—" Natalie broke down. "They don't know..."

Eleanor patted Natalie's back. "May you find peace."

The circle repeated, "May you find peace."

Ignis crawled across the mat to sit in front of Natalie. Her body thin and bony, she had the build of a child.

"There was a wildfire in my hometown. My family fled with the others until we were trapped between the fire, the sea, and the border. The patrol wouldn't let us pass. Papa told me not to look back, but I could hear it," her eyes widened at the memory. "Fire is so *loud*. It roared at my back. So many were trying to get to the fence, and they passed me ahead of them. Strangers and family, they pushed me first..."

Fire, Natalie recalled from her Latin classes. *Ignis means fire.*

"They lifted me over the fence, and I dropped down on American soil." Ignis dotted the bruises peeking over the collar of her uniform. "My father didn't fall when the patrol shot him. He only yelled for me to run."

Natalie waited for Ignis to shatter. She didn't. Instead, she leaned forward and whispered, "I can still hear it. The fire."

She's a child, Natalie fumed. *She needs a home and a dog and a damn good therapist. Not a spin cycle in Nautilus's brainwashing machine.*

"I am Ignis because of fire," she finished weakly.

"No," Natalie disagreed. "You are Ignis because of evil."

"May you find peace," Eleanor kissed the girl's forehead.

"May you find peace," the circle repeated.

The sharing circle proceeded on and to Natalie's horror, many of the stories had the same bitter theme.

"Maxine," Eleanor prompted, and Max shifted uneasily where she sat.

"My story isn't as dramatic as all that," she nodded in Ignis's direction. "It's simple: mum wasn't around, and pops never existed. I'm ready to be more than an afterthought. I'll make something of myself and lead others behind me."

"To peace," Eleanor supplemented.

"Sure thing."

"May you find peace," Natalie uttered with the group.

Max is not the enemy. Fire burned in Natalie's chest. *Ignis is not the enemy.*

"You see, brothers and sisters," Eleanor spoke softly. "Though we come from different places and celebrate different cultures, we all seek the same fate. Peace for the world, peace for our children, and peace for ourselves.

"Violence begets violence. Humanity relishes war, however, we find ourselves on the brink of destruction," Eleanor declared. "We need someone in power who will put peace first and Nautilus is finally in position to enact change.

"You will be the tenth class of recruits to graduate into full-fledged Nautilus members. A week from now, on the eve of your Graduation, Nautilus is prepared to give you the world. You must band together and be strong to build this unified society. The path to peace must be carved with blood before it can be paved in silver. We must bear the brunt of peacemaking for the generations that follow.

"Return tomorrow with rested minds, hopeful hearts, and mended bodies, for we will be learning the art of the bolt! Peace be with you!" With that parting sentiment, Eleanor dismissed them.

Natalie stayed seated as the rest of the group dispersed. The weight of what Eleanor said made it difficult for her to stand. Nautilus was planning something big, something to interrupt the course of nations and undoubtedly the search for her parents. Christopher had been right all along. The unrest trickling across the globe was no coincidence.

Nautilus is taking us to war.

CHAPTER 16
NATALIE

Natalie tapped the desk impatiently. "Where are we at, Owen?"

The snaking wires and mural of computer screens made his room more resemble the inside of a spaceship than a lighthouse.

"Nothing has changed since you asked five minutes ago."

"Don't lie, nerd. We all know you think faster than the speed of light."

Owen pinched his forehead. "Nothing's faster than the speed of light, Brant."

"Trust me," Tawney lounged on Owen's bed, tossing a tennis ball against the wall for Angie to chase. "The speed of thought is not a universal constant."

"Listen to all those big words you've learned!" Brant sneered from the floor with Enzi snuggled tight against him.

Tawney adjusted her grip on the ball and Natalie stepped between them, dropping a sweatshirt over Brant to extinguish the brewing squabble.

"Anyway," Natalie rested her elbows on Owen's desk. Gold

binary code filled the blacked-out screen. Though she knew her way around a handful of languages, this one eluded her. "You had some idea for a computer virus? Can you do it?"

"No," Owen wrung out the word. "Tawney mentioning a virus gave me an idea. This is exactly why I shouldn't have said anything. I'm not even sure it's possible."

"You'll make it possible." Natalie feigned more confidence than she felt. "And Graduation will be the perfect time to use it."

Owen typed as though the keys had personally offended him. "Why are we suddenly putting all of our eggs in my basket anyway?"

"Because," Natalie massaged a knot in her neck, "this is our best shot."

"Only shot, really," Brant added from the floor, muffled by the sweatshirt. "If what Eleanor said to Natalie is true."

Tawney stilled the tennis ball. "Do you really think they'll start a war?"

"Yes," Natalie and Owen answered together.

"Then how are we going to do anything about whatever it is they're planning?" Brant rolled over to better use Enzi as a pillow. "We won't have full access to the Helix until after Graduation."

"If what Eleanor said carries any truth, after Graduation might be too late." Natalie felt stiff and achy. "That's why we need Owen's plan to work. I'll figure out the rest."

"*We* will figure out the rest." Tawney poked Natalie square in the chest. "Sometimes you act like you're doing this alone."

The secrets buried in her wardrobe rattled so loud Natalie was certain her friends would hear. *I need answers to fill the voids they'll create.*

"So, step on it, Owen," Brant broke the awkward silence. "Be the best nerd you can be."

Natalie fidgeted with her bolt, tossing it back and forth and behind her back.

"Watch where you point that thing," Brant said nervously.

"It has to be rotated to activate, doofus. Until then it's just a pretty stick to hit you with." Tawney tossed the tennis ball at his head. Brant caught it outright and she feigned surprise, flipping off the bed to take cover.

"We should get going." Natalie reminded them. Enzi and Angie leapt to their paws, eager to accompany her down to the kitchen. "We'll play when I come home. Promise." Natalie positioned Chef's bolt beneath the jacket of her uniform where a line of magnets held it in place. Enzi's drooping tail made her heart ache.

"You're taking that?" Brant asked.

Natalie wondered how he'd react to the pistol hidden in her waistband. "We're sparring with bolts today."

"Already?" he asked longingly. "Curtanas don't start bolts for a few more days. We're still practicing hand-to-hand. I didn't realize there were so many ways to kill someone without a weapon." He chuckled.

She watched him adjust the pins on his uniform and push out the wrinkles. "You're not a Curtana," Natalie bit out the words. "You're Coelacanth. Don't forget yourself in there."

Brant planted a light kiss on her forehead. "I'm not forgetting anything. It was a bad joke, I'm sorry."

"If we're done getting all touchy-feely, I'm ready to split." Despite the sunlight reflecting off the sea, Tawney flung the door open to rain. "I'm so *sick* of beach weather. Pick something!" she yelled at the sky, tucking her red-dyed hair into her uniform.

They left Ancora to tack back to the Florida coast, letting several minutes pass between them as they set off for the Helix. Being in different Chambers, arriving together might draw unwanted attention. As always, Natalie went last.

Heat radiated off the blacktop as she mounted her bike and pedaled for the Helix. Slick with sweat when she arrived, the cold atmosphere of the compound was a relief. Funneled through the Core and into the Focus for training, Natalie navigated through several groups of recruits before joining her fellow Legates beneath a holographic tree.

"Morning Ignis," Natalie greeted the petite girl who stood staring at a stack of bolts propped up against the wall. Natalie played with a few of them before casually removing the one from her jacket. Ignis's frown deepened, though she seemed oblivious to Natalie's sleight of hand.

"I thought Legates didn't use bolts," Ignis mumbled.

"Sometimes the path to peace is treacherous," Eleanor's somber tone sounded behind them. "And violence lacks prejudice. We must all be prepared.

"Today's your crash course in the bolt," she announced to the group. "You'll learn to disarm and disable and receive your own at Graduation." She spun the silver rod, sending sparks from either end as it gained speed. "Think of it as your diploma, though it will serve you better than any piece of paper."

Eleanor broke down a few basic maneuvers and, after only a half-hour of drills, teamed them up tournament style.

Don't call attention to yourself, Natalie calmed her nerves. *Fall in the middle of the pack. I only need to make the top five to qualify for Legate status.*

Her first opponent was a heavy-set man lacking a single nimble bone in his body. He came at her with obvious, heavy blows and Natalie easily redirected his first swing, knocking his bolt to the floor. Her second contender tripped over her own feet and dropped her weapon, but the third was fast. He knocked Natalie to the ground with a sharp jab to her ribcage and, as she laid on her back, she realized the man lacked strength. When he lifted the bolt up over his head, Natalie grabbed the uncharged silver cap and yanked the weapon away.

She was so determined not to injure anyone, Natalie forgot to lose. Four opponents later she found herself in the championship match with Max standing opposite her. The dragonette flared her pierced nostrils.

"Remember," Eleanor warned, "we are on the same team. We

fight for each other, we fight for Nautilus, we fight for peace. Do not forget why you're here."

I won't. Natalie needed Max to win. She needed to keep her head down and blend in.

The defeated Legate recruits surrounded the mat, eager to see who would be the next to fall. Max sidestepped to her left and Natalie mirrored her, maintaining the distance between them. Watching with her peripherals, Natalie saw Max's respirations increase and her grip choke up on the metal rod. She caught every motion without ever breaking eye-contact.

Tawney may not have made Natalie a fighter, but she did make her a survivor.

Max spun and Natalie dodged the sparking metal.

"That's—" Eleanor's interjection was cut off by another swing.

Max threw herself at Natalie and Natalie let her. Deflecting another blow, Natalie allowed Max to pin her, and the girl's kneecap stabbed sharply against Natalie's sternum.

"I yield," Natalie breathed.

"Release her."

When Natalie attempted to rise, Max slid the body of the metal bolt along her collarbone. Electricity hummed through it.

"Pretty scars." She traced the white filigree that spread from Natalie's palm to her forearm. "They would be lovely across that pretty face."

Natalie didn't move. She could feel the searing heat of the metal baking the air next to her. Eleanor was yelling, holding her own bolt in the air. But if Max decided to kill her, there was nothing the woman could do.

"I don't want to fight you, Max," Natalie tried to sound small.

"You lied to me," Max snarled. "You came here for power. You will *never* be Legate over me."

"You're right," Natalie conceded. "You'll be Legate."

Max leaned closer to whisper in Natalie's ear. "You're weak and full of fear. That's why you couldn't save your family."

Natalie saw red. She elbowed Max in her jaw and brought her bolt up spinning. Shocked and growling like a wild animal, Max tried to crawl away. Natalie cut her off. She spun her bolt as a baton by her hip, watching the blood drip down Max's chin.

Eleanor stepped between them and a shot of fear overshadowed Natalie's anger, leaving her hollow and confused. She lowered her bolt. Max was nothing.

"Violence begets violence," Eleanor nodded solemnly.

She wasn't supposed to lash out. She wasn't supposed to draw attention. Still, watching Max's blood stain the front of her uniform, Natalie wasn't the least bit sorry.

"Then why does Nautilus teach us to fight?" Ignis asked from the sidelines.

"The roar of gunfire and screams of the innocent have deafened our tyrants," Eleanor explained. "They can no longer hear our soft words or feel our kind gestures. Save your anger for them and remember Nautilus gives you refuge, purpose, and peace."

Max stepped forward with her open palm extended. Natalie hesitated. She didn't have to like Max, but she couldn't afford to hate her either. She shook Max's hand and something slimy squished between them.

"Next time," Max promised, "I'll end you."

Natalie wiped away the spit on her pants.

Something else to look forward to.

CHAPTER 17
NATALIE

Dismissed for break, the recruits wandered to the Core in search of lunch. Slipping Chef's bolt under the jacket of her uniform, Natalie lingered in the Focus until only a handful of stragglers remained. She took her time, inspecting every inch of the hall connecting the central rooms, hoping her desperation to find *something* would pass as aimless curiosity to any passerby. The passage was short and dim, reliant on light from the two massive chambers it linked, and directly beneath the second-floor balcony stretched a few paces of darkness. Natalie stayed there until her sight adjusted and, when she could make out the laces on her shoes, she analyzed the wall in front of her.

Nothing. She wasn't surprised, still, she'd hoped. Natalie leaned against the cold painted surface, confirming its solidity and utter lack of anything. It was a wall. Nothing more, nothing less.

What were you expecting? Frustrated, she leaned her back against it, pressing Chef's bolt against her spine.

The information must be here somewhere, Natalie knew. *We need to get lucky.* Unfortunately, luck hadn't been one to do her any favors.

She mindlessly tracked a crack in the wall opposite her. If Owen's virus-thing worked, and that was a big *if*, it would only buy them a few minutes to raid the Helix. There wouldn't be time to dig around. She needed to know where to start, how to get in, and how to get out. There would be no room for mistakes.

And if Nautilus uses our parents for their global Graduation scheme, we may never have another chance.

The crack she studied spanned from the ceiling to the floor, a perfect division. Natalie had seen bombings and walked through the streets of the aftermath. She'd seen people shot and felt the sickening heat of their blood. Yet she couldn't imagine war any more than she could imagine a world without her mother and father. Adopted or not, she had to find her parents before Nautilus brought the world to its knees.

Natalie squinted at the wall. *It's not a crack...it's a seam!* Darting across the passage, she traced the divide. She clutched the defect and, pulling with all her weight, the panel slid silently into the wall beside it.

For a breath, Natalie stared down a black tunnel. The back of her neck prickled. It made sense Nautilus would mimic its architecture across its facilities, but the sight still stunned her. She could have been back in Antarctica, back in the pit with no sun.

Natalie could almost hear the seconds ticking by, wasted and gone, yet her feet refused to move. How could she go down there? Into another blind maze? She had only managed to escape the first time because of Chef. Who was there to help her now?

Tick-tock.

Voices echoed from the Focus. Recruits were coming. The darkness expanded into a void. She was losing time.

Natalie crossed the threshold and forced the panel closed behind her. She waited in the dark, listening to the recruits pass on the other side of the panel oblivious to the hidden passage beside them. When their conversation faded, Natalie remained frozen.

Eyes open, eyes closed, it made no difference. Fear clutched her heart in its icy palms. A hundred imagined monsters shifted in the shadows, more human than they'd been in her childhood and all in navy blue.

Move.

Listening for anything over the roar of her pulse, Natalie took a step. Light glowed to life by her feet, emanating from a space where the walls met the floor. She blinked at the empty passage ahead of her and sank against the door in relief. Light was good.

Alone was better.

She moved as fast as she dared down the hall. The ground sloped sharply while the wall curved constantly away, spiraling her deeper into the Helix. Shaking, she held her bolt at the ready.

It's different this time, Natalie told herself. *I know my way out.*

Natalie had no idea how far she walked; it could have been twenty paces or a mile. She was about to turn back when she found a door. She tried the handle. Locked. Instead, a scanner illuminated, and Natalie kicked the door in frustration.

Damn biometrics.

Merely a recruit, she lacked access to even the most basic locations, still Natalie hovered over the pad. What if she never got another chance?

She pressed her palm against the screen. It scanned, and her nerves wound so tight she hardly felt the pinch at the end. The pad's blue light blinked red. The door remained locked.

A booming *CRACK* shook the hall.

Then the lights went out.

Natalie took off. She sprinted up the pitch-black passage, expecting every step to be her last. She knew a hand would come out of the dark to pull her back. Surely a bolt would spark up and smite her down. She ran anyway.

It's a game, she reached out blindly. *Marco Polo in the pool. Feel your way through.*

Lungs burning, she tore through the Helix underground. The floor leveled out and the end of the passage rushed up to meet her. Slamming into the panel, she threw open the sliding door and barreled through. She forced it shut behind her and collapsed in the hall connecting the Core and the Focus.

"Raven, dear?"

A squeak escaped her, and Natalie covered her mouth. She searched for Eleanor, but she couldn't see her. She couldn't see *anything*. Panic closed her throat. What was wrong with her?

"Ah, here you are!" Eleanor's fragile silhouette shuffled closer. "Cursed blackouts. I didn't see you in the Core, dearie. Still can't see you now, I suppose," she hummed a laugh.

"Blackouts?" Relief washed over her.

"Yes, yes, growing pains. Speaking of, I know this can be a hard transition." Eleanor forced something crumbling into Natalie's lap. "Have a biscuit, child." To her surprise, Eleanor sat next to her. "Never seem to lose power when it's convenient. Not to worry, though. They'll open the doors soon enough—"

Daylight filtered in from the Core as the entry doors were propped open.

"Ah!" Eleanor nodded. "There you are dearie! Eat."

Natalie forced herself to take a bite of the biscuit.

"I was a wicked mess when Nautilus found me," Eleanor puckered at the memory. "So angry with the world for the suffering in my life, for the suffering of my children." The filtered light underlined the old woman's features. Darkness found refuge in the wrinkles etched into her forehead.

"You have kids?" Natalie asked.

"Biologically, no." Eleanor brightened. "Spiritually, yes. I've had many children. For thirty-two years I taught preschool in Washington, D.C. It was an honor," she patted her chest, "guiding children towards their potential under the watch of our forefathers. Despite my love for Nautilus," Eleanor spared a quick glance in either direction, "my teaching years remain the very best of my life."

It was difficult for Natalie to imagine Eleanor tutoring toddlers. The same woman who hunted her and her friends in Ancora I, who burned down her home, who had been content to see Natalie locked away for days in a sunless pit. No, that image would not compute.

"Why did you stop?"

"I told you before, dear: violence lacks prejudice. Ethnicity, nationality, age." Her sigh rattled her chest. "Not even a child can stop a bullet."

Natalie tried to subdue the swell of sympathy rising within her. She didn't bother with words of encouragement or condolence; there was nothing she could say.

"I see my pain in you, Raven. You feel that weight." Her misty eyes reflected what little light fell between them.

How much do you see, Eleanor?

Natalie forced down what remained of the biscuit. "I won't sink if you don't."

Eleanor beamed. "My dear, you won't sink because Nautilus will make it so! You live only in pain and regret. After Graduation you'll live for more. Before then you have work to do." Eleanor used the wall to help herself to her feet.

"Don't let past sufferings rob you and our world of the peace that's to come, child. You cannot make Legate with ghosts on your back. Heal. Then you can serve your purpose for Nautilus and for peace."

Natalie frowned at her. For a moment, the briefest stretch of time, she'd actually wondered if Eleanor could be freed from Nautilus's hold. Then the woman started spewing nonsense again.

"You're excused for the rest of the day. Go. Do what you must to give yourself completely to Nautilus." Eleanor pinched Natalie's chin between her thumb and forefinger. "Conquer your demons, dearie, lest they drown you first."

Natalie knew she needed to be at the Helix for her parents, for her friends, for any possible outlet to bring Nautilus down, yet the old woman's words found purchase. Graduation was coming. She needed to focus, and she couldn't clear her mind in Nautilus's silver cage.

The sun was still high in the sky when she reached the lighthouse, greeting Enzi and Angie with a treat at the door. The shower water ran black as she transformed back into herself, stripping her hair of every drop of dye. She loaded a backpack with water, a jacket, Chef's bolt, and a handful of cash. Ready to go, she didn't hesitate until she reached the stairwell.

Fate's a wicked beastie, Christopher's words haunted her. Natalie marched to the wardrobe and kicked open the bottom drawer. The bloodied copy of Dr. Seuss's *Oh, The Places You'll Go!* awaited her, its once bright cover muddied brown with blood.

Leo's blood.

He'd rescued her treasured titles from Ancora I when Nautilus forced them to flee. He'd saved Enzi's life, and when the time came for her to return the favor, she'd lost him.

Natalie drew a ragged breath. It wasn't enough to tuck his memory away, to ignore the empty chair at the kitchen table. She couldn't chase a fractured hope when her parents' freedom was at stake, when her friends were putting their lives on the line for a truth they didn't know was coming. If she wanted a real chance against Nautilus, Natalie needed to let Leo go.

My family needs me to move forward.

Dropping the book back in the drawer, she retrieved Enzi's purple harness from the top of the wardrobe and got him dressed. Meanwhile, Angie's high-pitched protests followed them all the way to the dock.

Under the covered boat slip, Natalie's stomach fluttered. She'd been breaking their rules all summer, tacking on her own to visit Uncle Chris, but this was different. This was risky. Yet her pace never faltered. Enzi sniffed the metal on Natalie's hip and sneezed in protest.

"A deal's a deal. The gun comes, too." She dangled the toes of her shoes off the edge of the dock.

Brant will find my message. Though the note only vaguely explained her absence, she knew he'd understand. He would cover for her.

This is for me, Natalie reminded herself. *So I can move forward. So I can focus on my family. So that when I look back, there are more than ghosts in my wake.*

Natalie held tight to Enzi's scruff and together they leapt off the dock, falling into a world of light.

CHAPTER 18
NATALIE

The bustling city of Le Havre seemed to have erupted straight out of the English Channel. High-rise hotels on cafe-lined boulevards abutted the narrow strip of sand where Natalie landed. The sweet aroma of fresh patisseries mixed with the cool salt air made her mouth water, but even the bouquet of French desserts and thrill of foreign soil couldn't shake her unease. An ocean away from Ancora and the Helix, Natalie still watched over her shoulder.

Eventually she stumbled upon the train station. Although her bumbling French helped break the ice, it took some back and forth with the teller before Natalie boarded a Paris-bound train with Enzi draped awkwardly across her lap. Preoccupied with the weight of her thoughts, the ride passed faster than expected. Enzi napped and she watched the towns flick by and when the train finally stopped, she followed the crowd onto the platform. Hurrying to the metro, Enzi tucked against her so tight his fur brushed her knee with every step.

"Four stops," she told him.

Enzi's head rotated on a swivel, watching people board and exit the subway car. A few passengers perused a book or a newspaper, though most lived absorbed in their phones. She couldn't help wondering if they'd seen the same reports she had. Along with suspicious explosions in Maryland and Lebanon, Paris had been the subject of numerous bomb threats in recent weeks.

Not to mention the fire, Natalie's heart wrenched.

The car screeched to another lurching stop and the monotone speaker announced their arrival at Saint-Michel-Notre-Dame Station. Natalie left the car of strangers behind and climbed a set of concrete stairs to emerge in the heart of the city.

"Woah." Awestruck, Natalie stopped, earning many jolting collisions from those still exiting behind her.

The sun hung low in the sky, gilding the boulevards between ancient buildings, and filtering down pavestone pathways. Bridges crisscrossed the Seine and green boxes lined its banks, sheltering the wares of local artists. Purple and pink flowers overflowed from hanging pots chased by wayward vines creeping up the café walls. And despite the tourists and cars and traffic, a collective hush blanketed the streets.

Across the river, the towers of Notre Dame commanded the attention of the square. Natalie had stood at the feet of skyscrapers and nothing made her feel so small as the cathedral. Though its whitewashed stonework exhibited charred scars from the fire, beneath the soot and scaffolding she could still make out magnificent sculptures and carvings.

Even burned she was beautiful.

Enzi rubbed against her.

"You're right," Natalie blinked away from the cathedral. "We're here for something else." She turned to a squat building tucked between two busy streets. Wooden bins overflowing with books lined the entrance, accompanied by the bitter aroma of coffee.

Ducking through the narrow entry, the murmur of the city muffled out to silence. Dust swirled in the filtered sunlight, spiraling around the towers of titles that filled the store from floor to ceiling.

"Bienvenue à Shakespeare and Company," a shopkeeper greeted

her. He tucked his long hair behind his ears and resumed a lighthearted debate with someone below the counter.

Natalie leaned over to see a man with deep brown skin and a radiant smile unpacking a box of books.

"Vous vivez dans les nuages avec des rêves et des souhaits!" The greeter sneered at the man on the floor.

"Better a dreamer than a bore!" His thick Indian accent echoed in the foyer and his coworker shushed him with a huff.

Natalie left the shopkeepers to their bickering, eager to lose herself among the shelves. Polished oak boards creaked their welcome and lingering notes of vanilla calmed her nerves. In the back of the store, she found a staircase painted with a quote to be read upon ascension:

—Hafiz
BEING
OF YOUR OWN
LIGHT
THE ASTONISHING
IN DARKNESS
LONELY OR
WHEN YOU ARE
I COULD SHOW YOU
I WISH

As Natalie traced the flaking white paint, her mind skipped back across the Atlantic, across the mountains and plains of America, to the rooftop of a yellow cottage on the Pacific coast.

All those stars, they're surrounded by an abyss of darkness, but they burn anyway.

"Imagine the courage that takes," she whispered aloud.

The fast thumping of paws on wood snapped Natalie back to Paris. On the second floor, Enzi's white tail swished around the railing and out of sight.

"Enzi!" Natalie bolted after him, knocking over a stack of books and barreling into more than one customer. She caught him just as he found it: a round tabby cat curled in the window. "Sit!"

Enzi dropped his haunches on the spot and sat with perfect posture. His tail flicked back and forth, a white blur against the braided burgundy rug. Natalie knelt between him and the cat who was still asleep in her personal ray of sunshine.

"No," her tone was low and serious. "Kitty does not want to play."

"Mademoiselle," the shopkeeper who'd greeted her approached. "Chiens interdits."

Natalie wasn't fluent in French, however her knowledge of Latin filled in the gaps: Enzi was not welcome.

"Je suis désolé," she apologized. "We'll—"

A hiss interrupted her, abruptly followed by a sharp yelp. The cat slinked away between the bookshelves, leaving Enzi crying and dripping blood from the gash on his nose.

"Enzi!"

He fussed pathetically, pawing at his muzzle and painting his front axe-murderer red. The shopkeeper cursed furiously in French as blood dripped on the rug and antique floor.

"Je suis désolé!" Natalie repeated as the man shooed them down the stairs. They'd nearly crossed the threshold when his cheerful coworker stopped them.

"Simon!" he gestured at Enzi. "The poor pooch is a bloody mess!"

"Notre magasin est un bordel sanglant! Et le pauvre chat!"

"Bah! Mythos can take care of herself!" The man knelt over Enzi.

Enzi took his cue and cried dramatically. His entire muzzle and front paws were streaked in a deep red that darkened as it dried, his white fur making everything appear bloodier than it truly was.

"Simon! Serviette!" His gleeful personality was infectious. Simon fetched a small towel and tossed it to his friend as two customers entered the shop. They gawked at Enzi's mess and Natalie apologized, embarrassed.

"I am Parth." He applied pressure to Enzi's cut with the towel. "What do you call this lovely creature?"

"Enzi," Natalie explained sheepishly. "And my name is Natalie. We appreciate your help. I can't imagine walking him through the streets like...what?"

Parth gawked at her and Natalie sensed Simon listening intently behind the counter.

"Natalie?" Parth accentuated each syllable. "Your name is Natalie? Natalie...Morrigan?"

She blanched. Ever since her parents disappeared, it never turned out well when someone knew her name. It was time to go.

Natalie broke for the street. Parth was faster and knocked her aside. Enzi showed his teeth and Parth jumped back, distracted but not deterred.

The store behind her was a dead end. She assessed the shopkeeper. He didn't seem like a bad person; he'd been willing to help Enzi despite the mess. But now he stood between her and the exit.

The only way out is through.

"Move," she demanded.

"Wait!" Parth looked from her to Enzi's bloodstained, snarling muzzle. "Please," he begged, refusing to step aside.

She scanned his attire for the Prestige pins that would match her own, for embroidered silver details that would appear ornamental to unsuspecting tourists. She assessed Parth from head to toe and did not find a single Nautilus decoration on him. It made no difference.

Question everything.

She pulled Christopher's pistol from her waistband and held it level with Parth's chest. "Let me pass," Natalie ordered again, "and I won't hurt you. I promise."

"You cannot leave!" Parth begged, ignoring the weapon. "I told you, Simon! I damn well told you!"

Simon dipped for something below the counter.

"Don't," Natalie warned. "I'll shoot you both before you even have the chance to raise your weapon. Drop it."

Simon rose cautiously. Natalie watched the door. If anyone entered the shop she'd be in a whole other mess of trouble. She didn't need the French police hunting her down because of these two Seashell idiots.

"I'm a bloody bookseller!" Simon's English was laced thick with French undertones. "I don't have any weapons!"

"Shut it," Parth barked before turning back to her. "Do you believe in fate, Natalie Morrigan?"

Natalie adjusted her grip on the pistol without lowering it. "No," she confessed. "I believe in what I can touch, what I can see. And right now, I see your life in my hands. Step aside."

"Give her the book, Simon," Parth commanded.

"I tried!"

A group of girls passed behind Natalie, winding their way from one cluster of shelves to another. Parth clasped his hands together and stretched them high overhead. He was covering for her. The action gave Natalie pause.

"What are you talking about?"

"There's a book reserved for you," Parth explained, delighted despite the gun aimed at his chest.

"I didn't reserve anything."

"We know," Simon pursed his lips. "Why do you think he's so damn excitable? Been waiting for you all year, he has."

"I don't understand."

"Books have a habit of finding us when we need them," Parth nodded towards her gun. "I'd say yours is right on time. Simon."

Simon ducked below the counter and emerged with a black box.

"This was put in your name fifteen years ago," he explained. "To be received sometime in August of this year."

Natalie's ears rang. Someone had guessed she would come to a random bookstore in Paris before she had even learned to read.

Parth took the package from Simon and offered it to her. "Would you consider opening it here?"

"Do not think he is merely curious," Simon cut in. "We have wagers on what title waits inside."

Parth shushed him. It took Natalie a moment to collect her thoughts enough to speak again.

"Are you with Nautilus?" Though it lacked poise, blunt proved effective. Simon and Parth exchanged a puzzled look.

"Is that a distributor?" Parth frowned.

I'll take that as a tentative 'no'.

Satisfied enough to rely on Enzi's protection, Natalie pocketed the pistol and took the gift from Parth. She sat cross-legged on the floor and with the box in her lap. A yellow-gold lump of wax sealed it closed, with an ancient looping symbol pressed into it.

The triquetra.

It had been on Christopher's map in Ancora I, the answer to the logic puzzle with the mysterious key, and had plagued Natalie's thoughts ever since.

Parth leaned closer and Enzi snapped him back. Undeterred, the bookkeeper rocked excitedly on his heels.

"If September came and I didn't, would you have opened it?" Natalie asked.

"No!"

"Oui."

Parth recoiled at Simon's response and Natalie relaxed a little more.

"What do you think is inside?" Parth wondered.

Natalie shrugged. She had no idea.

Breaking the wax, Natalie popped open the lid to reveal a leather-bound book on a cushion of velvet.

"*The Sceptical Chymist,*" she read aloud, "by Robert Boyle." The name rattled a forgotten trunk of facts in a dusty corner of her mind. It twitched once or twice before finally settling down again, content to be lost. "It's familiar," Natalie nodded. "The author, not the title. Is it what you expected?"

Their disappointment suggested not.

"Well, it is paid for," Simon said, his interest fading.

"By who?" Natalie suspected she knew. Who else could have achieved something so poetic with such ease? The real question was how did he know she would be there? Why wouldn't he give her the book before now?

Fate's a wicked beastie.

"Some bloke named Christopher. Ring any bells?" Parth's excitement rebounded.

"A few." Dazed, she stowed the book in her backpack and stood to leave.

"Wait!" Parth darted out of the room and returned with a fresh towel and a bottle of clear fluid. "You cannot let him wander Paris like that." Ignoring Enzi's uncertain snarl, he poured the liquid down the dog's front. Mixing with the blood in his fur, the peroxide bubbled and foamed until he was squeaky clean and sopping wet. "There!"

Simon leaned against the check-out counter, bored. "Come back and see us." He bid her farewell and disappeared into the shop.

"He was wrong, you know," Parth whispered. "He often is. Nonetheless, I think you know as well as I how very wrong he was."

Natalie's head was buzzing and Parth's hushed tone rambled too fast for her to follow.

"We defend the most powerful thing in existence. To some it's a weapon, to others armor, and, to a fateful few, it is destiny."

Alarmed by his passion, Natalie stepped back. "I'm sorry?"

"Knowledge, Natalie! It is there in your pack." He shooed her away, beaming. "I beg that fate is kind to you."

Not likely. Natalie emerged from the bookshop, her thoughts slow and disjointed, consumed by the mystery of Christopher's most recent gift. Or maybe it was his first.

How did he know? She asked herself over and over, blindly setting one foot in front of the other after Enzi. *How did he know I would come? Why leave the book for me here? Why leave me the book at all?*

Settling onto a bench, Natalie realized Enzi had led her into a secluded garden with the cathedral's charred buttresses barely visible above the hedges. With only the rose bushes to witness, she removed the book from her pack. The cover was soft and worn with the crumbling remains of leather tie-straps dangling from the spine. She turned the first page.

The Sceptical Chymist
Or
Chymico-Physical Doubts & Paradoxes, Touching the Spagyrist's Principles Commonly call'd Hypostatical; As they are wont to be Propos'd and Defended by the Generality of Alchymists. Whereunto is præmis'd Part of another Discourse relating to the same Subject

Baffled, Natalie massaged her temples. Studying the inside cover, the triquetra greeted her once again, accompanied by a single, messy sentence inked across the parchment.

Hoc solum scio quod nihil scio.

Natalie smiled. Something important waited within those pages. All she needed to do was find it.

CHAPTER 19
LEONIDAS

Lache tapped her foot. "You are not trying."

Leo worked a thick salve into his scar, hoping the cream might dull the throbbing ache beneath it. He had pushed himself too hard, impatient to regain all the strength he'd lost. Now his heartbeat pulsed against the tender line of flesh and with every throb he anticipated the searing pain to return. He breathed deep.

Painless.

Still, the discomfort reminded him it was easier to break than to mend.

"You should have already found him. I am sure of it."

His Nautilus uniform hung in the corner. He hadn't seen or heard from Edwin since Nautilus's secret meeting days prior.

Follow the gulls...

"Leonidas!"

"Hmm?" Leo buttoned his flannel shirt.

"You are not listening!"

"I am," Leo lied. "I'm listening."

"What did I ask of you?" Lache quizzed him.

"Why I haven't found Amir Amani."

"Wrong!" Lache cried. "I did not ask you anything. I accused you of not trying. Perhaps you are growing complacent, or worse."

"Worse?"

"Maybe your commitments are beginning to reflect your adornments." Lache tossed his uniform at him. Her acquired sisters leaned against each other in the hall, no doubt drawn in by the argument Leo hadn't realized he was having.

"You're crazy." Even as he said it, guilt raked him. He *had* found Amir Amani.

And he'd done nothing about it.

"Am I?" Lache closed the gap between them. "You spend every waking second staring at that stupid shell on your uniform. Admit it: you want another mission."

"Of course, I do! Completing a mission, a real mission, is my best shot for getting Nautilus to trust me. Then I might stand half a chance of finding something, *anything*, related to my parents. I'm still a dog on Edwin's leash."

"Why not fulfill your debt while you wait? Why do you hesitate?" Atro probed.

"Because that would throw the game!" Leo bordered on shouting. "Even if by some miracle I didn't get caught, assassinating a Nautilus Legate in the middle of their headquarters would cause a lockdown at the very least. I can't let that happen. Not before I find my family."

Lache resumed buttoning his shirt where he had left it. Behind her, Clo and Atro frowned.

"You saved my life," Leo tried to reassure them. "I owe you a debt and I made you a promise." He gritted his teeth. He'd already failed them once and, if he was lucky, they'd never know. Killing in defense was bad enough. Outright murder…

I have to keep my word, Leo pushed his reluctance away.

The Nautilus shell flashed a fluorescent white. Anticipation and excitement ushered him up on the balls of his feet. Edwin was back!

"Ah," Clo leaned against Atro. "Saved by the shell!"

"Show him," Lache blocked his exit.

"Lachesis, maybe we should—"

"Now."

Clo cowered beneath her sister's scrutiny as Atro pulled Leo into the common room.

"Show me what?" Apprehension dug in his heels, but Atro was stronger than she appeared. "Where are we going?"

She stationed him before their boxed television set and fumbled with a makeshift antenna. Atro adjusted the foil covered coat hanger until the screen only flickered every few seconds.

"Sit," Lache instructed.

"No?"

Clo stepped beside him, her green cloak balled up around her neck to the base of her spiked hair. "You should sit down, Leonidas," she coaxed.

Her stillness spiked his fear. He didn't want to sit down. And he definitely didn't want to see whatever was on the television. Regardless, when Atro finally stepped aside, he couldn't turn away.

The image was black and white. Leo caught the first few words the narrator said then the rest was lost as noise, a collection of meaningless sounds, like hearing someone speak in another language.

But Leo understood everything.

He understood the woman tied to the chair was a hostage. Shades of black delineated the bruises on her face and neck, and grey blood dripped steadily from her mouth. He understood the painted sign propped in her lap was a taunt of sorts. *Freedom isn't Free*, it read. As figures moved in and out of screen, he understood that the woman had not once shifted or drawn breath. And somehow, he understood Clo had known he would fall to his knees, even if she didn't know why.

"You have been wasting time," Lache snipped. "You said Nautilus holds you and your friends' parents captive. We gave you an opportunity to find them and now, well this is one of them, yes?"

Leo couldn't answer. Beneath him, Clo crumpled with a whimper and he wondered when he'd begun to lean on her. Why couldn't he stand?

"Leonidas?" Lache sounded uncertain. "You do know this woman...yes?"

Leo gasped. Why couldn't he breathe? The world blurred. Was he going to pass out? What kind of defense mechanism was at work? Perhaps a panic attack? He couldn't be sure. He didn't have panic attacks, did he?

Pressing his head against the floor, he begged the walls to stop spinning as he clung to soft green cloth. Clo. He clung to Clo. How strange. The edges of his vision frayed into darkness.

"Full opossum," he sputtered. *Opossum,* he grasped for solid consciousness. *Panic-fainting opossum.*

Marble hands comforted him. They were cold and wiped something away from his cheeks. Sweat. Surely it was sweat.

"He cries," Clo's terrified whisper sounded a thousand miles away.

"You know her." Lache's tone degraded to something resemblant of an apology.

Leo feared if he attempted to speak more than words might come out. Yes, he knew her. He knew the touch of her kiss on his hair when she used to tuck him into bed. He knew the feel of her smacking the back of his head when he misbehaved. He knew the way her nose scrunched when she worried. The memories burned like molten metal, closing his throat. He forced them back.

Yes, he knew her.

"If Nautilus gets its war," Lache appeared to rock back and forth. Or maybe he swayed. "The Ward will not need what prisoners they have left."

"More?" Leo croaked.

Lache bit her lip. "More?"

"More?" Leo pounded his fist against the floor.

"We have not seen any more like this," Atro stepped in.

"Amir Amani must die, Leonidas," Lache begged.

Nodding, Leo stood. He was wobbly, and nauseous as hell, but he was standing.

"He must die," Lache repeated.

"And anyone else who stands in my way," Leo growled.

A triumphant glee radiated from her.

"Is that what you want me to say, Lache? That I'll kill them all?" Leo asked quietly. "Try a stupid stunt like that again and I'll disappear."

"We do not care if you—"

"You're wasting my time." When Leo made off to fetch his uniform, Atro stopped him.

"Who was that woman?"

Leo took a long breath in through his nose. He was still in the game. He couldn't think about the woman, not now, not until it was over. He pushed the prisoner from his mind. He didn't tuck her away; he forced her out completely. "It could have been anyone."

"But she was someone," Atro countered.

"We're still in the game," Leo said bitterly. "We grieve our losses when it's over." Shoving past her, he hastily pulled on his Nautilus blues. His mind was so perfectly void, a glass vase would envy him. The Nautilus shell buzzed and glowed instantly. He'd have to make up some excuse to Edwin to explain his—

Thin arms enveloped his torso.

"I am sorry," Clo whispered.

He pried himself out of her grip. "I needed to know."

"Not like that."

Leo pictured the vase; he embodied the void. "No," he admitted. "Not like that." He slipped into his sneakers and had nearly cleared the door when she called him again.

"Leonidas?"

He dropped his head back to scan the rafters spanned across the ceiling. There wasn't a single cobweb between them. He wondered if the Moirai cleaned or if Scotland simply banished things so trivial as dust.

"Yes, Clo."

"What is a opossum?"

Minutes before, Leo would have smiled. He may have rolled on the floor with such laughter that his scar would have burst open. Part of him wished for that. A hundred gunshots would be less painful than what he'd witnessed. But he was a vase. He was empty. He didn't have anything to give her.

Leo stepped out of the cottage and closed the door gently behind him, leaving Clo still awaiting his answer.

CHAPTER 20
LEONIDAS

Leo didn't remember leaving the Moirai or tacking to Florida's coast. One minute, Clo was asking about opossums and the next he was walking into the Helix. It was twenty minutes of his life he'd never get back and he refused to dwell on it. The separation kept him from imagining a thousand ways to reduce the Helix to rubble.

Then I wouldn't have any leads to Natalie and the rest of my family.
Or what was left of it.

"Lev!" Edwin greeted Leo in the Core. "Long time no see!"
Clear and empty.

"Where have you been?" Part of Leo was genuinely glad to see Edwin. It sickened him. "Do you know how boring this shell-hole is?"

Edwin's smile did nothing to obscure the dark circles beneath his eyes and the chucks of hair that stuck up at odd angles. "Why do you think I spend all my time at the gym?" Edwin pulled him along. "Anyway, we have a new mission, yeah?"

Nautilus members greeted them as they climbed the grand staircase and Leo focused straight ahead, pretending they didn't exist.

He needed to survive in the Helix long enough to locate his family. After that... He was starting to favor Lache's way of doing things.

Leo felt their path was familiar, unfortunately the Helix was such a maze he couldn't be sure. It wasn't until Edwin stopped beside a heavy bolted door that Leo decided he was, in fact, lost.

"I've been waiting for a mission like this since I first came to the Helix," Edwin confessed. "This means something, Lev. It could determine the fate of the war."

Leo wondered if he meant the imaginary war for peace Nautilus constantly preached or the real one that could see the entire world razed by nuclear fallout.

"Ready to have your mind blown?"

Clear and empty.

"Try me." Leo followed Edwin onto the sunbaked roof. Surrounded by two higher floors of the Helix, the circular rooftop sheltered a flat white jet with a silver Nautilus shell on its tail.

"Incredible, right?" Edwin jogged to the plane's side. "The jets rotate, enabling a vertical takeoff. We'll complete a transatlantic flight in under an hour."

The plane's sleek metal skin hummed with power. "It's on!" Leo realized. "Wait, we're crossing the Atlantic how fast? That's impossible."

Unless you can tack.

"Nothing's impossible if you're willing to break the rules," Edwin winked. "She's hypersonic."

Reluctantly impressed, Leo whistled. He was familiar with Nautilus technology: their bolts, their holograms, the biometric scanners sprinkled around the Helix like confetti. The fact they had hypersonic flight should have come as no surprise, especially after witnessing the murder of—

"Our technology is always a step ahead," Leo shook away the thought. He still had the rest of his family to save.

Edwin cocked his head. "Didn't do too well in your history

143

classes, hmm? Supersonic flight is old hat, man. The hurdles lie in funding, not concept. But let's not hurt their egos."

"I did fine in history," Leo defended himself. "Owen was always better with the technical stuff."

"Owen?"

Oops. Clear and empty, clear and empty.

"Uh, yeah," Leo's mouth went desert dry. "He's my brother."

We're not friends. Leo reminded himself sternly. *Edwin's as lethal as the rest of them. He's as guilty as Amir. Lache was right; I'm too comfortable.*

"Did he come to Nautilus, too?" Edwin's curiosity seemed genuine, but the topic made Leo uncomfortable. It was too close to home, a forest fire smoking under his front door.

"No. Haven't spoken to him for a long time." *Too long.* "What does Nautilus need us to do?" Leo swiftly changed the subject as they boarded the jet.

"Graduation is in three days," Edwin's expression darkened. "Over a decade of planning and strategic positioning of global powers is going to come down to a single event. Nautilus has worked too hard to risk failure, so the Ward wants our biggest threat taken out of the game."

Then I have to make sure we fail.

The inside of the jet reflected its streamlined exterior. Black leather seats filled the aircraft and blue lights made Leo feel as though he'd sunk underwater. About to fly over an ocean, he hoped it wasn't some kind of omen.

Nearly every seat was occupied. His crew, men and women hardened through Nautilus's training, admired him with bloodthirsty grins.

He loathed them all.

"Remember," Edwin whispered, pressing a pistol into Leo's grip. "Falter and they will doubt you. Doubt breeds disobedience.

"Now," Edwin addressed the entire plane, "the Ward did not choose us for this assignment. The fate of our world, of everything

Nautilus has worked for, rests on this mission. With failure comes the possibility that the Ward's greatest ambition will never come to light. With failure comes fear the glory promised will never come to pass. So no, the Ward did not choose our Chambers for this crucial expedition." Edwin glowered at the Curtanas. "We volunteered."

The soldiers nearly leapt from their seats. They howled and hollered and stomped their boots.

"Impressive," Leo commented.

"Never underestimate the power of piety," Edwin said quietly.

Edwin secured a leather strap on the ceiling around his forearm and Leo mimicked him, grappling for balance as the floor swayed. Beyond the many small windows, the Helix sank as the jet climbed skyward.

"Oy!" Edwin shouted to regain their Chambers' attention. "Details. We're after a woman. Brown hair, green eyes, average height. She won't stand out and she'll disappear easily in a crowd, so focus on finding her companion: a large white canine. Find the dog, find the target."

It was happening again. The color drained from Leo's face. His lungs refused to fill. He was grateful for the leather strap holding him up because his legs had turned to Jell-O.

"Capture or kill?" Someone asked from their crew.

"Capture. Take her out of the public areas."

Leo couldn't remember feeling so out of control in his life, other than maybe about an hour ago. Adrenaline flooded his system with nowhere to go. He wasn't sure if he was going to collapse or be sick or some humiliating combination of the two.

"Once you're in a secluded area, call me." Edwin sounded a hundred miles away. "I'm ordered to take her down myself."

"Yessir."

He pictured her clearly for the first time in weeks. Edwin's description was wrong. Her hair was molten caramel. And her eyes, they weren't simply green.

They're flecked with amber. They're analytical and inquisitive and stubborn. The strap flexed under his weight. *So stubborn. How will I find her first? How will I convince her to run?*

"You alright, Lev?" Edwin rocked on the handhold like a rope swing.

"Don't like flying," Leo lied.

"No worries, man. I took this engine apart and reassembled it last night. She flies like a dream."

"You're joking."

Edwin tugged on the lobe of his pierced ear and a genuine fear of the open air rooted in Leo's stomach.

"Why on earth would you do that?"

"To see how it works." Edwin laughed heartily. "You're going to love the City of Lights. Tell me, have you ever had a macaron?"

Paris. She'd once confided her desire to go to Paris, only it wasn't for the food or the romance, not even the history. She was after their books. And he might be the only one on the plane who knew it. Leo surveyed the fifty-some Curtanas he had to outwit.

I have to find her first. I have to find her first or Nautilus wins.

I have to find her first or Natalie's dead.

CHAPTER 21
LEONIDAS

Hypersonic flight was smoother than Leo imagined. In fact, the only discernible difference from a regular flight was that the clouds passed faster than normal.

Much faster.

"I swear," Edwin chatted next to him, "macarons are truly the best part about France. Everyone always says baguettes, but macarons my friend," he sighed. "They're divine. Crunchy outside, chewy inside, light as a cloud, and filled with a confection-perfection."

Leo wanted to punch him in the mouth.

The jet decelerated, swinging Leo forward, and the clouds slowed until they appeared not to move at all. They hovered mid-air. Leo bounced on his toes as the rotational jets maneuvered within the wing until, slowly, they descended.

Something rigid pierced the cloud cover. Seared gothic spires riddled with gargoyles materialized so close to the window Leo imagined he could have reached out and touched them. He braced for impact and worked himself up into such a state that the soft thud of landing made him jump clear off the floor.

"She'll be nearby," Edwin checked the bolt on his back and loaded his gun. "Spread out and stay alert. Paris lures many down its cobbled streets with no regard to their intentions."

"Yessir!"

It took every ounce of self-control to keep Leo from sprinting out of the plane. He paced as wave after wave of Curtanas departed. However, upon exiting the hatch, he stopped short entirely.

Woah.

The jet had landed *inside* Notre Dame.

Scorched stone and soot-covered beams reached high overhead, opening to a watercolor sky. Though he'd never had the privilege to see the cathedral before the fire, he imagined it would have been breathtaking.

It still was.

"They'll rebuild." Edwin patted one of the pillars as a cloud of ash billowed above his feet.

Leo's scar throbbed. "It won't be the same."

"A scar only disfigures a thing if you let it," Edwin disagreed, a freshly lit cigarette dangling from his lips. "How you carry the past, how you move forward, that's what matters most."

"They're terrible for you," Leo nodded to the cigarette.

Edwin admired the impossibly huge stained-glass window and blew out a puff of smoke. "I'll never understand what happened here, even if it was for peace."

"I thought it was an accident." Leo wracked his brain for memories of the fire. It felt like a lifetime ago; so much had happened since then.

"I thought you were awake in there?" Edwin took another long draw from the cigarette. "We did this. Nautilus."

Leo stopped so fast he nearly fell forward. He wasn't sure why it surprised him. Nautilus lived to burn sanctuaries.

"Why?"

"War, man. It's the fastest way to reshape the world. We're

desperate for it." He flashed a weak grin. "Though it would seem not all violence begets violence after all."

For a moment, Leo wondered if Edwin might disagree with Nautilus's methods. Then that moment ended.

"Come on," Edwin followed an ash-cleared path to the door. "Let's take care of this and find some desserts for the flight home, hmm?"

Leo ducked beneath a maze of scaffolding and out to the pavestone square. He'd only experienced the City of Lights in movies, where it served as a serene crucible for romance, so the bustling chaos took him by surprise.

Hordes of tourists flooded past him. He heard more than five languages in the span of a hundred paces and spotted more nationalities than he could count. Cars beeped and sped down narrow streets while the red, white, and blue French flag flapped proudly atop every building in sight.

Most jarring of all, the Curtanas made no attempt to blend in. Even Edwin blatantly flashed his pistol as he followed Leo out of the burned cathedral. They'd barely crossed the square when a patrol of French officers emerged from the mass of tourists. Leo backtracked and Edwin slammed into him.

"Oy!" He laughed. "It's only the police."

Leo was less concerned about who they were and more about what they were carrying. Each officer held an automatic rifle at the ready and, as they assessed the Nautilus members flooding their streets, Leo expected to be gunned down on the spot.

To his horror, Edwin waved at them.

"What are you doing?" Leo asked, astonished.

"Relax. They're on our side."

Sure enough, the officers returned Edwin's greeting and turned their patrol in the opposite direction. Leo frowned. Exactly how far did the Ward's reach extend?

Meanwhile, the crowd appeared oblivious to the blatant display of power. Locals and tourists alike seemed to agree neither the police nor the Curtanas were worth a second glance.

Strange what people convince themselves is normal.

Like the murder of prisoners on TV.

Leo hurried forward. He couldn't think about her, not when he should be sabotaging a manhunt. Leo jogged around the outskirts of the crowd, clinging to the only advantage he had.

He knew why Natalie was there.

While the Curtanas inspected every tourist, Leo scanned the storefronts. The bright green and yellow sign wasn't hard to spot. He gripped his gun firmly in his pocket and crossed the street, skirting the entrance to a metro station.

That's it, he decided. *That's her way out.*

"Spread out," he ordered his already scattered team. "Form a perimeter around the square. She'll likely be drawn to the cathedral."

"Yessir!" His Curtanas assumed their commanded positions, far away from Natalie's escape route.

"I'll check the cafés. Let us be the ones to secure victory for Nautilus, eh?" Edwin grasped his forearm tightly before dashing away.

Leo suppressed the fear coiling in his belly.

Victory for Nautilus meant Natalie's death.

He had to find her first.

It's Capture the Flag. Leo invited the thrill of the game to distract from its stakes. *A big, fluffy white flag.* The sound of the streets grew muffled, and figures blurred together as he searched for Enzi's perked ears and swishing tail. Every sense was heightened, every inch of him focused on the goal.

Instinct rooted him to the shop's entrance. The first thing Natalie would do is explore the store, but she wouldn't stay there.

And if my team finds her while I'm inside, she'll be dead before I breach the door.

He sidewinded towards a nearby garden. The pavestone path had turned to pebbles when something big barreled into him. Drawing his pistol, Leo turned on his attacker.

A warm, wet tongue slathered him as a mass of white, bubbly fur knocked him backwards. The creature bowed playfully before jumping up and setting his heavy paws on Leo's shoulders.

"Enzi!"

The dog wagged his tail so hard Leo swayed side to side with him. Leo couldn't help it; he burst out laughing. He buried himself in Enzi's sopping wet fur and lifted him clear off the ground. The dog was the closest thing to home Leo had seen in months.

For a breath, Leo relaxed. He found Enzi before the Curtanas. Or rather, Enzi found him. Natalie had to be nearby. With an ounce of luck, he could slip them both into the subway station while distracting his Nautilus frenemies around the other side of the store. Everything was going to work out fine. Better than fine.

Then Enzi barked.

Leo clamped the dog's muzzle shut. Enzi hardly cared. He wiggled in Leo's grasp, trying to press himself as close as possible.

Holding his breath, Leo listened. The streets were loud and crowded, so there was a chance the Curtanas didn't hear him. Regardless, Leo knew they had to move.

A sharp whistle cut through the noise of the city. Enzi darted away and then she was right there, no more than ten meters from him, as perfect as the day he lost her. It was as though no time had passed at all.

Natalie.

Leo had imagined the moment a hundred times: she would run to him and he'd tell her he was sorry, sorry he lost them, sorry he couldn't get back to her. He would kiss her like he had in the depths of Nautilus's prison, only they wouldn't have to stop.

But she didn't run to him. And the longer he watched the more he realized she wasn't the same. His gut twisted. Whatever he'd missed in the past weeks, Natalie had changed.

A fact made clear by the gun she aimed at his chest.

Leo tried to call out to her, only to gape stupidly like a fish out of water. Why was she doing this? What could he have done to make her so angry? Then it hit him.

She doesn't see me.

Looking down, Leo saw his navy Nautilus uniform, his stupid Prestige pins, and the damning gun in his hand.

She doesn't see me*!*

Shouting broke out near the entrance to the bookshop and Leo risked a glance behind him. By the time he turned back, Natalie had jumped the hedge.

Leo sprinted after her.

She wove through tourists with the stealth of a street cat and Leo realized Edwin had been right: she *did* blend in. Enzi, however, did not. So, though Leo missed Natalie slip under the guardrail to the metro, he easily spotted Enzi doubling back to follow.

Yes! Leo pushed through the cramp in his side. If he could get her on a train, any train, she stood a chance of getting away. He didn't care that she didn't recognize him. He didn't care she didn't run to him. He needed her to escape.

He needed her to live.

"Get her, Lev!" Edwin's shout reached him from a block away, maybe less.

It's going to be close.

Leaping down two flights of stairs, Leo noticed Natalie on the first platform he came to. Nearly deserted, the girl hauling ass after the departing metro car was a hard sight to miss. Leo's heart sank. She'd missed it. The train sped out of sight, screeching into the narrow tunnel.

Cornered, Natalie spun to confront him. Enzi paced between them, his ears flicking forward and back, growling at the approaching Curtanas' shouts while cocking his head curiously at Leo.

Natalie's chest heaved. She held her pistol at the ready, looking from him to the tracks and back. She reminded him of a squirrel on the side of the road, debating if it was nuts enough to cross, but her calmness unnerved him. She glanced at the tracks again.

She's not the squirrel. Leo's ribs closed tight around his lungs. *She's already decided.*

Another train thundered towards them, drowning out the stampede of Curtanas descending the stairs. It didn't matter how close the car was.

Natalie had already made up her mind.

She won't let herself get captured.

Leo aimed his gun at Natalie. When Nautilus flooded the platform, they needed to see him threatening her. He hoped Natalie would see something else.

She didn't.

Instead, she inched towards the tracks. Leo needed her to wait ten more seconds. Ten seconds would put her on the incoming train instead of under it. Ten seconds. What would buy him ten seconds?

"Mortem ante cladem," he blurted.

For the first time, Natalie's eyes found Leo's, and in the moment it took him to clear the distance between them, she dropped her weapon.

"Leo?"

He collided into her, pulling her body against him. She was warm and alive and *real*. He cupped her neck and stroked her hair, desperate to feel every inch of her in the fleeting seconds they had left. After weeks of pain, he was home.

"Leo?" She whispered his name and it set his blood on fire. He pressed his forehead to hers. Five seconds left. He could kiss her. But the dead woman in the chair held him back, her body beaten and broken, breathless by Nautilus's brutality.

He'd die before they caught Natalie.

The incoming train blew Natalie's hair back from her neck. It rumbled to a stop as Enzi's ears flattened against his head. He bared his teeth and the first Curtanas ran onto the platform.

"Hit me."

Natalie blinked at him. The train doors slid open. The car was empty.

"Hit me!" Leo shook her. "And go!"

She stared at him. He couldn't tell what she was thinking, but she certainly wasn't moving. He didn't mean to say what came next. It was three small words yet giving them life was the hardest thing he'd ever had to do. Harder than physical therapy, harder than waking up every day in the Moirai's cottage knowing he couldn't go home.

And if he said them out loud, those three words became real. Permanent. He'd have to deal with what they meant, with the finality of every syllable. The declaration burned up his throat. It was coming out whether he was ready to tell her or not.

"My mom's dead."

Natalie woke up. The veil of confusion and disbelief lifted, and her expression turned hard as stone.

"Lev!" Edwin called across the platform. "Get her!"

Time's up.

"Are you with me?" Natalie asked.

For a second, Leo considered it. He wanted nothing more than to board the metro car and leave Nautilus's murderous games behind. But he'd made a promise to the Moirai, and if he left with Natalie, he'd be throwing away his chance to find who was left of their parents.

"I'll find you," Leo whispered. A warning alarm dinged, and the car door began to close. "Go!" he urged. "Hit—"

Natalie spun on her toes and dropped her hands to the ground, bringing her foot up sharp across Leo's jaw. Surprised, Leo crumbled. When he collected himself, she'd already retrieved her pistol and rolled onto the train. Enzi leapt after her, his tail whipping inside as the doors snapped shut.

Gunshots exploded across the Nautilus-infested platform. Leo covered his head. A few bullets dented the metro car while most bounced dangerously across the tunnel. The shots stopped as the train sped off.

"Lev," Edwin yanked him up off the cement. "You had her, man!"

Leo's jaw throbbed. He bit his tongue to keep from smiling.

A *lot* had changed in seven weeks.

The Curtanas' disappointed pouts were far less concerning than Edwin's calculating one. Despite his tone, Edwin appeared more suspicious than angry. Leo would have preferred him angry.

"What happened?"

She got away.

"I couldn't shoot her here on the platform." Leo spat blood onto the cement, trying his best to sound annoyed. "I was going to get her on the train with me so I could take her out alone, discreetly, as ordered. I got distracted warding off that *stupid* mutt. Didn't see the kick coming." Leo tossed his gun in a show of frustration. "Damn rookie mistake."

Leo had single-handedly cost Nautilus their target. He had cast the faintest shadow over their precious Graduation. And he couldn't care less how Nautilus punished him for it. They'd killed his mom.

And Natalie got away.

Edwin fiddled with his earrings. "We'll figure it out, man," he said loud enough for only Leo to hear. "You're the only true friend I've got in this place, but damn, you've made a mess. Someone has to take the fall for this."

"I understand."

"Captain Lev underestimated our enemy," Edwin announced to the gathered Curtanas. "Now we know she fights! Will we make the same mistake again?"

"No!" the Curtanas answered together.

"No," Edwin confirmed. "This is not the end of our fight. This time we have learned, next time we will win. For peace!"

"For peace!" The Curtanas trudged out of the station, back to the toasted towers of Notre Dame.

Edwin and Leo kept well out of earshot.

"No worries man, really." Edwin seemed much cheerier, perhaps roused by his own speech. "We'll get her. In the meantime," he produced a box of colorful cookies from his pocket, "macarons!"

Leo bit into one. It was exactly as Edwin described: a crunchy shell with a chewy, sweet center. The sugar stung a cut in his cheek and this time Leo couldn't contain his smile.

"There he is!" Edwin said with satisfaction. "Macarons make everything better. Delectable packages of perfection they are."

As the jet ascended from the carnage of the cathedral into the clouds, Leo's thoughts stayed far below, speeding away beneath the ancient streets of Paris.

Natalie was alive.

And she got away.

CHAPTER 22
NATALIE

Night had fallen by the time Natalie sprinted out of Le Havre train station. She barreled past the crowded cafés and schools of people wading through glowing ponds of city streetlights. The stone walls around her spun and snapped back into place and her stomach flipped as though someone had dropped her off the top of the Eiffel Tower. It was the best and worst she'd felt in weeks.

Leo was alive.

His mother was dead.

Every few paces she questioned the fate of her own parents, of Owen's and Tawney's, of Brant's father. What if they were too late? What if Nautilus had already killed everyone she loved?

Leo's alive. Natalie half sprinted, half stumbled for the beach. *He's okay.* She hoped that fact would be enough to hold her together until she reached the water. Enzi jumped the chain blockading the pier and Natalie followed close behind. They dropped onto a floating platform that bumped against the pylons with every wave, relying on the wooden planks above them for cover.

It wasn't perfect, but she didn't have time to search for anything better. She was fraying at the seams. She needed someone stronger, someone better suited to carry everything she threatened to crumble beneath: her parents, time-travel, Leo, all of it.

She needed Christopher.

With Enzi beside her, Natalie reached into the oncoming wave. Gravity dissipated. A tingling shot through her body and then there was only light: no dock, no water, no sky. She pictured the marina and the weight of the world pulled her down an ocean away from where she started. Blinking against the weak afternoon sunlight, Natalie slipped up the concrete boat ramp.

"He's alive!" Natalie let herself into the cinder block cottage. "Leo's alive!"

Enzi lifted his muzzle to inspect the countertops as Christopher sauntered out of the back bedroom. His bare toes peeked out beneath his jeans. He shuffled to meet her, scratching his salt and pepper beard as he yawned. Natalie could have smacked him.

"Leo's *alive*."

"Yeah, kid, I heard ya the first time." He nodded at Enzi. "Get the pup a treat for cryin' out loud."

Irritated, Natalie dropped Enzi a pumpkin biscuit from the counter and rounded on Christopher again.

"I saw him!" She paced the length of the kitchen. "I *touched* him!"

"Quiet down, you'll wake the dead carryin' on like that." Christopher eased himself into one of the kitchen chairs.

"Am I inconveniencing you?" she snapped. "Leo's *alive* and he said...he said—" Natalie stopped. The room tilted and she had to lean against the wall to right it.

"When's the last time you slept, kid?"

"Doesn't matter." Natalie pressed her palms against her temples. She couldn't exactly remember when she'd caught more than a few hours of rest in one go. "Why are you ruining this?"

"Never thought the boy was dead."

Because you know everything and say nothing. Natalie sank to sit on her calves.

"Why are you really here?" Christopher pressed.

How did she ever allow herself to have hope for finding their parents before the Ward killed them all? Mrs. Merrick was dead. How many more had already followed her?

"I can't do this, Chris," Natalie confessed. The room morphed into a single blur of color as she fought back tears. "I need you to come back with me. I don't know what I'm doing."

"Why are you here?" He slammed his fist on the table, making Natalie jump. "Use your head, Nat. What are you missin'? What questions aren't you askin'?"

Natalie couldn't answer.

"I wouldn't ask if it wasn't important." He gestured to the chair opposite him with a calloused hand. "Start with the obvious."

She didn't want Christopher's guidance. She didn't want his advice or opinion on how to proceed. She wanted him to take back the responsibilities he'd put on her. But that wasn't an option, so Natalie took a seat.

"Why didn't Leo come to Ancora III?" She sulked.

"Excellent," he scratched his chin. "Thoughts?"

"Because Nautilus still has him." It was the most obvious answer.

Christopher's dark eyes bore into her.

Okay...wrong answer.

She took a deep breath and quelled her frustration. She subdued her relief of Leo's return and tucked away her concerns about their parents. Her emotions clouded her judgement and obscured the facts.

"He found me in the garden," Natalie started slowly. "Enzi knew him instantly, of course. He wasn't distracted by the Nautilus uniform."

"Animals rarely pay mind to petty details like appearance."

"He was wearing their uniform. Nautilus must have him," Natalie concluded.

"They're lettin' their prisoners tour western Europe?"

"Well, I guess…" Adrenaline blurred the details. She remembered him chasing her, catching her on the subway platform with his gun. "My gun was up, too," Natalie relived the scene out loud. "His fingers weren't on the trigger…" *Right?*

"The Nautilus I know wouldn't be arming threats to their cause." Christopher watched the sun's slow descent beyond the window. "They'd be huntin' them down."

"If Leo wasn't a prisoner…" Natalie couldn't finish the sentence, not aloud.

"What'd he say to you?"

"That his mom was dead," Natalie's breath came quick and shallow. "That he'd find me." She felt dizzy and curled against the nausea churning her stomach.

"Then why hasn't he come to you sooner?"

Because he's not Nautilus's prisoner.

"He's one of them," Natalie whispered. She twisted her shirt, squirming against the pain in her chest. How could he betray them? Was it because of his mother? Because Nautilus killed her and threatened everyone else?

In the end, the reasons didn't matter. She was in the wrong place. She had to move.

We've stayed too long.

"I shouldn't be here." Natalie hurried out the door, leaving Christopher behind without so much as a goodbye.

"I know I'm not privy to your doin's these days," Uncle Chris yelled from the porch. "Humor me. Where did Leo find you?"

Natalie slid to a stop. Enzi panted at her side, exhilarated by the impromptu game of sprints. On her back *The Sceptical Chymist* weighed heavily in her pack. The book Chris reserved for her, a decade and a half prior, that she'd completely forgotten about in the shock of Leo's reappearance. Now she didn't have time to ask him what it was for.

"Paris," Natalie answered.

"Ah." The afternoon light cast him in a sharp silhouette. "Curious city."

"About Leo," Natalie added, "until I know if it's true...don't tell anyone."

"Not a soul."

Natalie couldn't afford the extra seconds to reach the covered boat slip. She had to get back to Ancora, to her friends. She'd left them alone to chase a childish dream and now Leo's whispered promise echoed menacingly in her thoughts.

I'll find you.

After seven weeks of quiet, Nautilus was finally coming for them. With Enzi by her side, Natalie ran straight into the sea, desperately hoping she wasn't too late.

CHAPTER 23
NATALIE

The heat found Natalie before gravity did. North Carolina was known for sweltering summers, but the sun itself seemed to have come to Earth. She pulled herself onto the pier and Enzi cowered behind her, his fur tickling her legs. It wasn't until she heard the roar that she realized what it was.

Ancora III was burning.

"Tawney!" Hungry flames licked out of the upper windows, outshone in brief bursts by the beacon still spinning atop the tower. "Owen! Brant!" Natalie screamed as she cleared the last planks of the pier.

A hunched figure fell out the front door. Shielding herself with her pack, Natalie guided them back to the safety of the dock. She pushed back Brant's mop of brown curls as he coughed and sputtered.

"Brant," she breathed, patting his back. "You're okay."

Nora's black duffle hung off him, the sleeve of a navy uniform and a container of hair dye poked through the zipper. He rocked on his hands and knees, coughing violently.

"Are you okay?" Natalie asked, less certain.

"Inside," he hacked again. "Amir..."

Natalie stiffened. "Give me your shirt."

Brant squinted up at her. Smoke and ash covered every inch of him.

"Give me your shirt!" Natalie nearly ripped the t-shirt over his head before Brant conceded to helped her.

"Think," he begged. "Don't," another coughing fit silenced him.

"Keep this safe." Natalie tied her spark to her backpack and shoved the bag into Brant's lap. She wasn't going to let Nautilus catch her, her spark, and Christopher's book all at once. Not if she could help it. "Enzi." She lifted her dog's muzzle. "Stay."

Natalie doused Brant's shirt with sea water and ran for Ancora. Five stories up the fire raged. Louder than a freight train, it radiated heat so thick it condensed into a palpable barrier around the lighthouse. Every fire drill she'd ever seen came to mind and not one of them covered how to enter a burning building. She pulled Brant's shirt onto her head and pushed herself beneath the inferno.

A blanket of cool air enveloped her upon entering the kitchen. With the floors above her providing some protection against the heat, Natalie caught her breath.

"Tawney!" Natalie yelled.

"You idiot!"

Alive.

Natalie took the stairs two at a time, careful to avoid the iron rail. The temperature rose with her and Natalie tasted the bitter tang of smoke as she searched the first landing for her friend.

It might have been easier had the room not been completely trashed.

The wardrobe laid overturned on its side, its contents scattered, workout equipment littered the floor, and two narrow feet stuck out from beneath the bed skirt.

"What are you doing?" Natalie asked incredulously.

"Me?" Tawney pushed herself out from under the mattress and jabbed Natalie hard in the chest. "You ran into a burning building!" She jabbed her again. "Stupid."

Natalie began to fire off a retort and bit it back. Tawney's soot smeared face was streaked with tears and her bottom lip quivered. She kicked the bed frame.

"Stupid mutt won't come OUT!"

"What?" Beams strained against the fire above them and Natalie rocked onto her toes.

Tick-tock.

"Angie!" Blood coated the fingers she motioned at the bed. "She bit me. She *bit* me!"

"She's scared," Natalie searched for options. "Toss the bedspread over her and pull her out, no time for coaxing. Where's Owen?"

"Gathering his precious tech," Tawney huffed, then paused. "He went up there a few minutes ago…"

"Get Angie," Natalie instructed. "Go straight outside. Meet Brant at the pier."

Without waiting for a response, Natalie hurried further up the stairs. The crack of flames grew louder, and smoke drifted in a haze. Sweat dripped off her chin as she bent at the waist to breathe.

"Owen!" Her coughing covered any response. Her eyes stung and watered, blurring her vision so she failed to see the amorphous mound on the floor that entangled her feet. She sprawled, collapsing on whatever had tripped her.

It grunted.

"Owen?" Natalie dug through the mound of clothes and exposed a head of red hair. Unconscious, his glasses dangled precariously from one ear as he clung to a stack of papers and a laptop wrapped in a thick rain jacket. She nudged him. He didn't move.

Somehow, she had to get Owen's gangly body down the spiral

staircase without dropping him, or burning him on the hot iron rail, or falling and breaking a limb. She dragged his body towards the stairs, groaning with the effort. *I only have gravity and the heat and the lack of oxygen against me. No big deal. I can do this.*

"Got him!" Brant appeared at her side and Natalie almost melted with relief, or just plain melted.

She supported Owen's head as Brant lifted him with ease and her hands came away sticky with blood. Suddenly, she couldn't remember if Owen had been breathing when she found him.

She followed Brant down to where Tawney stood in the center of her room screaming incoherently at the bed, the empty comforter clutched at her side.

Natalie snatched the blanket from her. She dropped to her knees to retrieve Angie herself, only to find someone already had her. She backed away as Enzi crawled out from under the bed with a mess of black fur between his jaws. He leapt down the stairs after Brant with Tawney close behind him.

Natalie was on the last stair when she stopped.

The key! Christopher's key and their adoption papers were four floors above her, still stashed away in her very flame-susceptible wardrobe. She'd paid a heavy price to fill her drawer of secrets. She'd lost her home, her life, her family. She couldn't leave it all behind to burn.

Natalie sprinted back up the stairs. The heat bordered on unbearable, and her exposed skin was singed as she struggled through the smoke. Above her, the ceiling cracked. Natalie draped Tawney's comforter over her and marveled at the state of her room.

The wardrobe door laid torn from its hinges. Her drawer of secrets and unanswered questions had been snapped in half. Books were torn from their covers and papers so heavily littered the floor she nearly overlooked the envelope among them. Natalie hastily gathered as many of the items as she could, taking care to shove

Chef's copy of the adoption papers deep into her pocket.

Something collided into her. She fell to the ground, her forearm tingling.

What the —

A low chuckle sent an unnatural chill down her spine. Natalie fought her way out from beneath the comforter, backing away from the man who haunted even her most pleasant nightmares.

"I told you, Ms. Morrigan," his velvet voice strained under his fervor. "You take what's mine; I take what's yours."

Amir Amani sneered at her. All his composure had melted away, leaving him wild eyed and utterly *mad*. Sweat poured down his forehead as he slung a weakly sparking bolt across the back of his soot-stained suit. He held a metal case in the air and Natalie's stomach melted through the floor. This was not the Amir she manipulated in the caves. This man was unhinged.

A flaming wooden rafter fell through the ceiling on the far side of the room. Natalie cowered behind the comforter, covering herself against the cloud of sparks and ash. Another fit of laughter erupted from Amir.

"You should have joined when you had the chance, Morrigan," he yelled over the roar. "Now it's too late! Now we don't need you."

Natalie's breath caught in her throat and it had nothing to do with the smoke. She threw off the comforter only to find Amir had already disappeared down the stairs, taking Christopher's key with him.

She threw herself down after him, chasing his black suit that kept slipping out of sight. She tried to yell and choked on the smoke that invaded her lungs. It was all she could do to keep breathing.

By the time she reached the kitchen, he was gone. She swept by the fireplace, scooping up every photograph before stumbling outside. Beyond the protection of the floors above her, the direct heat of the fire knocked her off her feet. Desperate, Natalie crawled, feeling as though she carried the sun on her back.

Someone lifted her. She wasn't sure if it was Nautilus or her friends. Natalie wasn't even sure she cared.

Amir has Christopher's key.

"Nat."

Someone shook her. A breeze wicked away her heat and induced an agonizing tremble throughout her body. The last thing she wanted to do was move.

"Nat!"

"Stop," she begged. Opening her eyes, Natalie did a quick head count. Brant retied her spark to her wrist. Tawney stood a few paces away with Angie in her arms and Enzi at her feet. Owen sat next to him, awake and pressing his makeshift jacket-package against his head wound. Everyone was accounted for.

The key.

Natalie painfully rose to her feet, scanning the surrounding dunes for any sign of Amir. All she found was the glow of emergency lights in the distance.

"Amir was inside." Natalie's throat felt like gravel in a blender. "He has the key."

Sullen faces turned away from her. She carried their shame. They had failed, her more than the rest of them.

I should have been here. Natalie pulled at her smoke-stained hair. *I should have been with them.*

She watched the lighthouse burn. The apex of the tower had long since caved in, destroying the beacon. Ancora III had given them sanctuary and she was leaving it in ashes.

Another floor of the lighthouse collapsed, and a roaring burst of flames forced her to turn away. Sparks danced in the billowing smoke plume that blackened the sky. Her blistered knuckles screamed in protest as Natalie's hands balled into fists. Glowing drops of sea spray rolled down her skin, charged with the power of aurichalcum but cut off from the sea.

I could undo this. Natalie could feel her power flirting just beyond her reach. She didn't know how to channel it, or summon it, or control it, but she knew if she stepped off the dock right then, the ocean would take her exactly where she wanted to go: any place, any time.

I will undo this.

Natalie turned towards the sea and came face to face with Brant.

"Don't," he said. "Let it burn."

A writhing pit of anguish and dejection consumed her. It converged on everything she was, expanding and contracting with her breath. She squirmed against it. Desperate to feel anything else, she braved the blaze again, drinking in the sting of the heat on her threadbare nerves. Of course, Brant was right. Even if she did manage to travel back in time, that didn't mean she should. The risk was too great.

Let it burn.

Natalie wondered if the fire could be seen from space. The possibility Ancora III's last signal would be its brightest brought her a sliver of comfort. At least until she thought of Christopher.

How disappointed would he be if he knew?

She wanted to watch the lighthouse burn to the ground, to not move from that plank until every last ember went dark. Sirens pierced through the crackle of the flames.

"We have to go." Brant slung Nora's duffle bag over his back. He was right. Fire and Rescue couldn't find them there.

"Where to?" Owen asked.

Natalie felt the pressure of their expectations. She selected one of Christopher's Ancora photographs at random from her pack and passed it to Owen.

"Don't you want—"

"No," Natalie cut him off. "Don't let me take us anywhere." Her mind was a mess. Her thoughts ricocheted like asteroids on a racquetball court: unpredictable and annihilating. The last thing she wanted to do was land them all in the Cretaceous period.

Brant took the picture from Owen. "And maybe not the guy with the head injury."

Owen nodded then winced.

Natalie pulled up her pack and took Brant's hand in her own. Enzi nosed his way between them as the others fell in line on either side, Tawney last and silent.

Natalie felt a familiar tug as Brant stepped off the dock. There was a flash of light, the tingling of static. She hovered in a moment of infinite nothingness and wished she could stay there forever.

CHAPTER 24
NATALIE

In the opening of a shallow cave, Natalie landed on a rugged shoreline fringed with thick evergreens. Mountainous islands framed the black water of the inlet and an orange sun hovered over the farthest stretch of sea. The scene was deceptively peaceful and fresh.

"Wow," Owen pressed his jacket against the wound on his scalp. "British Columbia, maybe?"

"Where is the house?" Natalie asked pointedly.

"Oh." Brant compared the beach to his picture. "Ah! This way." Scaling a wall of haphazardly stacked boulders, he disappeared into the trees.

"Brant," Owen hobbled after him. "Wait up, man."

Natalie made to follow when a half-choked cry sounded behind her. Tawney knelt in the pebbles, clutching Angie to her chest.

"Tawney?"

Tawney sobbed. Her entire body shook, and her chest heaved, and Natalie stood shamefully frozen in shock. She'd never seen

Tawney cry. Ever. Not when she'd been grounded for skipping ballet or when she'd hooked her thumb while fishing with Christopher. Tawney had always been their rock, her rock.

Sitting next to her, Tawney placed the small dog into Natalie's lap. She stroked Angie's soot covered fur, only realizing what had happened an instant before Tawney found the words.

"She's dead."

Natalie shook her head. That wasn't possible. She should have never gone to Paris. She should have made her friends leave Ancora III weeks ago, with or without Leo. She should have known Nautilus would find them eventually. Most of all she should have been there.

Should, should, should. Hot tears carved through the ash that caked her face.

"Hey, we found the—" Owen stopped short.

"Ugh!" Tawney stood and threw a slate of rock into the water, shattering the stillness of the inlet. She folded into herself and let out a guttural scream, clawing desperately at her own shoulders.

"Woah!" Owen dropped his jacket and trapped her arms down at her sides. "Stop it. Stop that!"

Blood traced the deep gouges Tawney etched into her skin. "I can't!" she screamed. "I can't do *this*."

Natalie covered her ears as Tawney screamed again.

This isn't happening. She stared at Angie's limp form in her lap. *This can't be happening.*

"Tawney, I-I'm so—"

"Where were you?" Tawney rounded on her. "With Christopher?" Pebbles scattered as Owen held her back. "Tell him what happened! Tell him Angie," she hiccupped, "that Angie's—"

Enzi drooped his soot-stained muzzle on Angie's chest.

My fault.

"Fix it," Tawney ordered.

Natalie knew what Tawney was asking, and Tawney knew she couldn't do it. Whatever she'd felt at the lighthouse dock had faded.

The power she'd glimpsed had recessed again far beyond her reach.

"I can't—"

"Can't or won't?" Tawney spat. "Fix her!" she cried. "Fix her for me, Nat!"

"I don't know how!" Natalie's throat tightened. It wasn't fair.

"Then why are we doing this?" Tawney hugged her stomach. "I'm done," she announced. "I want to go home." She shoved past Natalie, and Owen followed her into the woods.

Brant hurried to her side. "She didn't mean that," he said earnestly.

"Yes, she did," Natalie brushed back the fur from Angie's paws, hating herself. All she had done since the bombing in Norfolk was take her friends from one disaster to another. Because of her their parents were captured, Chef was dead, Christopher was shot, and Leo was lost.

My fault.

Even if she could change what had happened, she wasn't sure she would. Not without knowing the cost.

We don't know what happens when you mess with the timeline.

She'd never asked to be able to time-travel, and now more than ever she wanted no part of it.

"I know what you're thinking." His lips vanished in a tight line.

"I should have been there."

"It wouldn't have made any difference." Brant took his soot and ocean-soaked shirt from around Natalie's neck and draped it over Angie. "We let our guard down."

Violence begets violence, Natalie clenched her jaw. *I brought this on us.*

Brant pulled her up off the rocky shore and hugged her. She rested against his grime-covered chest and listened to the beating of his heart. The rhythm was familiar, like the ticking of a clock.

"Another one to carry, yeah?"

Natalie nodded, wiping away fresh tears.

"But not by yourself." He stroked the crown of her head before adding, "we should bury her."

Natalie sniffled. "I'll find something to dig with."

"I'll dig." Brant directed her towards the woods. "Get Tawney. She should be here."

Adrift in her guilt, Natalie left the beach. Slick rock gave way to loamy earth as the cedars stretched out their branches to snare her. Among them Ancora appeared to have sprouted from the earth itself. Platforms of polished stone and walls of dark glass reflected the young conifers standing guard against the sea. Its soft edges melted into the forest as though the building belonged to the landscape instead of infringing upon it.

Ancora IV.

Beside it, Tawney propped Owen against a boulder.

"What happened?"

"Passed out." Tawney refused to look at her. "Probably that head wound. Can't carry him myself."

At first, Natalie hoped Tawney was lying to help repair the rift between them. She was certain Tawney could manage Owen's weight. However, helping him to his feet, Natalie realized strength wasn't the issue. There was simply too much of him.

"You're all arms and legs, aren't you?"

"I'm fine."

"Oh yeah," Tawney rolled her bloodshot eyes. "Fit as a fiddle."

Together they hobbled to a tree framing one side of a massive window. Its bark encased an eerily familiar security system.

"Biometrics," Owen's interest piqued.

The entrances to Ancora were not usually as straightforward as the lighthouse had been. Ancora I could only be entered through a holographic projection or a hidden door, and Ancora II had required passage through a covered cavern.

"Still think Christopher's one of the good guys?" Tawney jabbed.

Natalie ignored her comment. The Coelacanth Project and

Nautilus had manifested similar technology before, everything from holograms to monitoring tacking signatures. Still, the biometric scanner made her uneasy.

"Could be a trap," Owen pondered darkly.

"No," Natalie studied the scanner. "Uncle Chris gave me the collection of Ancora photographs himself."

Right before we got him shot.

"Where's Brant?" Tawney peeked over Natalie's shoulder. "He can test it."

Before either of them could utter another word, Natalie pressed her palm against the scanner.

Not their fault, she held tight to the adoption papers still hidden in her pocket. *They don't know what I know. They don't know that he knows us better than we know ourselves.*

For a moment nothing happened. Bickering squirrels in the boughs above them stilled. Natalie forgot to breathe. Then the scanner opened and absorbed her hand up to her wrist.

She yelped in surprise. It didn't hurt. What she had assumed was glass now enveloped her like silicone. A second later the window creaked open, sliding into the body of the tree, and her hand was returned to her. The dark depths of Ancora IV opened up before them.

Natalie assisted Owen inside, guided by the lights glowing to life at their feet as they walked. At a long table, she eased him into a chair.

Unlike the lighthouse, Ancora IV was spacious. Dark wooden cabinets and furniture made the transition from the forest nearly seamless. Painted floors carried up the warmth of the earth and wide windows made it seem they were truly among the trees and not apart from them.

"Tawney can you grab the first-aid kit? Christopher keeps it—"

Tawney slammed the tackle box onto the table. "I know where he keeps it."

Biting back fresh tears, Natalie parted Owen's ginger hair. A two-inch gash grazed his scalp.

She grimaced. "Did you fall?"

"No. Everything happened so fast. It had to be a coincidence. Ouch!"

"Sorry," Natalie dripped lidocaine into the cut to numb it. "What do you mean?"

"I had slipped through the Helix's firewalls. I was in for maybe thirty seconds before Amir hit me. I'm not sure how long I was out," Owen admitted. "When I came to, he was going through my desk like a madman. He threw my computer monitor, he ripped open the hard drive. He kept saying he couldn't find it."

"Well, he did find it. Amir took the key."

Owen sat back against the chair. Tawney sank to lean against his shins.

"You need stitches." Natalie dug through their uncle's toolbox in search of suture materials.

"I'll do it," Brant joined them, dropping Nora's bag of supplies on the floor.

"You?" Tawney sniffled.

"Yes, me," he replied. "Unless you'd rather."

Tawney's curls puffed out soot as she shook her head. Enzi plodded into the kitchen. He sniffed around, checking Tawney's lap multiple times before trudging deeper into the house, his tail and head hung low. Natalie's heart sank. Bloody footprints marked his path.

"I'm stealing some supplies." As Brant worked the suture needle into Owen's scalp, she foraged the kit for burn cream, non-adherent gauze, and bandage wrap.

Enzi's prints, illuminated by halos of light shining from the baseboards, led her up a flight of open stairs. The second floor was as spacious as the first and dotted with cushioned seats and long bookcases. A wall of floor-to-ceiling windows overlooked the inlet where moonlight traced the craggy islands. It was breathtaking. It was always breathtaking.

Ancora captivates you with the beauty between the bars. I'm as free and illusioned as a bird in its cage. Ancora was as much a sanctuary as it was a prison.

"Down," Natalie instructed, catching Enzi half-heartedly nosing around a box of biscuits.

He supervised her warily as she assessed the damage. Pink flesh oozed on all four paw pads. They were burnt and blistered, and Enzi was not going to appreciate what she had to do. She gave him a pile of treats to focus on.

"Pace yourself," she warned. Instead, he turned his nose up at her offering, lying flat on the floor with a heavy sigh. She coated the foot closest to her in ointment and he kicked her.

"You're not a horse." Her thumb traveled over the pads of his toes and something between a hiccup and a cry stuck in her throat. Angie's paws were so tiny compared to his.

Natalie applied cream to his other paws and bandaged them loosely up to his wrists and ankles. Helping him stand, she evaluated her work. It was like watching a newborn fawn learn to walk. Enzi crouched low to the ground, uncertain of what had become of his limbs. He picked his feet up absurdly high and flicked his paws in frustration. Finally, he sat, and his ears dropped flat against his head.

"It's only for a few days," Natalie said. She worked the remaining salve into the backs of her hands which had taken the brunt of the heat. Gritting her teeth, she welcomed the sharp sting on her skin. She deserved it.

"Owen's done." Brant appeared in the stairwell. "You ready?"

"What for?" Natalie asked.

He knelt near Enzi and the dog nuzzled against him, pressing his muzzle under and around Brant's neck. They were both quiet and reserved, reflections of the jovial creatures they'd been only hours before.

CHYMIST

Brant swallowed hard and answered, "A funeral."

CHAPTER 25
NATALIE

Mist swirled about Natalie's ankles, teasing her with the possibility she'd become lost in a terrible dream.

"You should do it." Brant nudged Tawney, his cheeks wet.

At the edge of the tree line, a small bundle of fabric laid near a depression in the earth. Tawney shuffled towards it, lowering Angie into the grave with a sob that convulsed her entire body. "I'm s-so sorry."

Natalie stuck out her chin. She wanted nothing more than to turn away, but she refused. She would endure every one of Tawney's cries and feel each thud of dirt Brant pushed over Angie's body. This was her fault.

How many more will we bury before this ends?

Tawney forced her sobs into something of a controlled pout as Enzi nosed the freshly turned earth, stepping cautiously with his bandaged paws.

"Come on," Owen steered Tawney away.

She let him, only pausing long enough at Natalie's side to whisper, "I hate you."

Natalie nodded. She watched the moonlight play on the breaking waves of the inlet without really seeing it. Thoughts moved in and out with her breath and she let them go, too apathetic to do more than acknowledge their presence. Her body was exhausted and her mind a toxic void. The inlet seemed peaceful, though. She wondered how far out she could swim before she lost the strength to stay afloat.

Brant cleared his throat. She'd forgotten he was there, or maybe she'd been on the hillside so long he'd left and come back.

"Nat…"

She backed away. She hated the longing in his stare even more than the venom in Tawney's. He couldn't possibly mean to do this now, not with Angie dead under their feet.

My fault.

"Nat," he took her hand. "Hear me out."

Natalie pried herself away and marched back to Ancora IV. She wanted to bury herself under the covers of a new bed and sleep for a year or two. Instead, she found her way into the cushioned sitting room with Brant trailing close behind. Owen cradled Tawney against his chest, nearly as pale as the couch they sat on. Silence surrounded them, making Natalie feel as though she was a mile under water. The pressure was suffocating.

"So, Amir has the key," Tawney fractured the surface-tension just as Natalie feared she might drown. Her tone was flat, every word an emotionless fact.

"Maybe it's not so bad," Owen said.

Natalie busied herself by rubbing Enzi's belly. Owen was hit harder than she thought.

"Think about it." Bleary-eyed, Owen went on. "We've no idea what the key goes to, so maybe Nautilus won't either. Or maybe they will, and they'll lead us to it. Maybe it will be fine. Actually, it's better. Now that we don't have the key, we can go back home with Christopher."

No one said a word. Tawney unburied herself from his chest. Natalie shifted uncomfortably. Owen was hit *much* harder than she thought.

"Eat this, bud," Brant passed him a granola bar.

"There's more," Natalie began slowly. The shame heating her neck made her flame-kissed skin itch. "Eleanor told me...well, it doesn't matter what she told me. Point is, I ended up in Paris—"

"Paris." Tawney pouted.

"Yes, I went to—"

"Angie is dead because you went to Paris." Tawney cursed and stormed down the hall.

"Leo's alive."

Tawney froze mid-stride.

"I saw him," Natalie continued. "I touched him."

Her friend spun on her heels. Brant leaned against the table to stay vertical.

"I think I was hit harder than I thought," Owen announced.

"Are you sure?" Brant asked.

"Yep."

Brant kicked his foot. "Not you, you brilliant idiot. Her."

Natalie remembered staring down Leo's pistol. She remembered his declaration that his mother was dead and his promise to find them. All while wearing Nautilus blue.

"I'm positive."

"Where's Leo now?" Tawney pressed.

Natalie studied the textured ceiling, eager to be anywhere else. "With Nautilus," she answered. "I think. He was in uniform." Folding her arms behind her back, Natalie wondered if this was what it felt like to stand before a firing squad. "He said his mom's dead."

When no one spoke, Natalie's discomfort egged her to go on. "I sought out a bookstore," her gaze flicked to Brant's for a moment before she focused back on the ceiling, ashamed. "Christopher had something there for me."

They blinked at her.

"I mean, he wasn't *there*. He had placed it on hold," she hesitated. "Fifteen years ago." Natalie produced Robert Boyle's book from her pack, shoving the Coelacanth adoption documents to the bottom and out of sight.

"Fifteen *years* ago?" Owen managed through a mouthful of granola.

Natalie put *The Sceptical Chymist* on the table. No one touched it.

"We lost the key, the lighthouse, Mrs. Merrick, and...and Angie...for a book?" Tawney's entire body trembled.

All Natalie could do was nod.

"He's alive." Brant's complexion mottled to a pale green.

"He's alive," Natalie confirmed. "And Ancora burned only hours after we met."

"He's with them," Tawney growled. "Nautilus. I'll bloody kill him."

"No," Owen tried to sit up then seemed to think better of it. "Not everyone is with the enemy. It feels that way sometimes...well, all the time, but this is Leo. Leo!"

Natalie wanted to believe him. Unfortunately, facts were facts. *Question everything.*

"He was dressed in Nautilus navy," Natalie explained. "With a gun aimed at my head."

"He didn't shoot," Owen argued.

"It's Nat," Brant slumped against the table. "Of course, he didn't shoot."

"Why didn't he come home?" Owen's hair stuck out where he pulled at it. "What if he *can't* come home?"

"We don't have a home!" Natalie snapped. "We have a hiding place until we have to move to the next one, and again and again until we're dead or captured. Home is gone. We have to move forward."

"What if he's trapped somewhere—"

"Shut up," Tawney stomped back to Owen's side. "You're going to make your head explode and Brant just put it back together."

"Let me see the book." Owen examined every inch of it. Opening the front cover, he read the scribbled inscription aloud. "Hoc solum scio quod nihil scio."

Brant patted him. "Definitely a concussion."

"No," Owen swatted him away. "Well, maybe. It's Latin."

"I only know that I know nothing," Natalie translated.

"Boyle's credited as the founder of modern chemistry." Owen's eyes gleamed with more than the haze of head trauma. "But he wasn't actually a chemist."

"That's right," Natalie's pulse quickened. "He was an alchemist. The founder of modern chemistry," she repeated. "That was a question on my Assessment."

"This means something," Owen insisted.

"Isn't alchemy like witchcraft?" Tawney frowned. "It isn't real."

"Not exactly." Owen scrunched his nose to adjust his glasses. "It's a natural philosophy. The study of the transformation of matter; basically, turning one element into another. It fell out of favor in the seventeenth century as true, evidence-based chemistry took its place. But you're on the right track: it isn't possible."

Tawney shook some ash from her hair. "Why can't Christopher tell us straight up what's going on? Why does it have to be puzzles and clues and stupid Latin?"

"It doesn't make sense," Natalie agreed.

Owen closed the book decisively. "We should ask him."

Natalie frowned at Brant who clicked his tongue.

"On that note," he eased Owen to his feet. "You need to rest."

"The answer to everything could be right here," Owen whined.

"All the answers you need right now are in a dark, quiet room," Brant assured him.

"Why did you say that?" Natalie asked.

Brant turned back to her, supporting Owen's weight. "Because he needs rest?"

"No. Why a dark, quiet room?"

He shrugged, inadvertently jostling Owen. "It's safe."

"Safe." Her thoughts raced faster than she could keep up. "There's a passage under the second-floor balcony in the Helix. It's well hidden, dark and quiet. The key might be there."

"That's what you're going on?" Tawney sneered.

"It's all we've got. And it's the perfect place to hide something." Natalie's confidence grew with every word. She was right about this. She had to be. "We can't wait until Graduation anymore, not with Nautilus breathing fire down our backs. Owen, you said you got into the Helix's security system. How long will it take you to do it again?"

"Assuming they haven't adjusted their firewalls too much and I can access a secure network, an hour. Maybe two."

"And you can bypass the biometric scanners?" Natalie pressed.

Owen rocked a hand in the air. "I can probably manipulate one at a time. I'm working on something to bypass all of them simultaneously. It'll have major consequences and—"

"Get some sleep. Tawney, get him a computer, a router, whatever he needs." Natalie turned away with *The Sceptical Chymist* hugged to her. "I need you to get me through a locked door. Tomorrow."

Without waiting for inquiries or Tawney's stinging comments, Natalie fled up the stairs. Her ribs tightened around her lungs as the walls of their beautiful cage closed in on her.

She needed to get out.

Natalie rushed out onto the roof. Or what should have been the roof. Instead of a wooden deck or nailed shingles, the top of Ancora IV had been reclaimed by the forest. Kicking off her shoes, Natalie spread her toes onto a floor of soft moss.

She laid on her back, clutching Christopher's gift to her chest. Watching the trees sway with the night's breeze, she tried to remember what she was fighting for. She still wanted answers to her past. She still wanted to save her parents, no matter how much they lied. As for the rest of it...Natalie wanted out. No more secrets, no more surprises, no more tacking or time-travel. She knew she couldn't go home. She'd meant what she said downstairs: she didn't have a home. However, she'd settle for somewhere quiet, somewhere she wouldn't have to hurt anymore.

Through interlaced branches overhead, a sea of stars blinked down an eternity away from her. They were beautiful, but to shine they had to burn.

Perhaps pain is the price of existence.

CHAPTER 26
NATALIE

Trudging into the Helix the next morning, Natalie failed to mask her pain. Her muscles ached, her singed skin screamed with every step, and her head throbbed so intensely she feared it might actually crack. Every attempt she'd made to rest had evoked visions of Angie's skittering paws lost in a maze of fire and smoke, so she'd clung to Boyle's book as a distraction. Unfortunately, the old English text had proved to be more enigmatic than Christopher's logic puzzle. Now Natalie returned to the Helix alone, sore and sleep deprived, to tread water in the sea of Nautilus blue.

"Everyone's buzzing this morning," Eleanor grumbled. Upon further inspection she added, "You look like hell, child."

Natalie wasn't sure if she lacked the strength or the courage to reply. Despite being states away, news of the lighthouse fire had spread like...well, fire. And no amount of coconut shampoo or chemical hair dye could cover her lingering aura of smoke. Not to mention she resembled a walking blister. It would be nothing short of a miracle if Eleanor failed to put the pieces together.

"Did you face your demons?" Eleanor probed.

Hundreds of Nautilus members filed in around them, conversing and laughing, oblivious to the suffering they made possible. Natalie hated them. Every single one.

"I did," she cleared her throat. "There were more of them than I expected."

"That is often true." Eleanor steered her not towards the Focus, but up the stairs to the second-floor landing. "We pick and choose which troubles we confront and which we ignore, though it makes no difference." She leaned casually against the loft railing. "All of our demons grow restless eventually."

Natalie scanned the gathering crowd apprehensively. It wasn't like Eleanor to wander about for an idle chat. Something wasn't right.

An enraged shout cut through the Helix as two bulky Curtanas dragged a man to the center of the Core. Thin and gangly, he twisted and coiled against his captors like a snake. The guards locked their hold, corralling him towards the exit.

"He compromised a mission in Paris," Eleanor explained. "He failed the Ward and his people. He created his demons, now he must suffer them."

Paris, Natalie tried to hide her rising panic. *I was the mission in Paris. Leo let me go, he failed them, not...whoever this is. Why punish him instead?*

"Don't do this!" The man kicked and struggled as his procession continued steadily towards the door. "Please, I beg you, don't do this!"

"I don't understand," Natalie said. His desperation set her on edge. "What are they going to do to him?"

"Take his peace." Eleanor fixated dutifully on her feet. In fact, no one except Natalie seemed able to watch the Curtana be dragged towards the door. In a crowd of hundreds Natalie witnessed the stranger's expulsion alone.

"They're forcing him out?" She could hardly believe it.

"He will be punished in accordance with the severity of his failure." Eleanor's three-fingered hand rested on Natalie's burnt knuckles. "Do not watch, child."

Yet Natalie couldn't look away. The Curtana bucked and thrashed against his escorts and, when that didn't garner his freedom, he screamed. It was grating and primal and set Natalie's teeth on edge.

"Eleanor, what's happening?" Natalie begged.

Muffled sobbing near the exit interrupted the man's pleas, and if Eleanor ever answered Natalie couldn't hear her. A petite girl was shoved into view. The Curtana hesitated for a moment and then his efforts to free himself rebounded. Veins in his neck and arms rippled beneath his skin as he fought to reach her.

"Penny!" he yelled at her. "Penny please, speak for me, look at me!"

Penny wept silently towards the floor, never lifting her gaze. Whatever she felt for him, whatever their relationship, her vows to Nautilus proved stronger. He pleaded to her and she denied him, along with every other gathered member in company.

Natalie forced her way across the balcony, her legs moving on their own accord until Eleanor's cold grip yanked her to a stop.

"Remember where you are, child. Remember why we fight. Lessons must be taught." She shoved Natalie against the balcony rail. "The path to peace is carved in blood."

The man's screams reverberated in Natalie's bones.

"Remember this moment, girl," Eleanor stroked Natalie's raven black hair. "The next time your demons come knocking."

Natalie couldn't breathe. She waited for the crack of a bolt to smite the man down, for the explosion of gunfire to crumple him lifeless to the floor. She'd seen it before. She knew firsthand what Nautilus was capable of.

Yet the violence never came.

Instead, the Curtana's escorts paraded him out into the Florida heat and the frosted glass doors locked shut behind them. Nautilus members throughout the Core dispersed to their normal activities. Even the girl, Penny, dried her face and walked away. Meanwhile

Natalie stood frozen, unable to move, unable to think, entirely unsure of what she'd just witnessed.

"I don't understand," Natalie whispered.

"He no longer serves at the Ward's pleasure," Eleanor popped her lips. "He is stripped of his Prestige and his status. Anyone discovered to be in communication with him after today will be treated likewise. He is an outsider now. We condemn him."

"So...he's been kicked out?" The more Natalie's thoughts caught up with her, the more sense the scene made. Naturally, Nautilus wouldn't show their lower castes the truth of their bloodlust. And even without a show of force, the display they'd made was a powerful one. They didn't have to say join or die, only join or leave.

Because the last thing anyone wants is to feel alone.

Memories of Natalie's first moments in the Helix flooded back to her. Nautilus collected people of every age and race and demolished the differences dividing them. A mosaic of humanity crafted from the single hope of finding peace. It was beautiful. It was powerful.

It was intentional.

The Ward united their follower's fight for peace with their sense of belonging. Nautilus gave them titles, Curtanas, Doves, Legates, Artisans, while making anyone outside an enemy. It wasn't Nautilus's guns or bolts she needed to fear, it was their control over their people.

"Collect yourself," Eleanor snapped. Though she was firm, her touch was gentle. "That isn't going to happen to you. Fix your face, child, before someone sees. Quickly now."

Natalie ignored her. How could she hope to win against people like this?

"We are about to begin the most important fight humankind has ever known." Eleanor sounded fuzzy and far away. "The winner will determine if we succumb to the darkness of the human condition or rise into a glorious era of coexistence. We cannot tolerate insubordination." The old woman shuffled away, leaving Natalie alone with her thoughts.

I can't let these people keep Christopher's key. Natalie's heart thumped back to a normal pace. *Or our parents.*

I hope you're ready, Owen.

Natalie descended the stairwell as fast as she dared and slipped into the tunnel linking the Helix's two primary chambers. Passing through the hidden panel, Natalie enclosed herself in total darkness. Fear strangled her, but she refused to turn back.

The key could be just beyond this passage. Natalie took a tentative step forward, then another. *Information on our parents could be just behind that door.*

She moved quickly then, following the wall. Reaching the locked door, she fumbled for the biometric scanner in the dark. The rectangular box glowed to life and she pressed her palm against it. A brief pause and the scanner glowed red, beeping so loud Natalie jumped.

"Eyes open, Owen," she whispered to herself.

When the red light faded, Natalie returned her palm to the scanner. Again, it read and pricked her palm, the platform beeped, and its light bled red. She began counting.

One, two, three…

If everything went according to plan, two failed entry attempts would alert Owen to her location.

Ten, eleven, twelve…

Then he could unlock the door on her third attempt from his computer, a thousand miles away in Ancora IV.

Eighteen, nineteen, twenty…

A shuffling echoed down the hallway.

Twenty-five, twenty-six, twenty-seven…

She dried the sweat from her palms on her jacket.

Thirty.

Pressing on the biometric scanner, Natalie allowed the machine to prick her skin a third time. No lights. No sound. An eternity passed. Then the lock blinked white and clicked open, and Natalie rushed inside before she lost her nerve.

Pain erupted on the back of her skull. Natalie crumbled. The world spun as though gravity misplaced her. Squinting against a blinding light, she tried to crawl away. Her body wouldn't listen.

"Well, well," a man chuckled. His black eyes shone like beetles in the dark and an aroma of sugar and gasoline made Natalie's stomach churn. "Tell me, did you bring any macarons?"

CHAPTER 27
LEONIDAS

Admiring the summer green hillside, Leo half expected frost on the window pane. The Moirai's cottage had been frigid at best since his return from Paris as his hosts rewarded any attempts at conversation with a cold shoulder.

Leo couldn't stand the pointless tension and accepted their behavior as a challenge. He'd poked at Clo's orchid display so many times she'd developed a twitch, while Atro had mysteriously lost all of her right shoes. And he was just getting started.

The doughy scent of fresh biscuits drew him to the kitchen. He picked a particularly fluffy one from the pan only to have it snatched away. Atro fussed at him, the bare toes of her right foot curling against the floor. When she turned her back, he stole two new biscuits from the pan, only to have Lache round the corner. Thinking fast he tossed a biscuit over her head, sidestepped her awkward grab, and caught it between his teeth.

Clo giggled in delight only to cower beneath Lache's scowl.

Clo's shoulders sagged. "That *was* funny."

One down.

"You should be thrilled, you know," Leo announced aloud. He

didn't understand their anger and, frankly, he didn't have time for it.

Lache stole the biscuits back and marched off. Despite their exclusion and his grumbling stomach, Leo retreated to his room more optimistic than he'd been in weeks. He'd found Natalie *and* ruined Nautilus's plans to kill her. It was the best double play he'd ever seen. Especially after what had been done to his mom.

He didn't understand why the Moirai had frozen over instead of joining in his celebration. Locked away in her room, Lache didn't say a word to him all night and her sisters followed her lead. He'd assumed their silent vigil would break with the dawn but—

The door creaked. Leo instinctively reached for the gun on his bedside table only to have a pale hand snatch it first. Holding the weapon in the air as a truce, Clo peered sheepishly at him beneath her spiked silver hair.

"Clo." Leo convinced his heart to slow down. *Man, she's fast. And quiet. And still holding my gun.*

His visitor repeatedly checked the bedroom door until finally shaking herself with a sigh. "I brought you breakfast," Clo relinquished the gun and pulled three biscuits from the sleeve of her robes.

"Wow." Speaking to him was one thing. Leo never expected her to go so far against her sisters as to feed him.

She flicked another glance towards the hall and stepped closer. "I wanted— Lache...you see," she stopped. "Apologies, Leonidas, I have spoken to few others on my own outside of my sisters."

"I know." Leo sat on the bed, doing his best to appear less intimidating. When standing he was almost an entire foot taller than her. "Take your time." He chewed on a biscuit, letting the flakey crumbs melt on his tongue.

"I have tried many times to imagine what it must have been like for you to lose your family. Seeing how you reacted to the footage of that woman," Clo hesitated. "Should I go on?"

The dough turned to concrete on Leo's tongue. He didn't want to talk about his mom. He already couldn't stop reliving the images a thousand times a minute in his head; he didn't need Clo revisiting them as well. He felt a little dizzy and he wished he could swallow the freaking biscuit already.

"Just skip to the point, maybe?" he mumbled through a mouthful.

"Well," Clo went on, "I have not known anything like that. And I suppose it must be strange for you to try and imagine yourself as us, without any family at all." She wrung her hands. "We are not angry at Natalie's return. We are frightened and sad and selfishly so. Lache fears you will leave without honoring your debt, and I do feel we have earned your agreed terms."

AKA: Murder. Leo gave up and spit out the biscuit. "Did Nautilus teach you to speak like a diplomat?"

She blinked.

"I'm kidding, Clo. Relax."

"Last night, I tried to imagine losing Lache or...or Atro," she shuddered. "I truly attempted to envision my life forward without them and I could not. I could not do it. I tried and I think I felt what you felt during that broadcasting. The pain was too great, and I am no stranger to pain, Leonidas." Clo pulled up the sleeves of her green cloak to show the white scars carved across her forearms and up the curve of her neck.

Blood pounded in his ears as he turned away from her branded body. The sight made him sick. He'd heard Amir Amani torture his friends and watched him stain the tundra red with Chef's blood. He'd seen Amir's sanity fracture and chaos erupt from the fissures. The Moirai didn't earn their scars by cooperating, and Amir met their resistance with rage. Nautilus had treated his own mother with the same regard. Why shouldn't he do as the Moirai asked and return the favor? Why shouldn't he bring Amir Amani to his knees and then the dirt?

He couldn't for the life of him remember why he'd ever resisted their request at all. Amir deserved to die.

"I am happy you have found your family again," Clo's confession interrupted his thoughts. "Please forgive my sisters, the emotions are...confusing. We have never experienced something demanding both sorrow and celebration. It is peculiar. Quite unpleasant, I must admit."

Leo grinned.

"You are pleased by this?" Clo's silver brows knit together inquisitively.

"We're family now, too, Clo. Though a strange one, admittedly. I've been trying to tell you since last night: I want you all to come with me."

Clo draped herself on one of the bedposts and cocked her head at him. "The offer is generous. Though not yours to make. Do not assume your Coelacanth family will be open to us. You should speak with them first and know we will forgive you when you do not return."

Leo huffed. "When I find Ancora, you, Lache, and Atro *will* come with me. You aren't safe here by yourself. And my friends will welcome you because I do; I'm sure of it."

"Do not make more promises you cannot keep," Lache glowered at her sister from the doorway and Clo skittered from the room.

"This is the easiest promise I've ever made," Leo said. "It's been my intention from the moment you saved my life, though I won't force you to come like Nautilus forced you to be Moirai."

"Because you cannot."

"You're right," Leo admitted. "I hoped fighting alongside friends would be more appealing than cowering alone on this cliffside."

A pulsating glow emanated from a heap of clothes on the floor. Leo snatched up the uniform before Lache had even taken a step.

"You have grown too close to those devils," Lache sulked as he changed. "You cannot trust them."

"You know I don't. Everything will be better when we're back with my friends."

"We would not mix well with your Coelacanth company."

"Why not?" Leo was swiftly losing his patience.

"Because we grew up hating the very idea of you."

Leo nearly dropped his jumpsuit. All his fight died in his throat.

"The Moirai," Lache breathed out heavily through her nose. "We were not merely prisoners. We were part of a copy-cat assignment, a *project*. 'The Moirai Mission.'" The words dripped like venom from her tongue. "Nautilus tortured us because we failed to emulate you."

This time Leo really did drop his jumpsuit. He looked from Lache to Clo to Atro, who had slipped in beside her sisters. "I don't understand."

"Clearly," Lache's blue eyes pierced him. "As a child they preached the Coelacanth Project like gospel. I read about you. I studied you. I tried desperately to imitate you," she spat the words with disgust. "Amir Amani was tasked with replicating what the Coelacanth Project had accomplished. And no matter the concoction of chemicals they imbued us with, or the shock therapy they initiated, or the composition of water they submerged us in, we still could not do it. Temporal Associated Conditional Kinesis," Lache snarled. "Every night I wished you would die because perhaps then my fate might be freed from yours."

Leo sat on the bed only to have his nerves propel him up again. He paced, his mind reeling.

Nautilus was raising their own Coelacanth Project the whole time? That's why they started hunting us? Because they failed? Because Lache and her sisters never managed to tack?

On the floor, the shell of his uniform glowed again. He ignored it.

"Nautilus will never find us because we are already dead." Lache moved so only a breath existed between them. "The Moirai Mission became irrelevant the second Nautilus procured the Coelacanth Project. By order of the Ward, the mission was dissolved, and all remaining subjects sentenced to death." Lache smiled wickedly. "However, when we were escorted to the Black Chamber, three bodies already laid in the incinerator. Our executioner smuggled us out through narrow passageways that twisted forward and back. We were led out by a shadow, an Angel of Death who killed three others so they may burn in our place."

"Who was it?" Leo pressed. "Maybe they can help me. They could know where my parents are—"

Atro shook her bald head. "We do not know. As Lache said, they were merely a shadow."

"We were corralled into a van," Lache continued, "and when it stopped the ground still rocked and swayed. When no one came to free us, we intended to break open the door, only it was already unlocked. The driver was gone, and we were in the cargo hold of an ocean liner. There was a room key on the driver's seat, along with this note." She passed a worn piece of scrap paper to Leo.

Your life is now your own. Waste not those given for yours. See the ship to the end of the line. Friends will meet you there.

On the corner, three interlocking leaf-like shapes were flawlessly inked. The symbol had no beginning and no end. To Leo, it looked almost like a flower. He pursed his lips in frustration.

Natalie would know this.

"Any idea what this is?"

Atro leaned in. "A triquetra, of course."

"Great. What does it mean?"

"Oh, it depends on the context," Clo rocked on the balls of her feet. "The symbol has carried numerous definitions to various cultures over many centuries."

"What does it mean now?" Leo quelled his rising frustration. "To you?"

"Nothing." Lache took the paper from him.

The Moirai Mission became irrelevant the second Nautilus procured the Coelacanth Project. Her words echoed in his mind. *The day Nautilus captured us in Norfolk must have been the day the Moirai were sentenced to death. The Ward didn't need them anymore.*

A pain tore through his gut, the discomfort gnawing him from the inside out. Though none of it was his fault, though he'd never asked to be part of the Coelacanth Project, guilt consumed him. He understood Lache's desire to cull the entirety of Nautilus society and doubted her thirst for blood would be quenched by the death of Amir and the Ward alone.

"And now you're after revenge," Leo tested her intentions. "Justice isn't enough. You want to hang Nautilus for its crimes."

"Our agreement was contingent on Amir Amani's death," Lache answered calmly, however Leo sensed the hatred coiled patiently behind her words. "For now."

"So, one corrupt leader is enough to condemn them all?" he challenged.

"No one is forced to follow the Ward."

"We all know that isn't true." Leo exposed the crisscrossed pattern on Lache's forearm. "You escaped because an ingrained member of Nautilus chose to free you. We might have more people on our side than we think."

"Oh, they were not Nautilus," Clo said dismissively.

"What?" Leo frowned. "You said—"

"A panther in wolf's clothing," Atro said.

"You mean 'a sheep in wolf's clothing,'" Leo corrected her. "You think your rescuer was an impostor? Like me?"

Lache huffed impatiently. "No, they were no sheep. No one would have risked freeing us out of mere pity. Whoever they are, they have power. Their pockets run deep and their reach spreads wide. Not Nautilus, though equally surreptitious. They aimed to smuggle us from one prison to another."

Covert doesn't necessarily mean corrupt. Leo smiled.

"What is it?" Clo leaned forward eagerly.

"Florida is known for its panthers."

Lache retrieved the Nautilus uniform from the floor and folded the slick fabric. "Do not pretend to know the game you are playing when you cannot even see the board." She pushed the jumpsuit against him before ushering her sisters from the room.

Leo pulled on the still-blinking uniform. "You couldn't have waited five minutes?" he muttered to it.

The Moirai's history gnawed at him as he dressed. He had been helping the Moirai because he owed them his life. Now that there was a real chance to go home again, a chance he could be reunited with Natalie and Ancora, he couldn't leave Lache and her sisters behind.

As he hurried down the cliff and left the Scottish cabin behind, he realized his rescuers had become more than a debt. He owed them each a lifetime they could never get back.

The least he could do was kill the man who destroyed them.

CHAPTER 28
LEONIDAS

Edwin wasn't waiting for him in the Core. Leo hovered awkwardly for several minutes near the glass doors, tapping his thigh and scanning Nautilus members for anyone familiar. Assuming Edwin had been held up, Leo wandered restlessly to the second-floor overlook. Over the other side of the balcony, clumps of recruits swarmed the Focus and, unsure what else to do, Leo watched them spar or sit in circles. He spotted a head of wild grey hair and turned his back to avoid Eleanor catching any glimpse of him. He leaned against the railing.

How long am I supposed to wait?

The few members near Leo bowed their heads respectfully as a clutch of high-nosed Legates approached. Leo followed suit, noticing the flecks of pearl in the tile floor catch and bounce the light. It wasn't until the Legates were merely paces away Leo recognized the velvet-smooth voice among them.

Every muscle tensed. His breathing dropped deep and even as the clicking of Amir's polished shoes approached. Hatred surged through him until his temples throbbed with it. Amir had kidnapped him and his friends. He'd tortured the Moirai relentlessly, innocents caught in the fallout of what the Coelacanth Project had produced. And worst of all, Amir was responsible for their parents' capture, the murder of his mother.

Amir and his entourage passed, and Leo gave them no reason to look his way. Silent and still, he waited until the Legates had nearly crossed the balcony before lifting his head. He couldn't take out Amir in the Core. However, he'd seen the depths of the compound. There was more than one good place to hide a body.

Leo shoved his fists in his pockets and when Amir's group turned the corner, he set off casually after them. His role felt unsettlingly natural, and, despite weeks of separation, Christopher's advice rose from his memories.

"If you ever have to do something you shouldn't, don't run, walk."

Rain dripped sweat into his eyes, yet he didn't stop. Hoisting his knees waist-high, he ran up one side of the bleachers and down the other, racing the second hand on Uncle Chris's watch. Puddles splashed over his cleats, soaking his socks. He knew he'd curse the blisters in the morning. He also knew making the team would be worth every one of them.

"If I walk," Leo said over the ting of raindrops on the steel stadium, *"their offense will catch me."*

"Movement catches attention. If you're slick enough, kid, the enemy won't even know you're there."

Sure enough, Leo reached the end of the balcony without turning a single head. Far in front of him, Amir's company dwindled as Legates took branching passages. Leo practiced patience, hovering one turn behind, knowing the further Amir led him into the Helix the lower their chances were of being discovered. It wasn't until Amir's entourage dropped to a single other Legate that doubt tightened around Leo's chest.

He deserves this, Leo reminded himself as his target continued alone, apparently at ease with his hands cupped behind his back.

Leo tailed him down an empty passage. And another. And another. Sweat slicked the pistol clutched in his pocket as the walls narrowed in. He could have taken the shot already. He could have taken the shot fifty times over.

Think about Christopher, Leo worked his jaw. *And Natalie. And your friends. Remember what he did to the Moirai, what they did to Mom.*

Leo gripped the gun so hard his nails dug into his palm. *Don't choke, Merrick.* He stared at Amir's shiny black head. *He deserves this.*

Steeling his resolve, Leo released a slow breath between his lips and studied the bounce in Amir's step. He would have one shot to get it right, one shot to avenge his mother, to honor the Moirai and his family. He shifted his finger to the trigger, pulling the weapon from his pocket—

"Lev!"

Leo spun his back on Amir.

"There you are!" Edwin cheered. "I know I was late, but you've got to be careful around here, man. Lose yourself in these tunnels and no one will find you for a decade or two."

Glancing back, Amir was gone, and Leo's swell of relief was polluted by shame.

Weak, he berated himself.

"I was headed for the gym," Leo lied. "Guess I missed a turn."

"Or twenty," Edwin snickered. "Almost found my place though! Must be my magnetic personality."

"Right," Leo relaxed. "I'm sure all the ladies come knocking down your door."

"More and more as of late."

Descending a narrow staircase, Leo wondered how many Nautilus members called the Helix home. It made sense for those who didn't live nearby or lacked the luxury of tacking. Leo spent every second so focused on his con that he never stopped to wonder where Edwin was from, let alone where he lived.

"How long have you lived here?" Leo asked as they started down a musty hall.

"Long enough to get comfortable, not long enough to call it

home." Edwin stopped at one of several identical doors and scanned his palm on the biometric pad. Pushing open the door with his knee, he gestured for Leo to enter first. "Do try not to break anything."

Leo let out a low whistle. More reminiscent of a junkyard than an apartment, Edwin's place was a wreck. Dismantled electronics littered every inch of what appeared to be an upscale hotel suite. A narrow footpath connected the kitchen to the living room and spare rooms beyond. Most objects were dissected beyond recognition however Leo spotted a few wristwatches, the belly of a vacuum, and several large-scale model-planes and ships. Stripped wires wound through the debris like ribbon and one in the corner even sparked occasionally.

"I tidied up yesterday." Edwin proudly surveyed his hoard.

Leo was so distracted by the graveyard of technology, and the fact Edwin sported jeans and a jacket instead of his normal uniform, he nearly overlooked the ocean glittering outside the window.

"How do you…" Leo didn't finish his question. It didn't make sense. Underground and inland, turquoise waves crashed against a shell littered beach.

"Oh, that," Edwin tapped the glass and the sea scene evaporated into a thick, sun-filtered forest. "It contributes to our psychological well-being."

Leo scanned the apartment again. *Well, that's obviously not working.*

"Maybe we should, uh, do something about…this," he gestured around the room.

Edwin chuckled the comment away and Leo suspected he was not the first to be shocked by his living situation.

"I need to know how things work," he stood happily over his collection of junk. "Sometimes to know a thing, you have to take it apart. Most folks think it's an obsession. It's not," he defended himself. "I was a bit of an inventor back home, constantly tinkering and fixing." His demeanor constricted as though they'd wandered into unwelcome territory. "It's funny though, the pieces never fit the same once I've taken them apart. Still can't figure out why that is."

"Well," Leo clapped Edwin on the back. "Hopefully, you didn't call me here to figure out how I work."

"Nah, that's what the books are for." He kicked a cheap bookcase sagging under the weight of twenty or so textbooks. Their topics ranged from anatomy to botany to astrophysics. "Besides, humanity is more a study of chaos theory than anything else; makes for difficult subject matter."

Leo didn't want to ask why Edwin had summoned him there. In fact, given how badly he'd messed up Paris for Nautilus, he wanted to avoid the subject as long as possible. To his relief, a muffled noise in the next room caught his attention.

"You have a dog or something?" Leo brightened.

Edwin shoved some LED bulbs out of the way to make room for his forearms on the kitchen counter. "Never had much interest in anything relying on me for its care."

"Fair enough." Sweat dampened Leo's brow. Edwin wasn't watching him, he was scrutinizing. "What about a fish?"

"Living in a cage is no life for anything," Edwin curled his lip, "even a fish."

Leo nodded as tension condensed between them. Seconds stretched into minutes, emphasized by the ticking clock on the wall. He cleared his throat. It echoed louder than thunder.

"Okay, man," he said finally. "If this is about Paris—"

"Lev," Edwin cut him off. "Don't say another word if it's anything other than the truth."

Leo almost felt an actual rug slip out from under his feet.

Stupid. He had been so *stupid* for getting even the slightest bit comfortable. Edwin worked for Nautilus. Edwin lived in Nautilus. Leo fumbled for the excuses he'd worked through the night before.

"I made a mistake," Leo scrambled. "I choked. I didn't expect to have to kill some girl. I hesitated and she got the better of me. It won't happen again."

Edwin's expression didn't change. "We'll get to Paris," he promised darkly. "I want you to start with your name."

"My...my name?" Leo looked to the forest outside the fake window as though it was some means of escape.

"Yes. You know my name; it's only fair I know yours."

Leo weighed his options. He'd never make it out of the Helix without Edwin raising some sort of alarm. And that was assuming he could escape Edwin's apartment and get away before the Captain bested him. Worst-case scenario, he'd be caught, tortured, and killed. Best-case scenario, Edwin would skip right to the killing part.

Another muffled sound came from the adjacent room. His heart raced. It had sounded disturbingly *human*.

"My name is Lev," Leo lied. "You know me, man. What's in there?" He nodded towards the sound.

Edwin frowned. "If you don't want to talk then I have to show you. Come on."

Edwin led the way into the adjoining room, stepping over a boombox that appeared three or four decades out of place. The new space appeared intended for socializing, only all the furniture had been rearranged. Chairs lined the walls and the coffee table had been flipped on its side. Edwin halted near a heap of blankets piled on the floor.

"Last chance," Edwin stood next to the pile with his palms opened out. He appeared conflicted, as though he wasn't sure about what he was going to do next, as though he wasn't sure if he was demanding or begging. "Just tell me your name."

"My name is Lev."

Do whatever you want to me, Edwin. My name is Lev until the moment I die. I will not betray the Moirai; I will not betray my friends or my family or Christopher. Death before defeat.

"Okay," Edwin shook his head. "I tried to help you." He tossed the blankets aside and Leo recoiled.

A woman lay curled on her side with her wrists and ankles bound.

Dried blood caked the side of her mouth and stained her navy Nautilus uniform while a purple bruise blossomed across the left side of her face. Her hair was tousled and so black it was almost blue. Edwin pulled her into a sitting position, and she grunted, the sound muffled by the gag between her teeth.

"Edwin," Leo gaped, unable to say more.

"This one thought she could sneak through the Helix undetected. A bold assumption. Deadly at best. Remember what I told you about cats around here? And my, my did she have plenty to say about you. Now, tell me. What's your name?"

Leo shook his head. He wasn't following. He didn't understand.

Edwin forced up the girl's chin. He flipped a knife from his jacket and pressed the blade against her throat.

"You're going to tell me exactly who you are and why you're here," Edwin warned. "Or she'll never see the light of day."

Her green-amber eyes met Leo's and his breath caught in his chest.

Natalie.

CHAPTER 29
LEONIDAS

Blood pounded like a war-drum in his ears. His pistol was aimed at Edwin's head before he'd even finished the thought. Though not as good a shot as Brant, Leo was certain he wouldn't miss. Not this time. The world would burn before he lost her again.

"My name is Leonidas Merrick," he answered Edwin's question through bared teeth. The Nautilus uniform she wore, the color of her hair, the knife against her neck, it was wrong. It was all wrong. How did Natalie escape Paris only to end up on her knees with a blade at her throat?

Natalie looked from him to his gun and gave a subtle turn of her head. Bound and gagged, she was trying to tell him something. Leo wasn't sure if he wanted to shake her or kiss her.

"Where are you from?"

"Florida."

Edwin pressed the flat of his knife against a throbbing vein in her neck. Natalie didn't even blink.

"Virginia," Leo snapped. "Let her go."

"You mean like you did in Paris?"

"She's not part of this."

Edwin picked at Natalie's uniform. "It seems she's very much part of this." He wagged the tip of his blade from Leo to Natalie. "Tell me, how does this work? What are you trying to do? Overthrow the Ward?"

Leo ignored him. Natalie looked at the gun and jerked her chin. She didn't want him to shoot. Why? What choice did he have?

"Why are you here?" Edwin pushed.

"I am here to find peace," Leo growled. "Just like everyone else. Starting with my own."

"Explain."

"Nautilus took something of mine," Leo said slowly, watching Natalie test her restraints.

"Something or someone?"

Leo didn't answer. Natalie stopped struggling, her expression unreadable.

"I caught your metro rat trying to slip into the Helix's central cell," Edwin explained. "Rumors are flying that it holds the key to Nautilus's victory at Graduation."

Natalie's glare bore into him as though she was waiting for him to do something. Was there some signal he was supposed to give? Or something he was supposed to notice?

"I find it hard to believe your friend here would risk her life for something so equivocal," Edwin continued. "Tell me why you're here or she dies. It's that simple."

And it's that hard. If Leo told Edwin the truth, that would be it. He wouldn't be able to search the Helix for information on their parents, he wouldn't be able to honor his debt to the Moirai or avenge his mother. He couldn't tell Edwin why he was there, and he wouldn't let Natalie die. He tightened his grip on the pistol and traced the trigger.

I have to kill him.

It wouldn't be enough to simply shoot him down. Edwin could

raise an alarm or pursue them, and it would already be hard enough escaping the Helix without leaving him as a loose end. Still, Leo hesitated.

Natalie pulled against her captor, distracting Leo from his thoughts. She blinked at him once, slow and deliberate. He shook his head, and she repeated the motion. Her message was clear.

Trust.

She wanted him to tell Edwin the truth, which was suicide. Still, there was the slightest chance she knew something he didn't, that they could escape without Edwin bleeding out in their wake…

"They have our parents," Leo bit out every word, deciding if Edwin did raise hell, he would shoot him then.

"Why?"

"They're inventors, researchers. The Ward probably wants to use them."

"What do they work on?"

Again, Leo hesitated. Natalie had begun to cry and shook her head adamantly back and forth.

"We don't know," he lied, taking her cue. Thankfully, Edwin didn't press.

"This girl is your sister?" Edwin frowned at Natalie.

"No," Leo flushed. He tried to channel the adrenaline overpowering his senses. It was fogging his mind; he could have sworn he saw Natalie flicker.

"Ah," Edwin grinned. "Girlfriend?"

Natalie scowled in Edwin's direction.

"I told you what you wanted to know," Leo said. "You have me. Let her go and I won't shoot you."

"One more question," Edwin flipped the knife skillfully in the air. "Who forged your transfer papers to get you inside the Helix?"

Leo didn't say anything. He couldn't. He wouldn't let the Moirai suffer any more than they already had.

"Interesting answer." Edwin sliced Natalie's throat.

"NO!" Leo forgot the gun. He launched himself at Edwin. He couldn't see. He couldn't hear. He felt as though he fought underwater with a mountain on his chest. Every breath was agonizing and utterly impossible.

"You're dead!" Leo bellowed. "You're all DEAD!"

Edwin dropped his knife in surrender. Leo didn't stop. He wanted to feel Edwin's pulse thread out beneath his hands. He wanted to see him broken and lifeless and bleeding at his feet.

Leo shoved Edwin against the wall and punched him. His knuckles split open as he felt the satisfying crack of Edwin's nose and he reared back to punch again. Edwin would die for this. Nautilus would burn. The world would burn for her.

"Any day now," Edwin coughed.

Blood dripped freely from his nose and the sight of it made Leo hungry for more. He wanted Edwin to feel every second of agony. He punched him again and Edwin's black eyes rolled back into his head.

"Leo."

Leo squeezed around Edwin's throat. Edwin sputtered and gagged. His face turned ugly shades of purple.

"Leo!"

Something soft cradled him, pulling until his mind tripped on the details. Strips of fabric hung loosely from her wrists. Purple and red pigment painted her skin. She fell into focus, a perfect impossibility.

"Leo, let him go."

Edwin sagged against him as Natalie pried at Leo's grip. She even felt real.

"Let go!"

Natalie. Natalie was yelling at him. She smelled like vanilla and coconut and smoke. Leo dropped his hold and Edwin collapsed to the floor. Natalie knelt to his side and Leo yanked her up.

He forced her against the wall. He felt the rise and fall of her chest with her breath and the red painted curve of her neck. She felt so *real*. Natalie winced as he traced over patches of burnt skin. He didn't stop and she didn't ask him to.

"Hi," she said.

He kissed her. Not careful or gentle, but hungry. His touch traveled up the sides of her hips and through her hair. She went rigid, which he failed to notice until she bit him. He pulled away in surprise.

"I'm—" she stopped and started again. "I had to know what side you were on."

Leo tensed. He examined the room, struggling to put the pieces together. The paint on Natalie's face. The loose restraints on her wrists. A collection of projectors hidden in the clutter, all used to create Natalie's image.

"This was a set-up," he said weakly.

She nodded. "I was in the other room. In case you tried to do something ridiculous."

"I nearly killed him."

"He knew you wouldn't."

"Paris?" Leo itched at his scalp. "That was arranged, too?"

"No," Natalie said firmly. "That was an accident."

"Like hell it was."

"Guys?" Edwin croaked.

Natalie stepped back and Leo sensed the movement was more than physical. There was a wall between them that had never existed before. Natalie had been a lot of things to him, opaque was never one of them.

"I had to know whose side you were on," Natalie repeated. She inspected the bruises already darkening Edwin's throat and staunched his bleeding nose with the fabric from her wrists. "I think you two have some catching up to do."

"You failed to mention he might hit me." Though Edwin's retort was muffled, his joviality rang through.

"Suppose we're even then." Natalie headed for the door, waving lazily as though she saw them every day, as though he hadn't spent the past seven weeks agonizing over being apart. "See you," she said.

"Will you?" Every cell in his body screamed to stop her but doubt grounded him. She had wanted to test him. And when he leaned in, she stepped back.

Instead of answering, Natalie tapped her pockets in a little rhythm and disappeared into the Helix.

Edwin gave him no time to wallow. He coughed violently and spit up a mouthful of blood. Leo watched his fellow Captain struggle his way into a chair.

Liar. Traitor. Nautilus. Sneak. Definitely a sneak.

"Don't look at me like that, man," Edwin groaned.

"How do you know Natalie?"

"Met this morning, actually," Edwin sucked on his split lip. "Guess things escalated quickly from there. Her idea." He gestured at the projectors that created her hologram.

"She's always been clever," Leo said darkly, "never cruel."

"You think that was cruel?" Edwin shook his head. "This was the kinder of her ideas, believe me."

Leo resisted the urge to start pummeling him again.

"Look," Edwin massaged his bruising neck. "When I found her sneaking around, she was able to disarm and pin me in four moves, and that was after I nearly gave the girl a concussion. I'm damn lucky she didn't kill me."

"Her?" Leo pointed at the door Natalie left through.

"Oh yeah."

"Huh." It made sense now why Edwin disappeared after the meeting of world powers in the Helix, why he didn't report Leo for failing in Paris. Leo had been fooled by Edwin for weeks. Natalie saw through him in seconds. "If you're not supporting the Ward, then who are you working for?"

"Myself mostly," Edwin explained. "I think we can all agree peace would make the world a better place, and not everyone is fooled by

Nautilus's promises or aligns with their methods. Your friends are not alone in that."

She told him about the others, Leo realized. *But not about tacking?* He would have to tread carefully to not give away more than she already had.

"Then you only know I'm not with Nautilus because Natalie told you?" Leo clarified.

"No," Edwin chuckled and spit out more blood. "I suspected it from the moment you arrived, though I wasn't certain until you saved her life in Paris." He coughed again.

"Then why go through the trouble of questioning me?"

Edwin shook his head. "Already told you, man. I didn't need convincing. She did."

Great. Leo ran his tongue over where she'd bitten him.

"Anyway, we have a lot to do. Graduation is in two days and if we don't stop the Ward, we're going to have front row seats for World War III, 4-D edition."

"How can I trust you?" Leo asked, irritated by Edwin's nonchalance.

"Your girlfriend seems to trust me. Isn't that enough?"

"She's not my..." Leo shifted his weight, unsure why Edwin's classification of his and Natalie's friendship made him so uncomfortable. Maybe it had something to do with the fact she didn't seem to want to be anywhere near him. "No, it isn't."

"Hmm." Edwin squinted at him.

Leo couldn't help feeling he was being sized up. Again. Finally, Edwin smiled.

"Good! Maybe this will change your mind." Edwin hurried into another room, shockingly light on his feet for someone who had nearly been strangled to death.

Leo followed him into something that might have once been a bedroom. Another fake window decorated the space above the bed with an image of actual space. Millions of stars flickered and blinked in the darkness.

"Over here." Edwin's head shot up from the other side of the bed. He popped out a piece of flooring and produced stacks of crumpled papers and photographs.

"What is all of this?"

"Evidence," blood coated his teeth. "Everything I've done to slow Nautilus's advances. I've been dismantling their operation for nearly a year now. Idiots. Here," he pushed over a picture of St. Petersburg. "This is where I first heard of Nautilus. They were marching around claiming to bring peace in our time. I was curious how that would work, the logistics and all, so I followed them here.

"I was going to add saving Natalie's life to the pile. Now that's your thorn in Nautilus's side. Well played." Edwin dug deeper into the box and produced a thick piece of paper. "This, however, I thought might earn me a ticket back home."

Leo studied a shredded document that had been taped back together. He read it once, then again, unsure if he understood what he held.

"Follow the Gulls," Leo read aloud. "That's what you said after the world powers met with the Ward. What does it mean?"

"No idea."

"Gather all the information you have on Graduation." Leo headed for the door. If neither of them had any clue to the meaning of the cryptic message, then he needed to find someone who did. And the Moirai were as good a place to start as any. "Meet you back here tomorrow."

"Tomorrow?" Edwin balked. "We don't have that kind of time!"

"It's the best I can do," Leo was already picking his way back through the piles of junk.

Edwin began to argue then seemed to think better of it. He tiptoed his way to a corner desk and powered up a line of computers.

"What are you doing?"

"The best I can do," Edwin answered without turning around.

213

"Tomorrow, Leo. No later."

Leo set off into the Helix, trying his best to pay attention to where his feet were taking him as his mind raced. He knew whatever 'Follow the Gulls' meant had to be important. But the harder he focused on the mystery, the more his thoughts trailed back to Natalie. They'd grown up together, they'd tacked together, and they'd finally collided into one another in Nautilus's tunnels. For weeks he'd thought that had meant something. Every moment he'd ached to be next to her. Now, when he'd finally found her again, she didn't trust him? What did that mean?

Looking up from his shoes, Leo found himself back in the Core with the exit doors in sight. Shoving his hands into his pockets to resist the urge to run, he discovered something folded and smooth. His heart skipped.

Ancora.

He didn't dare remove the photograph inside the Helix. Only when he'd reached the bus stop did he risk a peek.

It wasn't a lighthouse. A long, squat building protruded from a mountain of rock as though the earth had grown it there. Though Natalie shied away, she was still leading him back to her.

No mistakes this time, Leo vowed. *I'm coming home.*

CHAPTER 30
LEONIDAS

Lache sat still as stone. "No."

"I didn't even ask yet!"

"It was implied." She countered. "The answer is no."

Leo leaned his head back and reconsidered his approach. The Moirai were like a mountain: no amount of pushing or shoving was going to make them move anywhere. If he was going to convince them to go to Ancora, he'd have to work up something more efficacious than 'please.'

"My friends need your help," he insisted. "They don't know about the Nautilus copy-cat project, about what was done to you. They've been snooping around the Helix blind to what they're up against."

Not bad, Leo complemented his own devious play.

"This is our home," Atro said. It wasn't an argument or an excuse; it was the truth.

Leo deflated. He crouched to where they sat together on the couch. "We want to bring Nautilus down. Permanently. I don't think we can do that without you. And if we succeed, that silver shadow in your nightmares disappears. This can still be your home. I don't understand how you can object to a chance to live without fear."

"I am sorry," Lache stonewalled him. "Nautilus will graduate to the world stage in two days. It is done."

"You're giving up?"

Atro peered out the window to the cliffs while Clo busied herself adjusting her robes.

"Two days is not enough time," Lache said finally. "You made us a promise and you broke it. We will not risk what we have left for your naive dream of dismantling a global organization in a matter of hours."

Leo stopped her from pulling away. "I've failed you with Amir, I admit it, but it isn't too late. This Graduation can be Nautilus's downfall. They're throwing the world into war just for the power to tack from shore to shore."

"Tack from shore to shore," Atro repeated.

Clo's icy gaze dashed from Leo to her sister. "Lachesis, he thinks—"

"Okay," Lache spoke over her. "You are right."

"Really?" Leo asked, shocked. "I mean, I generally am but it's a treat to hear you say it."

Lache's lips disappeared in a thin line. "We will help you sabotage Graduation, then we are coming right back home."

Leo could hardly believe it. After nearly two agonizing months, he was finally going home. "Great. Let's go, right now. Get your things."

In hardly ten minutes they were packed, though it took another five to pry Clo away from her precious plants. She sniffled back tears as each potted shrub was watered and every flower positioned perfectly on the sill.

"What if we do not return?"

"We will," Atro promised her.

"Why don't you bring one with you?" Leo offered.

Clo lit up and he fiddled impatiently with the hem of his jacket as she decided which lucky twig would come along. Finally, with a potted eucalyptus in tow, they set out for the beach. Leo caught both Atro and Clo sneak more than one glance back at the cottage shrinking behind them. He tried to think positive, to tell himself they would be back in a few days, only the illusion wouldn't hold. So far, every home he left he'd never seen again.

"What made you change your mind?" Leo asked Lache as they navigated the steep path single file. He was curious which part of his argument had taken root. "Not that I'm complaining," he added quickly.

"It became apparent you do not know as much as you think you do. Saving your life was no small feat. I would like to ensure our efforts were not in vain."

"I don't think I ever apologized for all the trouble."

"I will consider the fulfillment of our agreement apology enough."

Leo's heart sank. Their agreement. Right. She turned on him then, temporarily halting their procession.

"I know you are expecting a homecoming," she sighed. "I pray you steel your heart, Leonidas." She hurried towards a stone arch where Atro and Clo waited.

Leo lacked the bandwidth to juggle Lache's cryptic concerns along with the giant knot of anxiety tangling his insides. He hadn't seen his friends in almost eight weeks. If the brief moments he'd stolen with Natalie carried any weight, this reunion was going to be more complicated than he'd originally anticipated.

"Ready?" Leo tried to shake away his concerns as he joined the Moirai beneath the arch.

Lache fixated on the horizon as her sisters-by-circumstance huddled beside her. They were about to do the one thing Nautilus had nurtured, mutated, and tortured them for, and none of them looked pleased by the prospect.

"What is it like?" Atro asked nervously.

"It's like," he paused. Tacking had become as elemental as breathing or walking. How could he explain something as natural as the sensation of his lungs filling and emptying of air to someone who had never drawn breath?

"It's like you're suspended in static. It's not painful, though it's not exactly comfortable either. There's a moment where time stands still or maybe you're entirely separate from it. It's just you, weightless and alone. You can't see, you can't breathe, but everything happens so fast you don't need to. I'm here," Leo drew a line in the sand with his shoe, "and then I'm somewhere else. It's like the world realizes you're missing and pulls you back down. If you aren't entirely focused on where you want to go, you could be lost."

"Magic static," Clo scowled, her eucalyptus trembling.

"Just do it," Lache curtly jutted her chin.

Leo envisioned the Ancora enveloped in the woods, carved from stone into the earth. With the Moirai arm-in-arm, he stepped into the wave trickling up the sand. A familiar white light enveloped them, and the Scottish shore faded to nothing beneath his feet. His entire body hummed, voltaic as energy pulsed through his veins as natural as blood. In an instant, gravity reclaimed him, and the light left him momentarily blinded.

The knot in his stomach had wound unbearably tight. He had no idea if he was elated or terrified or about to be sick. He blinked rapidly, desperate to know if it had worked.

"Leo?"

He had never heard Tawney sound so small.

Leo breathed out a laugh as she barreled into him. She scaled him like a tree, wrapping herself around his torso and covering him with a veil of curls. The stars faded from his vision only to be blurred again by an upwelling of tears. He clung to her, terrified she'd fade away.

"You're okay," she breathed against his chest.

"I'm okay." Leo squeezed her so tight he feared he would break her. Hot tears overflowed and he knelt on the pebbled shore, still holding Tawney to him. Enzi circled them, licking anything he could reach.

"Leo," she patted his back. "Leo, I can't breathe." Loosening his grip, Tawney filled his vision, studying him. "Sheesh," she gawked. "Leave you alone for a few weeks and you get all hippy with your hair."

"Hey, man!" Owen threw his gangly arms around them.

"Nerd!" Leo wiped his face dry of tears and Enzi's slobber.

"Alright, alright." Brant pried Tawney's limbs away from Leo's chest. Leo flipped her onto his back as Brant helped him to his feet.

"We thought you were dead," Brant's brown eyes were misty.

"Ye of little faith," Leo clapped his friend on the back, aiming for jovial, however there was no escaping Brant's pain. Taking a closer look, Leo realized every one of his friends appeared tired and strained.

He spotted Natalie instantly, drawn to her presence like a magnet. She hovered in the tree line, her hair back to its normal caramel brown. Owen's freckled-and-bespectacled-self carried notably more muscle while Brant seemed almost sickly, as though he'd dropped ten or fifteen pounds.

"Welcome back." Natalie hovered out of reach. Any anger he'd held for her plot with Edwin dissipated. It didn't matter. None of it mattered. He was home.

Leo scratched Enzi's ears, hoping it would calm him down. It didn't. The dog howled and yipped and bounded excitedly through their group. The Moirai yelped collectively as Enzi approached them, his nose high in the air. His hackles lifted as his tail was wagging, as though both threatened and excited by the strangers.

Lache, Clo, and Atro clung to each other, even paler than normal. It struck Leo it could be their first time ever seeing a dog, and Enzi proved quite the formidable creature when he wanted to be. Leo patted his thighs and Enzi ran back to him.

"It's okay," he assured the girls. "He won't hurt you."

Tawney shifted on his back. "So long as you behave."

"Who are they?" Natalie asked, frankly.

Admittedly, he hadn't allowed himself to dwell on how his friends would react to the Moirai. Partly because he hadn't felt he'd had a choice. And partly because, deep down, he'd known bringing the two groups together would be no easy feat. After what they'd been through, he couldn't expect his friends to welcome strangers with open arms. Leo could only hope they'd trust him long enough to give the Moirai a chance.

"This is Lache, Clo, and Atro."

"Sorry," Natalie said, though her tone suggested otherwise. "Ancora isn't a halfway house. No tours, no strays, no strangers."

"We came to help you," Lache snipped back.

"That's sweet," Natalie stood taller. "We don't need you."

"Because you're beyond tacking from shore to shore?"

A strange tension rippled through his friends and Leo didn't miss the looks exchanged between them. Tawney crouched on his back like a cat prepared to pounce. Introductions would come to blows if he didn't intervene fast.

"Nautilus is after them," Leo stepped between the two groups. "They're like us."

Owen straightened, intrigued. "How much like us?"

"More than you think," Lache answered.

Tawney worked her fists. Clo cowered.

"I'd be dead without them," Leo looked straight at Natalie. "I would have bled out on their beach if they didn't help me."

"Bled out?" Brant blanched.

"Yeah, I—" Leo pressed his thumb against his forehead. "It's a long story, actually. Can we do this inside?"

Natalie approached the Moirai, assessing each in turn. "Betray us and it will be the last thing you ever do. Understand?"

Conviction rang in every word. Perhaps she wouldn't take his agreement to assassinate Amir so badly after all.

Atro pursed her lips, holding protectively around Clo's waist. Lache cocked her head.

"You are more insignificant than I expected."

Tawney dropped from Leo's back. Assuming flattening the three girls into the ground wouldn't be a great foundation to build a friendship, he scrambled to catch her. He brushed the back of her collar as she slipped past. He waited for blood and screams, however instead of swinging her fists, Tawney extended her hand.

"I'm Tawney."

Lache stared at it until Clo reached beyond her and shook it.

"You are the fighter," Clo said wistfully.

"Uh, yeah," Tawney glanced questioningly back at Leo. "I guess so."

"Will you teach me?"

"I don't know," Tawney surveyed Clo's willowy frame. "You seem fragile."

"As do you," Clo observed.

Tawney pulled hard on Clo's wrist and spun her, locking her arm behind her back. Beaming she said, "Lesson one: don't shake hands with strangers."

"Thank you." It was directed at all of them, though Leo looked at Natalie as he spoke. "I owe them my life."

"And more," Lache added.

Brant scratched his head. "It's kind of perfect actually."

"How so?"

"This Ancora has more rooms than we needed," Natalie's expression was flat and guarded. "Exactly four more."

"Wait," Leo skimmed the beach. "Is Christopher inside with Angie?"

His friends froze. Tawney dropped her hold on Clo, hugging her own tiny frame instead.

"Angie's dead," she whispered. Enzi nosed her and Tawney

kneed him away.

Something inside Leo crumbled.

"Dead?" he repeated, the word thick like cotton. Lache's warning resurfaced. She'd told him to steel his heart. He thought he'd been prepared, but not for this. Not for a grave.

"Christopher," Leo shook his head. "Chris must be devastated. That dog was his life."

"You were right," Natalie soured as though it pained her to say it. "We should talk inside." As she strode away, Leo couldn't help noticing how close Brant stuck by her side, how easily his touch found refuge on the small of her back...

"Come on," Leo scooped Tawney onto his back and nodded for the Moirai to follow.

"May I carry that for you?" Owen nodded to Clo's plant and she clutched the shrub to her chest. "I'm not going to steal your eucalyptus," he laughed.

"Oh." Clo awkwardly let Owen take the pot and hovered by him like a bird. "This is strange."

Tawney rested her chin on Leo's shoulder. "Leave again and I'll pummel you," she whispered in his ear.

"Noted."

"I'm serious, Leo."

"Me, too." Leo watched Enzi trot between Lache and Atro. Each took turns nervously stroking him from nose to tail. "I'm sorry about Angie. What happened?"

"Fire," Tawney sniffled.

Fire, Leo reeled. *That explains the burns on her skin.*

"Is that what's wrong with Natalie?"

"Depends," she said coldly. "Are you referring to this minute or the past few hours? Days? Weeks?" She cracked her knuckles around Leo's neck. "Nat does what she wants and doesn't care who she hurts."

Leo's stomach sank. He knew that wasn't true, though he didn't feel comfortable relaying that insight to Tawney with her hands so near his throat. If he hadn't gotten lost, if he had been able to find Ancora III after getting shot, he would have been around to help them. Maybe then things would be different. Maybe—

Lache's light laugh blossomed behind him and he saw Enzi prancing around in front of her with Atro clapping in approval at her side.

Only I would have never met them.

"If I were you," Tawney advised, "I'd get your explanations out quick and dirty and get her alone."

Leo hoped the gathering darkness hid his flush. "Uh, what?"

"Ew," Tawney kicked him. "You're *such* a guy. I meant get her alone to *talk* to her, you dweeb. She won't open up to any of us, but she's always had a bit of a soft spot for you."

"Always?"

Tawney kicked him again.

"I'm confused," Leo admitted. "Are you angry with her or not?"

"It's her fault Angie's dead," Tawney declared. "I'm pissed with her. It will always be her fault," she slumped against him. "But I still love her," she grumbled in resignation.

He couldn't believe Natalie was the cause of Angie's death, however he sensed he'd be opening a can of worms if he pressed for more. Ancora loomed over them and he set Tawney down on the pine needles.

"She'll come around. I'll explain everything. We'll be right where we left off."

"Uh-huh. Like I said, quick and dirty. She won't give you time for anything more eloquent."

"She will."

"You're as arrogant as I left you." Tawney playfully tripped his step.

"Arrogance is the pinnacle of confidence."

Tawney laughed. It was a real laugh that bubbled up quick and loud and reminded Leo of simpler times. Times before bombings and disappearances and tacking, when they were five normal teens going out for a round of ice cream.

"Yeah," Tawney hiccupped. "Nat is gonna punch you in the mouth."

CHAPTER 31
NATALIE

Owen and Brant took turns catching Leo up on what had happened since Antarctica. Natalie knew she should have been happy Leo was back, though it was hard to move past the baggage he'd brought.

They stuck to his side like leeches.

Their rigid posture and silent observance made Natalie uneasy, and their obnoxious cloaks did little to hide the fractals etched into their skin. Natalie recognized the bolt-born scars the second she saw them. They were a perfect match to her own and yet their shared suffering did nothing to defrost her scorn. They were strangers, and the last thing she needed was another enigma to keep tabs on.

Clo wandered childlike about Ancora with her plant while her so-called *sister* followed with scrutiny, the contrast of their complexions woven in their interlocked fingers. Meanwhile, Lache sat perfectly still, captivated by every move Leo made.

Natalie shook herself. It didn't matter if Leo and Lache were involved. He never made any commitments to her before he disappeared. In fact, they hadn't really talked about anything. Every intimate moment between them had followed an intense fear of losing one another. She could easily argue their attraction was more adrenaline than affection. Again, and again, they collided together beneath the threat of death: Nautilus hunting them in Ancora I, escaping the compound in Antarctica.

Nearly bleeding to death.

A curved pattern of white scars on Leo's forearm caught the light and Natalie's bad mood turned bitter. The longer she thought about it, the more convinced she became Leo's attention towards her was situational.

It's not important, Natalie scolded herself. Their parents were still missing, and Nautilus was merely days away from claiming the center stage of global politics. If they'd ever had a window of opportunity, it was closing. She didn't have time to worry if Leo cared for someone else, if he shared their secrets or their bed, if he longed for them as she did for him.

"So then, when Natalie went back to find you, she—"

Natalie snapped back to attention. Owen caught her reaction and stumbled over his words.

"She, uh, she couldn't?" It was more of a question than an explanation.

"You must have already gone," Natalie clarified. Short, sweet, and devoid of detail. That's what Leo would get so long as his leeches were listening.

"I have snacks." Brant balanced a platter of sandwiches, passing three directly to Tawney. Angie's passing seemed to have quelled the constant feud between them, at least for the moment.

Not hungry, Natalie lugged her pack of books out into the open air. On the mossy rooftop, she escaped the expectations of Ancora's walls and Enzi slipped out around her legs, content to roll in the grass.

Settling near him, Natalie propped *The Sceptical Chymist* in her lap. She'd inspected the cover inside and out time and time again for any clues from Christopher and, finding none beyond the Latin inscription, she'd decided to simply try reading it. It was slow, tedious work. Boyle's language was old and eloquent, his words arranged as much for prose as point. Natalie had to read and reread a single sentence three or four times before fully comprehending its meaning. So far, she'd found nothing more than semi-lucid ramblings about alchemy and a plea for reform in the definition of elemental substances presented as a debate amongst friends.

Too tired for analytical work, Natalie let the pages fall open to wherever they felt comfortable. She was vaguely aware when Enzi finally sat beside her. At least, she had assumed it was Enzi, until a very human sigh made her jump up in alarm.

"Sorry," Leo scooted away. "I thought you knew I was here!"

Natalie sank back against a tree, willing her racing heart to slow. Searching the rooftop, she didn't see her dog anywhere.

"Where's Enzi?" she asked in alarm. "He was right here."

"He's downstairs trying to convince the Moirai to sneak him snacks." Leo grinned. She hated him for it. "He seems to be the only thing that hasn't changed."

"The Moirai," Natalie tested the familiar phrase in its new context. "Interesting choice for a nickname."

"It's more of a curse, actually," Leo's expression darkened. "I know it's not ideal. I promised them it's temporary. Regardless, it would be a lot easier if you didn't hate them."

Natalie wetted her lips. "I don't hate them."

"Yeah, you really rolled out the welcome mat."

"What do you want me to say?" Natalie bristled. "We wanted to bring *you* here. We don't know them. We can't trust them."

"I trust them. Isn't that enough?"

"No." Frustrated, she slammed the book shut and rose to leave.

Leo sprung up and blocked her. "What did I do to deserve that, Natalie?" he asked, pained. "To watch you die? Do you have any idea what that's like?"

She rounded on him, shoving *The Sceptical Chymist* against his stomach. "I've watched you die a thousand times over!" she countered. "Every night I relive it, losing you in the darkness, in the middle of those freaking ice floes."

"You're acting like this wasn't hard on me, too!"

"Tell me." She would not cry, not in front of him. "Tell me the truth. Did you think about coming back to us? Even once? Or were you satisfied with your pretty company?"

"Natalie—"

"You have no idea what we've been through. No clue."

"I know I wasn't here—"

"Why not?" Natalie was stuck somewhere between yelling and begging. "What was so important about them you couldn't bear to come back to—"

"I was shot."

Natalie blinked. Thoughts slipped through her mind like smoke, intangible yet smothering.

Leo guided her hand beneath his shirt to press against a ridge of pale pink flesh. Boyle's book fell to the moss. She traced the scar, pleading her brain to work faster.

Leo was shot. Leo was shot in Antarctica?

He lifted her palm from his stomach and pressed it lightly against his cheek. He leaned into her and the smoke in her mind thickened. She didn't know how to feel other than confused.

"You were shot," she repeated dumbly. Enzi pushed his way between them.

"Shot?"

Natalie stepped back as Owen approached, acutely conscious of the lack of space between her and Leo. Owen carried the few remaining sandwiches with Lache, Clo, and Atro close behind him. Tawney and Brant both paused beyond the doorway, Leo's announcement having stopped them in their tracks. Brant blanched. Tawney stood frozen with a sandwich halfway to her open mouth.

"Maybe you lot should sit down," Leo suggested.

Natalie listened to his story intently. The beginning was rocky, with big chunks missing where the Moirai filled in. Natalie's insides knotted a little tighter every time Lache underlined Leo's helpless reliance on her and her sisters. By the end she felt positively nauseous.

"Wow," Owen breathed in amazement.

"Why didn't you come back once you healed?" Natalie cut straight to the point.

"I wanted to," Leo insisted. "I just…" He turned to Lache.

Natalie bit her tongue. Loathing scorched through her.

"I owed them a debt," Leo finished finally.

Natalie exchanged a glance with Tawney, who then seemed to remember her own anger and promptly turned away.

"You all grew up in Nautilus?" Brant frowned at the three girls. "They were trying to make you…make you like us?"

Clo nodded without lifting her head from Atro's shoulder. "We are the survivors of the Moirai Mission. Nautilus created us in your image to tack and," she hesitated, cut off by Lache's glare. "And serve Nautilus on their path to peace," she finished weakly.

Natalie chewed her cheek. If Nautilus was trying to recreate the Coelacanth Project, then Leo's companions knew about time-travel. And Natalie hadn't missed the unspoken exchange between Lache and her sister. She was willing to bet whatever they knew, Leo did not.

"Moirai," Natalie said aloud. "As in *the* Moirai: Lachesis, Clotho, and Atropos. The three Fates."

"Indeed," Lache confirmed.

"Oh!" Owen's hand shot up towards the sky. "The Moirai! Goddesses of destiny!"

"Is that significant?" Brant asked.

"Depends," Natalie hugged her knees into her chest. "Was Nautilus successful?"

"No," Lache answered coolly.

Natalie felt her friends relaxing. She kept her focus on Lache. "And…?" She inclined her head towards Leo.

The exotic girl gave a subtle shake that sent a ripple through her curtain of silver hair.

They do know, Natalie confirmed. *Only Leo doesn't.*

"Some things are better received from friends. At least, so I have been told," Lache offered an apologetic smile. Natalie wasn't buying it. If the Moirai withheld information from Leo, they must have had a reason.

"Christopher needs to meet them," Leo announced. "Maybe he can help them, too."

Natalie rose to her feet, brushing moss and grass from her pants. "No."

"Natalie—"

"I said no."

"Oh, come on!" Leo cried in disbelief. "With Graduation coming up we need all the help we can get. We don't even know what Nautilus is planning! Maybe he'll have some clue to what 'Follow the Gulls' means. There isn't time to hide anymore. I can hardly believe you convinced him to stay put as it is." He widened his stance. "I deserve to see him, Natalie."

Owen cleared his throat. "...he's not wrong."

"No." She felt Brant press against her. It was almost as uncomfortable as Leo's scrutiny. Natalie jerked away. She couldn't take Leo to see Christopher. Not now, not after Angie. How could she? What would she say?

"Nat," Tawney cut through her rising panic and Natalie's heart wrenched. Maybe there was hope for their friendship after all. "If you don't take him, I will."

Natalie pulled at her sleeve. She wanted to disagree, only there was no avoiding it. Leo would have to see Christopher eventually.

"Fine." Without waiting for anyone, Natalie marched him down the hill towards the shoreline. Enzi led the way, his white tail swishing between the young cedar trees. She'd nearly reached the water before Leo's hand slipped into hers. Her heart soared and she pushed it down. She didn't want to feel anything. Not now. With Enzi beside them, Natalie summoned an image of the marina and stepped into the water.

As far as Natalie was concerned, the weightless nothingness could have extended into eternity. She wanted to stay in that light forever, to be absorbed into it. She didn't need the world to return beneath her feet. She didn't want to deal with what waited for her at the end of the ride. Yet gravel crunched beneath her shoes as the light inevitably faded, depositing them beneath the awning of a boat slip.

Enzi burst out of her grip, darting into a thick growth of grasses where crabs skittered fearfully into their holes. Leo lit up at the familiar sight of the shabby cement cabin. He set out for Christopher's house so quickly he'd nearly cleared the porch steps before Natalie caught the back of his shirt.

Her throat tightened. Unable to speak, she shook her head.

"Oh, in the marina?" Leo asked, seeking out the corrugated aluminum building.

Natalie mouthed the word 'no' and guided him up a dune behind the cabin. Sea shrubs gave way to thorny thickets which eventually succumbed to a clearing of green grass and fragile white flowers. Nearly level with the cabin's roof, the hilltop offered a gorgeous view of the shoreline and ocean beyond. Natalie didn't care to look. It took everything she had to simply put one foot in front of the other.

Natalie knew when Leo realized where she was taking him. Halfway across the clearing, he forced her to a sharp stop. The motion was desperate, frantic, and she refused to meet his gaze. She didn't want to see.

She continued alone to the edge of the clearing where saplings tested their leaves. Inhaling a sharp breath of salty air, Natalie knelt among the wildflowers that bloomed around a polished slab of stone. She knew then what Brant had said was true: no amount of time would ever make it easier. The granite was as cold and permanent as the day they'd laid it in the ground.

Her vision blurred, but she didn't need to read the inscription to know what it said. The lump in her throat choked her and she coughed as the sobs surged. The pain in her chest consumed her from the inside out, burning and cracking like fire. She couldn't breathe. She clawed at the ground, desperate to scream, to be free from the agony suffocating her, but nothing emerged. Pain had carved a home in her.

Eventually, Leo joined her. He didn't speak or try to make it better. Instead, Leo held her close and wept.

CHAPTER 32
CHRISTOPHER

In Perfect Silence with the Stars

Christopher E. Reyes
Beloved Uncle, Treasured Friend
At Rest At Last

CHAPTER 33
NATALIE

Natalie wasn't sure how long they sat by Christopher's grave. The sun shone hot and sticky in a cloudless sky, its rays reflecting off the endless expanse of ocean. At some point, Enzi grew tired of crab chasing and plopped down to nap in the flowers. Gulls circled and cried overhead and an occasional breeze wicked sweat off her neck. The hillside was beautiful and calm. Though Natalie wasn't eager to leave, staying was equally painful.

My fault.

"When?" Leo asked eventually.

"The night after we lost you," Natalie's throat felt. "Amir shot him. Do remember that?"

Leo nodded, transfixed by the gravestone.

"He lost a lot of blood," Natalie explained hoarsely. "A girl and her mom got him to a hospital in Virginia Beach. He survived the surgery, a nurse said he was conscious for a few minutes." She gestured to the grave. "We never got to say goodbye."

"I should have been here."

"There was nothing you could have done." Natalie knotted a blade of grass. "I wasted time dragging him to shore. I should have realized the salinity gradient sooner. He wouldn't have been in Antarctica at all if it wasn't for me."

My fault.

"Amir will die for this," Leo swore. "I promised Lache I'd kill him for what he did the Moirai. I couldn't do it before," he clenched his fists. "Chef, Christopher, Mom, Angie...hell, I have to kill him. He's not going to stop."

Alone, Natalie studied Leo openly. He appeared as tired as she felt. Dark circles underlined his eyes, and his jaw was constantly tight, squared with his resolve.

"Does that make me one of the bad guys?"

The question surprised her. Not because she hadn't wondered it before or because he might be right, but because it simply didn't matter.

"Well, if you are, I am." Natalie shifted to kneel in the grass. "If we ever cross paths again, I'll kill him myself."

Leo huffed out something of a laugh. "And to think I was worried you'd hate me."

"I doubt I could ever hate you," Natalie twirled a meaningless pattern on the polished granite. "I think no matter how hard we try we all do some good and some bad in the end."

"Even Christopher?"

"Especially Christopher." Natalie hugged her backpack as a reflex. The Coelacanth adoption papers remained hidden inside along with her bloodstained books. She changed the subject. "There are a few things we left out at Ancora."

"Because of the Moirai."

"Well, yeah. Sorry," Natalie said, not sorry at all. "We solved Christopher's logic puzzle in Ancora III, and it produced a key. Amir stole it before we figured out what it opens," she took a breath. "Nautilus burned the lighthouse after I found you in Paris."

"I found you in Paris," Leo corrected her. "And it doesn't matter. I'll take the key back as soon as I stop him from breathing."

"I was searching for it when Edwin found me."

"You think it's in the Helix?"

Natalie lifted a shoulder. "Honestly, I have no idea. It seemed like a decent place to start. And when Eleanor said Nautilus is going to do something big at Graduation—"

"Hold on. You *spoke* to Eleanor?"

"Every day for the past two weeks."

"And she didn't recognize you?" Leo gaped at her.

"Not yet," Natalie grimaced. "She's kept busy with Recruitment and Graduation. Regardless, nosing around by myself wasn't smart. I guess losing Ancora III pushed me over the edge. I got impatient. Reckless."

"You?" Leo asked sarcastically. "Never."

Natalie shoved him. "*Anyway,* thankfully Edwin caught me before anyone else did."

"Does 'Follow the Gulls' mean anything to you?"

"No," Natalie replied. "He already asked me. I'm hoping Owen can find something once he's recovered from that head wound."

"Yeah, maybe."

"There's, uh, something else you need to know," she tucked a stray strand of hair behind her ear. "Something happened while you were away." Holding her breath, Natalie realized she'd been dreading this moment since Paris. She couldn't explain how she'd managed to time-travel, nor could she duplicate the experience. Leo was going to have to take her word for it. He was going to have to believe the impossible on only her word. He was going to have to trust her.

Leo leaned back casually in the grass. "If you're happy with Brant then I'm happy for you."

Natalie flushed from her toes to the crown of her head. "I'm sorry, did you say—what?" she bumbled through her shock. "I'm not...we're...no. No."

Leo sat up tall, focused on something behind her. "Someone's here."

A petite figure stumbled up the hillside towards them, her auburn hair whipped by the wind. Enzi sprinted to her and bowed playfully in her path. She rushed past him and Natalie sat up straight. Something was wrong.

"Who is that?" Leo's gun sat ready at his side and Natalie moved it to rest in the wildflowers blooming between them.

"A friend." Hurrying to meet Nora, Natalie slid to a stop ahead of her. Her blood boiled with rage. She wanted to throw something, to break something. She wanted to blow the entire freaking dune skyward.

Two silver pins shone on Nora's jacket.

"When?"

"I didn't have a choice."

"When?" Natalie demanded.

"They took mom four days ago. If I didn't cooperate, they said, they said they'd—"

Natalie didn't make her finish. She could guess the rest.

She had been selfish to ask for help from Nora and Mrs. King. She'd been reckless coming back to Christopher's cottage over and over. She'd been stupid in hoping the ghost of his memory could solve the riddles he had left behind.

My fault.

"Nora." Enzi pushed his head between them. "Do everything they say, you hear me? You follow every order."

"They're going to kill her," Nora whimpered.

"No," Natalie said firmly. "We're going to get you out. Until we can, do what they say, and they won't touch her."

"I can't do what they want," her lip quivered again.

"Then I'll do it."

Nora choked out a small sob. "I can't do it and they're going to kill her!"

"Nora, is it?" Leo stepped in. "You said the Ward has your mom?"

She nodded and Leo threw Natalie a loaded glance. He'd personally been on the wrong side of this deal.

"Are you Leo?" Nora wiped her nose and put her hands on her hips. "Where have you *been*? Do you know what she's done to find you?"

"I found her," Leo corrected. "Tell us what Nautilus wants you to do. We can help."

"You can't."

"Why not?"

Nora stomped her foot and pointed at Natalie. "Because they want me to kill her!"

Natalie tensed. She thought of Leo's bloodthirst for Amir, of her own desperation to find her parents. She couldn't help wondering if the situation were reversed, would she sacrifice Nora to find her family? Only the two scenarios weren't identical. In a scientific comparison, the argument would never hold water.

Nora is innocent. I am not.

"I won't fight you," Natalie said. Anything Nautilus did to Nora and Mrs. King was her fault. She'd dragged them into this.

Nora feebly pulled a bolt from her back and tested its weight. "I can make over a blemish and a bad hair day, no problem. All you need is a good distraction and a quality cover up," she trembled. "I have to fake my way out of this, Nat. I can't kill you."

Leo paced. "Two months ago, the Ward wanted us more than our weight in gold. Wanted us *alive* to be clear. What's changed? What's changed since Antarctica that Nautilus doesn't need us anymore?"

Amir's mad laughter cackled in Natalie's memory. *Now it's too late! Now we don't need you.*

"They have the key."

Leo tossed a pebble back and forth. "A key can't do what we can do. And they no longer have the Moirai Mission to fall back on either. So, what's changed? And how do they expect Nora to kill all of us?"

"No," Nora spoke up. "Just her."

"That doesn't make sense either," Leo frowned.

Natalie shuffled her feet in the dirt. That part actually made plenty of sense.

If I'm not on their side, they want to take out time-travel as an option. Whatever they're planning, they want to make sure it's permanent.

"We have to go," Natalie said aloud. "Come with us."

Nora stood her ground. "My mom's dead if I don't come back. And they'll kill her if I come back empty handed."

"Not if they see you put up a fight." Though the comment was directed at Nora, Natalie felt Leo's attention on her. "It has to be you," he added, tossing her the pebble. He was right, of course. That didn't make it any easier.

"No cover-ups, you hear?" Natalie said pointedly to Nora, clenching her fists in preparation. "You let them see this."

Before she could think better of it, Natalie swung her elbow hard across her friend's face. Nora collapsed on the spot. Blood poured from her nose and her shocked cry turned to a choked gurgle that made Natalie wish she'd skipped breakfast.

"We'll come back for you," Natalie swore.

"No!" Nora rocked on her knees. "Don't come...back." She dripped blood over the white wildflowers, painting them red. "Get out of here."

Without another word, Leo had hold of Natalie's hand and suddenly they were running. Enzi flew ahead of them, a white blur leading them back to the sea. Passing the cottage, Natalie glimpsed Christopher's silhouette in the window. With a brief salute, he dissolved into the shadows.

She tripped on the uneven planks of the dock. Beneath the sheltered boat slip, Leo took hold of Enzi's collar and ran them all straight off the edge and into the water. The familiar tingling sensation spread through her and she leaned into it, desperate to get as far from Nora and Christopher as possible.

Nautilus. Coelacanth. Natalie knew it didn't matter what title she chose or whose uniform she wore; she was a monster in every color.

Liar. Traitor. Coward.

Leo never broke stride as gravity reclaimed her. He half dragged her across the rocky shoreline and into the cedar forest, slowing only once the branches blocked out the sky. Natalie followed Enzi around the curve of Ancora's walls and scanned her palm on the pad.

Inside, they stopped. There was no sign of Owen, Brant, or Tawney, not even the Moirai. Ancora was silent. Leo began to speak, and Natalie hushed him. Adrenaline threaded her pulse, making every motion deafening. Beside her, Enzi's ears perked up and, before she could stop him, he dashed up the stairs and out of sight.

Natalie pulled Chef's bolt from her back and Leo mimicked her, readying his gun. He crept silently up the stairs ahead of her. They had nearly reached the second floor when Tawney shattered the silence.

"You have *got* to be kidding me!"

Natalie pushed past Leo and found her friends standing triumphantly around a single kitchen chair.

"Serves him right," Leo mused, pocketing the pistol.

Natalie slumped against the wall, the fading rush of adrenaline leaving her tired and weak. She dropped her bolt on the counter and poured herself a glass of water.

"Take that, Nautilus!" Tawney shouted proudly from her perch on the kitchen table. "We have our own prisoner!"

While Owen and Brant shared a celebratory fist-bump, Enzi dropped his large front paws on the prisoner's lap and licked his ear.

Tawney pulled him away. "No, Enzi! We do not give prisoners kisses."

"I thought I told you to wait at the Helix?" Leo leaned the prisoner's chair back, amused.

Under the assortment of twine and bedsheets that bound him, Edwin managed to shrug. His black eyes glinted with mischievous satisfaction.

"I've never been particularly fond of following orders."

CHAPTER 34
NATALIE

Edwin smiled. "I'd be happy to explain," he promised. "If you'll call off your hound."

Enzi shamelessly attempted to condense himself onto Edwin's lap and Natalie shoved her fists in her pockets. What was Leo playing at? First, he brings along three strangers and now Edwin, too? Did he want all of Nautilus knocking down their door?

I trusted him too soon.

"Aw, scared of Enzi?" Leo teased.

"What? No, no." He rubbed Enzi's head with his chin. "The pooch is adorable. The girl, on the other hand." Edwin cut a look at Tawney, who blinked innocently.

Enzi put his paws on Edwin's shoulders and the chair tipped backwards to the floor.

"Help. I'm drowning in affection over here."

"He claims to be the one working with Leo. After Ancora III we weren't about to take any chances," Brant explained.

"It was awesome," Tawney said triumphantly. "Owen picked up the plane on Ancora's radar system. He was surrounded before his wheels hit the dirt."

CHYMIST

Natalie soaked in the joy radiating from Tawney. As much as she hated Leo for giving away their location, maybe this was exactly what her friend needed: a victory.

"Guys?" Edwin called again.

Leo tilted the chair back onto its legs. Edwin appeared moderately disappointed when Leo made no move to untie him.

"He is who he says he is," Natalie confirmed. "Everyone, meet Edwin. Edwin, this is Brant, Tawney, and Owen. And you seem to have made quite an impression on Enzi." A creak in the hall reminded Natalie of their other guests. Three ice blue stares fell fearfully on the Nautilus man tied up in the kitchen.

"Hey." Leo coaxed them forward like kittens from a barn. "It's okay. This is Edwin."

Lache gingerly took his hand and Natalie doused the fireball blazing in her belly.

"Edwin, this is Lache, Clo, and Atro," Leo introduced them.

Edwin blanched. "No." He strained against his bonds to better glimpse the Moirai. "No, you're not supposed to be here."

"It was you," Lache stepped closer.

"What are you doing here?" Edwin fussed. "You're supposed to be in—" he growled through gritted teeth. "You're supposed to be *home*!"

Lost, Natalie watched Leo's attention flick from the Moirai, to Edwin, and back again. "You're joking," he begged. "It was *him*?"

"I would recognize his voice anywhere," Atro said.

To everyone's surprise, Clo threw her arms around Edwin's chest, including the chair in her embrace. "Thank you."

He grunted. "Don't thank me yet."

"You rescued them?" Natalie challenged Edwin, making sure she understood what was happening. "Why?"

"They didn't belong there. And they don't belong here."

"You could be a bit more cordial." Tawney kicked his chair.

"Sorry," Edwin backtracked. "So glad to see you are alright."

Quite unfortunate you didn't make it all the way. It's very important though, afraid I must insist: why aren't you," he squirmed, "somewhere else? The note I left specifically told you to ride the ship to the end of the line."

"We did not trust you." Lache said bluntly.

"Ah, well," he relaxed into his bindings. "No helping that I suppose." Enzi draped his front half over Edwin's lap again. "No matter," Edwin went on. "Unlikely they would've let you in without the key anyway."

No one moved.

"What did you say?" Natalie breathed.

"Home. You need the key to get in."

Natalie sank against the chair closest to her. "A key."

"Uh-oh," Tawney whispered.

"Where is 'home' exactly?" Natalie asked. The floor swayed like a boat beneath her. She could feel the stares of her friends and she ignored them. Breathe in, breathe out. It was all she could do to stay standing.

Edwin flinched. "I, uh, can't...can't really say," he shook himself. "Security measure. You've heard of her, no doubt. If Nautilus ever found it...well, war would be the least of our worries."

"We need to know what's at stake, Edwin." Natalie sat across from him, so close their knees brushed. "Tell us where the key goes."

"Would if I could."

Natalie resisted the urge to elbow him as she had Nora. She figured his face was bruised enough from Leo as it was.

"Let's say, hypothetically, Nautilus has this key," Owen pulled at his thickening red beard.

"I don't like this game," Edwin peered at Owen.

"Ditto," Brant picked a loose thread in his cap. "I'd rather be playing Jumanji at this point."

Clo giggled. "You're funny."

"No, he isn't," Tawney scowled. "I'll let it slide this time, you're new here."

"You don't know what a opossum is, but you know about Jumanji?" Leo looked at Clo quizzically. She grinned.

"Okay, folks, can we focus here? Right here, on me." Edwin became as stern as he could while still bound to his chair. "Are you saying Nautilus has *the* key?"

"Maybe," Owen said sheepishly.

"Very possible," Tawney agreed.

"Yeah," Natalie confirmed, not a doubt in her mind. "It was...willed to us."

"Describe it."

"Rustic. Made of hammered metal with a triquetra on the handle and some kind of metallic green chip in the bit."

"Shit." Edwin dropped his head back. "First of all, it isn't rustic, it's a freaking treasure. Second, you're sure Nautilus has it?"

"Uh-huh." Brant bounced one of Clo's eucalyptus fronds and she smacked him off.

Edwin nodded. "I could really go for a smoke right now," he complained.

"Ick!" Tawney scrunched her nose in disgust. Stomping over from the pantry she stuffed a pink taffy into his mouth. "Smoke-free zone," she declared. "Suck on that."

Edwin's shock melted into delight as he chewed. "This is delicious! What is it?"

"What is it?" Tawney shook her curls. "It's salt-water taffy, doofus. What rock have you been living under?"

"Oh, a big one, trust me. May I have another?"

Brant removed Edwin's restraints and offered the entire bag.

"I think our uncle would have liked you," Owen smiled sadly.

"The green one is exquisite!" Edwin marveled as Enzi nuzzled him. He squinted at Natalie, speaking between bouts of chewing. "Are you telling me...you had the key...and you didn't know...where it leads?"

"That about sums it up."

"How is that possible?" he probed.

"I don't know."

"Who are you?"

That's a tricky one, Natalie bit her cheek. If Edwin knew about the key and wherever it went, she guessed he knew a lot more. She couldn't say anything about the adoption in front of her friends, not until they had their parents back. It wasn't her truth to tell.

When it became apparent Natalie wouldn't be answering his question, Edwin moved on. "Well, we're going to need to get that key. Like now. When I tracked Leo's suit here, I noticed something odd on the database."

Natalie's throat closed up. The Moirai all turned to Leo who regarded Edwin as though he had sprouted a second head.

"What?" Edwin unwrapped another taffy.

"Did you say 'tracked'?" Leo pinched his brow.

"Of course." An uncomfortable silence followed, filled by the crinkle of candy wrappers stowed in Edwin's pocket. "There's a tracking unit in the shell of every Nautilus uniform. It's standard issue."

Owen put his glasses on the table and pressed against his eyelids. "They can track any suit?" Leo clarified.

"Of course. How else would they make sure all their members are following orders? The shells have a signaling device, too. You saw it when I called you back to the Helix all those times."

"Who invited this guy again?" Brant sank to the floor with his head between his knees.

Tawney kicked over a chair. "They've known where we are the entire time! The lighthouse, the stupid Helix!"

"Woah! It's okay!" Edwin said. "I don't think they have. Or at least they didn't care. According to the log they've only been tracking senior Legates involved with Graduation. That's what was weird: none of the trackers had been accessed since Paris."

Natalie paced the length of the kitchen. It didn't matter what any log said. Nautilus could locate them any moment they wanted to. So why did they wait until Paris to burn Ancora III? Had they finally accepted she would never join their side? That she would never tack or time-travel for Nautilus?

"Amir Amani found us yesterday," she thought aloud. "We were careful with our...commute," Natalie caught herself. "He must have looked us up in the database."

"Doesn't explain why they waited eight weeks to do it." Tawney said.

"If Legate Amani found you, it wasn't through the database," Edwin argued firmly. "Why would they be monitoring you guys anyway?"

No one answered. Owen became quite captivated by the joints of the table again.

"Because of our parents," Leo offered eventually. "Like I told you before, they're researchers. Very covert stuff. Controversial."

"I guess Nora's disguises really did the trick then," Tawney noted with some surprise.

Natalie chewed her cheek.

Why send Nora after me instead of true Curtanas? Unless it's about more than killing me...unless it's personal.

"So, that's how you found us?" Brant clarified. "Trackers in the uniforms?"

Edwin nodded.

"Leo pinged here a few hours ago. I signed the jet out for a practice flight and sped on over."

"Doesn't the plane have a locator?" Tawney probed.

"A simple magnet causes enough interference to trick that box of bolts."

"Can the suits be disabled?" Owen asked hopefully.

Edwin pulled a metal square from his pocket. "Been jamming the signal since I got here," he frowned. "Which reminds me, I couldn't wait for you to get back; I think we're running out of time.

"The signals from Legates and senior members have gone dark. Nautilus is getting ready. And if they have the key," Edwin opened another piece of candy, "it's going to be one interesting evening."

"I don't get it," Owen pouted.

Edwin pressed his lips together.

Impatient, Natalie pushed on. "What does it matter if the trackers went dark?"

Edwin played with a candy wrapper. "Trackers are never deactivated. If the Legates aren't being detected, it's because the satellites can't pick them up."

"So...?" Tawney made a swirling motion for him to continue, though it was Owen who jumped in.

"So, they're probably in bunkers."

"Bunkers?" Brant managed to sink even lower to the floor. "They really are getting ready for war."

Natalie's heart pounded in her chest. Edwin was right. They were running out of time.

"We have to find out where they're keeping our parents."

Edwin leaned back in his chair with a low whistle. "You've been nosing around the Helix for almost two weeks now. How long does it take to bust out a couple of old folks?"

"Maybe I would have found something if you hadn't tried to knock me senseless," she said sharply.

Edwin sat up straighter. "Are you telling me you don't know *where* they are? Geographically?"

"Why else would we be in the Helix?" Natalie snapped.

He rubbed his chin. "I don't know, to free them, maybe?"

Natalie's mouth dropped open.

"Our parents are in the Helix?" The color drained from Leo's cheeks.

"Are they truly as important as you said they are?"

Natalie and Leo exchanged a glance.

"Then, yeah," Edwin caught the unspoken confirmation between them. "Absolutely."

Natalie didn't know if her heart pounded in anger or relief. She'd been so close the entire time, possibly only rooms away.

"Why didn't you tell me?" Leo raged.

"I didn't know you didn't know!" Edwin surrendered. "It wouldn't have mattered anyway. Security is airtight. You'll need something like Graduation to even stand a chance."

"We have to free our parents," Natalie blurted.

"We need to get that key," Edwin countered.

Natalie ignored him.

"What about two teams?" Leo suggested. "One to get our parents and one to find the key."

"Do you really think Graduation will be a big enough distraction?" Tawney asked skeptically.

"Oh, we really couldn't ask for anything better," Edwin assured her. "It's a ball."

"Not going to be that much fun, mate," Brant mumbled from the floorboards.

"No, a *ball*." Edwin swayed his hips and danced with his bag of sweets. "A masquerade."

"We're going to need one hell of a game plan," Leo noted.

"And some masks."

Everyone in the room turned to stare at Clo.

"We did not come here to simply keep running away," Lache announced. "We are here to break Nautilus down."

"I think I can help with that." Owen's glasses reflected the glow of his laptop. "Well, not the masks."

As everyone crowded around, Edwin squeezed in next to Natalie.

"You're holding out," he whispered.

"Monkey see, monkey do."

"You're going to have to trust me."

Natalie thought of Nora, of her kind mother Mrs. King, suffering because of Nautilus. She thought of Mrs. Merrick, and Chef, and who knew how many others, dead by the Ward's order. She didn't care who Edwin said he was. If he sported a shell on his uniform, nothing else mattered.

"Trust isn't an option."

CHAPTER 35
LEONIDAS

Hours of staring at Owen's computer screen left Leo's eyes itching and his head throbbing. While Brant and Natalie opted to keep studying Owen's mindless maze of maps, Tawney had set out to acquire some masquerade masks. Leo seized his opportunity and slipped out after her. Adrenaline had pooled into his muscles and he was desperate to move, to run.

He hadn't seen the Moirai since dusk. While the plan ensured they would never go back inside the Helix, they would be close. Certainly much closer than the three of them had ever hoped to be again. He was relieved the Moirai didn't appear as he found his way outside; he felt drained enough as it was. However, he wasn't alone. Stepping through the sliding door, a giant mound of fur snuck out behind him.

"Where is your mother?" Leo teased as Enzi circled the clearing, obviously not caring one bit if Natalie approved of a run on bandaged paws. He resembled a pony proudly sporting a new set of shoes. "Alright," Leo conceded. "Don't come whining to me when you get in trouble."

The crisp air pricked his lungs as he jogged the natural paths of the forest. A thick bed of pine needles cushioned his steps and sent Enzi sprawling more than once. It was refreshing to do something other than plan the impossible. Part of him wanted to keep running forever, though it seemed neither fate nor his recovering stamina would allow for that.

Returning to Ancora, he rocked from foot to foot as the scanner assessed his worth and granted him entry. Enzi promptly disappeared and Leo meandered to the seating area, captivated by the inlet beyond the windows. It was the kind of view Uncle Chris would have loved: quiet, starry, and without a soul in sight. He wondered if Christopher had ever stood where he stood now, had ever looked out over the same jagged shoreline, had ever doubted every move that put him there.

Leo caught himself massaging his scar with his palm and stopped. Dwelling on what happened on the cliffside wouldn't change anything, still he wished he'd at least thanked Christopher. Not only for saving their lives, but for every second that came before, even the ones that were hard to take. He wished he could have told his mother how brave she was, how he hoped to make her proud...

Something shifted on one of the couches and Leo reached for his gun.

"Apologies," Lache sniffled, smoothing non-existent wrinkles from her cloak.

"Don't worry about it." Not entirely sure how to proceed, Leo secured the pistol back to his hip. Lache had been a rock of frustration and stubbornness from the second he met her. He'd never entertained the notion she could cry, let alone the possibility he'd ever be tasked with consoling her. "You don't have to go through with any of this."

"Oh, it is not that." A shake of her head sent silver ripples down her hair. "As a Moirai, I only ever wanted to escape Nautilus. Freedom," she huffed. "I never knew exactly what it meant yet I wanted nothing else."

CHYMIST

Leo knew his experience in Nautilus's cells had been a vacation compared to the Moirai's lifetime of torture and seclusion. Still, he could understand her fear. He patted her back in an awkward attempt to reassure her. He wasn't sure why it worked, but it had always seemed to make him feel better when his mother had done it.

"Nautilus won't take you."

"You do not understand. I do not fear them."

He attempted to nod, and she clutched his jaw, holding him still.

"Do not pretend to know what I am saying before I have said it," she scowled. "I do not know what to do, Leonidas. To want anything is dangerous." She leaned in and he could smell the fresh Scottish air still clinging to her skin, the remnants of yet another life she'd left behind.

Her breath caught and her rose lips parted, and he realized then what she was going to do. He had never thought of Lache in this way, and the unexpected play left him frozen. Seconds dragged on and in their brief eternity he diagnosed himself captivated by curiosity, not affection or any of what drew the color to Lache's cheeks. She was hardly an inch away when Leo finally stopped her. He knew he'd let her get too close.

Even before the glass shattered.

Leo leapt up from the couch so fast Lache fell into his vacant seat. Natalie gaped in the hallway with the remnants of a glass cup scattered around her bare feet.

"Natalie," his gut clenched.

At the sound of her name, Natalie busied herself with the broken bits of glass. He rushed to her side. Nothing had truly happened, yet he wanted to apologize, to say it was a misunderstanding, to explain he didn't feel anything for Lache at all. But how could he spout all those things with Lache standing right behind him? And helping Natalie pick up the glass, with her face unreadable and plain, every combination of words terrified him.

"Are you alright?" Lache bent to help.

Natalie fled and Leo didn't waste a second. If she left then, before he could say anything, it would only get worse. He had to fix this now, fast, before she got away.

"Natalie!" He jumped over the glass shards and grabbed her hand. Searing pain shot through his palm and he hissed through his teeth, blood dripping to the floor.

Natalie's collection of broken glass glittered to the floor. "Leo," she gasped.

"It's nothing," Leo hid the cut behind his back, silently begging she'd understand what he truly meant. "Back there, Natalie, that was nothing. It will never be anything."

Lache reappeared and he wanted to swat her away like a fly. She wrapped a cloth over his palm, and he grunted against the pain. He'd grown tired of Lache constantly needing to bandage him.

Without another word, Natalie disappeared down the corridor.

Leo yanked out of Lache's grip and hurried after her. With no luck in the common rooms or her bedroom, he knew it was no use. She wouldn't be found until she wanted to be. His palm stung and he frowned at the blood already seeping through Lache's cloth.

"Want some help?" Brant peeked out of his bedroom.

"Hey," Leo greeted him weakly. "Yeah, I guess so."

Brant whistled. "What'd you do?"

"Something stupid." Leo slid his back down the wall and sat on the floor. His head was spinning in a bad way.

"Woah, alright, hang on. Don't move okay?"

Leo didn't bother to answer. Where would he go? He tapped his head against the wall.

Stupid.

A cold towel draped over his forehead and he heard Brant click open what he could only assume was a Christopher Reyes first-aid tackle box special.

"There's water next to you."

Leo grunted in response. Wincing as the suture needle punctured his skin, he distracted himself with conversation.

"What's the first thing you're going to do when you see your dad?"

"Punch him."

Leo laughed out loud.

"I'm serious. What about you?"

Leo moved the towel onto his neck. It wasn't the first time he'd pondered the question.

"I don't know," he confessed. "Sometimes I want to hit him. After finding out about mom...I think I just want to hug him. I guess we'll find out soon enough."

"Maybe." Brant tied off the last stitch, leaving Leo's palm throbbing. "What happened here?"

"I broke something. Natalie," he cleared his throat. Leo had seen the way Brant looked at her, the way he drew circles on the small of her back. "She saw me drop a glass."

Brant snorted. "Smooth." Closing the tackle box, he pulled his knees up by his chest. "Look man, about that night on the cliff. When you were shot—"

"Don't," Leo cut him off. "That was no one's fault. I'm grateful none of you were hit."

Brant fixated on the wall beside Leo's head. "I'm sorry about your mom."

Leo didn't know what to say. Nearly ten years prior their roles had been reversed. When Brant's mother passed, Leo sat with his friend through the night. There'd been no talking or joking, no pick-up games; they held their vigil until the sun rose. He'd thought he understood what Brant had gone through. He'd been wrong.

"Guys!" Tawney joined them with a bounty of formal contraband. "Check out the awesome masks I—" She spotted the bloodied rag and stopped. "Seriously? I left you guys alone for what, thirty minutes?"

"I'm fine," Leo deflected, reluctant to relive his idiocy. "You bought masks?"

"Sure, I bought them." She tossed him a two-toned silver and black mask, color-blocked right down the center. "Natalie picked this one for you."

Leo frowned at the two-sided implication in his lap.

"I thought you weren't talking to her?" Brant received his own mask from Tawney. It was flat black with swirls of shiny satin that reminded Leo of the scars on the Moirai.

"Silence is counterproductive," Tawney lifted her nose in the air. "I'm more than capable of talking to her and despising her simultaneously."

"I know you're upset about Angie," Leo coaxed. "But you two never fight. She loves you."

"Things change. Get used to it. She's not who she used to be."

Leo shrugged. "None of us are."

"You don't get it. She doesn't *care*," Tawney said. "She doesn't care what we want and isn't there when we need her. She didn't care about Angie. She's a freaking iceberg."

"Wait," Brant cut in. "How come he can talk back without getting his ass handed to him?"

"Come back from the dead after eight weeks and I'll see what kind of deal we can work out." Tawney stuck her tongue out at him.

Leo ran his thumb over the tender line of stitches. If Natalie wasn't opening up to Tawney, then who was she talking to? Brant? The thought made his pulse pound in his ears.

"She'll come around," he distracted himself. "After we get our parents back."

"There's that eternal optimism. Missed that." Tawney skipped away. "Get some rest, boys. This is probably the last nap you'll get before we all die."

CHAPTER 36
LEONIDAS

Despite Tawney's suggestion, Leo couldn't sleep. Frost on the windows blurred the ocean and glacial peaks into a bleak grey puddle. He pulled the covers up to his nose and listened to Brant's snores radiate down the hall. He tossed and turned, and Enzi grumbled at his feet until eventually sulking off, no doubt bound for Natalie's bed.

Leo imagined following him there. He pictured Natalie in his arms, letting the soft rise and fall of her chest lull him to sleep. He ran his fingers through his hair. What was he going to do about her?

"You awake?" Natalie fidgeted in the doorway with Enzi begrudgingly at her side.

Leo sprung upright, his stomach fluttering. "Can't sleep?"

"Only for a few months or so." Natalie closed the door and if Leo hadn't been awake before, he was then. The possibilities of what happened behind a closed door vastly differed from those of an open one. He took care not to move as she lay next to him, fearing any wrong motion might send her away.

"I'm sorry about the glass." Natalie curled on her side and inspected Brant's repair work on his palm. "And Enzi." She dotted the pinpoints left behind by the dog's teeth in Ancora I. "And this…"

He shivered as she traced his scar. "None of that's your fault."

Enzi jumped ungracefully onto the bed to melt in the bend of her knees, his muzzle propped on her hip.

Grappling for something to talk about, Leo clung to the first thought that came to mind. "Owen told me you visit Christopher often, that you talk to him." Leo grimaced. Not his best move.

Natalie stiffened. "I'm not crazy," she whispered.

"Nothing about grieving is crazy."

"I don't go looking for him," she relaxed again. "He's just…there, as puzzling as ever."

"I guess not even death changes that."

Natalie cocked her head. "Kind of a reassuring thought, actually."

Leo wondered what he'd say to Christopher if he could. An apology came to mind, followed by a few dozen questions. Then he thought of his mom. He'd never truly allowed himself to dwell on the fact that his mother was dead. It would have to wait. Yet already her memory blurred, warped through the passage of time, though it still felt as though no time had passed at all.

"Even if we manage to pull this off," Natalie whispered, "even if we do get our parents out of Nautilus, nothing will ever be normal. We'll never be normal."

"You're not wrong." Leo could smell the remnants of the fire in her hair. "But being normal doesn't make you happy. Everyone has to seek out those good moments, to hold onto them. We forget to love what we have."

"I didn't forget." She twisted a corner of the sheets into a knot, the bravery of her mouth falling short of her eyes.

Everything Leo had worked for since he was shot condensed into the span of heartbeats between them. He wanted to tell her she's the reason he survived, that his longing to find her wrenched him from his hospital bed and to his feet. He wanted to tell her the torture of therapy, the harrowing walks around the Moirai's cottage, were all spent chasing her ghost, her fleeting mirage that flirted just out of reach. But he was certain a thousand declarations wouldn't be enough. How could they be?

The grey puddle through the window condensed back into lines and shapes. Filtered moonlight edged the mountain peaks and the entire world appeared stagnant, caught in an infinite twilight. Despite what he saw, Leo knew the dawn would break. It was a certainty he took for granted.

"In Antarctica," Leo spoke slowly, hoping his mouth knew what it was doing. "In Nautilus's holding cells, we didn't see the sun for days."

Natalie nodded, her unblinking stare vacant and miles away.

"Hour after hour ticked by and through the window the clouds faded, the stars turned, but the night never lifted," Leo guided her hand from his scar to his chest. "Not until Paris."

She stilled next to him. Her breath caught and she averted her gaze, so he lifted her chin, pulling her closer until the window was lost to a world of green and amber.

"I could have lived in darkness forever and still never forgotten the sun." He pressed his lips to hers and instead of stepping back, Natalie leaned in.

When they parted, she sank against him. She rested her head on his shoulder and tucked in close. She fit perfectly and he melted into her, pulling her tighter to him. He savored the rise and fall of her chest and the way his arm curved on her back. He ached to kiss her fully, to be lost in her, to abolish any memory of Brant from her being until they were the only two souls in existence. And at the same time, he never wanted their quiet stillness to end.

Leo had no idea how long they laid together. Minutes lapsed into hours and he replayed their brief conversation on a loop. He wanted that forever, whatever it took.

"What happened earlier with Lache, that was nothing. Nothing. Okay?"

Natalie didn't stir. Her breaths had fallen rhythmic and deep. Leo tried his best to stay awake, to drink in every second, but as the first rays of sunlight burned through the morning fog, he couldn't help closing his eyes.

"Hey, man," Brant called a second later. "It's time."

Leo sat up. Alone, dark shadows haunted the room, the sun deep in its descent on the other side of Ancora. Though his body didn't believe it, he'd slept for hours.

Hovering in the doorway, Brant looked sharp in a solid black tuxedo. An identical suit hung on Leo's open door, no doubt a product of Tawney's questionable shopping excursion. The moment his feet hit the floor Brant pulled him into a tight embrace.

"Uh, good evening?"

Brant slapped him hard across the back and stepped away, as goofy as ever. "Just making sure you're really here."

"Want to catch a game after this?"

"Which one?"

"Anything," Leo insisted. "Any sport, any team. We can go watch chess for all I care."

Brant laughed. "Sure thing. If we survive this, we'll catch a chess game."

"Deal."

Leo changed and followed Brant outside. The cut on his palm throbbed against its stitches. He felt like he was entering the locker room before his team took the field. His nerves lit him up.

Upon reaching the beach, Leo's optimism faltered. Natalie paced, her bare feet inches from the waves and a pair of heels dangling from her wrist. Tawney and Owen walked off on their own and their intertwined hands made Leo do a double take. Lache, Atro, and Clo hovered in the tree line while Edwin repeatedly circled the jet, triple-checking the engines and landing gear.

Leo rubbed his scar. How were they going to work as a team when they couldn't even share the same stretch of beach? As Brant marched past the Moirai, Leo ushered them alongside him.

"They do not want us to come," Lache complained.

"Tough luck," Leo said, rougher than intended. He started again, "You have your own part to play. Feeling up to it?"

Despite a unanimous nod, fear radiated from them.

"Our success depends on all of us," he said. "If you don't want to be involved, I need to know right now."

"We are in," Atro assured him.

"Glad to hear it," Leo said truthfully. "Because we need you."

Natalie appeared at his side and an open-back black dress outlined every curve she'd pressed against him that morning. To call it distracting would have been an understatement.

"If you let us down," Natalie spoke with all the warmth of a frozen lake as she strapped a pistol to Lache's waist. "I promise you'll never see morning."

Lache didn't even blink. "You are not strong enough to kill me."

"I didn't say I'd kill you," Natalie frowned. "Imagine what would happen if the Ward discovered their experiment was running free."

Lache paled, something Leo hadn't even believed possible. Her porcelain skin turned nearly translucent in the weak evening sun.

Leo cleared his throat. "We can trust them."

Not acknowledging his comment, Natalie addressed the group. "Should we run it one more time?"

"Please, not again," Tawney muttered.

"I think we're as ready as we're going to be, Nat." Brant traced the length of Natalie's bare spine and Leo clenched his fists. Fresh blood leaked out between his stitches.

Enzi darted his way between the Moirai. He bowed and Clo tentatively tapped his head.

"Come here, you," Natalie called him over and slipped the bandages off his paws. "Not bad." She pressed her temple to his. "Be safe, you hear me?"

Enzi licked her nose.

"All aboard!" Edwin called from his perch on the jet.

"Tacking would have been faster," Tawney noted under her breath.

"We have to keep up appearances," Natalie explained. "Edwin's been helpful, but he's hiding something. I don't trust him."

"So many secrets," Lache sneered.

Leo suspected he'd missed something, but whatever feud brewed between his friends would have to wait. It was game time.

They boarded Edwin's hijacked jet as the setting sun cast burgundy rays behind the rocky isles.

"Red sky at night, sailor's delight." Natalie recited one of Christopher's favorite superstitions. "Looks like we have his blessing." Her expression was hard and determined. "We're going to get them out."

"We are." Leo promised.

As she joined the rest of their crew on the jet, Leo rocked from his heels to his toes. He'd never dreamed they'd be facing Nautilus without Chris. That was never supposed to be the plan.

He would have laughed at me for that, Leo knew. He secured the black and silver mask into place. It itched and cast dark shadows in his peripherals, emphasized by an unanticipated punch in the bicep.

"Hey!"

"Hey yourself!" Tawney spat, her hands on her hips. "I've asked you three times!"

"Asked me what?" Leo rubbed his arm indignantly.

"Are you ready?"

"Oh, yeah, sure." He followed her up the ramp and strapped into one of the leather ceiling-holds.

Edwin sealed the hatch and as Ancora IV disappeared into the forest, Leo suspected he'd never see the sheltered sanctuary again.

I hope you're with us for this one, Chris.

CHAPTER 37
LEONIDAS

Leo bounced his knee impatiently. Five minutes had passed since Natalie and Tawney ventured through the rooftop access of the Helix. He was sick of waiting.

"We won't be undetected up here for long," Leo warned the Moirai. "Defend the jet. If Owen gets interrupted, we'll be stranded."

The three girls nodded and Lache fiddled with the gun Natalie gave her.

"You know how to use it?"

Lache gave him a quizzical look. "Point and shoot."

"That about sums it up," Leo admitted, not at all reassured. "We'll be gone fifteen minutes," he adjusted the collar of his suit. "Twenty tops."

"Leonidas," Clo folded her arms. "Do not make us save your life again."

While Owen and Brant monitored another march of penguin-suited Nautilus members in the solar panel field below, Leo jumped out of the jet and entered the Helix alone. He descended into the Core, casually complementing the attire of his fellow partygoers, and worked through the playbook again. It should only take a few minutes to dismantle Nautilus's operation from the inside out. But the plan required everyone to play their part flawlessly.

That was what worried him.

Entering the party, he couldn't deny the Helix was impressive. Blue and white beacons shone from the foundation and silver balloons cascaded down the walls. A nautilus shell carved from ice stood surrounded by linen-draped tables laden with chocolate, cider, and fine wines. More than once Leo stopped himself from searching the crowd for his friends. After all, getting in wasn't the tricky part of the evening.

It's getting out that might kill us.

On the second-floor balcony, distinguished members gawked over the parade of their success. Legates modeled floor length formal gowns garnished with Prestige pins and peacocked around a grandly vacant mahogany throne.

Guided by a navy-blue carpet, Leo proceeded into the Focus. Previously the training station for new recruits, the disco ball sparkling from the ceiling bordered on bizarre. Leo wasn't sure what he'd expected Graduation to look like, however the prom-like scene before him definitely wasn't it. His high school once attempted to transform their gymnasium into something of a night club to a lackluster effect. In comparison, the Focus was downright impressive. Not to mention the dancing was cleaner.

Much cleaner.

"I was actually starting to miss Formal Friday's before I put on this infernal thing." Tawney passed him a cup of soda. Her red-dyed hair had been pressed straight and pulled into a long ponytail. "Sometimes it seems like they're doing something right beneath all the wrong."

"I don't follow," Leo sipped the cola. He swayed to the tune, grateful for the reassuring pressure of his gun on his hip.

"The dancers," Tawney explained. "Nautilus is their safe haven.

"The Helix is their Ancora."

Leo looked again at the swirling vortex of color on the dance floor. It wasn't merely a mosaic of gowns and masks, but of humanity. On the surface it appeared Nautilus managed to undermine prejudice itself, uniting strangers through the common goal of peace. It was a beautiful lie. Nautilus hadn't eliminated any boundaries between people.

They've only rearranged them.

"Why does the good have to go, too?"

"Because it isn't real."

"I know," Tawney snapped, then sighed. "I know. What if people aren't capable of peace?"

Leo marked the Ward's empty throne. "Every day we choose whether to celebrate or scrutinize our differences. Nautilus showed these people peace is possible. After they see the truth behind the Ward's actions, they could still choose peace on their own terms. But as long as Nautilus stands, they'll never have that chance."

"On that note," Tawney offered her glass. "Let's burn it down. For Christopher."

"For Christopher," Leo tapped his cup to hers. *And Mom.*

She winked at him. "Go get 'em, *Lev.*"

Tawney hip checked him, making Leo stumble and spill his drink on the person standing behind him. He spun, grabbing for the woman to try and keep them both from falling. In the end, it was her stability that saved them.

"I'm sorry," Leo blurted. "Are you okay?"

"She packs a mighty punch for a tiny package."

"Natalie," Leo breathed, both relieved and alarmed he'd barely recognized her. "Dance?"

"Not yet." She wiped soda off his tuxedo. "Security is heavy."

"We knew we'd need a distraction." Leo examined his empty cup. The adrenaline of their heist and the anxiety of being so close to her spun a nauseating concoction.

"Think he's up for it?"

"I know I've missed a lot, but that's a joke, right?"

"Yes," Natalie discarded his empty cup. "It's a joke."

The music stopped and a spotlight illuminated Legate Shaye on the balcony. With political decorum, she lifted a tall glass of champagne and a minor flicker rippled through her body as she began her speech. Natalie gripped his arm; she had seen it, too.

"She isn't here."

"Maybe she'll do a grand entrance," Leo whispered back. "Maybe she'll come out with the Ward." He fed the false hope to her as much as himself.

Perhaps it's for the best. One less obstacle between us and our parents.

Yet his skin prickled with unease. If Nautilus planned on making its move at Graduation, why wasn't one of their highest-ranking officials there to orchestrate it?

"Welcome," Legate Shaye addressed the crowd. "Brothers and Sisters, Legates, Curtanas, Doves, and Artisans all. Welcome to our Graduation Gala to celebrate our newest members!"

Deafening applause answered her. Though her words projected all around the Helix, members abandoned their spots in the buffet line to better glimpse Shaye's image.

"Though we miss our Ward in our celebrations," a collective slump of disappointment passed through the audience, "his absence is not for nothing. By sacrificing an evening of delight, the Ward will bring us into a new age. Tonight, the Ward ignites our path to peace!"

Beside him, Natalie tensed as the hall erupted with cheers. Legate Shaye paused before raising a holographic hand for silence.

"Let us take this time to honor the newest members of our society. First, the Doves, who spread our message for peace and prosperity." Legate Shaye proceeded to read off a list of names, none of which Leo recognized. As they were called, recruits made their way to stand together at the center of the Focus. A senior member moved swiftly among them, fastening a new Prestige to their formal wear. "Congratulations and welcome home. May you serve Nautilus well. Peace be with you."

"And with you," the new Doves cooed, dispersing into the crowd as Shaye proceeded to the Artisan inductees. Again, there were no names Leo recognized, though a familiar gangly figure caught his attention.

"Thomas," Natalie repeated Owen's alias. "And Patricia and Bobby."

"For Robert," Leo's chest swelled with pride at the sound of their parents' names. It felt right.

It felt mutinous.

"Our newest Artisans will bring us ingenuity. Peace be with you," Shaye dismissed them. "Let us now honor our inducted Curtanas, who will serve to protect our peace from threats and untruths."

Tawney and Brant joined the large group gathered beneath the balcony. Leo wasn't surprised the Curtanas were by far Nautilus's largest Chamber. Despite their constant call for peace, he had witnessed more of Nautilus's violence than anything else.

"Peace is not given," Shaye prompted.

"It is taken!" the Curtanas answered.

"And we would be nothing," Legate Shaye continued, feeding off the energy of the crowd at her holographic feet. "Without our leaders, our mentors and trainers. Let us honor the Legates!"

After 'Raven' was announced, Natalie swiftly left his side. She strode to the center of the room with three men and a tiny figure in an orange dress. To his horror, Eleanor climbed up the stage behind them. She hugged Natalie tight before personally pinning a new Prestige to her dress.

Cold sweat beaded on Leo's neck and he pushed his way to the front of the crowd as Natalie hurried back to him.

"That's— she's—"

Natalie hushed him, focused on Legate Shaye's speech. She

preached about working together, Chamber with Chamber, to accomplish their goals.

"They made you a Legate?" Leo clarified. "Correction, *Eleanor* made you a Legate?"

Natalie nodded, watching Shaye.

Leo scratched his chin. "It's almost cruel. If it wasn't for Graduation, you could have found out everything. All we needed was more time."

"It is cruel," Natalie agreed. "Especially for someone who can theoretically time-travel."

Though he knew he'd misheard her, Leo had no idea what she could have meant instead. As Shaye's speech ended, his attention was drawn back to the play at hand. Edwin already loitered near the violinist.

"Tonight, we will rise, and the day will break on our achievements." Legate Shaye skillfully wound up for a finale. "Tonight, tyrants and dictators and nations will fall, and we will rise. Tonight, the Ward's promise will come to fruition, and from it *we will rise*!

"Nautilus will unite our world as one people: one for peace, one for prosperity, one for all! Eat and dance and celebrate the new age that is coming, for tomorrow begins our fight!"

Nautilus members screamed and cheered and many even cried. As Shaye vacated her podium, the band kicked up and their audience danced with renewed vigor.

"Now?" Leo asked.

"Now." Natalie was smooth as water as she pulled him onto the dancefloor.

They had moments at most, and Leo wasn't about to waste them.

"My lead then." Leo supported her waist and her breath on his neck inspired goosebumps when he dipped her.

She smacked his wrist. "No nonsense!"

"Perfect time for nonsense." He spun her, fully aware her fingers slipped between his own. "Have you had any fun while I've been gone?" Leo pushed her away before sharply pulling her back against him, his grip tight on her hips.

She smiled.

"I thought not. You don't have to spend every moment preparing for the next disaster. This one can be ours."

She stopped him and he traced the line of her jaw with his thumbs. He wanted to kiss her again. It might be his only opportunity before their plan pulled them apart.

"You're wrong," she whispered. "Alone, together, asleep; I live and breathe in terror. It keeps me alive. It keeps them alive."

Before Leo could respond, Brant interrupted, and Natalie fixed her expression as he dropped to one knee. Leo's insides felt like concrete. He shook Brant's hand emphatically, wanting to crush him. Instead, a metal square passed between them, calibrated by Owen moments before.

Game on. Holding the button tight in his fist, Leo made his way to the back of the room.

"Ladies and gentlemen!" Edwin boomed into a microphone. "We have a proposal!"

The Focus jittered with excitement. Bodies crowded him as Leo weaved against them, forcing his way towards the grand staircase. He passed a few stray guests, all too intoxicated to care. When he reached the spiral stairwell, Tawney was already waiting.

"Have I mentioned how grateful I am to be running to my death with you instead of Brant?"

"Only six or seven times." Leo didn't slow as she fell in step beside him.

Shell-shaped lanterns illuminated their descent while Owen's instructions replayed in his mind. According to Edwin, Nautilus's computer servers were housed in the depths of the Helix. If Owen's plan was going to work, Leo needed to go as deep as he dared while still sparing enough time to escape.

It was going to be a race.

"Here." Stopping, he envisioned the play. He imagined Edwin already slinking towards the roof while Brant and Natalie shared a celebratory spotlight dance, holding the attention of the crowd as long as they could. Leo stretched the space between his ribs.

Painless.

"Last one to the top does the dishes for a month." Tawney assumed a runner's stance, barefoot with a shoe in each fist. They shook.

"And the grocery shopping."

"Oh, it is so *on*." She deepened her lunge.

Owen calculated it would take Nautilus four minutes to recover from the electromagnetic pulse. That gave him and Tawney two hundred and forty seconds to free their parents, Natalie and Brant two hundred and forty seconds to steal the key, and Edwin and Owen two hundred and forty seconds to reboot the jet.

Leo pressed the button and darkness enveloped them.

Two thirty-nine.

Leo began to sprint.

CHAPTER 38
NATALIE

Natalie froze as the masquerade ball dropped into darkness.
Four minutes.
Panic gripped the gala. Occasional, isolated blackouts were common in the Helix. Complete darkness was not. Natalie couldn't see her hand in front of her face.

She ran anyway.

With Brant in tow, Natalie sprinted off the dance floor. Haunting memories of Antarctica's black tunnels threatened to slow her pace and she forced them out of her mind. Instead of fumbling for a way out, Natalie pushed herself deeper. She wasn't running away this time.

Natalie subdued the lump in her throat as she started up the stairs. Every cell in her body screamed to turn around, to go down through the passage beneath the balcony, past where Edwin had caught her to where he claimed Nautilus held their high-level prisoners. Instead, she continued to climb.

As though hearing her thoughts, Brant shifted to run alongside her. "Tawney and Leo will find them. We need to focus on the key."

After losing Leo and Christopher's death, it felt wrong to put anything before her family. The thought alone made her heart sick with anxiety. She knew Edwin was right before: Nautilus shouldn't be left with Christopher's key, no matter what it led to. And protecting what he'd died for was the least she could do, but if she failed her parents in the process...

"Here." Brant diverted her path.

With every corner drenched in shadow, Natalie had no idea if she'd entered a ballroom or a coffin. Imaginary shapes stalked her vision and she blinked them away. Every step carried the possibility of Nautilus's silver grip closing around her neck.

It's only the Helix. I know these monsters and—

A door slammed.

"Damn flashlights won't even work!"

Natalie stopped. A sharp crack made her jump, followed by the rhythmic sloshing of fluid. She knew that noise. As children, Uncle Chris had let her and Tawney string up his boat radioactive-green on clear summer nights.

Glowsticks.

The blue light filtered down the hall and Natalie fruitlessly scanned the dark for somewhere darker to hide. She could already make out the Nautilus member's frustrated frown. The moment he turned around they'd be caught. Their heist was over.

Brant shoved her against the wall, forcing the air from her lungs. Before she could protest, he knotted her hair, and his mouth explored her neck.

"What are you *doing*?" She squirmed beneath him.

"Saving our asses." He planted an orchard of kisses towards her collarbone.

"But we—" His kiss silenced her. It was awkward and rough, and she cringed against it. He wasn't a bad kisser, he just felt...wrong. She closed when he opened. He turned when she didn't. Natalie squeezed her eyes shut and waited for it to be over.

"Oy!"

Brant pulled away. Natalie flushed a thousand shades of red as the man raised his glowstick to look them over.

"Get a room," he grumbled and marched past them.

"See," Brant sank against the wall beside her. "Just a couple of randy teens."

Natalie wasn't listening. The encounter had cost precious seconds, and in her panic, she'd lost count of exactly how much time they had left.

Tick-tock.

"Let's go." She pulled him to the door the guard emerged from and fumbled with the scanner. No lights, no beeping. It appeared as dead as Owen promised it would be.

Please open. Natalie turned the handle and the metal clicked. She was in.

Beyond the doorway the same white-blue light of the guard's glowstick threw imposing shadows against the walls. Black computer screens marked desks like tombstones. Whiteboards filled with equations and formulas formed a semi-circle around a giant metal plate.

"Edwin thought the key would be here?" Brant asked.

Natalie inspected the metal square of floor. It was wider than she was tall, and more wires than she could count wound their way below it. Clumps of debris littered its surface. She kicked a mound with her shoe.

Rocks?

The chunks of gravel became smaller and finer until they disintegrated into sand in the center of the platform. Crouching, she sifted through the fine bronze-gold substance.

It's not sand... Natalie sat on her heels. She knew then why Christopher left her Boyle's book. She knew what caused the blackout the day Eleanor told her to deal with her demons.

"What's that?"

"It's aurichalcum." Even in the low light Natalie was certain the powder was composed of the exact same metal that made up their sparks. She examined the room again. Wide partitions functioned as shields to protect any scientists cowered behind them. And the metal platform was powered by electricity. A lot of electricity.

Enough to alter chemical composition?

"What are you saying?" Brant let out a nervous chuckle. "Nautilus *made* aurichalcum? Seems a little advanced, don't you think?"

"It's not advanced," Natalie stuffed the pockets of her dress with the powder. "I mean it is, but it's old. Pre-Scientific Revolution. They're changing random rock to aurichalcum. It's not chemistry." Her mind jumped to the jet where her backpack waited with Owen. "It's alchemy." What else had she missed?

"What about the key?" Brant spun in a small circle. "Edwin said the key would be in a safe. I don't see one. Do you?"

"No." Natalie stood and wiped her palms clean.

"What do we do now?"

Natalie was shocked he even asked. "We help Leo and Tawney find our parents."

Panicked shouts from the masquerade guided them back to the Focus. A toxic luminosity welcomed them as nearly every guest radiating with a glowstick or two. Despite Legate Shaye's efforts to make herself heard over the noise, Natalie only caught a few words before they hurried beneath the second-floor balcony.

"Nat?"

"What?" She could feel Brant fidgeting beside her as she fumbled blindly for the seam.

"Maybe we should talk about this."

The panel stood ajar when Natalie found it. Her skull throbbed at the memory of her last journey inside. As far as Brant's reservations were concerned, there was nothing to talk about. She was freeing their parents one way or another.

"I'll meet you on the plane."

"No, Nat, I—"

She didn't wait to hear him out. And though she was pleased to hear his footsteps following her, she couldn't slow for him to catch up. Every breath made her feel lighter. She hadn't gotten into this mess because Christopher wanted to play treasure hunt with some key. She'd left home to find her family.

So that's exactly what she would do.

Natalie burst through the door at the end of the hall and a weak cough stopped her in her tracks. She whipped her bolt from its holster on her thigh. Ten seconds passed without a sound.

Ten priceless seconds.

Tick-tock.

I don't have time for this.

"Mom?" Natalie called boldly. "Dad?"

A sharp crack resonated, and light expanded beneath the floor tiles. It spread like a river, illuminating the ghostly gates of at least twenty empty glass cells. Disheveled cots and soiled clothes were all that remained.

"Tawney and Leo must have already helped them escape!" Brant said happily.

Natalie might have believed him, if not for the wavering voice in the darkness.

"I had hoped for peace for you, child."

CHAPTER 39
NATALIE

Eleanor bowed her head. "Miss Morrigan."

Natalie winced. "How long have you known?"

"Since before the beginning," Eleanor confessed in a sigh. "I authorized your invitations."

Before the beginning.

Natalie's knees threatened to give out. She thought they'd been clever. She thought she'd slipped in undetected. She'd thought...well, it didn't matter what she'd thought. She had played right into Nautilus's silver-plated scheme.

"Where are they?" Natalie brushed away angry tears. If her parents weren't there, if they were gone...

"I told the Ward you had come home," Eleanor's wrinkles deepened. "I disputed your capture. I convinced them you *needed* us. They were right, though. The Ward is always right. You resist your own peace."

"Where are my parents?" Natalie nearly screamed at her.

Eleanor didn't answer, lost in the swirling glow of the floor. "I risked the fate of our cause."

A pang of sympathy rocked her. She should hate Eleanor. She *did* hate Eleanor. And yet the woman seemed so small.

"We need to go," Brant urged.

"No," Natalie brushed him away. "She knows where they are, don't you?"

"Who is it you search for, dearie?" Eleanor shuffled towards her.

Natalie held her ground, a feat only possible by the fact the old woman appeared unarmed, and her own legs had turned to jelly. "Mr. and Mrs. John and Mary Morrigan? Or Benjamin Shepard and Madison Finch?"

Natalie clenched her fists.

"What is she talking about?" Brant paused his efforts to leave.

"Nothing."

Eleanor's sorrowful frown morphed into a twisted, confused pout. "Brant, do you not know? Your parents aren't your own. You and your friends...your lineage is unclear. Testing at the Antarctic Center confirmed that much at least."

Brant looked from Eleanor to Natalie, shaking his mop of curls. "You're lying."

Natalie stayed silent.

"It's not true," Brant shouted. "My mom...my mom died and my dad...if they aren't my parents..." He crouched and dropped his head between his knees, cradling his mop of brown hair.

Natalie empathized. Unfortunately, she didn't have time for him to play catch up. "Where are they, Eleanor?"

"They aren't here," Eleanor gestured to the empty cells. "They'll ignite the final act to join nations in Nautilus's reign of peace. I envy their sacrifice," she nodded, "and pity them for they will not live to see our glory."

Natalie wanted to scream. She was in the wrong place. Turning to leave, she'd never know if it was mercy or fear that stalled her. The swirling blue river of light beneath their feet underlined Eleanor's frailty. Natalie had no doubt the Legate would be punished for her failures, and she suspected banishment would prove inadequate.

My fault.

She strapped Chef's bolt to her thigh and her own words shocked her. "You don't have to die here."

Eleanor smiled sadly. "I won't run from my demons, dearie," she said. "I still carry hope for you."

Natalie knew the burden of hope, its expectations, its iron anchor constantly pulling her under.

So many weeks treading water, Natalie thought bitterly, *only to arrive at an empty cell.*

"The Ward is lying to you."

"No," Eleanor shook her head. "The Ward cares for us. He understands people. He understands our suffering. He understands the path to peace isn't always peaceful."

"Nat," Brant yanked her firmly. "We're out of time."

Natalie retreated. Knowing there was no way to save her, to make her see things clearly, she offered Eleanor the only comfort she could. "Peace be with you," Natalie said weakly.

"And with you, dearie."

"I don't believe it," Brant mumbled a moment later. They navigated the dark halls back up to the sliding panel beneath the balcony. "I won't believe it."

"I have proof." Natalie was thankful she couldn't see him.

"Proof?"

"Documents."

"How long have you known?"

She quickened her pace.

"How long, Nat?"

Not now. We have to get to our—

Brant pinned her against the wall, locking her arms by her sides. "How long?"

"Weeks."

"Does anyone else know?"

"No," Natalie answered, exasperated. "What was I supposed to say, Brant?"

"You could have started with the truth."

"It doesn't change anything!"

"It changes everything, Nat! Everything!" He dug painfully into her singed skin and a whimper of discomfort escaped her. He didn't let go. Instead, he gripped her tighter. She felt every shaky breath he drew in and let out. "I have to tell you something."

"Once we get outside—"

"No," his lips brushed her collarbone. "I have to tell you now, before—"

Brant was gone. Natalie shrank to the floor in his absence. She pushed herself against the wall as a sharp yelp sounded near her, followed by a deep grunt.

"You can let me up, Tawney."

"Oops. How'd you know it was me?"

"Guess there's something special about the way you flatten me into the dirt."

Natalie relaxed and reached into the dark. Tawney found her first and gave her a quick hug.

"You okay?" Tawney asked. Though it wasn't exactly friendly, it wasn't *not* friendly, which was more than Natalie could ask for.

"They aren't here."

"We know," Leo sounded somewhere above her. "Get the key?"

"Not exactly," Brant said gruffly. "And our parents—"

"Aren't here." Natalie cut in. "We need to move." She set off towards the Focus, dragging the closest body along in her wake and all the while grappling with the fact Nautilus had been on them from the start.

Does all of Nautilus know? Or only Eleanor and the Ward? What about Legate Shaye? And Max?

"If our parents aren't here, how are we supposed to find them?" Tawney stomped in tow.

No one answered because no one knew. Natalie threw open the

panel at the end of the passage. She could hear Legate Shaye speaking again and a larger hologram lit up the center of the stage. Before Natalie could make sense of what she was seeing, Brant turned her towards him.

"Natalie."

He had her full attention. He never called her by her full name and the more she studied him the more concerned she became. His brown eyes flitted nervously away from her and his jaw worked as though uncertain how to form the words.

Natalie tried to back away. *He's determined to do this now? Here?*

"Natalie, I'm in—"

"I'm not," she blurted before he could finish.

Brant's expression clouded over, and he drew back, hiding his hands in his pockets.

"I'm sorry." Natalie hugged her stomach. "What you're feeling...I'm not."

Brant gave her a strange look and her gut wrenched.

"Nat."

"I'm sorry, I truly am, only—"

"Nat, look."

In the Focus, hundreds of Graduation guests clustered beneath a projection floating near the ceiling. Flecks of light bounced and flashed as the disco ball began to turn.

"This isn't right," she muttered, fiddling with the hem of her dress. "Owen said we would have four minutes."

"Owen said we *should* have four minutes," Leo clarified.

Legate Shaye's projection spoke again. "Tonight, Nautilus will take the old regime out of existence! Even a reluctant warrior cannot ignore an attack on their own soil. Our Ward will lead us from purgatory to peace."

Natalie skirted around the back of the crowd to better view the image. It was fuzzy and flickered, offering mere flashes of clarity. It was enough.

"It's them," Natalie pushed closer. The background was a haze, offering no clues to their whereabouts. Only the rectangular bundles they carried were clear. Back and forth, in and out of frame, to and from the pile of grey bricks, stacking them higher.

"This is what happens when disorder is left unchecked," Legate Shaye warned darkly. "The hostage scientists were abandoned by their country to suffer their violent end. No peace was left for them. Their only option? To join with those who brought them violence. To turn against those who abandoned them."

"This isn't real," Natalie's reality frayed.

"These poor souls will take the only route left to them," Shaye went on. "They seek to burn monuments to tip the world to war. But do not fear, my brothers and sisters. Nautilus will confront their chaos with peace! This is our time! This is how the world will see us!"

"Our parents would never do this," Leo seethed. "And since when is Nautilus the one stopping the bombings?"

"You're right," Natalie's thoughts raced. "This is how the world will see us," she repeated.

"It's like the festival," Tawney crossed her arms. "The people don't know that *is* Nautilus. But why feed their own followers this propaganda?"

"Because it's not only Nautilus seeing this." Brant thumbed towards the red banner along the bottom of the screen that read *Breaking News*. "The world is watching."

Then the image changed.

Two parallel lines of yellow orbs snaked across a black background. As the camera panned closer, dark waves filtered into focus. The orbs condensed into streetlights, cutting a familiar arc into the darkness.

Natalie reached for Leo as he reached for her.

"Follow the gulls," they said together.

"No!" Tawney inserted herself between them. "They can't!"

They'll ignite the final act to join nations in Nautilus's reign of peace. Eleanor's words resurfaced. *I envy their sacrifice.*

Natalie shoved her way out of the crowd.

"What?" Brant slid behind her. "What is it?"

"Follow the Gulls! The Ward's going to blow up the Chesapeake Bay Bridge-Tunnel," she growled between breaths. "And they're all going to bloody watch."

CHAPTER 40
NATALIE

The words were hardly out of Natalie's mouth when gunshots echoed through the Helix.

Brant tackled her to the ground and her chin bounced off the tile floor. People screamed. She tasted blood. Whatever order Legate Shaye managed to recover after the blackout shattered.

"I don't see a shooter!" Leo struggled to cover Tawney, who fought tooth and nail beneath him.

Shots echoed again. Natalie had been in a firefight more than once and the shots sounded almost...muffled?

"Because they aren't here!" Tawney rose indignantly.

"The roof." Natalie took off again.

The roof was supposed to be safe.

The roof was supposed to be their escape.

She took the stairs two or three at a time. The roof access door swung in the breeze and moonbeams bounced in, outlining a sturdy silhouette topped with a toxic green up-do.

"*You,*" Max snarled.

Natalie stopped the procession behind her. "Let us go, Max." Another shot echoed from outside, making Natalie jump.

"I knew you weren't here for peace." Max spun her bolt to sparking.

Natalie squared her stance. If Max wanted a real fight, she would get one. Leo tried to shelter her behind him and though she would have resisted, she didn't have to. Tawney held him back.

"Trust me," Tawney said, "this is a long overdue."

Max closed the distance between them with swift steps. Her frustration glistened on her forehead and reverberated in the sharp pant of her breath.

Good. Natalie stepped to the side, drawing Max away from her friends. *Get angry, Maxine. Make a mistake.*

"Natalie," Leo pushed against Tawney.

Natalie pulled Chef's bolt from its holster and held it lightly with nimble fingers.

Mere paces away, Max bared her teeth. "They chose *you* over me. They'll see who's better now. They'll see who should truly be a Legate."

Max swung her bolt and Natalie rolled, the movement more awkward in her dress than during Tawney's sparing lessons. Max screamed and swung again, and Natalie saw sparks. She jumped back, blinking. Fear doused her like cold water.

Max aimed to kill.

"We don't have to do this." Natalie waited for the turn of the girl's elbow or tilt of her hip. She watched for any sign of where Max would swing next.

Leo broke past Tawney, and she dove for his legs, bringing them both down.

Distracted, Natalie reacted a second too late. With a guttural cry, Max swung for her. Natalie blocked and the momentum sent her toppling with Max on top of her. Everything was a blur. Green hair, navy dress, the sting of deadly electricity thrumming inches from her skin.

It lit her up.

Natalie kicked Max's bolt away and pushed into their tumbling to pin her.

"Yes!" Tawney boasted as Natalie knelt on Max's chest.

"We're leaving," Natalie informed Max. "If you want to live, stay down."

Max's smirk gave her pause. Before she could piece together what the dragonette was thinking, Max stole Natalie's pistol from the strap on her thigh.

They sat frozen. The barrel was so close, the cool metal radiated against Natalie's forehead. It was Christopher's gun.

Natalie wondered if he would be proud of what was about to happen.

"Surrender," Natalie advised softly.

Max sneered. "Find peace in your grave."

Natalie doubted anyone else saw Max pull the thin curve of the trigger. And she was certain the faint click of the empty barrel fell silent to all except the two of them. So, the confusion that rippled across Max's face was a pleasure reserved solely for Natalie.

"Perhaps one day I will." Natalie slipped her unloaded gun from Max's hold. "Nautilus isn't what you think it is."

"Oh, *shut up*." Max attempted to start punching again and Natalie did the only thing she could.

She knocked her out.

"Who taught you to get disarmed so easily?" Tawney critiqued disapprovingly as Natalie left Max snoring on the floor.

"I couldn't have helped you," Leo interrupted. "I didn't have a clear shot."

"I was fine."

"Uh," Brant cleared his throat. "Hello there."

A petite figure in an orange cocktail dress stood over Max, an inactive bolt held loosely at her side. The girl watched her with round eyes and Natalie did the only thing she could. She lifted her hands in surrender.

"Nat," Tawney warned.

"I won't fight her," Natalie vowed. To the girl she added, "I'm not going to fight you, Ignis."

Ignis approached cautiously, looking over each of them. Natalie fumbled for some sort of diversion, something that would make her look the other way.

"I can explain."

Ignis jerked her chin towards the roof, swishing her black braid. "You should hurry."

Natalie could hardly believe it. "You're not with Nautilus?"

Ignis swished her braid again.

"Come with me."

"I can't," she tapped her bolt on the floor. "My mum and pop burned to get me across the border. They gave everything so I would have a better life."

"I know they paint a pretty picture, Ignis, but you have to believe me: Nautilus is *not* a better life," Natalie implored her.

"You do not understand."

"Don't give up your life for this, kid," Tawney stepped in.

Ignis's expression was set. "The guards who watched my family die," she lifted one bronze shoulder, "they had shells on their uniforms."

Natalie's gut twisted with rage and she hugged Ignis against her. The girl no longer felt as frail as she appeared. "We'll stop them."

"Get out of here," she insisted.

Natalie held Ignis out to look at her. "My friend Nora King has been taken, along with her mother. Can you find them for me? Get them out?"

"I'll try," Ignis promised. "Go."

Still, she had to know how Ignis would avoid the Ward's wrath in aiding their escape. "What will you tell them?"

To her surprise, the corners of Ignis's mouth turned up. "That a raven has left their castle."

Leo dragged Natalie so swiftly to the door she barely managed to say goodbye. On the roof, two Curtanas lay bleeding and whimpering. Natalie didn't let herself look too closely as she sprinted past and leapt inside the jet.

"Anything else?" Edwin sealed the door and returned to the cockpit. "A spot of tea? Catch up with more friends perhaps?"

"Get us the hell out of here." Tawney fastened her seatbelt.

Natalie collapsed into the first seat she reached. Enzi pounced on her, nuzzling his head up under her arms, and she obliged, scratching him without having to think about it.

"I see you're as stubborn as I left you," Leo grumbled. "That was reckless, Natalie."

She wanted to snap back a snide comment. Sheer exhaustion stole her words.

"I don't see anyone new with you," Edwin noted. "Did we get anything we came for?"

"Nothing and more," Brant cut a look at Natalie.

"Edwin," she called to the cockpit as they rose vertically into the cloud cover. "Go North."

"Where to?"

"The Chesapeake Bay Bridge-Tunnel," Leo answered. "Follow the gulls."

"Come again?" Edwin flipped various switches on the dash.

"It's road signs," Tawney explained wearily. "Follow those signs anywhere in Hampton Roads and you'll reach the Bay Bridge-Tunnel."

"Local slang?"

"I guess it is." Natalie didn't like the idea of Nautilus drawing any inspiration from her hometown. It made the Ward's intentions feel less focused on global tensions and more personal.

As though the attack was made for them.

"Well, that's a sure-fire way to bring America to war." Candy wrappers overflowed from Edwin's suit pockets as he worked. "Not the biggest target they could have aimed for, but also less protected. The Ward's a lot of things; stupid isn't one of them."

"Yeah, woo-hoo for them." Owen unzipped several nested black bags, exposing a laptop.

Brant paced the narrow aisle. "How are we going to stop them from blowing up a freaking *bridge*?"

"Tell your pessimism to shut its pie-hole," Tawney turned her attention to Owen. "Did your falafel bags work?"

"Faraday," he corrected.

"Semantics."

"Oh, big word," Brant teased. Tawney tripped him.

Owen ignored the spat and connected his computer to the jet's control panel through a series of cables. "The bags should have saved my computer from the effects of the EMP. It'll stand in for the operating system. All the jet's mechanics should maintain functionality, provided my laptop can instruct them what to do."

"That's a big 'if' to save right for the end, nerd," Brant frowned.

"You took out the Curtanas on the roof." Leo patted Lache's back and Natalie forced herself to look away.

"I did not kill them," Lache's tone bordered on disappointed.

Seconds stretched painfully long as Owen worked. In the brief silence, Tawney's stomach grumbled.

"I should have eaten at the party."

"We have snacks on the jet," Brant assured her.

"Really?"

"No."

"I hate you." Tawney sulked in her seat.

Natalie bit her lip. She wanted to make Owen work faster, to remind him their parents were waiting. She managed to hold her tongue.

Edwin didn't. "I need some direction, man."

Owen slammed against the keyboard. "We're going north, aren't we?" he snapped. "Keep the ocean on your right and don't hit anything."

"Huh," Edwin smirked. "Simple. Logical. I like it. It'll slow us down, but work with what you've got, eh?"

Natalie shifted in her seat. '*Reckless*,' Leo had called her.

I'll show you reckless.

She moved her gun to her waist and fastened Chef's bolt down her thigh. "Get us over water."

"What are you doing?" Brant tensed.

"Whatever it takes."

"Hell yes, you are," Tawney leaned across Leo and gave her a high-five. "Let's blow this popsicle stand."

"Are we sure about this?" Owen flashed an uncertain glance in Edwin's direction.

"Not at all. Lower," she directed to Edwin.

"Any lower and we'll be in the drink."

"Exactly."

"Is this even possible?" Atro questioned.

Natalie didn't bother answering. She pulled open the hatch and the wind whipped her hair as the jet hovered precariously close to the ocean's surface. Kicking out the rope ladder bolted to the floor, she lowered herself outside. Ocean spray flecked silver on her skin, stinging the burns that had yet to heal.

She had never tacked anything so large before. Alive and inanimate objects alike never had an issue following her through the light and static, but this was a *plane*. This was over a hundred thousand pounds of baggage. Afraid to let herself think on it any longer, Natalie teetered on the last rung of the ladder.

She thrust her hand into the oncoming wave.

The familiar tingling of tacking washed over her. Static shot through her body, charging every cell. Picturing the mouth of the Chesapeake Bay, and the cut of Virginia's coast, the light rushed in and swept her away. Natalie fell back through gravity's net and the light swiftly receded. Before she heard the waves crashing on the beach, before she felt the continued hum of the jet, Enzi's ecstatic barking fell on her ears.

The plane listed roughly, nearly throwing Natalie into the sea. She grappled with the ladder, painstakingly climbing her way back up. Crawling inside, she looked up the barrel of Edwin's gun.

"Who are you?"

CHAPTER 41
NATALIE

He won't shoot you.

"I'm really sick of guns in my face, Edwin," Natalie replied sternly.

"I'm sick of defending my home every waking second." He clicked the chamber into position.

Natalie tensed. This wasn't the same Edwin who snuck salt-water taffy or tinkered with the inner workings of a microwave. This Edwin glowered with unfiltered contempt. This Edwin was dangerous.

"The truth. Now. Unabridged."

He won't shoot you. Though she was less certain than before.

Tawney coughed. Edwin glanced at her and Leo swept in from his blind side to punch him in the stomach, popping the weapon right out of his grip.

"I'm sorry, man." Leo comforted him as he doubled over. "We don't have time for the unabridged version. You're going to have to trust us."

"Trust isn't an option," Edwin groaned, glaring at Natalie.

"Guys!" Owen cried from the cockpit.

"Doin' great, nerd!" Brant shouted dismissively. "Don't hit any pelicans!"

"We can tack. That means—"

"I know what it means!" Edwin spat. "Tacking is an *honor*. I thought I'd ended the Ward's experiments by freeing the Moirai, but *you*. You slipped right through, didn't you?"

"Nautilus didn't make us." Tawney wrinkled her nose in disgust. "Who then?"

"The Coelacanth Project." Brant's bitterness wasn't lost on her. Natalie held his stare, silently pleading him not to say more.

Meanwhile, Edwin recoiled as though Leo had punched him again. He adjusted the three hoops on his right ear. "That's not possible."

"Where are you from?" Natalie pressed.

Edwin shook his head. "Can't tell you. Though I'm thinking...I might need to show you." His anger melted into blatant curiosity. "I've never asked your full name, Natalie. How rude of me."

He reeked of hope, and until Natalie knew why she wanted to appear as ignorantly innocent as possible. "Morrigan."

"No," Edwin smiled. "That's not it, is it?"

A terrified squeak sounded from the pilot's seat and Owen shouted, "Hold on!"

The jet tilted. Up became down and ceiling became floor and Natalie dropped like a ragdoll.

"Out!" Tawney yelled. "Everyone out!"

It was a great plan, only Natalie had no idea which way the hatch was. She clung to a now vertical row of seats and managed to grab hold of the bars, looking up in time to see the ocean rush up and meet the windows.

The impact sent her flying. She crashed against another row of seats and slammed into the wall. The rush of water filled her ears. Or was it her head splitting?

Someone dragged her. She felt the familiar tingling of tacking and she leaned into it, desperate to go away, far away from Edwin and

Nautilus and hope. Gravity returned. When she managed to blink her eyes open, Natalie lay with her cheek in the sand, watching the jet sink beneath the waves.

"That," Tawney coughed next to her, "sucked."

"You got me out?"

"For someone...so smart," Tawney managed between breaths, "you're really...an idiot." She held Natalie's hand. "I love Angie and I'm still pissed." Thick tears rolled into her hair. "I know you'd save her if you could."

Natalie didn't respond. The truth was, she wasn't sure she would save Angie. Without someone to guide her, without someone who knew more about the consequences of time-travel, she couldn't risk it. Not even for Tawney.

But what was another lie between friends?

"Do you have my backpack?" she asked aloud.

"You really have a one-track mind sometimes, you know that?" Tawney shoved the outwardly soaked bag of books against Natalie's chest. "Be grateful I got you the waterproof pack."

Clutching the bag, Natalie scanned the beach. Enzi shoved his muzzle into the crook of her neck and roughly pawed her bare legs. Lache, Clo, and Atro helped each other to their feet, all drenched from head to toe. Owen checked them for injuries while Leo and Brant supported a very pale Edwin between them. A thin line of blood trickled out of his black hair.

"Are you with us?" She questioned him.

Edwin examined the spark on her wrist. "How'd you come by your power to tack?"

"Genetic mischief." Natalie jutted her thumb towards the Moirai. "Same as them."

"So, you remember it? The pain of every cell's alteration, of every molecule's reconfiguration?"

Natalie knew what he was really asking: did you suffer as they did? Can you be trusted to withstand Nautilus's torture as they did?

"No," Natalie pulled back. "We don't remember a thing. We only found out a few months ago."

Fascination replaced the disdain he'd expressed on the jet. She imagined how his electronics must feel before he picked them apart.

"Indeed. Then let's save the world, Miss…?"

"Morrigan."

"Right."

Satisfied with their fragile alliance, Natalie stifled her own questions. She wanted to ask about his knowledge of tacking and the jabs at her lineage, but her family needed her more.

Disheveled and armed to the teeth, their company made an odd bunch. She drew herself up and confronted them head on.

"If the bridge falls, our family falls with it and the world after." Natalie followed the lights of the Chesapeake Bay Bridge-Tunnel from the beach beside them as far out as they could see. "I don't know what we're up against. I don't have anything even remotely resembling a plan. If you want out, tell me now."

Silence answered her.

"Okay," Natalie smoothed her ruined dress. "Good."

"I still do not understand," Lache watched the lights. "Why is the bridge important?"

"It's a national treasure," Edwin turned wistful. "Over 17 miles long with two tunnels; it's an engineering marvel."

"He's right," Owen added off-hand. "It's withstood numerous hurricanes, even a few barge impacts."

"Now it must survive a bombing," Clo murmured.

"What's up with that?" Brant motioned across the bay.

Where the line of lights should have continued across the water, there was darkness. Far beyond, Brant pointed out the solitary orange glow of a streetlamp, its distant beacon no brighter than a firefly.

Natalie squinted, attempting to judge the distance. "I think it's on the third island. There should be miles of lights between here and there."

"Island?" Lache asked.

"Man-made islands mark the entrance to the tunnels. Two tunnels, four islands." Natalie explained. "Pair up."

Tawney teamed up with Clo and Owen, while Brant and Leo stood on either side of Atro and Lache. Enzi wandered a bit before finally settling in between Edwin and herself. She rubbed his ears as much for his comfort as her own.

"No cover?" Brant considered the sky.

"They already know we're coming." Natalie wiped the blood from Edwin's forehead, pleased to see the cut had stopped bleeding on its own. "We lost the advantage of surprise at the Helix."

Owen held his cracked glasses against the starlight to inspect the damage. "What's our advantage now?"

"That they've managed to piss every single one of us off," Tawney huffed.

Natalie gravitated towards the moonlight flickering on the oncoming wave. She pictured the third tunnel in her mind, tucked in among seventeen miles of concrete. As the water rushed up to meet her, she felt an unexpected surge of confidence.

For weeks she'd been playing by Nautilus's rules. If the Ward wanted to take the fight to her own backyard, fine.

She'd die before they burned it down.

Mortem ante cladem.

CHAPTER 42
NATALIE

Whichever streetlight Brant had seen was extinguished on their approach. Either that, or the weightlessness of tacking had finally misplaced her.

She'd never been anywhere so *dark*.

In fact, the more Natalie blinked the more certain she became that *dark* was an understatement. Nautilus's Antarctic cells were dark. The blacked-out halls of the Helix were dark. Midnight in the middle of the Chesapeake Bay was more than *dark*.

It was an abyss.

Thick blackness enveloped her like a shroud. The echo of her own pounding heart competed with the roar of the surf as she begged light to come from somewhere. Slick with algae, the concrete beneath her feet provided little traction and she slid dangerously with every gust of wind.

A wild wave crashed on the rocks, sending droplets of sea spray glittering bright against her skin. She savored the brief glow and spotted Enzi's pearlescent fur as he sniffed along the bank.

"What happened to the light?" Tawney asked nearby.

"I don't know." High above her, the bridge was detectable only as a black river against the stars. There were no stoplights, no headlights, nothing at all.

"Nautilus would've seen us," Owen warned.

A nervous laugh escaped her. Tacking was bright in the noonday sun. A flare would have been less conspicuous.

"I know I am new to this," Clo hugged herself beneath her robe. "However, this does not feel right."

"That's because this is a trap." Edwin stuffed a taffy between his teeth.

"The entire summer's been a trap," Natalie dismissed him. "Come on."

Turbulent water churned where ocean tides collided with the bay. The salty air stung as wind gusts battled violently to claim her. Crawling her way up and across the boulders, she guided them single file towards the road. Natalie's arms ached when she finally crouched against the guard rail. Though not particularly scared of heights, scaling a salt-slick mound of rocks in the dead of night was more than enough to set her teeth on edge.

One by one her friends joined her where the northbound and southbound roads converged beneath the Chesapeake Channel sign. Eager to gobble them whole, the tunnel gaped wide before them, lined with weakly flickering bulbs like teeth.

"Are we sure this is a good idea?" Brant challenged. "Who are we really going trying to sa—"

"We're getting our family back." Natalie didn't let him finish.

We are so close to the truth, she added silently. *And I won't stop until we get it.*

Tawney peered into the depths awaiting them. "Let's show these Seashell Sissies what's up."

Natalie descended into the tunnel and Enzi trotted ahead of her with his ears pricked to attention. The long bulbs along the ceiling flashed weakly, casting puckish shadows that tormented Natalie's nerves. Their footsteps echoed ahead as the unrest of the sea faded behind. Having only ever driven through the tunnels, Natalie had never noticed the thin streams of water dripping down the concrete walls or the slimy, soot-coated ceiling.

"Disgusting," Atro avoided an oily puddle.

"Honestly," Owen scoffed. "This is what our tax dollars are paying for? Half-hearted road upkeep?"

"Shut up, nerd," Tawney nudged him. "You don't even pay taxes."

"I might," he grumbled. "If by some miracle I live long enough to do so."

Natalie slipped on a mysterious patch of slime and someone broke her fall.

"I'm with you."

Leo's trembling sent a chill of fear down her spine.

"You alright?" She glanced sideways at him. He appeared the same as ever: slight bounce in his step, small smile on his lips. But she knew what she'd felt.

"Never better. In fact—"

A disembodied groan silenced him.

Their parade halted as the sound bounced around the tunnel. Another grunt was chased by a colorful curse that prompted Clo to blush and Enzi took off, sprinting out of sight.

"Remind me: why don't we leash him?" Tawney frowned.

Natalie followed Enzi as fast as she could manage. Her pack bounced uncomfortably against her back and the pale lights blurred together as she splashed polluted puddles up her bare legs. Enzi barked madly, his high-pitched yips only bouncing once or twice before falling on her ears. Catching up, Natalie ran harder.

The back end of a shipping truck materialized in the muted glow and Enzi paced at its base. Natalie nearly barreled him over in her haste to open the latch. Her sweaty palms slipped free of the metal and she tried again, forcing her entire weight against the bar.

It popped open as Brant yanked her away. He stood alongside

Tawney with their pistols trained together on the sliver of exposed darkness. Edwin covered the Moirai as Leo took hold of the hatch and motioned the count.

Three, two, —

Enzi nosed the door open and slipped inside. Tawney shot Natalie an irritated look and she ignored it. Her heart thrummed inside her chest so hard she feared it would burst.

"Enzi! Oof, too much. Down! Down, boy."

"Dad." Something inside Natalie shattered and mended all at once. She moved in a daze, flinging open the container door and scraping her knee on metal step. One moment she was surrounded by tunnel pavement and the next she melted into her parents' embrace. After over two months of being apart, they didn't feel real.

"You're here." She let out something between a laugh and a sob.

"There's my little bilby." Her father breathed into her hair. "I see the Ancoras served you well."

"They were a disaster," Natalie groaned into his chest.

Despite their bruises and the blood caked in their clothes, they beamed at her. Her father had greyed and the lines on his face etched deeper than she remembered. Her mother's strength seeped through the bags under her eyes and the split in her lip.

"Natalie," she soothed.

"Mom—"

Her parents stiffened and reality rushed up under Natalie's feet. She remembered herself. She remembered where she was, and for the first time, she noticed her adoptive parents' wrists were chained and bolted to the floor.

"About that," her father cleared his throat.

"I already know." The fog of euphoria evaporated. Natalie was vaguely aware of Edwin picking Mr. Merrick's restraints, his brow furrowed as he manipulated the lock. It snapped open and he moved on to the next one.

"You know?" Natalie's mother confirmed.

Chained in two lines, their parents rose as Edwin tended the locks tethering them. Natalie scanned each of them again, confirming who was missing.

"Is Mrs. Merrick truly dead?" Natalie digressed, noting the void between Leo and his father. "And where's Mr. Smith? And...and Mr. Davis?"

"We were aware of the risks," her father said somberly.

No. Natalie couldn't stop shaking her head.

Across from her, Tawney melted unblinkingly into her mother's embrace, staring at the empty space left by her father. Leo wept against Mr. Merrick's chest, clutching at his shirt as his father pulled in Brant beside them. Brant, pale and alone, was the only other one among them who knew the truth about their adoption. Now he was orphaned once again.

Natalie couldn't take it. Their family was fractured, broken beyond repair.

She'd found them too late.

"Natalie, sweetheart." Her father's thumb on her chin broke her trance. "You have to know, we aren't—"

"You're not my parents," she finished in a breath. "Yeah, I know."

Given a hundred years, Natalie doubted she would have guessed the next words to pass her mother's lips.

"Then why are you here?"

CHAPTER 43
NATALIE

*W**hy am I here?*
"I came to get you out?" Her explanation devolved into a lingering question.
"Where's Christopher?" Her mother asked sharply.
"Dead," Natalie fumed. "Would you rather he'd come instead?"
"Adopted?" Tawney's shout rang in the shipping container. "*Adopted?*"
Natalie stopped as similar cries of confusion echoed from her friends. Though she empathized with them, though she felt their pain, she exhaled in relief. Their devastating truth finally spilled out for everyone to see. However, her reprieve proved transient. Without having to carry their secret anymore, Natalie had expected to feel lighter.

She didn't.

Instead, her coiled chains of hope snaked higher to lick at her throat. What did the truth matter if the tunnel became their tomb?

Her parents aided Mrs. Davis' efforts to calm Tawney down and Brant promptly filled their void. Pale as a ghost, he leaned so casually against the side of the container she suspected she knew the joke was coming before he did.

"Scale of one to ten: how's my kissing?"

Natalie wished he wouldn't hide behind the humor.

"A fifteen," she lied. "Brant—"

"I guess it's best I found out earlier." His lips twitched as though trying to smile. "You know, since there's no one here to tell me."

"I'm sorry," Natalie whispered. "Your dad, he loved you and your mom—"

"Don't." His speech carried a sharp clip to it. "No one can say I didn't try, right?" Brant's legs shook from the effort to stay upright.

Though unsure what to say, Natalie wanted to console him. She scooted closer, only to have her parents return even more agitated than before.

"You have to leave."

"What?" Natalie balked at them. "Why?"

"You knew about the adoption," her father frowned. "You shouldn't have come at all. Lehana promised to tell you the truth of it, to end your search for us. You have the key?"

Natalie's head was reeling. *Lehana?*

"No," she managed to respond. "Nautilus took the key. Who's Lehana?"

Her adoptive parents shared a hard look. "Nautilus can't have the key."

"Well, they do." Natalie's rage boiled over. Did they not care what she'd gone through to find them? After two months of separation and torture, were they not happy to see her? "Why did you pick us? Why—"

"No," her father stopped her. "There's a bomb in the truck."

"We saw the footage." Edwin pushed himself between them. "Where's the detonator?"

Natalie blinked. She'd already forgotten about the Ward's plan to blow the bridge-tunnel. Tunnel. Passages.

"Lehana was Chef, wasn't she?" Natalie felt sure of it. "She gave me the Coelacanth documents when we were imprisoned. She got us out."

Her mother ruffled Edwin's hair. "Who are you?"

"Depends on the day, really." Edwin jerked away indignantly. "Detonator?"

Her dad shook his head. "Haven't seen either."

Only half listening, Natalie admired Chef's bolt.

Lehana's bolt.

"Owen, investigate the bomb. Deactivate it if you can," Edwin ordered. "Lachesis, a word?"

A little green, Owen dropped out of the container and jogged towards the front of the truck without so much as a wave to his parents. Meanwhile, Edwin and Lache whispered intensely off on their own. Natalie drifted towards them, eager to listen in on their conversation, when her father stopped her.

"The Ward will be nearby. He'll surely have the key on him."

"Fine." Natalie caved. "First we're getting you out of here."

"Natalie—"

"You've suffered enough for my mistakes. You'll tack out with one of us, then I'll worry about the key."

"That's not an option, princess."

Her gut wrenched at the nickname. "I'm making it one."

"The tunnel's surrounded." Her mother stroked Natalie's hair, her once soft skin cracked and calloused. "Our best chance is—"

"Getting you out," Natalie stood firm. She presented a pinch of aurichalcum dust from her pocket. "Whatever Nautilus is planning with this war, whatever the Ward wants, they're about to get it." Natalie lifted her chin. "I won't let them have you, too."

Edwin nearly knocked her sideways in his rush to inspect the aurichalcum.

"You know what this is." She wasn't asking. It was obvious.

"We need that key," Edwin blanched.

"We don't even know what it opens!" Natalie pulled at the itchy sleeves of her dress. "We need to get them out of here! The Ward has what they want—"

"Not yet they don't, but they're close. They're headed for," the veins in Edwin's neck bulged as he struggled to force out the words. "Ugh." He rubbed his face. "Ever heard the phrase 'the key to the city'?"

Natalie gave a curt nod.

"This one's the original."

"It's the only way to get you home," her mother added.

"I don't have a home." Natalie growled her frustration. "Nautilus burned it. They've burned *everything*."

"The Ward can't burn this." Edwin presented a well-creased photograph.

It didn't look like home to her. All she saw was a black sand beach framed by dizzying cliffs. There wasn't so much as a shack in sight.

"This is where we need to go," Edwin implored her. "As soon as we have that key."

"Care to be more specific?"

"He can't," her father said proudly, and she wondered what he saw in the photograph that she couldn't. "For those entrusted with Her truth, it cannot be uttered beyond Her walls. Science is truly a magical thing."

"You must make it home," her mother interjected.

Something broke in her, and the narrow thread binding Natalie's life to her parents' frayed and snapped.

"I *must* do nothing," Natalie decided. "You may have made me what I am, but what I become isn't up to you. Not anymore."

Her mother said nothing. She studied Natalie with her thin brows pinched.

"Are you truly so *dense*?" Edwin cried. "Your future awaits should you only reach out and *take it*. Wake up, Nat," Edwin begged. "Why aren't you like the Moirai? Why don't you have the scars of creation? Why don't you remember the pain of your every molecule bending to the will of chemical alteration?"

"Because I was too young!"

"Wrong," Edwin's eyes shone like lit coals. "You were not *made*," he poked her chest. "You live and breathe by fate's wicked malevolence."

She held fast to her defiant scowl as his words stole her breath. Their implications sprinkled across her mind like seeds, sprouting deep, prodding roots.

Fate's a wicked beastie.

Her blood curdled in her veins. If her power to tack, to time-travel, wasn't concocted in a lab, then where did it come from?

What exactly was fate demanding of her?

Huffing from the effort, Owen pushed himself back inside the shipping container. "The bomb isn't wired."

"What?" Leo looked to Edwin. "That can't be right."

"I checked twice. The explosives packed in the truck cab aren't active. No wires, no detonator, only enough C4 to clear out a few city blocks," Owen adjusted his glasses, "or one big bridge."

Lache pressed her temples. "You said blowing up the bridge will bring the world to war...is that not what Nautilus wants?"

Edwin scuffed his shoe on the ground. "They probably expect the threat alone will be enough to lure what they want from the shadows."

"They're feigning an attack," Owen agreed.

"And Congress will take the world to war anyway," Atro studied her feet.

Edwin gestured at the entirety of the shipping container. "Trap."

"So," Natalie wrung her hands, "the Ward pretends to stop a terrorist plot on American soil."

"We'll be captured, and Nautilus will be heroes," Leo rubbed his side.

Brant opened his arms wide. "And that's the way the cookie crumbles."

"Shit," Tawney summarized.

"Hate to interrupt," Owen's father cleared his throat. "We've got company."

Far down the tunnel, where the road lifted towards open air, the glow of flashlights bounced and swayed. Natalie cursed under her breath.

"Let me talk to them," Leo drew himself up tall. "Think of a way to get us out of here."

Those that remained of their parents huddled together and spitballed ideas. On their own for so long, Natalie had forgotten what it was like to have someone to fall back on, someone to always take the reins.

"Could shoot our way out," Mr. Johnson suggested.

"Too risky," Owen's mother disagreed. "Kids could get hit."

"March peacefully?" Mrs. Davis offered. "Nautilus might hold fire long enough for them to reach the water."

Comfort rushed in and receded like a wave, eroding away Natalie's confidence. Their parents were no better equipped than she was.

"No one else controls your fate," Edwin whispered at her side. "Help me find a way out of this."

Natalie turned to the grime-coated walls for inspiration, and they responded with the echo of Nautilus's approaching steps. She was running out of time.

Tick-tock.

Time-travel. Tacking. Those were the obvious options. Except the salty water of the Chesapeake Bay was half a mile away with a sea of navy between them.

Her pack weighed heavy with Boyle's *The Sceptical Chymist* tucked inside. Why had Chris left the book for her? To understand Nautilus's production of aurichalcum?

Or as guidance for how she should act next?

"We have to think of something new." Edwin toyed with the

silver hoops capping his ear. "Something unexpected."

Natalie dropped out of the shipping container and viewed the truck in its entirety.

"What's the play?" Paces away, Leo guarded the opposite direction, waiting for Nautilus's marching boots to appear.

"Eleanor knew the entire time," Natalie felt sick. "So why let us in?"

"Why not kill us right away?" Owen's eyebrows cinched together.

"Nautilus doesn't want to kill you," Mrs. Davis chimed in. Their parents' fruitless conversation had fallen silent. "At least, not all of you. They need someone to get them inside."

"Inside where?" Tawney snapped at her mother.

No one answered.

"Eleanor knew I'd never abandon our parents. She knows me too well," Natalie nibbled at her lip. Once again, she led them exactly where they shouldn't be. But these were their parents... "She knew I'd take the bait to come here. She knew I couldn't let—"

It was suddenly so painfully obvious.

Her mind flew through the books stashed in her pack: Crichton, Plato, Boyle. People Christopher had urged her to emulate. Visionaries who didn't merely deviate from traditional thought patterns.

They destroyed them.

"We don't need a new idea," Natalie breathed. "We need an old one. One Nautilus already thought of."

"No," Owen wagged his finger as though reprimanding a dog. "Absolutely not."

"They wouldn't expect it," Leo admitted as Lache gave Natalie a curt nod.

"It would get us to the water," Edwin smirked.

Brant kicked a stray pebble. "Yeah, as fish food."

"What are we talking about?" Mrs. Davis asked the group.

Tawney stared her down coldly. "Doing whatever it takes."

A train of handshakes rippled through Natalie's bruised and broken family. It was decided whether she liked it or not.

"We're going to blow it up." Natalie could hardly believe what she was saying. "We're going to blow up the Chesapeake Bay Bridge-Tunnel."

CHAPTER 44
LEONIDAS

This is madness.

"How?" Brant asked incredulously. "There's no detonator! Are we going to drive it into the wall or something?"

Owen cleaned his glasses with his tie. "That only happens in the movies. Real explosives need real detonators. A collision isn't enough."

"I could probably fashion something from the engine," Edwin unwrapped another candy.

The vacancy in Natalie's gaze made Leo's stomach turn. "What are you doing?" he asked quietly. "We're not killers."

"You're right," she conceded. "We're survivors. I'm trying to take out their assets, not their people."

"You won't have any control over that."

"Like that's new."

"You can't do this."

"I'm saving my family," she cut back at him. "With or without your help." Turning to Owen and Edwin she added, "Can you hotwire the truck?"

Owen blanched but Edwin lit up with a grin.

"I thought you'd never ask."

"Perfect." Natalie climbed inside the cab. "We'll ride it out of the tunnel and back to the bridge for the fireworks. I'll drive."

"No!" To Leo's surprise, Edwin and Brant both mimicked his response. Edwin pulled her roughly from the driver's seat, sending puffs of aurichalcum powder up in clouds and all over the cab.

"Anyone except you," Edwin said seriously.

"I'm the reason we're here," Natalie fought back. "No one else should take the risk."

"There's a small army awaiting us." Leo's father squeezed his shoulder, but the last thing he felt was reassured. "Any driver will be easily killed without help."

Adopted. Leo resisted the urge to shy away from the man who was now a stranger. So long as they sat trapped in the tunnel it hardly mattered who he was. They needed every able body and mind available to even dream of making it out alive.

"Hello, hello." An airy sigh interrupted them, and Legate Shaye's lacquered lipstick reflected the glint of her flashlight. "Welcome to Graduation."

Game time.

"Legate Shaye." Leo stepped forward, drawing her attention to him as he bent into a mocking bow. He gestured to the ragged group of family and strangers crowded around the truck behind him. "Welcome to the revolution."

Shaye grinned. If their parents' release from their bonds rattled her, she didn't show it.

Still our parents.

Sizing up the Curtanas blocking them in, Leo's stomach knotted. He took hold of Natalie's wrist, securing her next to him. There wasn't time to worry about the lies his parents wove, or the fact the woman who'd forever remain his mother was dead. He couldn't mourn the loss of his family, his lineage, or himself. No matter how damaging.

He had a game to win.

"I must admit, though the Ward cleverly predicted the actions of your friend, you, Leonidas, surprised us. The consensus was you perished in Antarctica with your infuriating uncle."

"That particular oversight falls to me." A man emerged from Shaye's entourage. His polished shoes and angled features glinted as sharp as his suit.

Amir.

Lache and her sisters advanced beside him and Leo's heart leapt into his throat. He'd let the Moirai down more than once. He'd made them a promise he couldn't keep. How could he expect them to maintain composure when Amir should already be dead and buried?

My weakness will be our undoing.

Leo managed to block Lache's path while Edwin pushed himself between Atro and Clo, his arms draped over their shoulders.

"The Moirai?" Shaye narrowed her eyes. "Edwin."

"Surprised? Good."

Shaye and Amir exchanged an uncomfortable glance. Nautilus's greatest failure stared defiantly back at them, and behind the Legates, whispers spread like wildfire.

"I should have killed you myself." Amir Amani's thin lips pressed together until they disappeared. "A mistake easily remedied."

"You will never suffer as I have by you," Lache growled. "Though, I will do my best."

Shaye laughed, a bubbly sound far out of place in the tunnel. "You will fail in that endeavor the same as every other task Nautilus presented you."

"Now, now," Amir's lighthearted tone had a tightness to it. "The past is past!"

Shaye flourished a gloved hand through the air. "Yes, of course. You are right. What matters now, dear Lachesis, is how you and your *companions* leave this filthy place: as prisoners of war, or alive and free."

Whatever conversing took place by the truck flatlined. Shaye was making them an offer.

"We're listening," Leo assured her.

"We each have something the other wants. The Ward is prepared to give you your freedom in exchange for *her*," Shaye nodded at Natalie.

"Done," Natalie stepped forward.

"Not done," Leo pulled her back.

"I do not fear imprisonment, and I fear death least of all," Lache zeroed in on Amir. "Your offer lacks substance."

"I wonder if your friends would agree?" Legate Shaye's smile was venomous. "Though I suppose you're right. You are so hungry for vengeance, Lachesis. Shall we make a deal, you and me? Natalie for your peace?"

Two Curtanas abruptly seized Amir.

"What is this?" He pulled against the Curtanas, glaring at Shaye. "What are you thinking? I am a *Legate*."

"You are a pawn."

"I found the Ward his key—"

"Do not claim victories that aren't yours," Shaye spat at him. "You can have Amir," she promised Lache. "You may punish him in a manner befitting his *many* crimes. All I require is Ms. Morrigan."

Leo felt more than saw Lache raise her gun. "Lache," he warned.

"Not so fast," Shaye blocked her shot. "Natalie first."

Lache wetted her lips.

"Sister?" Clo whined, though Leo couldn't tell which side she was on.

"They can't get Nat and the key," Edwin breathed behind Lache. "You know this, Lachesis. All will be lost."

"I am not afraid of death," Lache ignored him. "Nautilus inundated me with chemicals and radiation. I was electrocuted and drowned in attempts to tack. Twice, the universe showed me mercy and stopped my heart. Twice, Nautilus resurrected me into Hell."

Lache advanced on Amir, her marble complexion scoured with anguish. "I was not even named until my twelfth year." Her tone was even and cold. "Seventeen others died before then."

Leo clenched his jaw. He should have taken out Amir when he'd had the chance. "Lache," Leo reached for the gun.

"I am not afraid of death!" she yelled at him. "You have no right to take this from me."

"Well, I do." Tawney wrenched Lache's pistol from her grip. "Find peace in Hell, you sick son of a—"

Everything became a blur.

Shaye leapt aside as Tawney's shot exploded in the tunnel. Amir crumbled backwards onto the pavement. Bleeding, breathless, dead. His blood mixed with the dirt and oil caked into the road. Edwin and Natalie fled with the Moirai to the truck. And Leo stayed with Tawney. Even as he dragged her away, the girl kept shooting.

"That's for Christopher!" Tawney fired again. "Chef!" And again. "My lying father!" And again. "And Angie!"

Leo pulled her into him, and she pounded her fists against his chest. A thick haze filled his ears, the residual zing of gunfire.

Shaye's silent scream captivated him. The woman pushed past any and all in her way, sprinting up the tunnel, retreating.

Retreating? That couldn't be right. Leo expected a rain of bullets in response to Amir's execution.

Murder, he corrected.

Shaye glanced back, her horror distorting her pressed composure.

She's afraid? It didn't make sense. They were outnumbered five times over, yet Shaye fled, and her army of navy followed her.

"Go!" Tawney's shout filtered through the fog like a whisper. She could have been a hundred miles away.

Brant shoved him. "Run, man!"

Suddenly the tunnel was deafening. Thunder rolled on and on, pierced by the terrified yelps and cries of Curtanas and Captains tripping over themselves to escape. Leo hurried back to the truck and launched himself inside the shipping container.

It was vibrating.

Tawney crouched out the back and violently vomited up her dinner. As the truck lurched forward, Leo snagged the back of her dress to save her from tumbling over and out.

"Thanks." Shaking and white as a sheet, Tawney sagged against the metal wall.

"You didn't want to kill him," Leo realized out loud.

Owen lifted her hair and blew softly on her neck. Between breaths, he planted a light kiss on her collarbone and, most shocking of all, Tawney let him.

"We needed a distraction." Turning green again, she squeezed her eyes shut. "So she could get to the cab."

Leo stiffened. "So who could get to the cab?"

Tawney didn't answer.

Enraged, Leo shoved through what little remained of their family. "Where is she?" he demanded. "Where's Natalie?"

"I'm right here."

Leo pulled her against his chest, relishing the solid feel of her. *Exactly where you should be.*

"Who's driving?" Though a quick scan of those in the container told him everything. His scar throbbed. He held Natalie away from him. "Where is Lache?"

Natalie plucked him off her biceps and inspected the red marks left behind before answering. "She volunteered."

"This is her *life*! Do you understand?"

"And this is her choice," Natalie said coldly. "Do you understand that?"

"They're going to shoot her. She'll break through their ranks and—" Leo choked on the reality of what was about to happen.

Breaching the tunnel, Nautilus would aim to kill. They'd jump to the water and tack somewhere far away.

And Lache would never leave the bridge.

"Lache!" he shouted towards the cab. "LACHES—" Leo's cry was stifled by Clo's chilled hand over his mouth.

"She chose this, Leonidas. Do not waste it."

I am not afraid of death. She'd known the plan. No, she helped make the plan.

Lache outplayed him.

"We can't let her do this." Leo looked desperately from Natalie to Edwin, even to his father, yet no one spoke up. "There has to be another way." The truck jumped forward again sending most of them to the floor.

Tawney hugged her stomach. "Didn't Nautilus ever teach you to drive?" She glowered at the two remaining Moirai.

"She had her first lesson about two minutes ago," Edwin explained. "I'm an excellent teacher." An ear-splitting screech interrupted him as the truck grazed the tunnel wall. "Though you might fancy something to hold on to."

Leo wanted to scream. Christopher, Chef, Angie, Brant's father, Mr. Davis, his own mother, and now Lache. Was their freedom worth so many lives? Was tacking worth so many deaths? It wasn't fair. Leo punched the wall of their metal cage.

"Yeah," Brant sounded hollow next to him. "Me too."

Shots echoed off the outside of the container and Leo instinctively ducked, cupping his ears against the roar. Nautilus had started shooting.

And Lache was their primary target.

"Lache!" Leo pressed against the wall separating them.

"They have formed a blockade," she yelled back over the tormented whine of the truck's engine. "There is a huge helicopter behind it."

Edwin snapped his fingers. "That'll be the Ward."

"Get out!" Leo begged. "I'll switch with you."

"She's not picking up enough speed." Leo heard his father speaking, though it didn't quite register. "The girl's going to need a hole."

Determined to take Lache's place, Leo was nearly out of the container when the man he'd always known to be his father hugged him. He smelled like a barn in midsummer and his unshaved scruff scratched Leo's neck.

"When you clear the tunnel, run. Get the key. Your mother and I…well, we loved every second." He leapt out into the darkness.

And Leo never said goodbye.

Despite the deception, despite the lies, the man remained his father. Leo had half a mind to follow, yet something rooted him still. His friends needed him more. Adopted or not, his family made a choice to set him free, so he turned his back to the empty space and went to Natalie.

"Christopher promised this endeavor would cost us everything." Leo felt intrusive as Mrs. Morrigan cupped her daughter's face. "We thought he meant our identities and belongings, or perhaps we were to die for our cause," she spoke with impossible strength. "Now we know it's sending you home. He was right, of course: you are everything."

Natalie's parents pulled away. Leo found her hand as much to comfort her as to ensure she didn't follow. He wouldn't lose her again.

He couldn't survive it.

Natalie's father slipped Christopher's pistol from her side and the robbery jolted her awake.

"Wait!" She strained against Leo. "No! Wait!"

Natalie's mother accepted Edwin's offered gun without looking at him, nor anyone else in the shipping container. Not even her screaming daughter.

"We'll clear the way," Mr. Morrigan vowed. "You know what

must be done."

Edwin nodded solemnly and her parents dropped away.

And Leo clung to Natalie like the Sun anchors the Earth.

CHAPTER 45
LEONIDAS

Leo wasn't sure if he was still weak from his old wounds or if Natalie had gotten stronger. It took every ounce of will to keep her from tearing after her parents.

"No!" She clawed against Leo's hold, leaving shallow gouges behind. "You can't! You *can't!*"

Enzi paced with his ears flat against his head. He rubbed the back of Leo's knees, the closest he could get to Natalie without risking getting kicked.

"Christopher," Natalie bucked against Leo, entirely beside herself. "I promised, I promised—"

Tawney's mother and Owen's parents had followed Natalie's. Leo thought of his father, undoubtedly running towards his own death, and the memory of his mother's murder haunted his mind like a shadow. His lip quivered and he set his jaw.

Don't waste it.

"I need you here," he begged Natalie. "Are you with me?"

The truck lurched forward with awkward leaps. Gunshots echoed and sparks flew from ricochets off the concrete.

"No!" she sobbed. "It's my fault."

"I fear we are about to encounter some turbulence." Edwin crouched near the container's open doors.

Shot after shot hit the truck and every impact made Leo flinch. He waited for the icy-hot bite of a bullet. He waited for Lache's piercing scream. Neither came, and before he knew it, Edwin shoved them towards the exit.

"We've got to get to that chopper. Stay behind the cover of the container."

"We can't keep pace with a *truck*," Owen said, aghast.

"Sure, we can," Edwin countered. "I never taught the girl to shift."

Another jolt threw Leo off balance and Natalie slipped free, jumping out of the container.

Leo darted after her.

"Don't wait for us!" Edwin's orders rang down the tunnel and, to Leo's shock, he fell in stride beside him. "She's a stubborn one, eh?"

"What are you doing?" Leo yelled at him.

"We can't go home without the key." Edwin nodded to Natalie sprinting ahead of them. "Or her."

Leo didn't have the breath to argue. Shot after shot rained down from the barricade of navy-blue ahead and, wedged between the shipping container and the tunnel wall, Leo knew they made easy targets.

Yet none of the bullets found their mark.

"Headlights," Edwin shouted. "She's blinded them!"

Though the Curtanas couldn't see beyond the truck's glare, from Leo's position the truck lit up the bridge-tunnel like a runway. He saw everything. Including Natalie sprinting several paces ahead of him.

Before he'd been shot, Leo might have caught her easily. Now she drifted beyond his reach and he knew he'd never catch her, not before she crossed the truck's path and overtook her parents.

A white blur streaked past. Ears flat and head down, Enzi flew over the pavement. He nipped at Natalie's heels, herding his rogue sheep, and when she didn't stop, Enzi leapt ahead of her and dropped his belly to the road.

Natalie had no time to react. She tripped and they became a tangle of arms and legs and fur. Enzi yelped sharply and scampered to his paws, nosing her where she screamed into the concrete. Though her forearms and legs were slick with bloody scrapes, Leo didn't stop to inspect the damage.

He pinned her on the spot.

"Natalie!" Leo yelled at her.

She writhed beneath him until a gurgled cry snapped her head up towards her parents. Far ahead, Mrs. Morrigan doubled over, clutching her side.

"No," Natalie breathed.

The truck cleared the tunnel and with the Curtanas no longer blinded, bullets began hitting their targets.

"We have to go," Edwin stood over them.

Leo knew he was right. The truck was about to pass through a hole in Nautilus's ranks they couldn't afford to miss. If they didn't catch up, they'd be trapped.

"No!" Natalie screamed at her parents. "Run! RUN!"

Leo helped Edwin pull her, watching as Mr. Morrigan covered his wife with the gun he'd stolen from Natalie. He raised the pistol, aimed, and...nothing happened.

Her father studied the gun as another Curtana fired at him. He collapsed against Natalie's mother, and they lay in the street.

Quiet. Still.

And Natalie was anguish incarnate.

She screamed and screamed and there was nothing Leo could do except watch her implode. She clawed the ground, fumbling, searching, and he guided her hands to his.

"We have to go!" Edwin yelled impatiently.

"You have to move." Leo pressed his cheek to hers so she would hear. He lifted her to her feet, ready to grab her should she try to run.

"Christopher's gun…"

"It's just a gun—"

"No," Natalie curled in on herself. "Wasn't—it wasn't—"

Clarity struck Leo like a bell. It explained everything: her composure with Max at the Helix, why she still relied on the bolt for protection. Despite her intolerance for firearms, Natalie once promised Christopher she'd carry a gun.

Then she found herself a loophole.

"It wasn't loaded," Leo shook his head. "That's not your fault."

"Liar," she choked.

"The chopper," Edwin reminded them.

"Are you with me?" Leo asked her.

Natalie wiped her face, smearing blood with her tears, and nodded.

"Attagirl," Edwin coaxed her forward.

They made for the helicopter. Natalie's pack bounced on her back as she ran, and Leo steadied her more than once. They gained on the truck and Edwin slapped it twice. Lache reached out the window with a thumb up. Ahead of them, the chopper's blades began to turn, but it didn't matter.

Leo's chest swelled. They were going to catch it.

Their parents' surprise attack bought Lache the few precious seconds she'd needed. The Curtanas scattered as the truck made straight for them, horn blaring, blazing a path to the Ward's private ride. The truck careened on as they veered off towards the helicopter and Leo watched it go, his stomach bound in guilty knots.

As gunfire echoed around them, Natalie reached the chopper first. She threw open the hatch and a burly body hurtled out of it, sending them both to the ground. Leo stepped over her, his gun at the ready.

"Ugh." The man at their feet moaned as Enzi sniffed every inch of him. Leo tossed his head back with relief. He'd know that red cap anywhere.

"Brant," Leo shook him. His right eye was swollen, and blood dripped from a deep gash on his forehead. Brant dabbed at it with the sleeve of his jacket.

Natalie attempted to help him up, but Brant shied away, standing on his own. Glancing from the helicopter to her, he groaned again.

"Did you get it?" Edwin probed.

Brant shook his head and winced. "Ward and the key are long gone."

"No!" Despite Brant's statement, Edwin searched the helicopter himself. "No, no, no!" He paced, pressing the butt of his gun against his head. "We can't let this happen. We only needed a little more," he stopped and stared at Natalie, "time."

A fresh shower of gunfire snapped Leo back to attention. If the key was out of the question, he needed to save Lache. "We need to get to the truck."

"We need to get off this bridge," Edwin herded them towards the guardrail.

"I can't leave her here!" Leo shouted. "She won't let Nautilus take her alive. She'll die first."

"Tack to the beach—"

The gaping entrance to the tunnel erupted into chaos. Nautilus had regrouped after the truck passed, trapping Tawney and Owen behind a cement barrier. Two figures huddled with them that Leo couldn't make out.

"Go!" Edwin shouted at them.

Fighting her protests, Owen pulled Tawney and their company over the edge of the bridge out of sight. Seconds later, a brilliant white flash cut through the night.

They made it, Leo realized. *And there's still time...* If Edwin wanted to go to the beach, fine, but he wouldn't leave Lache behind. The headlights cut through the darkness, turning along the closest curve of the bridge.

"I can still get her," Leo turned to Natalie. "I'll tack further down the bridge. I'll head her off."

"And then what?" Natalie sniffled. "Even if you manage to tack ahead of her and scale the seven-story pylon before she passes you, how do you plan on stopping her?"

"The next island," he explained quickly, already backing towards the guardrail. "I'll flag her down and—"

A grating screech cut him off. Instead of sweeping across the bay, the truck lights turned down towards it. Lache was no longer driving along the bridge. She was driving off it.

"She's gone over the side." Natalie covered her mouth.

"Go!" Edwin yelled. Bullets bounced off the concrete at their feet. "Go now!"

With a hard shove to his back, Leo was falling. Tangled with the others, he whipped through the air, desperate to keep the truck in his sights. If she'd jump from the cab, he could tack to her. He could find her and bring her to the beach.

The explosion lit up the night like the noonday sun.

No! Hot air enveloped him as the air reverberated against his skin. He had no idea which way was up. The distant fireball flickered in and out of sight as Leo tumbled towards the water.

It didn't make sense. It shouldn't have exploded, not without a detonator. Owen said so himself. His scream tore out of him and he was numb to it, barely conscious beyond the single thought of her name.

He'd promised her freedom and led her to her grave.

The sensation of falling succumbed to weightlessness. In an instant it was over. The impossible explosion was gone, and Lache along with it.

CHAPTER 46
LEONIDAS

Leo collapsed in the thick black sand from Edwin's photograph. After the fight on the bridge, the world was unnaturally quiet. A breezy grey sky dotted with clouds replaced the roar of the explosion. Waves lapped at the shore and birds cried overhead.

"It shouldn't have exploded." He said it for no other reason than to tell the universe it was wrong. There was nothing else he could do. Lache was already gone.

"Come here," a gruff voice mumbled nearby.

Dad?

His father pulled every kid he could reach into his arms. Owen and Tawney pressed hard against him, with Clo and Atro squeezed in between. Even Mrs. Davis inserted herself among them.

"They did it for you." Despite the anguished twist of his mouth, his father's strength held out. "This was our choice. This is what we live for: to love and protect you. I'm sorry," he hugged them tighter and looked directly at Leo. "I'm so sorry."

The meager gap of sand between Leo and his father stretched into a chasm. Lache was dead. Most of his friends' parents were gone.

His own mother was murdered.

Sorry wasn't going to cut it.

Soaked in sweat and sea spray, Leo shivered in the chill. The black sand was warm and soft, and he wanted to melt into it, to become another boulder among the rocks. But he could feel Natalie's absence, and the need for her closeness forced him to his feet.

He spotted her several paces away, where Edwin had secluded her from the group. Leo shuffled carelessly through the sand, overhearing snippets of their conversation as he approached.

"It doesn't matter," Edwin gripped her bloodied arms. "You have to do this."

"I don't have to do a thing."

Furious, Leo broke them apart. "Enough! Half of our family just *died*."

"And she would have it be for nothing!"

"I can't do what you're asking!" Tears brimmed Natalie's eyes. "Don't you think if I could go back and save my parents I would? I *can't*. I've tried a thousand times."

"Not hard enough," Edwin seethed. "Not for this. Your parents gave their lives to save yours and get that key. If you act quickly, we can still go back."

Leo felt as though he'd waded into an unfamiliar territory. They weren't making sense. "What are you talking about? The key is long gone."

Edwin ignored him. "Your *father* took your gun to buy your escape, not his own. Their choices made all the difference in the world." He pointed at her. "Which is why you can't change it. You can't go back for them, but the key—"

"Shut up," Leo shoved him.

"You can still save what they died for!" Edwin yelled past Leo. "You can honor them! There's still time! We have a window of opportunity, Nat, but it's closing fast."

Leo didn't know what to do except knock Edwin out cold, and

he'd been looking for an excuse to punch something anyway. He reared back when Natalie stopped him.

"You know the rules?" she asked Edwin.

Sick of being talked over and around, Leo removed himself from between them.

"You have done it," Edwin smiled. "I *knew* it!"

Natalie scuffed her shoes. Leo was completely lost.

"Their sacrifice cannot be undone," Edwin managed to smear a smidge of respect over his excitement. "Their deaths paved our escape and our chance to go back and save the key. Do you understand?"

"I can't," Natalie hissed through gritted teeth.

"You owe it to them to try. The key is everything."

"Leave her alone," Leo warned. "What's done is done."

"Well," Owen dropped down next to them, cleaning soot and tears from his glasses. His own parents, who'd been together in the truck, were not among them on the beach. "That's not entirely true."

Clo sniffled. "Is it possible?"

"No," Tawney argued. "It's too dangerous. She couldn't risk saving Christopher or...or anyone else." Her chest rose and fell rapidly. "Why does she get to go back for a stupid key?"

"Because if we can't get home, we've lost more than the war. Whatever the consequences, this is necessary," Edwin explained. "We have to do this."

"What are you talking about?" Leo worried he might have a concussion. "There's nothing to go back to! The key is gone, Lache is...Lache is..." He couldn't finish.

"I can't do it," Natalie repeated.

Edwin guided her towards the water. "You can."

"She can what?" Leo yelled. "Someone better tell me what's going on."

"I tried to tell you before," Natalie stared at the water as though it might swell up and drown her. "You might want to sit down."

"Wait," Tawney marched towards them.

"I know you're upset about Angie. I get it—"

"No," Tawney spun around. "I mean, *yes*. Upset doesn't even begin to cover it." Her hair whipped as she searched the beach. "Where's Brant?"

Owen's freckled nose was red and dirty. "Don't drag him over here," he sniffled. "If he needs a minute or twenty let him have it."

"No, Owen, I don't think he's—"

"Brant can wait," Edwin cut in. "The key cannot. You have to go now, Nat."

"I swear if someone doesn't tell me—"

"I can travel back in time," Natalie said bluntly.

Leo blinked. "Right," he laughed. "Did I die, too? For real, this time?" He patted his chest and his stomach. He suspected if he was dead his body wouldn't ache so terribly.

But he wasn't sure of anything anymore.

"No, impossible," Leo bit out, all humor lost. "Then why didn't you travel back for me in Antarctica?"

"I did," Natalie turned on him. "I nearly drowned searching for you, and I might have but...I couldn't stay there. Uncle Chris needed help. He was bleeding… You were gone."

"You went back for me," Leo said dumbly.

She lifted one shoulder.

"Don't do that again."

"Don't disappear and I won't have to."

"We can all do this?" Leo pressed, lacking the energy to argue with her.

"No," Edwin said soberly. "Only her."

"Who are you, exactly?" Owen frowned.

"A friend, luckily for you. Come on, Nat, the sooner the better."

"For who?" Tawney challenged.

"Her." Edwin scooted Natalie to the water's edge. "And us, should we hope not to perish on these shores and leave the world to ruin."

"See, nerd," Owen leaned back on his palms. "No pressure."

"I'm going with you," Leo announced.

"No," Edwin stopped him.

"Who are you to—"

"Tell me, honestly my friend, if I sent you back with her, would you try to save Lache?"

Leo heard the two Moirai suck in a single, pained breath behind him. He worked his jaw.

"You are too close to this," Edwin warned him. "Now move aside. Time is of the essence."

CHAPTER 47
NATALIE

Every inch of Natalie hurt. The coarse black sand shifted uncomfortably under her feet and Enzi's fur rubbed like sandpaper against her legs. With every blink, her parents' mirage shimmered before her.

Still. In the end, they had lain so *still*.

My fault. It was her decision to storm the tunnel entrance. Her choice to turn Nautilus's own tactics against them. Violence begets violence. She should have surrendered. She should have done whatever the Ward wanted. She should have let the world fall. According to Edwin, it might anyway.

And still he asked too much of her.

"I'm sorry." She knotted her dress.

Sorry. What a hollow word.

The agony on the bridge resurfaced as though from a dream. A searing hot iron burned from her stomach through her chest and up into her throat, and she couldn't get it out no matter how hard she screamed.

Now, a thousand miles away on a beach of black sand, nothing existed beyond the rift inside, a black hole of black iron, that expanded and cracked. From their capture to their death, Natalie led Nautilus right to her family.

Their blood wasn't just on her hands. She was drowning in it.

Natalie squeezed her fists closed, digging her nails into her palms. The pain brought relief, leeching the anguish from inside her chest.

"You can't save them, Nat," Edwin's stare bordered on adoration and she shrank beneath it. "Their sacrifice was pivotal. They're the reason you survived. We can't risk that."

Why are you here? Her mother's final question haunted her. How could Natalie go back knowing she couldn't save them? Knowing she had to leave them behind?

"We go for the key," Edwin instructed. "And the key alone."

"I've been trying for weeks. I can't do it."

"You must."

"I hate you." The words slipped past her trembling lips. How dare he put this on her. How dare he ask her to go back to salvage anything other than her family.

"Good," Edwin shocked her. "Lean into that."

There was nothing to do except show him it was impossible. She stepped into the path of the oncoming wave and, as it rolled towards her toes, Natalie focused on the facts. She pictured the bridge, the flood of Nautilus members firing at them, the truck gaining speed as it broke through their ranks, Lache at the wheel…

Natalie knew the instant the ocean found her. A tingling sensation spread through her, static making every atom in her body alight with energy. White light shone intensely beyond her eyelids and a buoyancy claimed her for a fraction of a second before dropping her back into darkness.

"You can do this, Nat," Owen encouraged.

Natalie huffed a breath out of her nose in irritation. She already told them she couldn't. The first time, with Christopher, it was a fluke.

Edwin stepped in front of her, the waves splashing up around his ankles. "Don't think about the key," he advised. "That's not enough for you."

"You said I can't think about my parents!"

"Edwin," Leo warned.

"Shh. We're having a little lesson in emotional intelligence." Edwin refocused on Natalie. "I didn't say you couldn't think about your parents; I said you can't save them. Your mom and dad *died* for you."

Natalie recoiled as though he had struck her.

"Stop running from the truth," he urged. "You need to feel it. Use it." Edwin pushed his thumb up beneath her diaphragm making her gasp. "That pain, that emotion, that's how you'll get there. You can't think your way through time, you have to *feel* for it." He steadied her. "This one's going to hurt. Let it. Lean in."

"How does that work?" Owen asked.

"Emotion is the only thing more influential than active thought," Edwin explained off-hand. "It's older, instinctual, and incredibly powerful. Thought, merely picturing a destination, doesn't provide the temporal conductivity necessary for time-travel. Emotion, however," Edwin tapped his head. "With enough passion, a person can crumble cities and raise empires. Elation, rage, misery: they're gasoline to a fire. Or, in her case, ions to electricity."

He took Natalie's hand. "It has to be now. Lean into it."

Telling her to lean in was one thing, but actually doing it, allowing the flood gates of her inner turmoil to come down, was another. It was terrifying. The pain had a will of its own, and she wasn't sure she could survive it, let alone channel it.

Sacrificing logic and rationality for raw, threadbare emotion wasn't natural and she instinctively pushed the pain away. She subdued it into a cellar in the recesses of her being and pretended it wasn't there. For weeks that's how she'd been able to put one foot in front of the other; for months that's how she'd managed to keep breathing.

Now he's asking me to drown.

And how could she not? Too many had given their lives for her. Drowning was the least she could do.

So she did.

Natalie plunged into herself and the beach was gone. An invisible knife twisted her gut and the pain alone was blinding. Throat burning, lungs screaming, she welcomed every miserable truth to pour over her. She leaned in.

And her demons pulled her under.

Christopher's blood stained the Virginia Beach sand. Chef collapsed silent in the snow. Angie's fur caked in soot. Mrs. Merrick. Mr. and Mrs. Johnson. Mr. Smith. Lachesis. Mom and Dad, dead on the pavement. So still.

Natalie reached out for air. She was losing control. She couldn't think. She wanted the dark fissure inside of her to end it, to consume her whole, to suffocate her so she wouldn't have to feel anything anymore.

Something white shone beyond the veil of agony. A tingling gripped her, and she feebly summoned an image of the Bridge-Tunnel lights twinkling across the bay. Then gravity struck her down. A steady force led her to the rungs of a slick ladder. She clung to it, trembling, drinking the night air.

"Woah," Edwin breathed next to her.

"Did it work?"

"Oh yeah. Man, I've always wanted to do this!"

Natalie looked around, uncertain. They'd arrived not on the third island, but rather one of its nearest pylons. Salt and algae caked the concrete slab underfoot. "You're with me?"

"I'm with you," Leo promised.

She turned and sure enough, it was Leo still holding her up.

"I told you not to come." Edwin's stern tone gave way to a boyish grin.

"Guess I'm not fond of following orders."

"I'm glad you're here," Natalie confessed.

Leo gestured up the ladder. "Time-travelers first."

The Chesapeake Bay Bridge-Tunnel stretched high above her. Slipping up the ladder, Natalie distracted herself with thoughts of the stranger behind her. Edwin hadn't only known time-travel was possible, but how it worked.

Which is more than Christopher ever shared.

Nearing the top, Leo cleared his throat. "What's our play? Ah, no, better question: what are the rules here?"

Natalie almost smiled. Almost.

"Rule number one: stay with me." She wished she had a better answer for him. She didn't know the rules beyond what few she had gleaned from Edwin, the most specific being she couldn't save her family. "You can pick rule number two."

"Only meddle where necessary," Edwin advised below them. "And don't talk to people in the past unless you must."

"Because you'll go insane," Leo added confidently.

"Nah," Edwin chuckled. "The mind is incredibly inept with things it can't explain. Instead of focusing on what doesn't make sense, it tends to glaze over the details until arriving at an explanation that does. It's like trying to envision the vastness of the universe. You can't do it. Even now your mind is shielding itself. See how calm you are?"

"Thought I just performed well under pressure."

Edwin snorted. "It's your brain, think whatever you want."

Natalie pulled herself ungracefully onto the pavement and crouched against the guardrail to catch her breath.

"Then why don't we talk to people?" she asked as he and Leo joined her.

"We only change what we must."

"There aren't any consequences to this then?" Leo probed.

"I didn't say that," Edwin peered over the guardrail. "Some are exempt from the luxuries of a shielded mind."

"What do you mean?" The water crashing against the pylons

seemed to keep pace with the throbbing pulse of Natalie's entire being.

Edwin either didn't hear her or chose not to answer. He pointed across the roadway. "There."

Beyond a knee-high cement barrier, all that stood between them and the tunnel were two hundred yards of open road and an army of Nautilus soldiers armed to the teeth. Shots echoed in the tunnel and every single uniformed man and woman readied their weapons.

"Here we go," Leo tapped his thigh.

"Stay with us," Edwin told him firmly.

Leo fixated on the tunnel without responding.

Pulling her bolt from her thigh, Natalie watched Legate Shaye emerge with a flurry of navy Curtanas in her wake. A great rumbling emanated from the passage, shaking the very pavement Natalie clung to. Leo pressed against her back to steady her.

"You could have told me," he muttered.

"Right," Natalie huffed. "Great to see you, by the way, I can sometimes travel through time. We cool?"

"You wound me," Leo mocked. "Am I not the epitome of calm?"

Natalie glanced at him. She caught the way his gaze flitted repeatedly to the truck. To Lache.

"Ask me again when we're back on the beach."

"Okay," Edwin shifted positions. "Here come your folks."

Natalie didn't want to see. She knew she couldn't help her parents, not without throwing away everything they had accomplished. They may have been proud to die for their cause, for her, but that didn't mean she was proud to let it happen. Tears burned her eyes. She writhed in their hiding place, itching to move, to take the bullet that killed her parents instead, knowing full well it wasn't what they wanted. Desperate, she turned her attention to the helicopter.

"Let's go now," she begged.

Too late. Leo covered over her ears to block out the noise. It wasn't enough. She heard the gunfire. She heard her mother's choked cry. Natalie studied Leo's coat pocket. The stitching was flawless. She wondered how perfect it would be to be so small. Surely the point of a needle never felt any pain. Natalie bit her fist to stifle the scream that would give them away.

What kind of daughter allowed their parents to perish? What kind of daughter would abandon their sacrifice to save them? She was torn, split down the middle, unable to do anything but take the pain.

"Hey," Edwin shook her. "We have to move."

Trembling, Natalie pried herself from Leo's chest. She felt sick, but again her parents' fight bought Lache the precious moments she needed. The crowd of navy-blue uniforms scattered as the truck burst through their ranks.

"Now!"

On Edwin's command, she darted out from behind the barrier and sprinted for the helicopter. It was easier than Natalie expected. All eyes were on the truck and she sought the strain on her body. She wanted to push, to feel the heat in her muscles, to focus all her energy on the next breath and the one after that. Edwin reached the helicopter first. With his gun at the ready, he gripped the handle.

Natalie spun Chef's bolt in a silver arc of sparks and launched herself inside. She turned in a swift circle, her bolt held out defensively, only there were no guards or Curtanas, and certainly no Ward. Despite the spacious cabin, there was only one other person in the chopper. He leaned against the control panel.

"Hey, Nat."

The bolt dropped to her side, its charge dissipating into nothing. Suddenly she was back in Nautilus's caves drawing pictures in the dirt, lost in a world with no sun.

I missed something.

"Hello, Brant."

CHAPTER 48
NATALIE

As soon as Brant's name passed Natalie's lips she was no longer so certain it was actually him. He had the same confident stance, same broad shoulders, and jutting jaw, only his playful demeanor had been stripped away. He looked hollow. And as he pulled his pistol from its holster, he looked dangerous.

"I don't understand," Natalie confessed meekly. *When did this happened? At Graduation? At the Adoption? Somewhere in between?*

Brant grinned and for an instant he was whole again. "I wouldn't expect you to. Or maybe now I would."

"You're why Nautilus doesn't need us anymore?" Natalie struggled to put the pieces together. "They already have you."

Brant nodded.

"When?" she blurted.

"Don't ask me that."

"When?" Natalie reached for him, and his gun snapped up level with her chest.

"I said don't."

She'd seen Brant at target practice. A mile away she'd duck for cover. Here, point-blank, she'd die before her body hit the ground.

"For someone who prides themselves on finding the facts, you had no trouble feeding your fantasy."

Natalie flushed. "I thought..."

"Oh, I know what you thought. I can't even blame you for it." Brant's ghost resurfaced with a chuckle. "I did try to tell you. Over and over again, and every time you dismissed me as some hormone-drunk knucklehead instead of hearing me out as your friend." He paused. "I was your friend, Nat."

Was. The finality made her eyes sting. All this time she'd thought he'd wanted to confess some twisted romance built on destruction, death, and destiny. Only now she saw he hadn't been hovering close out of affection. The pack on her back seemed to grow heavier.

"You sent me to Paris," she accused. "Eleanor convinced me to go, but it was your idea." The Earth tilted beneath her. "And the fire?"

"Was deadlier than intended."

Natalie's lungs felt as though they were collapsing in; she couldn't get enough air. "You're the reason Angie's dead. You sent me right into Nautilus's hands." She shook her head in disbelief. "Amir didn't give the key to Nautilus, *you* did. What have you done?"

"What I needed to," he said darkly. "The path to peace isn't always peaceful."

She slammed the end of her bolt against the floor of the chopper. "Why?"

He didn't answer.

"They're brainwashing you!" she yelled at him. "Can't you see it? Look at what you're doing." She stepped towards him, pressing the cold barrel of his gun against her chest. "Would you, *Brant Smith,* put a bullet in me? Would you carry that pain every day for the rest of your life?"

He glowered at her.

"Answer me."

Brant hesitated, then lowered his gun.

"Come home," she begged.

"I am home. And I don't have to shoot you to hurt you."

"What then? You're going to start hunting us, too? Trying to pin down our every move until—"

Gunfire echoed from outside on the bridge.

I don't have to shoot you to hurt you.

"Did you know?" Natalie trembled. Whether it was from rage, or fear, or some murky combination, she wasn't sure. "Did you know about Graduation? About," she gestured towards the firefight.

His silence was damning. He'd sent her parents to slaughter. Natalie saw red. She had no idea when she'd begun to spin the bolt. It sparked with life as it arced high above her.

Brant dodged her wild blow and pushed her hard against the wall of the chopper. He held her there as a grunt sounded from outside the hatch, and a familiar figure crawled inside. His tousled hair shone with sweat, and blood dripped from his busted lip.

Natalie's fight seeped out of her. Brant was no longer forcing her down but holding her up.

"Brant," the man stammered, "my boy. Thank heavens." Mr. Smith rose shakily to his feet. He swayed where he stood, his manic gaze darting from one door of the helicopter to the other. "We have to go. Quickly now, son."

"Mr. Smith?" Natalie stood dumbfounded. "I thought...well, my parents said..."

"The Ward," Mr. Smith inhaled sharply, "separated us. Tried to break us. We are stronger than that. Mortem ante cladem, yes?"

Natalie shrank against the wall of the chopper as Brant helped his father to the control panel. It was nothing short of a miracle. She could see Mr. Smith right in front of her, beaten and bloodied, solid and real. And yet...

Question everything.

"Edwin?" she called feebly towards the hatch.

"Come Natalie," Brant's father motioned for her to join them.

"We must get airborne. We have to get you all far away from here."

"Edwin?"

"We can't wait, kiddo," Mr. Smith attempted to close the hatch. Natalie knocked him away with her uncharged bolt. Anger darkened his expression and she saw him clearly then.

He wasn't bruised and starving like her parents. Tanned and dressed in a freshly pressed suit, he had a solid Nautilus shell pinned to his lapel. From the grunts emanating beyond the hatch, she guessed Mr. Smith's busted lip was Edwin's doing.

"You're with them," Natalie's anger bubbled and frothed. "Brant's following *you*. You're with Nautilus."

He dabbed his bleeding lip with a handkerchief. "I am not *with* Nautilus, Miss Natalie. I am Nautilus. I'm its creation, its center. I am the salvation that will surface the truth of this world. I will bring peace by whatever means necessary, and you're going to help me."

"You're the Ward," the words felt foreign, as though she was speaking another language. "Why? Why are you doing this?" Natalie shuffled a step backwards, feeling with her heel for the open hatch. Her parents died to secure her freedom. She wasn't about to let them down now.

"I must say I thought your parents' capture would have swayed you to see things my way," the Ward remarked almost wistfully. "Perhaps if Lehana had not intervened."

He spoke of those killed as though they were pieces on a chessboard, as though they were pawns instead of friends. Formal Friday's and birthday parties flickered in her memories. This man, this *Ward*, was not who she remembered. When did they lose him? Surely the other parents would have noticed. Or Christopher? Someone must have known.

She studied Brant again. There was an assured calmness to his stance, a quiet, deadly certainty.

Someone did know. And he tried to tell me.

Natalie clutched Lehana's bolt and took another step back.

Outside the helicopter, Edwin groaned again.

Wake up, she begged.

"I never would have helped you," she said, buying a few seconds to think. She had to get out of the chopper.

The Ward rubbed his head. "Still so naive. Everyone has something they'll give themselves for. I thought I had found yours. No matter. I no longer require your services anyway."

Brant aimed his gun at her again. Natalie held his gaze. If he was going to kill her, she would make him watch every second of it.

"You can't time-travel without me." As soon as Natalie said it, she knew it was true. She believed what Edwin said. Time-travel belonged to her, and only to her. "I saw the aurichalcum in the Helix. Congratulations. You could have a thousand tons of it and it still won't work. Not without me." Natalie blinked slowly at Brant, silently begging him to come back to her.

"There are powers at work you do not understand, dear Natalie. With or without you, I will get what I want. I have aurichalcum. I have the key. My son will—"

"No, he won't," Natalie interrupted. "Ask him yourself. He knows he can't do it. None of them can."

Outside, Edwin cursed groggily. Whatever the Ward had done to him, he was coming to. She spun her bolt to keep the attention on her. Brant's mouth pressed into a thin line and Natalie nodded towards the door, imploring him to follow.

He responded by cocking the pistol.

"Take a seat," the Ward blew her off. He produced Christopher's key from his jacket pocket and laid it on the dash. "You're leading us to victory."

"Sorry, old chap," Edwin propped his elbow on the floor of the helicopter, aiming directly for the Ward. "You're not invited."

His shot flew harmlessly through the control panel, sending up a flurry of sparks. Natalie darted between Brant and his father and stole the key off the dash.

"Argh!" The Ward yanked Natalie down flat on her back and she brought her foot up to kick him clear across the jaw. Rolling to her feet, she came toe-to-toe with Brant. She wanted to beg him to come with her. He found his words first.

"Tell Leo I'm sorry," Brant frowned. "The fall was tricky...he wasn't supposed to get hit."

Natalie felt as though she'd been dropped off another cliff. She wanted to destroy him, to claw and tear him apart until nothing remained, nothing except for blood and dirt and the tainted memory of someone who'd once been her friend.

She settled for punching him in the face.

He stumbled back, a cut bleeding near his hairline. Still dazed, the Ward fumbled blindly for her and she dodged him, dropping out of the helicopter to pull Edwin to his feet.

"Hello, friend," he greeted her groggily. "I could really go for some taffy."

"Where's Leo?"

Voices floated to her from the opposite side of the helicopter, most notably her own. Hobbling as swiftly as she could with Edwin at her side, she spotted Leo's silhouette several yards down the bridge.

There was a crack of gunfire and Edwin howled in pain. She turned in time to see Brant step back inside the helicopter, pocketing his pistol.

"Edwin!" Natalie attempted to stop, and he pushed her on.

"I'll live," he grunted, applying pressure to his bicep. "Nice friends you have."

"He let us go." Natalie's head felt murkier than a saltmarsh.

Mr. Smith is The Ward. Brant's freaking father.

"He shot me!"

"Brant doesn't miss," Natalie said. "He let us get away."

"He just told you he missed and hit Leo!" Edwin countered.

"Special circumstances."

"Bah." Blood seeped into the cloth of his suit. "Got the key?"

She nodded, feeling its weight in her pocket with every step.

"Fantastic," Edwin trudged through the pain. "Now, let's keep your bullheaded boyfriend from getting himself killed, shall we?"

"He's not my—"

But Edwin had hurried ahead, his bleeding arm tucked against his chest.

CHAPTER 49
NATALIE

Natalie reached Leo before Edwin did. He sat crouched behind a line of orange traffic cones, much farther down the bridge than he'd been when Natalie first spotted him. What he'd hoped to accomplish as the truck came and went, she had no idea. Nor did she have the heart to ask him about it.

Leo hastily wiped his face as she approached, and Natalie pretended not to notice. She gripped the key tightly in her pocket, watching the truck fade farther away until only its headlights remained visible in the dark.

"She ignored me," Leo said flatly. "Or didn't see me. I don't know which is worse."

"This was her choice." Edwin arrived beside them. Clutching his wound, the tightness of his words betrayed how much pain he was in.

Natalie cleared her throat. "Perhaps we should," she nodded to the guardrail. They all knew what was going to happen next, she didn't see a reason to suffer through it again.

"Is there any harm in staying?" Leo asked without looking at them.

Edwin shrugged, then winced. "I suppose not."

"Then I want to stay until...until the end."

Even as he spoke the truck abruptly turned. Its lights arced down towards the abyss of the bay and, despite knowing what was coming, Natalie held her breath. She saw the flash of the explosion before she heard it. White light lit up the night, chased by an orange fireball bubbling up from the surface of the water.

Natalie rushed to the guardrail and leaned as far as she could over the edge. The rumble of the blast shook the metal she clung to, but she didn't care about the truck. Instead, she focused on the open sea, where the darkness offered a reprieve from the fireball. She could have been mistaken. She might not have seen what she thought she had. Maybe it was simply part of the blast...

Either way, she didn't want to miss—

"There!" Natalie gestured so hard she nearly toppled over the edge. "Did you see that?"

Far down the bridge, back towards Virginia Beach, she was certain she'd seen it. The flash was so brief that if she'd blinked, she would have missed it.

"See what?" Edwin squinted out over the endless expanse of black.

"It looked like…" Natalie paused. She couldn't afford to be wrong.

"Impossible," Leo shook his head adamantly. "They can't do it. She...Lache, she can't..."

Edwin shoved Leo into Natalie and suddenly she was falling. She scrambled mid-air, twisting and turning, desperate to get a hold on both of them. Between Leo's startled yell and Edwin's manic laughter, Natalie couldn't even hear herself scream.

She couldn't see the water beneath them. At least she hoped it was water. She pictured the wide cement pylons and forced her mind to think of something else.

To think of the light on the beach.

Sooner than she expected, the white light engulfed them. Her body folded in on itself, carrying the momentum of the fall into a world without gravity, letting it dissipate and fade as she floated, every atom tingling. Then she dropped on her back in warm sand.

Natalie leapt to her feet. She didn't hurt, at least no more than before. The key was safe in her pocket and Edwin and Leo pushed themselves up on either side of her.

And they were not alone.

"Lache?" Natalie rushed to the girl's side. She laid several paces away, flat on her back. "Lachesis, can you hear me?"

"I am in shock," Lache said wryly. "Not deaf."

Natalie couldn't help it. She laughed.

"Well, either is a hell of a lot better than dead." Edwin helped Lache up with his good arm and pinched her chin. "You are a scientific marvel, my dear."

"Lache?" Leo hovered off to the side, ghostly pale. "You're okay?"

"I am most certainly *not* okay, Leonidas. Though admittedly alive, I am nauseous and—"

Leo embraced her so tightly Lache couldn't continue. Natalie turned away, unable to stand the ache in her chest at the sight of them. It felt selfish and pointless given all they had lost, who she had lost, and yet there it was. Green and ugly and painful.

"You tacked!" Leo exclaimed with a mixture of admiration and shock. "How is that possible?"

"I think...this." A fine powder coated Lache's hands.

"The aurichalcum dust," Edwin grinned. "Nautilus didn't crack the alchemy until after they'd sentenced you to death. They never tested it on you."

"And it spilt all over the cab! That must have been what caused the explosion," Leo laughed in relief. "You! Tacking! All it took was—"

"A spark," Natalie interjected. "We should probably be getting back."

"Indeed," Lache brushed the dust off on her robes.

Edwin clapped her proudly on the back, then added to Natalie, "Let's go home."

Home. An odd sense of elation peeked out beneath her pain and rage. She let it bubble up, rising until she immersed herself within it.

The black beach and soaring cliffs floated in her mind and where she should have stepped into the water, there was only light. Gravity slipped away. She floated in an infinite nothingness until rough sand dragged her down. Falling to her knees, the blinding light receded into a world of grey. The cliffs and the sea wound themselves together and, too dizzy to fight it, she collapsed.

Familiar voices called to her, but soft oblivion beckoned, and she leaned into it, cascading in on herself and thinking for once it would be nice to feel nothing at all.

CHAPTER 50
NATALIE

She woke to the aroma of charcoal and chocolate.

"I told you she'd come around," someone boasted. "My girl can't resist a good s'more."

Natalie pulled her covers tighter around her. Her head throbbed and as consciousness claimed her, she became increasingly aware of the pain branching outwards down her back and, well, everywhere.

Something sticky poked her and she swatted it away.

"Tawney! Leave the poor dear alone!"

Mrs. Davis? Blinking, Natalie squinted against the firelight. She took inventory of her injuries and found her initial assessment proved correct: everything hurt. Though nothing seemed broken. Sitting up, she discovered her covers weren't covers at all, but a layer of jackets. Formal ones.

A bonfire burned beneath the shelter of the cliffs. She supposed someone carried her to it. A starry sky shone down on the black ocean, glittering as far as she could see. Even with the fire the breeze had a bite, and she pulled on one of the jackets.

"No, *Patricia,*" Tawney sneered back at her mother. "Last time Nat time-traveled she slept for two days. She needs to wake up."

"It's true," Owen's gangly form blurred into focus.

"Unfortunately, we don't have that kind of time. Here," Edwin offered a gooey mix of marshmallow and chocolate squished between two graham crackers. "You need food."

Natalie took it reluctantly, nibbling on the corner. "Is everyone okay?"

The group shifted and Natalie grew suspicious. Owen's eyes were bloodshot behind cracked frames. Tawney burned four marshmallows at once, sitting pointedly on the opposite side of the fire as her mother. Mrs. Davis herself appeared a little disheveled, and much thinner than Natalie remembered, but otherwise alright. Edwin hoarded a box of graham crackers and bartered with Mr. Merrick for marshmallows. And Lache, Clo, and Atro huddled so close together their foreheads met, while Leo sat with his elbows on his knees, staring absently into the fire.

The bridge came rushing back and Natalie flinched at the memories. Brant was gone. Thanks to him and his father, her parents were dead.

"I mean, I know none of us are *okay,*" she backtracked quietly.

"We're alive." Mr. Merrick hoisted a marshmallow in cheers. "Thanks to our friends. And to you."

Enzi slinked over and snatched the s'more from her. She wrestled it from him, the effort making her head scream.

"No, sir." She tapped his nose. "No chocolate for canines. Ugh." She pressed against her throbbing temples. "Where are we?" She fumbled for something safe to talk about.

Edwin beamed. "Iceland." The gunshot wound across his bicep had been roughly bandaged with scraps of cloth. A small patch of fabric still shone dark with blood.

"Iceland," she repeated dumbly.

"Amazing how close the historians get sometimes," he winked at her. She didn't get it.

"Where's Brant?" Leo interrupted.

She watched the fire pop, pondering the real question: when did she lose Brant? In Antarctica? On the cliff? Or had he ever been hers at all?

"Where is he, Natalie?" From his tone, Natalie suspected Leo already knew, or had at least managed a good guess.

"He chose a different side," Natalie's throat felt raw and burned when she spoke.

Tawney's marshmallow hit the sand. "He did *what?*"

"Brant's father...he's the Ward."

Dumbfounded faces stared back at her.

"No." Mr. Merrick's scruff blurred as he shook his head. "No, you're mistaken. He's one of us. Mr. Smi—"

"Don't call him that," Natalie snapped unexpectedly. "That's not who he is anymore. He's the Ward. That's it."

"He devoted his life to you kids," Mrs. Davis said sadly. "We all did."

Natalie had no way of consoling them, so she simply stated the facts. "Brant set the fire in Ancora III. He knew," she clasped her fists to stop them from shaking, "he knew what the Ward planned tonight." Natalie didn't try to stop the upwelling of tears for fear the effort would make her head explode. "He tried to tell me a hundred times and I wouldn't listen. I never thought…"

My fault. Her fists clenched in the sand.

No. His choice.

"He's going to wish he'd never been born," Tawney growled.

"I can't believe he'd do that," Owen slumped in shock.

Of all her friends, her and Owen thought the most alike: calculating, analyzing. And she had to agree. Nothing Brant had said to her made any sense, and the absence of logic only made her angrier. She took Christopher's key from her pocket and passed it to Edwin.

"Whatever it is you're protecting, Nautilus knows."

"Well, everyone *knows*. The trick is no one knows how to get *in*."

Edwin shouldered her, giddy as a kid at Christmas.

She whimpered as the motion sent searing pain through her head.

"Oops, sorry." He offered a ripped piece of his suit. "For your nose."

"What's wrong with my—" As she spoke, a trickle of blood dripped from her nostril. "I don't get nosebleeds," she claimed defiantly, her heart quickening. "What's happening?"

Leo leaned over and wiped his thumb across the base of her ear. It shone with a thin layer of crimson.

Natalie froze, fearing any sudden movements might make the bleeding worse. "What's wrong with me?"

"Nothing." Edwin's adoring stare only heightened her concern. "You're perfect. It's a side-effect."

"This didn't happen before!"

Edwin's smile faltered. "Yeah," he wiped a spot of blood from the base of her other ear. "It's...cumulative."

"Cumulative?" Natalie squeaked.

"Don't worry." Edwin pressed his thumb to the center of her forehead, and to her relief, the pain lessened. "The discomfort will pass soon."

"How do you know?" Natalie's attempted yell escaped as a pained whine. "How do you know anything?"

"How does anyone know anything?" he countered. "Research."

"Oh! Follow-up question," Tawney tossed a marshmallow into their conversation. "A birdie told me you knew about the adoption already." Her birdie aimed a kick for her shin that she easily dodged. "Going to have to be faster than that, newbie."

Natalie found her pack lying at her feet. She reached past the books she'd carried with her from Ancora I, the mysterious family photograph, and *The Sceptical Chymist*, to finally produce the Coelacanth document.

Tawney snatched it away and scanned the paper a few times

before passing it on to Owen. Natalie hoped she wouldn't ask the question that would hurt her most.

"When did you get this?"

Natalie hung her aching head.

"Nat," Tawney pushed. "When?"

"It doesn't matter, sweetie," her mother cut in.

"You don't get to speak." Tawney threw a marshmallow at her.

"Nat?" Owen lifted a brow.

Edwin barely held the document for a second before Leo took it, his frown deepening.

"Chef gave it to me," Natalie confessed. "Back in Antarctica...before we escaped."

Tawney leapt from her seat. Owen leaned back with a low whistle. Though Natalie couldn't bring herself to look at Leo, he pushed the paper back to her.

"I didn't know how to...I thought," Natalie stopped and started again. "I thought it would be better for you to hear it from them." She nodded towards Mr. Merrick and Mrs. Davis. "Maybe some part of me hoped it wasn't true. I worried if you saw it, you might not want to find them. I was scared."

"You had no right!" Tawney yelled. "No right!" She charged towards her and, when Tawney reared back to punch her, Natalie declined to defend herself.

She knew she should have felt guilty for lying to Tawney and everyone else, but she didn't. She'd made her choice, and after watching her parents die it hardly seemed to matter anymore. Natalie only wanted to go back to sleep.

"I messed up," Natalie admitted. "Would you have risked your life to find them if you knew?"

Tawney decided against hitting her and kicked a clump of sand into the fire that sizzled and popped. "Of course, I would have Nat. Didn't you? They'd been lying our whole lives anyway," Tawney shoved her into the sand and the pain in Natalie's head sent a flutter of nausea through her stomach. "But *you*," Tawney shoved her again. "You were supposed to be better than them. You were supposed to be my friend."

Natalie heard more than saw Tawney march off and, as badly as she wanted to go after her, her body wouldn't allow it.

Leo changed the subject, addressing his father directly. "So, uh, Mr. Kurr, is it? Where are we really from then?"

"I'm afraid I cannot say."

"Unless you've got Plato in that bag of books, I'm afraid you'll have to wait until morning," Edwin added.

Natalie sat up too fast and was temporarily blinded from the headrush. "I do!"

"You're kidding." Edwin gawked as she dug through her pack.

She passed him the now beat-up copy of *Plato's Complete Works* she'd taken from Christopher's library in Ancora I. It felt like a lifetime ago.

"What nerd carries around Plato?" Edwin mused, fanning through the pages.

"Ours," Owen smiled.

"We all have our vices," Natalie winced as she spoke, though curiosity won over discomfort.

"Here!" Edwin tapped the page excitedly. "*Timaeus and Critias.*"

Natalie pursed her lips. She knew the story. She'd studied it in her government and history classes numerous times in grade school.

"Plato's portrayal of the perfect government," Natalie's memories resurfaced aloud. "It's his idea of Utopia."

"Precisely."

"So, the Minoans?" Natalie guessed. The Mediterranean civilization had often been suspected of being the inspiration for Plato's story. "We're from Greece?" She hardly considered that worth the secrecy their adoption had posed.

"Everyone always thinks it's the Minoans." Edwin needled them. "Where do you think the Minoans learned everything?"

"Oh," Owen blanched and then sat bolt upright. "Oh! You can't mean—" he stopped abruptly, his mouth wide-open as though choking on his words. He turned red, his eyes bulging from the effort. Edwin smacked him on the back with the book and Owen sucked in a sharp breath.

"You can't force it," Edwin laughed. "The synapse block won't let you. There's a rumor people have actually died trying."

"I can't say it," Owen marveled. "I literally cannot say it!"

A wild idea formed in the back of Natalie's mind and she fought against it. If Edwin meant for them to take Plato's text verbatim, then it only left one city on the map. One no one had ever been able to find.

"You're not serious," Natalie looked from Edwin to Owen.

Owen directed her to a single word on the open page. She reread the tiny print and her pulse throbbed, transforming the ache in her head into burning bolts of lightning.

"Is this a joke to you?"

Edwin's smile fell. "Uh…"

"My family is dead." Natalie passed the book angrily to Leo and woozily stood to leave the fire. "And you're feeding us this…this delusion?"

"Wait, Nat," Owen stopped her. "Say it."

She glared at him.

"Come on. For me."

Natalie meticulously smoothed her ruined dress. The idea was preposterous. Yet when she tried to speak, the word stuck in her throat. Her anger evaporated like mist in the sun. She tried again, and couldn't utter a sound.

"What is this?" Natalie asked apprehensively.

"This," Edwin stood, "is your homecoming."

"You magically know where *this place* is?" Leo asked.

"It's not magic. I'm from there, too."

"Well, where is it then?" Tawney asked, irritated.

"Right here."

Natalie pinched her forehead. Recalling Christopher's maps in Ancora I, the ones she replicated on her own walls, provided some merit to Edwin's impossibilities. He'd had a triquetra drawn at the height of the Atlantic Ocean, remarkably close to Iceland. The same triquetra that embellished the key he'd left her.

"We have to wait until sunrise to get inside. We'll need the key," he held out the hammered piece of metal. "And a right good amount of luck." Edwin muttered loud enough for Natalie to hear.

"Why Iceland?" Mr. Merrick asked.

"It caps two major tectonic plates."

"The North American and Eurasian," Owen rattled off.

"Yes," Edwin continued. "The diverging plates create a homely subterranean pocket with the added bonus of the occasional earthquake." Edwin rubbed the back of his neck. "It's good to have the cover of a quake when things go...awry."

"Cover!" Owen exclaimed. "We didn't have any cover when we tacked here," he pulled at his hair. "Nautilus is going to know exactly where we are!"

"You'd be surprised how many get this far," Edwin waved him off. "Without the key, the Ward will never see more than the beach."

Atro squinted down at the book. "This is a fantasy."

"One of the first," Edwin agreed.

Tawney wrinkled her nose in disbelief.

"You'll see, come first light," he nodded towards the horizon. "Trust me."

Natalie dug her toes in the sand. *Trust* was asking a lot. She wasn't sure she'd truly *trust* anyone ever again.

But stranger things had been known to happen.

CHAPTER 51
LEONIDAS

In the predawn hours, the bonfire gathering fractured. Leo observed his father as he talked with Mrs. Davis. Edwin helped Owen forget his sorrows in Plato's book, while Tawney jogged restlessly up and down the beach. With Atro and Clo huddled close by the water's edge, Lache paced as far away from the ocean as she could get.

"Keep at it and you'll hit seawater." Leo inspected the trench she had inadvertently shuffled into the sand.

She blanched at the comment and stopped moving.

"It's a joke, Lache. Nothing will happen without the aurichalcum. The water's safe."

"I know," she said defensively, then deflated. "Thank you for coming back for me. I might have died in shock on that beach."

"Thank Natalie. She saw the flash," Leo confessed. "Why did you volunteer to drive the truck?"

Her red robe billowed in the wind. "I should have died a long time ago, Leonidas. If I could save you and my sisters by giving my life, it was a small price to pay."

Leo stepped into her trench, savoring the coolness of the deeper sand on his feet.

Lache trudged a few more paces before turning back to him. "I am grateful to you, Leonidas."

"You are?" he asked, surprised.

Lache rolled her eyes, a talent he was certain she'd picked up from Tawney. "I was the right one to drive that truck. I do not fear death," she said ruefully. "I have met it twice before. However, I never had so much to leave behind. So, when the truck hit the water and I knew I wanted to stay—"

"You were tacked to the nearest beach," Leo traced the Coelacanth symbol etched into the spark on his wrist. "I suppose we'll have to find you a spark of your own now. Clo and Atro, too, I'd bet."

"Perhaps." She pulled at the collar of her robe as though unsure how the idea fit her.

"You knew about time-travel, then? And," he cleared his throat of the name his mind wouldn't let him say, "where I'm from?"

"Of course."

"And you didn't care to tell me?"

"Everyone has secrets, who am I to tell you yours?" She dug through her pockets. "This is for Natalie."

He inspected the plain envelope she gave him. "Why don't you give it to her yourself?"

"Must you always ask so many questions?" Lache glanced at her sisters and added, "You promise the water will not take me again?"

Leo inspected her hands one at a time, diligently brushing away any remnants of the aurichalcum dust. "There," he said afterwards. "You won't be going anywhere."

"Thank you," she said with sincerity. "I suppose we are even now, yes?" Without waiting for his opinion, she left to join her sisters.

Scanning the beach, Leo spotted Natalie lying flat on her back beside the bonfire with Edwin sitting cross-legged at her side. He sifted through the sand towards them.

"I'll take the next watch."

"I don't need a babysitter," Natalie protested from her bed of sand.

"Overruled." Edwin rose and Leo took his place at Natalie's side. Right where he was supposed to be.

Looking her over she seemed more or less alright. Her dress was torn, and superficial scrapes crossed her body. Her hair knotted at the nape of her neck and a drop of blood had dried under her ear. Despite the puffy redness around her eyes, they were open and sharp.

"Do you believe him?" Natalie asked. "About—" she made a face. "About *the city*."

Leo leaned back on his elbows. "Do you?"

"Yes."

"Really?" From her reaction earlier, Leo expected her to reject the idea. "Why?"

"Well for one," she lifted the wrist with her spark, "aurichalcum. It's mentioned in *Timaeus and Critias* as well. I should have recognized it right away," she sighed. "Maybe I did. Maybe I just didn't want to see."

"And second?"

She nodded to the sky.

Leo sank beside her in the sand, close enough for his side to press against the length of hers, and admired the star-studded ceiling of the Earth. There were more stars than he'd ever seen. If any of the few constellations he knew were among them, they were lost in the sheer volume of light.

"Uncle Chris would have loved it here," she said quietly.

"Do you think he knew about Brant?" The question escaped him before he'd even registered the thought.

He didn't want to think about Brant. He didn't want to deal with the fact his best friend had betrayed him, but it was like pressing his tongue against a sore tooth. Despite the pain, he couldn't stop.

Natalie started to respond, stopped, and finally breathed out a laugh. "I was about to say of course not, but then again..."

"Question everything," they said together.

She looked right at him then. "Brant said he shot you in Antarctica. He said it was an accident."

Leo nodded, his scar throbbing in response. The ache didn't quite hurt. He rubbed against it anyway.

"I guess he was aiming for Chris."

"That doesn't make me feel better," Natalie confessed. She flicked the paper in his palm. "What's this?"

Leo propped himself up on one elbow. "Apparently it's for you." He offered her the envelope. "From Lache."

Natalie inspected the gift with suspicion, not rising from her back. "What is it?"

"Seriously?" Leo nudged her. "She doesn't tell me anything."

Natalie unsealed the packaging and picked out a stack of print outs and magazine clippings. Leo flushed as she inspected each image silently before setting them to rest in a pile on her chest.

So much for not revealing other people's secrets...

"Natalie," he shifted awkwardly. "I wanted to get back to you, but I didn't have my spark. And when I did, I couldn't remember—"

She gave him one of the clippings, a tall lighthouse with black and white spiral stripes. "I guess you were closer to Ancora than you thought."

Leo stared at it. The lighthouse once seemed so important. Ancora was all he'd lived for: to be home again. Now it seemed hollow. Empty.

Natalie pressed against him and several moments passed before she spoke again. "You know what's strange? I haven't spared a thought to who our true parents are. Now that we're about to be home," she paused, "they could be right there in the city."

"Do you want them to be?"

"I don't know." A tear streamed down the side of her face to be lost in her hair. "I loved the ones I already had."

Leo mirrored her conflict. He didn't think he wanted any more parents, yet. Maybe not ever.

"What if they don't like me?"

Leo laughed. It was deep and genuine, a light feeling he hadn't known in months. It seemed absurd to worry about what strangers might think of them after all they'd been through.

"What?" Natalie leaned away from him. "It's a legitimate concern."

"Honestly, Natalie, stop thinking too much," he begged. "Please. For me."

"Fine."

They sat in silence then, watching the ocean and the brightening sky and Enzi curled against Leo's side with a heavy sigh. When Leo finally did speak again, it wasn't what he'd expected to say.

"Do you think we're still the good guys?"

"No."

"Ouch." Leo winced. "You sound awfully certain."

"I am," Natalie responded firmly. "For a while I wasn't. I was so desperate to believe our parents were flawless, that everything they'd done was for some master plan. But now," she side-eyed him, "it's obvious they weren't perfect at all. They lied, they manipulated, they quite possibly stole," Natalie held up her spark as evidence.

"They weren't bad people," she went on. "We're not bad people. I think we're better than Nautilus. That doesn't make us *good*." She hesitated. "I'm not even sure what *good* is anymore. Are you good because of what you do, or because of what you don't do? You could have killed Amir and chose not to. Whether or not that makes you good is a matter of perspective. It depends on whose side you're on. It's subjective."

"No, I didn't kill Amir," Leo's anger propelled him upward and he sat with his knees tucked to his chest. "Tawney did. They'd better have therapists in, ugh—*where we're going*—because she's going to need a good one. I should be bearing that burden, not her."

"We're doing what we must to survive," Natalie argued. "We're trying to keep breathing. Maybe in the city we can figure out what good is again."

"Hmm." Unconvinced, Leo dug his heels in the sand.

Natalie sat up and rested her head on his shoulder. "Don't forget yourself."

After losing Christopher and their families, after traveling back in time, it seemed a bold request. He brushed his sandy thumb across her chin, sliding to the base of her neck and pulling her closer. It wasn't their desperate collision in Nautilus's Antarctic prison. He wasn't clutching tighter for fear of losing her. He reached across the void because he wanted her. In that moment and every stubborn, chaotic, and quiet one after. There was nothing to pull them apart, no impending call of duty. That piece of time could have stretched into eternity.

Then Natalie leaned in.

He felt her sigh on his lips and when he kissed her, Iceland dropped away. Every touch left him craving another. The waves colliding against the sand fell silent and the breeze no longer carried a chill. Gravity itself surrendered them as the ground melted into nothing.

There was only Natalie.

"Oy!" Edwin shouted at them. "This is it!"

A golden glow raced across the horizon, bathing the beach and cliffside with light. Leo rested his forehead against hers and traced the length of her jaw, certain the dawn could have waited another century or two.

Leo eased Natalie to her feet, and they followed Edwin together, falling in line with what remained of their fractured family.

He took a deep breath in and a long breath out.

Ouch. Every inch of him hurt. Badly. Still, he was grateful for it. He was alive. And as the sun broke upon the shore, he knew the pain wouldn't last forever. It would throb, it would ache, and it would scar; one day callusing over into a memory he would grow from.

All it would take was time.

CHAPTER 52
NATALIE

Edwin splashed in the surf at the base of a tall cliff. "This is it. Right here," he explained, "is the first place the light touches upon breaching the horizon. This is the entrance."

Natalie inspected the solid rock skeptically.

"Okay," Tawney stood as far away from Natalie as possible. "How do we get in?"

"Excellent question."

"You don't know?" Tawney balked.

Natalie blocked them out. If Edwin claimed the cliff was the entrance, then she believed him. All that was left to do was find the place where the cliff stopped being rock and became a door.

She surrendered her spark to Leo and joined Edwin in the surf. The cool water swirling above her ankles made her breath catch in her chest. When had she last *felt* the ocean? She grappled the slippery crevices of rock, grazing every inch of stone she could reach.

"What are you searching for?" Leo asked.

"I'm not sure," Natalie balanced up on the tips of her toes, spreading her fingers wide. "But if the key is made of aurichalcum, wouldn't the lock be?"

"You can tell the difference in stone by feel?" Atro asked, impressed.

"Normally, no. But ankle-deep in sea water, yeah," Natalie nodded. "I think I can." Reaching higher on the rocks, a dull glow emanated from the water around her.

"Go back!" Edwin directed.

Natalie retraced the rock and the glow returned. She tapped a gap much smoother than the surrounding stone.

"Pass me the key."

Edwin cradled Christopher's key as though it was made of pure gold. Which, Natalie figured, wasn't far from the truth. Aurichalcum had to be worth more than something as simple as gold.

She guided the key into the hole and, as she'd guessed, it fit perfectly. What she did not expect was the announcement that accompanied it. She jumped back in surprise.

"*Vos autem inventus est clavis. Et inventus est civitatem. Sed quid enim didici te?*"

"What did it say?" Tawney whispered, her eyes wide.

"It is Latin," Clo beat Natalie to the translation. "'*You have found the key. You have found the city. Yet what have you learned?*'"

Owen pinched the bridge of his nose. "It wants a password?"

"Well," Leo addressed Edwin. "You're the expert."

"I've never done this before," Edwin shrugged. "I'm a resident, not a guest."

"Christopher wouldn't have given us the key without an answer to go along with it," Tawney suggested.

Natalie splashed back to dry land. "You're right." Rummaging through her pack, she laid *The Sceptical Chymist* in the sand.

"Where did you get that?" Edwin dripped next to her. He lunged for the book. "That isn't yours," he said sourly.

Natalie swiped it beyond his reach and looked up at him with a raised brow. "It was a gift."

"That doesn't make it yours."

"Do you want to get inside or not?"

Edwin fiddled with the hoops on his ear and finally shrugged.

Flashing him another annoyed look, Natalie flipped past Boyle's argumentation of the elements, reached the end, and started again. She skimmed cover to cover twice more, her anxiety mounting with every fruitless pass. Surely this was why Christopher had left the book for her in Paris. So why couldn't she find anything that even moderately resembled an answer to the key's question?

The throbbing in her head mounted again. What had she learned? Natalie scoffed. She'd learned her life was a lie and her parents were strangers. She'd discovered a power—no, two powers—she'd harbored at least most, if not all, of her life. She knew she'd cost the lives of her Mom and Dad, Christopher, Chef, and Angie. Yet, despite everything she'd endured, everything that had come to light, she still had more questions than answers. Natalie wondered if that was precisely what Christopher had intended.

Question everything.

She turned to the inscription on the inside cover.

"I only know that I know nothing," she translated aloud. Grinning with relief, she pushed her hair back from her forehead. "That's it."

"The answer is nothing?" Tawney frowned.

"Of course." Edwin splashed back to the aurichalcum vein of stone. "You can't discover something new without first accepting ignorance."

"Hoc solum scio quod nihil scio," Natalie read the Latin text aloud and a loud crack shattered the quiet of the dawn. A flock of black birds fled the top of the cliff as the rock ahead of them retracted into the earth. Above the water's reach, a passage tall enough to crawl through stretched open. Natalie peeked inside before lifting her attention to the birds.

"They're ravens," Edwin noted. "Brilliant creatures. Particularly good at puzzles."

Natalie watched as one by one they landed again. Part of her wanted to stall on the stoop of the city forever. Part of her wanted to be one of the birds.

"And," Edwin dragged her attention back to the tunnel, "they're excellent thieves. We've used them to track global advancements for millennia."

"Hmm." Though Edwin's words were clear, few of them made any sense. She made a mental note to have him clarify when her head felt less like the inside of a racquetball court.

"So, this is home," Leo peered down the dark passage. "Can't say it's what I expected."

Edwin shoved him inside. "This is merely the driveway, man. Hold onto your butts."

With everyone inside, Natalie removed the key from the cliffside and followed Enzi in as the rock slid closed. The air was dense and cool where the passage emptied into a grand antechamber. Its stone floor was sanded smooth, and its chiseled walls were weakly illuminated by a huge holographic triquetra.

"I'm not sure we are meant to see this," Mr. Merrick confessed. He hovered off to the side with Mrs. Davis, and Natalie figured they must feel as out of place as they looked.

"Oh, most definitely not," Edwin confirmed.

"You're coming with us," Natalie said stubbornly.

"If anyone has an issue, they can take it up with me. And I have no doubt they will," Edwin added under his breath.

They fanned around the ominous triquetra, with Enzi settling beside Natalie's feet. Unsure what was coming, she scratched lightly around his scruff, ready to take hold of him at the first sign of danger. With a quick wiggle of his fingers, Edwin reached into the center of the hologram where the three concentric ovals joined. The triquetra dissolved and the figure of a child took its place. Draped in a modest floor-length robe, its round blue eyes scrutinized them each in turn.

"Hi there," Edwin began awkwardly. "It's me: Edwin."

"Were you invited?"

Though Natalie knew the child was the product of projections, its flat and lifeless tone unsettled her.

"Ah," Edwin flushed. "Well, I'm a native. I was born here, and—"

"And asked to leave. Were you invited?"

"No, not exactly. You see—"

"Entrance is granted by invitation only. Please follow the path the way you came. No memory of this place will accompany your departure."

The child began to dissolve, and Natalie lunged forward.

"Wait!"

Half dissipated, the hologram inspected her curiously. "Your name?" it asked her.

"Natalie Morrigan," she answered, inexplicably breathless. "You have to let us in. My family lived and died to get me here. Nautilus is on our heels. We'll be lost without your sanctuary."

Across the room, Edwin brightened. Though the concept of sanctuary was international, she had no idea if it would work. She hoped it extended beyond fissures of aurichalcum as well as it did borders.

"Sanctuary," the child repeated, leaning closer. "Your hand, Miss Natalie."

Natalie obliged. The hologram felt unexpectedly solid against her skin, though void of texture or temperature. It admired, or maybe studied, her spark.

"Where did you come by this?"

"It was a gift."

"It belongs in our Temple of Thoughts, along with the book you carry." The child nodded to *The Sceptical Chymist* tucked under her arm.

Natalie lifted her chin. "We didn't take them."

The child released her and addressed the group. "An attack occurred on American soil hours ago. Do you deny your part in its development?"

Leo cleared his throat.

"No." Natalie answered. "We were—"

"You are dismissed."

"Nautilus was going to have its war no matter what happened on that bridge." Natalie took another step forward. "Nautilus is a parasite. They'll rot the world from the inside out to see themselves on top. They tried and failed to use us to achieve that power and every choice we've made, I've made, since they bombed the Norfolk Naval Station has been to stop them."

She paused for breath, frustrated by the child's lack of expression. It was only then that she realized she wasn't speaking to the child. Not really. There was someone on the other end, watching through its eyes and talking through its mouth. Digging Nautilus's Adoption invitation from her pack, she threw it at the projection's feet.

"Here's your invitation," she stood straighter. "We've escaped the Ward more times than I care to count, and this is the end of the line. Denying us sanctuary won't only mean our blood spilt. Nautilus is coming for you," she unclenched her fists, "and I think it's because of me, because I can travel through time. I need a teacher, I need sanctuary. We'll die by their hand if you don't extend yours."

The projection stood still, silent and expressionless. Natalie didn't hold her breath. She didn't bite her lip or clench her jaw. Either their passage would be granted, or it wouldn't. Whatever the child decided, they would deal with the decision together.

"Our Regent grants you sanctuary upon one condition." It spun slowly to each of them. "As you have arrived on our step with no invitation and strangers in your wake, you must assume responsibility," the child's gaze fell coldly on Edwin. "Should misgivings follow your arrival, the punishment shall be your death. Swear it so."

Natalie shook her head fiercely at Edwin. With Nautilus practically at their gates, *misgivings* were almost guaranteed. She'd rather him risk death outside in the world than march straight to the gallows."

Edwin bowed his head respectfully. "I accept responsibility for the consequences of our arrival and our sanctuary. I swear on pain of death we have no malicious intent."

Satisfied, the child disappeared. Natalie expected darkness in its absence, but instead the room grew brighter.

"Oh my," Mrs. Davis marveled.

Across the round room, an ornate metal door swung outward, flooding the passage with impossible, brilliant sunlight that outlined a tall silhouette in its archway.

"Well met, friends," an olive-skinned woman in a green gown nodded in greeting. "I am Regent Aislinn." She opened her arms to the city behind her. "Welcome to Atlantis."

Atlantis.

Home, her parents had called it.

Her home was in Williamsburg. Home had a gravel driveway, and parents, and a steady supply of popcorn. Her home was in ashes, but for once the memory filled her with pride. Though there was nothing back there for her, she found herself staring not through the archway into the city, but back into the passageway.

She wondered if Christopher had ever stood on that spot, if Chef had ever seen the city, or if her mother and father had known the truth of her ancestry. None of the answers mattered. Each had done what they'd intended. Atlantis might never truly be her home, but it could prove her haven, her purpose.

The knot that had tightened her stomach for months unraveled. She rolled her shoulders back and her lungs expanded with sweet, salty air until they ached. She could *breathe*. She felt light enough to fly. Encased in a cliff of rock, she could have been on top of the world.

Her parents dedicated their lives to the secret of the age. Christopher left her clues, even in death, to guide her down the rabbit hole, to wake her up, to make her question. She was never meant to save them, but she could honor them. She could become the hope they'd carried. She could choose to walk through the archway and confront her fate with certain steps. She could choose to embrace the Coelacanth Project, to accept the impossibility of what she was and rise to meet it.

"Thank you," she whispered.

Natalie stepped forward and Edwin blocked her path. "Eyes and ears open, Nat. Stay awake."

"Hey," Leo leaned back through the arch, beaming. "Looks like home to me."

Enzi landed two big paws on her chest before darting through the doorway after Leo, his sleek white tail flicking out of sight.

"Atlantis," she tested the weight of it on her tongue and smiled. It felt *good* to smile. No, Atlantis wasn't home. It was more.

It was hope.

EPILOGUE

She fidgeted with the bird-shaped Prestige.

"You are joining at a most fateful time, Dove Nora."

Moving anything other than her fingers woke the bruises that covered her body. Nora felt numb to the world beyond her skin. The white-washed walls blurred together, the passages of the Helix wound into an impossible knot, and the sinking balloons from Graduation gradually floated to the floor. Days could have passed in the time she sat.

"Put it on."

Nora secured the Prestige to her uniform. She sniffled and cringed. Her broken nose still ached.

"Pull your hair back," the Legate ordered.

Nora secured her auburn hair up and back.

"Sit up straight."

She was their doll, their marionette. Act out, speak up, and she'd be reunited with the business end of a bolt. She was an *Acquisition,* not a Recruit. Forced to follow the Ward's commands, she was welcomed with none of the glow and glamour of the willing inductees. Nautilus broke her. She was beaten and strung back together; an empty vessel for them to fill. A puppet for them to play.

"Follow me, Dove. Pay attention."

Nora followed. Nora paid attention. The Legate led her out of the Focus to the Grand Staircase. She catalogued every turn. Left here, right there. If asked to replicate their route, she must do so flawlessly. She was the rat trained through the maze: one wrong turn and they'd shock her into last week, they'd make her start all over. Up this flight, down that one.

Finally, the Legate stopped in a vast room. Shipping containers lined the space and irritating fluorescent lights flickered from the ceiling. At the farthest end of the room, an impossible brightness shone through—

"You have a choice."

Nora started. Nautilus didn't give choices. She narrowed her eyes suspiciously, awaiting the Legate's test.

"This is a one-time offer, Nora. You hear me?"

The fog of forced obedience and pain shifted in Nora's mind. She nodded.

The Legate flashed a quick glance in either direction, swishing her long, dark braid, before dropping her voice to a whisper. "I can get you out. Right here, right now."

Nora blinked. Nautilus was *cruel*.

"Nora?" The Legate shook her lightly. It was enough to radiate pain across Nora's entire being and she hissed through her teeth.

"Peace will be my freedom," she answered robotically.

The Legate's dark eyes narrowed with...sympathy? Nora was confused. How did the Legate want her to respond? Was declining the opportunity to flee not enough? Should she bow?

"Your mother is already free. I got her out last night."

Nora's composure cracked. "How *dare* you," she said quietly. "This is beyond cruelty, this is...this is…"

"It's the truth." The Legate turned her to face the distant sunlight. The hope it offered was intoxicating and Nora succumbed. Did she care if they beat her for it? No, maybe she didn't. It was nothing she hadn't endured already.

371

"Nautilus...doesn't have her?" Nora asked cautiously.

The Legate offered a genuine smile. "No. She's safe. For now, at least."

"Why?" Nora searched the Legate's face. "Why are you doing this?"

"Mutual friend," she said wryly. "This tunnel will spit you out well past the solar panel fields. Or," the Legate gave her another Prestige pin, "you can stay."

There it was: the test. Nora studied the pin. It was a simple black flame. She longed to be reunited with her mother. She longed to see her brother again and go *home* where things were normal.

"This isn't a trick, Nora," the Legate's strange sympathy returned. "If you stay here, if you join with me, you will no longer be part of Nautilus. If they catch you, they will kill you. Do you understand? There's no coming back from this."

She's right, Nora knew. *Even if I did go home, this would never be the same. There's no going back. Not while Nautilus still stands.*

"You're not Nautilus?"

"No."

"Natalie...they're saying Natalie escaped."

"I knew her as Raven."

Nora's eyes flicked up. The Legate's demeanor was sharp and determined.

"But yes. From what I hear, the Ward lost her and more. The Legates are scrambling for Plan B, whatever that is."

Nora shuffled her feet, still uncertain.

"A forest burns fastest from the inside out," the Legate urged. "It will only take a few of us Flames to cause chaos."

"My mother is safe?" Nora asked skeptically.

"I escorted her out myself."

With shaking fingers, Nora pinned the black flame to the inner collar of her jacket. Hidden from sight, it pressed cold against her neck.

"Well," she smoothed down her hair. "Can't let Natalie have all the fun, can we?"

"I'm Ignis." The Legate extended her hand and, as Nora took it, she spun her to face an adjoining corridor. "Let's go meet the others."

Her bruises hurt as she walked, and she welcomed the pain. Nautilus would pay for what they did to her family, to Natalie's. They would pay for their lies and deceit and false promises of peace. They would pay for every bruise and scar they'd inflicted on her body.

Nora was welcomed into a room full of strangers. They hugged her and shook her hand and wiped away the tears of relief that flooded her cheeks. Ignis led her to a rotating wall packed floor to ceiling with schematics and diagrams: the inner secrets of the Helix.

No, Nautilus will do more than pay, she grinned. *They will burn.*

SARAH NEWLAND

THE ADVENTURE CONCLUDES IN BOOK
III, THE FINAL INSTALLMENT OF THE
COELACANTH PROJECT:

REGENT

AUTHOR'S NOTE

First and foremost, thank *you* reader for joining me on this adventure. This book proved significantly more difficult to write than *Extant*. From the first word, I knew exactly where Natalie's journey would take her, however, linking the beginning and the end through *Chymist* was no easy feat. I wanted to give you some answers and raise new questions. I wanted to craft an adventure not central on the impossible powers at play, but on the strength, resilience, and sometimes fragility of the characters forced to carry them. Fingers crossed I pulled through. If you've embarked on *The Coelacanth Project* thus far, an honest review would be genuinely appreciated. I want to inspire a renewed love of reading and questioning – and I cannot hope to achieve that without you.

Thank you to my husband, who is there through every draft, pushing me to question the story but never its potential. And of course, to Big Kitty, Little Kitty, and Meowse, for never missing a writing session and enforcing breaks for snacks.

Thank you, Lauren, for your keen eye, your honesty, and for establishing #TeamBrant. You met Natalie first, before the Coelacanth Project existed, and believed this story was possible before I believed it myself.

Thank you to my parents and family for your unwavering support, and to my siblings, Autumn, Chloe, and Dean, for reminding me to peek up from the books from time to time. An incredibly special thank you to my soul-sisters Leah and Megan. You help me see the world in new colors and provide support around every chaotic turn of my life. To my Beta Readers and Advanced Copy Team – I don't know where I (or Natalie) would be without you. You mean the world to me.

And to the City of Suffolk, Sweet Beans Coffee Shop, Dog Eared Books, AFK Books and Records, and my local Barnes and Noble's, thank you for welcoming *The Coelacanth Project* with open shelves and hearts.

I am beyond grateful to all of you.

SARAH NEWLAND

DISCUSSION QUESTIONS

Level 1

- What was your favorite part of the book and why?
- Did you have a favorite quote or passage from the book? What was it?
- Who was your favorite character and why?
- How do you think Natalie changed throughout the story?
- Which character do you think is the bravest? The most selfless? The most selfish?
- What do you predict will happen to Natalie and her friends next?
- What advice would you have given Natalie to help with her grief?
- Why do you think so many people follow Nautilus?

Level 2

- Why do you think Natalie tacked to Paris even though she knew it was dangerous?
- How does the dual point-of-view affect how the reader experiences the story?
- Where do you think Nautilus's power comes from?
- What themes did you notice in this story?

- Do you think Natalie should have turned to her friends sooner for help? Why didn't she? Who do you turn to for help when you need it?

- Natalie and Leo discuss whether or not they are still the "good guys." What do you think?

- What do you think is the significance behind the name "Moirai"? How does that significance fit in with the overall themes of the story?

Level 3

- What do you think of how Uncle Chris was presented in the story? What does this suggest about Natalie's character?

- How did Leo learn to trust the Moirai? How did Natalie? How do you determine if you can trust someone?

- We all make mistakes. What are some mistakes Natalie made? And Leo?

- At one point in the story, Natalie realizes "their parents were no better equipped than she was." What does this mean for Natalie? What does this mean to you?

- People experience and handle grief differently. Compare and contrast how Natalie and Leo experienced their grief.

- Why do you think Nautilus's methods of guiding public perception are effective? Do you think those methods are moral?

SARAH NEWLAND

THE CHESAPEAKE BAY BRIDGE-TUNNEL

As a Virginia native, the iconic CBBT is one of my favorite places to visit. But despite numerous trips to the Eastern Shore, I still get a little nervous about halfway across. 17.6 miles of open bay is no joke! If you're ever in town, and the winds are favorable, I highly recommend the drive. It's stunning, and there are scenic stops where you can pull over and take it all in. In the winter months, from late December to February, you might even spot a whale or two.

This photo is my own, taken on a fishing trip led by my father, the great Captain Deano. In the image, Fisherman Island is behind us. Can you see the gull over the water?

CHYMIST

THE CHESAPEAKE BAY BRIDGE-TUNNEL

The image below depicts the entirety of the CBBT. In *Extant,* Natalie and her friends drive from Virginia Beach to the Eastern Shore side to find Christopher at his marina. In *Chymist,* we are focused mainly on Island 3 and the Chesapeake Channel Tunnel. More information, including the history and future plans for the Chesapeake Bay Bridge-Tunnel, can be found at www.CBBT.com.

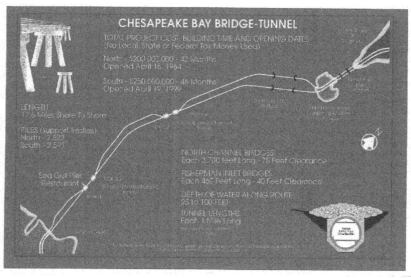

Image source: http://www.cbbt.com/about-us/facts/

SARAH NEWLAND

SHAKESPEARE AND COMPANY

In case it wasn't obvious, I love Paris. Yes, the macarons are *exquisite*, but I don't go for the pastries, or even the books. The history of Paris practically pulses through the soles of your shoes. Every street has a secret, and every brick holds a story.

Somehow, this is the only image I took during my visit to Shakespeare and Company. I wandered between the shelves, I pet the store cat, and I started writing *Extant* a week later. I wanted to pay tribute here in *Chymist,* and have Shakespeare and Company guard Natalie's path home. I dream to one day have one of my own books housed amongst their shelves on the bank of the Seine.

To find out more about Shakespeare and Company, and order bookish delights from their shop, you can visit their website at www.ShakespeareandCompany.com

Made in the USA
Middletown, DE
21 April 2021